Belief

Belief

A Novel

STEPHANIE JOHNSON

St. Martin's Press ✠ New York

www.stmartins.com

ISBN 0-312-29110-8

First published in New Zealand by Vintage, Random House.
First U.S. Edition: May 2002

10 9 8 7 6 5 4 3 2 1

For all of William's descendants, near and far.

PROLOGUE
1880

If you had been there, in about 1880, and if you had looked in that dusty little square of glass, a pane veiled by a cobweb spun by a spider no larger than a mite, then you would have seen a man in a red robe soaked with seawater to a foot above the hem. You would have seen him slumped in a chair kept in the stables for his daughters to sit on while they pulled on their riding boots. A little, fine-boned chair that shuddered with the man's weight.

You would have seen the man's legs part to admit a small boy to stand between them. The child is ten, maybe twelve years old with hair impossibly black and glossy – until you see that it is wet. Indeed, all the boy's clothes are wet – his jacket and plus-fours, his scuffed boots, his pale shirt showing at the soggy cuffs. He lifts one arm and hooks it with infinite gentleness around the man's neck. How old is he, the father? It is difficult to tell because his head is bowed and what you thought at first was his grey hair is in fact a wig. A crisp, curly grey court wig.

'Poor Father,' whispers the boy.

There is a small, dull clatter and you see by bending your eye to the floor that the man has dropped a riding crop. The boy bends his head into his father and feels the strong heart beating under his ear, which has caught a cut and bleeds a little onto the red robe.

He closes his eyes and sees his father on the beach, the view he had of him from the water, the quick gulping glances he took whenever his brother Henry stopped struggling for an instant. His father's robes were flapping, an entourage of men in dark suits surrounded him, and the boy who ran for him panted from his long run up the hill to the court and back. But then Henry pulled William under again and the

9

group on the beach were lost to him – his important father in his red robes, the men and the boy.

The group on the beach stared; they watched the brown chop wash around the boys' shoulders. A warm grey westerly hissed summer rain along the sand; they stepped closer to the sea with each dunking. His father waded out to his knees.

Then one of the men from the court, seeing that William had calmed his brother, who at fifteen was surely big enough to hold a man underwater, peeled off his jacket.

'I can swim,' he announced, the only one who could or would, and he swam the short distance, only a few feet away from the shore, and brought the brothers in.

How memory obfuscates and obscures – a single incident, a beating among many beatings. Until the night on a hill many years later, William's mind endlessly returns to it. He remembers how he sensed what was inevitable, the way he talked fast and seamlessly all the way from the bay to the house, his father cold and silent in the cab, his brother sodden and slobbery between them. Henry had been in the water so long his flesh was marbled blue, his teeth chattered, his big head wobbled, the skin beneath his eyes so purple it was almost black. He thinks of it when he is on a schooner bound for England. When he is lying with women, when he raises his hammer on building sites around Sydney, when he is dead drunk, when he is unwillingly sober, he thinks of how he had expected the hero's welcome for saving his brother and how he had been beaten for it. He takes the memory out, a cold stone shot with quartz, and turns it to the light.

'For Henry now.' His father poised at a middle point, the riding crop raised, to begin the cuts on the other son's behalf, the son who was not right in the head, who could not take his punishment.

Afterwards the child slipped a comforting arm around his father's neck. Poor Father had it wrong: he couldn't see that he had been trying to save Henry, not to drown him. He believed what was not true and the boy knew how his father railed against false belief, how daily he passed judgement on the deliberately wicked, the trespassers and the merely misguided who came before him. In Samuel it says: 'If one man sin against another, the judge shall judge him: but if a man sin against the Lord who shall intreat for him?' It was one of his father's favourite passages. As the boy remembered it, a sudden pillar of fire burned through him, from the top of his damp head to the soles of his chilly feet, quick and pure, the voice of God, whom by meting out wrongful punishment his father had sinned against. The fire burnt conviction into the child: the man had done wrong, but the boy, who was strong with the Lord, could pardon him. He pressed the swelling in his cold, bloody face against his father's robe and whispered forgiveness for his false belief.

At this moment, if you had kept your eye pressed to the window all this time without being seen – either by the man and boy themselves or someone in the house behind you – you would surely have drawn away. If you were one of Will's gang you might have made an idle wish that the spider who made the web was a great deal bigger, that the web's construction was of coarser fibres more densely woven.

Perhaps you are Gordie, the family cook, and you decide at this instant that you must hurry away to fetch the black salve and gentian violet and plasters.

Perhaps you are Henry and you lumber bewildered into the house to a scolding from your sister, who is calling you for a hot bath.

Or perhaps you are the boy's mother, who crept through the garden and across the lane with her heart in her mouth, who hoped to arrive at the end of the beating, not at the beginning of it.

Perhaps you are a woman who one day will love him.

Swing open the heavy door. Still the father's hand.

11

PART ONE

NORTHLAND, NEW ZEALAND 1898

CHAPTER 1

He is ascending and as he ascends his soul cries out to the night: 'Oh my God, my Lord. Is it you?'

The sky is dark, light pricks through from a million stars glimmering between scudding clouds. Vertical, feet towards the earth, his head is bathed in divine phosphorescence. The stars are the angels: the gold strings of their harps, the blue of their eyes and their heads of yellow hair flash through the gossamer membrane that divides Heaven and earth. Speeding towards them, he passes the moon that hangs, fixed, paler and less brilliant than himself. His arms hang loosely by his sides, he bows his head to gaze below his white feet.

There are continents on earth more vast than these islands his pale soles now rise above, the bush below furred and dull, continents it takes weeks to cross on shining new railways. He has crossed in the sky a vertical distance the breadth of America, of the wide hip of Russia, as far as the sea-licked curl of the Holy Land. Far below is his hill, glowing with embers, the last stand of rimu and kauri a tassel on its crown. Between the hill's foot and the stream, gleaming and narrow as a silver hair, are his narrow flatlands wedged between Pukekaroro and Bald Rock. Above that fertile green stands the foolish house on its wet feet, on the southern side of

Bald Rock, its damp walls three sides surrounded by kahikatea.

Smoke – at first he thinks it is smoke – rises from the chimney. But why would his wife have stoked the fire so late at night? No, it is something else, rising not from around the crumbling chimney copestone, but from the earth itself, the farm and the bush and the near sea, from the grieving woman who lies sleepless, the woman revealed now lying as still as if she herself were dead, the walls and roof having achieved for him an unearthly transparency. He wonders at the consistency of the threads – they are ship's ropes, grey snakes, wafting chiffon, spider webs, stalagmites, old woman's hair – reaching for him, travelling faster than he is, he sees now, as if they would pull him down, fetch him back. He inclines his head, offers his face to the rushing, fast-approaching dome of the sky and kicks his feet like a swimmer.

Faster, he thinks, and cries out despairingly, 'Lord, let me see you,' and as the first gleaming, viscous restraint reaches him and nudges at his sole, he foots it away and feels it to be made of glass. A length of it snaps, breaks off; he hears the tinkle and smash in the thin, high air as it shatters and begins its fall to earth. Again and again he kicks out, breaking the fragile and beautiful ties that would bind him to his young wife, to their marriage, to the lost infant and their life together on the dreary farm.

Above him the membrane opens to peel apart like the softest of thighs, and painlessly, without blood, he crowns the gap to enter – he thinks for ever – the Kingdom of Heaven. How warm I am, he thinks. I am loved beyond measure. I am forgiven. I am washed clean. He opens his newborn eyes, his child's face turning slowly in a rotation as ancient as earthly birth, to perceive a tumbling inhabited light. The devotion surrounding him is eternal, without judgement. He knows this as certainly as he feels, ruffling his brow low and cool, a celestial exhalation of breath: William McQuiggan is about to hear the voice of God.

Sweet, sweet oblivion. An absence of sensation, of bewilderment, of all responsibility. There is no voice but neither is there silence. Light and movement absent themselves like midwives, but neither do they leave him in the darkness. There is no symmetrical exchange of one phenomenon for another: pain for pleasure, melancholy for bliss, body for soul. All he knew before, should he be able to remember it, if memory were a function of Heaven, is gone. Future does not exchange itself for the past, or need for satisfaction.

Were William to return to earth, he would not be able to describe where he is – or is not. Even if he were an educated man, or a man with no hunger for the garrulity of the bottle, he would have no language for it.

Save perhaps one word. A word feeble for its paucity of exactitude, a word men use to describe that which is far beyond their ken, beyond their wildest prophecies, their sad doctrines of violence and hypocrisy. He would be forced to use that word, the only word left to him: three-lettered, guttural, hard, voiced explosion of air from the back of the throat.

CHAPTER 2

In the parlour the clock ticks, unheard by the tiny, waxen ears of the baby. Next door, in the dark bedroom, Myra's wakeful breath rises and falls. William will know what to do, she thinks. He is twenty-eight years to her twenty, he grew up in a city, he is a man of the world, he ran away to sea at fifteen. He can send to his father for money for the funeral. He will mourn with her as long as she is silent in her grief, he will be her rock and her stay as long as she is contained. In the other room is the child she laid out herself on a folded quilt between two wooden chairs.

That morning, after Myra had discovered her dead, she had wrapped her in the fine crocheted white receiver she had made before the birth, torn up her best petticoat and swathed its soft, white folds around the makeshift cradle. Throughout the day she had paused in her work, running to fetch treasures and lay them beside her. There was her mother's Limoges brooch with its orange-breasted lady, and a trinket box that had belonged to her grandmother. It was right that little Alithea should see the lovely things, all that she had. One day, had she lived, they would have been hers. At the child's feet sat one-armed Poppet, whose painted features had faded almost entirely away. Myra stole a moment to run outside and pick some ferns. She pinned them to the torn petticoat and wished she had some roses. She hadn't seen roses since she was married, the white ones on either side of the communion rails.

Just before the bread was ready, she had a sudden inspiration and took the china teapot from the shelf. At the door of the parlour she held it in her hands. It was her only wedding present, cream coloured, fat, with pink painted roses gathered in posies above a golden rim. A draught from the fireplace scattered ash across the floor and gave her skirts a gentle tug. Myra closed her eyes and had the child alive, older, dimple-armed and tottering, reaching for the pretty thing.

'Look,' she said, 'I'd give it to you to hold, but you might break it, dear.'

She sent the news of the death with the dinner up to the clearing gang. Through the long, cool afternoon she waited then for her husband, sitting on the floor beside the two chairs, every now and then stroking the baby's tiny forehead with a gentle thumb, wondering at the translucent bony face. The first baby and she was a stranger. After Riha left, the day after the birth, there had been no one to ask. The eyes, before she'd closed them, had been the colour of smoked glass.

High in the Brynderwyns he woke rigid with cold, a pain burning in the cortex of his brain. Under his pulsing ear and heavy head was a stone, beside the stone an empty bottle. He peeled his tongue away from the acrid roof of his mouth, felt himself scrabbling about in his empty skull on rat feet. How had he come here? The mare was nowhere to be seen. He must have left her with the clearing gang. His mind threw up a picture, an image appearing in an empty frame in the space of a pulse: the boy who had fetched the dinner clambered towards him across the ravaged ground.

'Bad news, Mr McQuiggan. The little one's passed on.' He remembered the men's faces as they watched for his grief, his rage. He knew they thought him cold, irritable, above himself, a black sheep sent away from Auckland. He didn't give them the satisfaction. Instead, he left them to the food and went a distance away in the bush. He didn't weep, though he had felt his mouth draw down in an unwitting contortion at the news of the child's death. Among the trees he'd hidden himself away and wondered if he should go down to Myra, but hadn't she suspected the child wouldn't live long? Hadn't she been exasperated by its perpetual crying? It kept her from her work and her rest. Perhaps there had been something wrong with the child from the moment it was born, and it was as well it had died. Momentarily he felt relief, but it vanished, and was replaced by dread. What would he have to endure from Myra on his return? Torpid, mute despair; the enveloping melancholy of her. He would not be roused to anger, he vowed; he would not shout at her or lock her away from him as he had done on so many occasions.

At sunset he'd left the gang in the hills and set off on the five-mile walk. But he hadn't gone home to her. Below Bald Rock he'd turned instead into a narrow rocky valley, following a clear stream deeper into the bush, to his still. It was dark by the time he'd got there and dug up a bottle, the bottle now empty.

He shifted on the hard ground and a memory, tepid, vague, trickled away at the back of his moonshine-battered brain. It was the shade of another journey, an overwhelming sense that he had failed to meet his destination. For a moment he ceased to breathe, his heart raced, he clamped his hands together between his thighs for comfort and warmth, shied away from the truth that gripped him now, forced him up to his knees, his aching head thrown back to the pale dawn sky above the clearing.

'I did not resist you! Why have you restored me?'

There was no answer, though the bush around him fell silent to receive one. He dropped his eyes, his poisoned head governing the downward movement until he was arrested by the sight of his beloved still: the fireplace of tawny bricks, with a blackened copper set into it. Beside that there were two other coppers, gleaming softly now in the moonlight. These he had carefully rivetted together, so that they might support the stillhead, which was itself connected by a length of pipe to a barrel. It was the barrel, tenderly patched and pitched, made water-tight, that contained the curling worm, the heart of his operation. The worm was where the mysterious alchemy took place, where the whisky vapour was condensed.

The whole contraption was fed with water conveyed by iron piping from the nearby stream. William closed his eyes a moment to listen to the water and saw the still as he'd had it in the spring, flames raking the sides of the fireplace copper, smoke billowing into the heavens. But the ashes had been cold for months: since clearing began he had neglected his blessed machine.

Groaning, he got to his feet and staggered against a punga, which smelt of his mare. It was where she'd rubbed her back during the long days of last spring when he was building the still. Here and there the spiky trunk had caught pale, silvery hairs from her rump. The horse knew more about this place than his wife, who knew nothing. Of a morning, last spring, the horse would turn her head towards the track to the still without any direction from him. He took into his head, suddenly, a plan: he would show Myra his magnificent contraption. She wouldn't know what it was for, he would have to explain. He pictured her suddenly, in their white bed, felt her white arms across his shoulders, the way her breath came in tiny puffs. His lips remembered the soft dip of flesh between her collarbone and young throat.

He plunged off into the bush, his amnesiac heart aching for Myra, wanting her.

A photographer, making the journey from Auckland to Dargaville, had disembarked with his horse from a timber boat at Mangawhai and spent the night on a neighbouring farm. Word spread quickly as words will do that concern themselves with death, and when he knew there was call for him, he thought he would make a diversion. His hosts warned him there was no road to the McQuiggans' place, though the bridle path that led over the Brynderwyns could be used to go some of the way. The old man of the house took him aside and told him that if he played his cards right he could win a bottle of this – and he showed him a bottle of whisky, corked. McQuiggan never attended the church in Hakaru, he said; he was an outsider, and from what they knew he was making a mess of things. The photographer nodded and smiled. Once on the Kaipara gumfields he'd drunk a concoction of logwood, fusil oil, opium and syrup. He'd not been able to bend his head to his camera or hold anything in his stomach for weeks and he'd hardly drunk a drop since, though people had offered him plenty: he had the red swollen face of the dipsomaniac.

On the evening of William's ascension he photographed his hosts on their veranda. Then he packed his equipment into its boxes and strapped them to his horse so as to be ready to make a start after dawn.

He reached the farm at the foot of Pukekaroro just before nine, where he kept the bereaved young mother from the kitchen. A pot boiled over there while he fussed about in the parlour. First, he took the pennies from the infant's eyes.

'We won't be needing these,' he said. 'His eyes will be closed now, good and proper.'

'Her eyes,' Myra told him. 'She is a girl.'

Then he'd tried to move the child closer to the window and the baby almost fell between the chairs.

'For the light,' he explained, his red sweaty face earnest in hers. 'I don't want to disappoint you, ma'am.'

Myra helped him by holding the baby in her arms. It seemed a natural thing to do, to bend to the child and lift her, though in the six weeks of the child's life she had never lifted her quiet. Until the day before, the small red mouth had always been open, the little fists enraged and clenched against her slippery cheeks. Myra had been relieved when the baby had learned to cry less and she had had to struggle to feed her less often.

'Lay her down here, Mrs.' The photographer had rearranged the quilt, but not as nicely as she had had it. Some of the white lawn had fallen away, the Limoges brooch had dropped to the floor. Suddenly, as she replaced them, the drooping ferns, the torn petticoat, Myra felt ashamed. What must the photographer think? The old brooch, the battered doll, the dented trinket box, the worn *Book of Common Prayer*. She was a little fool. Since he'd brought her to the farm William had told her so, and more than once. She brought her hands to her face, covering her shameful, weeping eyes. More tears – they seemed endless. She remembered a girl at the Home in Sydney who'd taken nothing to drink for two days in the vain hope that her tears would stop, that her eyes would find nothing to manufacture them from.

But the man had his back to her, opening his cases. The tripod was brought out from a canvas bag, his camera fitted to it. He glanced at her now, to where she had retreated by the empty fireplace.

'Don't cry, Mrs,' he said. She seemed so very young, tiny and fined boned, her face as white as the pieces of torn cloth she had snatched up. 'When I've finished my work you'll have her to keep for ever. You can get a grand frame and hang her up there.' He gestured to a place above the mantelpiece. Myra nodded. It would be the only picture in the room. The photographer opened the third box.

'I've got a few bits and pieces here,' he began. 'Some ladies like to have a look. You can borrow them, for the picture. No extra charge.'

The red face was turned to her again. Myra looked up into his pale eyes and away. He was a kind man, perhaps. The face was square with a wide mouth and the red, she saw now, was not from heat. It was a sort of rash, vivid at his neck and chin. She wondered if it hurt him.

'Help yourself,' said the man. 'Whatever you like.'

There was a white cross set with yellowing artificial flowers, a pair of white candlesticks, a length of creamy muslin and a wire hoop. Myra knelt and lifted the hoop, a simple arc with a hook at either end.

'Ah,' said the photographer. 'In this instance we won't – you see that is for – for when –'

Her face, from where he stood above her, was ineffably sad. Dark shadows stood under her eyes. She was so alone here, the still-maker's wife. The room was cold. It smelt of ashes and bruised ferns. She was gazing at him now.

'For when the child is in a cradle, or basket,' he finished lamely. 'To make a hood.'

'But we could do this!' Myra stood, her earlier solace from the laying out returning. 'Here!' She stretched the wire out, opening it further, hooking the ends at the side of each chair. 'And hang the muslin over!'

'Ah,' said the photographer. He nodded, saw how strong her hands were, small and square. The skin was chapped and raw, her nails bitten to the quick and her knuckles red against the pallor of her face. 'I'll do it for you. You run and get some candles.'

She did not move; there were only two left in the kitchen dresser, one partly burned. Myra wondered if they must be the same length for the photograph. The photographer thought her pausing was to do with concern over payment.

'No extra cost,' he repeated. 'I need them. For the light.'

Myra passed quickly out of the room. Behind her, the man shook out the muslin.

There had been so much to do since the arrival of the gang that she had not had time to take the candlemaker down from its hook, to boil the tallow and fix the wicks. Perhaps there would have been time this morning if she hadn't kept running into the parlour.

Set into the kitchen wall, above the bench where she kept her dish-pan and rag, there was a tiny window scarcely bigger than her face. It looked west, through the tall legs of the white pine, the Brynderwyns running down one side of its view, the paddocks giving way to bush on the other. Something caught her eye: movement beyond the trees, a tall broad-shouldered man walking with his head pushed forward, his arms loose at his sides. It was William, shambling more than walking. Something must be wrong with him. Perhaps he had wept when news of the child's death reached him with yesterday's dinner, although she doubted it. He hadn't much liked the child. The crying had made him irritable and he hadn't liked her going to it during the night.

She took the last two candles in the house: one three-quarters burnt away, the other bent, through to the parlour.

His wife and a raw-faced fellow in city clothes were arranging muslin over a frame; a flowered cross had been tacked to the chair back behind the little head. Two scruffy, misshapen candles stuck out at odd angles from two chipped white candlesticks. William forced his eye from the sputtering, smutty flame to the child's face and it occurred to him suddenly that such a minute infant had never been properly alive: it had made the journey to the temporal world as incompletely as he had to the other. The notion was an immense comfort to him and he fell to his knees, snatching up the small red book from where it had fallen on the floor.

'William?' The muslin fell from Myra's hands; the photographer gathered it up. William reached for her and she stepped towards him. Too hard – he heard her pained intake of breath – he clasped her fingers, drew her down beside him. Wondering, the photographer bowed his head.

'"If I ascend up into Heaven, Thou art there; if I make my bed in hell, behold, Thou art there."' Grief took men in different ways, the photographer thought. It was a peculiar psalm to choose and the man's voice was strange, high and breathy with emotion.

"'If I take the wings of the morning and dwell in the uttermost parts of the sea —"'

The photographer raised his eyes to see the young wife, perturbed, touch her husband's chest with her free hand. It was swatted away.

"'Even there shall Thy hand lead me —"'

'Please, William,' began Myra. She would pray with him if he wanted her to, but after the photographer had gone away.

'Stay!' hissed her husband. 'Stay.' His chin dropped lower, he closed his mouth. Myra watched his full lips press close together. The child had a mouth like that, the same deep bow at the centre of a long upper lip, the lower lip plump and soft. Would she have had his nature too? It would be impossible to be female and be like him, governed by want and rage.

The three living were as still as the one passed on. All of a sudden the tiny body was bathed in light: the sun had moved around to the window. Quietly, the photographer seized his moment. He slipped the plate into the camera, dived beneath the black hood and made the picture. He was aware, at his back, of the man and woman rising and leaving the room, but the picture took all his attention. He realised he hadn't asked the child's name. There was no outward sign of why it had died but then, in his experience, there rarely was. He moved the tripod to make a closer representation of the child's face and head. It had the mother's wide brow and tiny chin, a sprinkle of dark hair in the centre of its head. Through the fine open weave of the shawl he could see the tiny fingers laid carefully one between the other of the opposing hand, pale and shiny as freshwater pearls.

Her fingers were the fastest advancing part of her above her tripping feet, aching and buzzing, gripped tightly in William's hot hand. They passed through the stand of kahikatea, skirted the half-built barn, made a zigzag at the base of the hill where it rose suddenly from the green paddock. This was surely a concession to her dress, she thought: she had seen him from the tiny window taking those few feet at a bound. Then there was the ridge, which they hurried along, her husband towing her even faster now, before they entered the forest which still clad the hills.

Myra didn't know the names of the trees. She hardly distinguished their different forms. This sort of bush unnerved her. It wasn't like the scrubby bush around Yarrabin that was full of light: you could pass through it on horseback and provided you didn't meet with a rare, discontented black or irritable snake it was a pleasant place to be. Eucalyptus air smelt clean and fresh and lifted the soul, unlike this pong of damp and rot which filled her gasping nostrils and made her think of death, of sea voyages and cramped dirty beds, of cold nights and discomfort. But there – a parson bird called out nearby, his beautiful song lifting from his tufted throat. There was a tui that came close to her on washdays at the creek by the house, to the tree with the long yellow flowers, like wattle. At first she thought it a shame that such a song should rise from a plain, dowdy bird, until she looked closely at him and saw the iridescence in the black feathers, the purity of his white ruff. Some Australian birds were bright pink and red, green and gaudy, with voices designed to carry over vast distances. They sounded like sheep, or cross babies, or trains clanging in the sidings. Why did God not put the two together, Myra wondered now, the bright feathers and fluting song? Perhaps such a bird would be too perfect for this world, as perfect as she had thought William to be.

On the narrow track her husband released her hand and hooked her fingers through the waistband of his trousers as if she were a child or a simpleton. She watched the rise and fall of his strong shoulders, glowing in his red flannel shirt, as he climbed the steep incline ahead of her. Pressed between his belt and shirt her fingers sensed the heat of him, the shift and pull of muscles in his strong back. Sometimes, in their bed, she would lift her hands from the sheets and lie them across his back as he made love to her, heavy and hard. Her body remembered the sensation of his mouth at her neck, his hot, scouring face against her shoulder, and her mind attempted to shut the sensation off, but her cheeks were burning, her hand had dropped from his belt and her feet in their thin boots halted their struggle after his heavily shod ones. She wanted him to turn now and take her in his arms, to kiss her and stroke her hair. A deep breath filled her lungs; she wondered at her trembling. The sky was almost concealed by the heavy canopy. A sprinkle of rain crossed her lifted face, bringing with it the perfume of the broad leaves above. The tui called out again, from behind them now.

He was coming back towards her. Had he had time to get that far ahead? she wondered. She'd paused only for a moment. His face was odd: she'd never seen his mouth take that shape before. He took her roughly by the arm.

'Did I tell you to stop?' he asked.

The whiff of happiness vanished as quickly as it had arrived. She shook her head.

'You do as I tell you.'

Her hand had been taken up again, held so tight against his turning body that she tripped, her face falling against him. He smelt of sweat, ash, sheep and something else. Shellac, was it, or turpentine?

'Are we going to the gang?' she asked, pushing the flat of her hand against his back to right herself. He didn't answer. She couldn't bear it, the cold unfeeling silence. It was only because she'd forgotten, in that instant and the instant before, how he'd been with her since the birth of the child, that she spoke on.

'Because if we are, I could've brought the bread with me, and the stew –'

He whirled around so quickly she had no time to duck or raise an arm in defence before she was knocked backwards, a sharp sudden pain running across an axis in her head, ear to ear, and taking consciousness with it.

From a greater height than his almost six foot he watched her below him. Her pale dress was slicked with mud, a thread of blood emerged from one ear and wound into her hair. William took in these details as if he watched from the tops of the trees. He could see himself also, the bowed crown of his hat, his clenched fists. He would not hit her again, he was certain. It was not Myra he had struck, it was not what he had meant. It was God he had whirled against: His rejection of him. Why could he not remember what had happened after he had passed into the Kingdom? He clearly remembered the ecstasy of his approach, his entry and after that . . . nothing. He watched himself, contrite now, felt tears on his own cheeks as he bent to lift the woman from the ground. Her errant hand, the one that had caressed him before it fell from his belt, lay finger and palm flattened in the mud. She was so tiny, her waist narrower now than it was when they married.

There was a voice, rising in the still noon of the world outside the bush.

'Mrs McQuiggan –'

The caller was distant, male. The photographer had finished his work.

Her weight on his shoulder brought William back to himself. He carried his wife up the hill.

They were in a clearing, a kind of camp. Myra's eyes opened to an exposed sky of high grey cloud. From nearby came the sound of a torrent – loud, water falling on rocks. Crouched before her was William, dipping the tail of his shirt into a tin cup of water. He'd laid her on some sacking. Gently, he eased her over to face him and sponged the blood from her ear. It seemed now the torrent was inside her head, a rushing thunder that grew louder still, deafening her to her husband. His lips were moving and tears filled his eyes, brimmed and fell to his cheeks. Myra's heart constricted and she reached up a hand, softly wiped the tears away, looked into his eyes. They were the deepest blue, almost black, ringed around with long eyelashes that were damp, stuck together with his remorse. Perhaps he hadn't meant to hit her. Perhaps he had lost his footing on the slippery track and spun with his arms flailing. She would believe that. He let his head fall onto her breast.

'It's all right, my love,' she said. 'Please don't. It's all right.' Her husband's shoulders were heaving; she could feel warmth and moisture through her bodice from his mouth against her clothes. There was an odd vibration against her chest, as if he were speaking, but she couldn't hear him.

'You are muttering, my darling,' she told him. 'I can't hear you.' Her own voice was muffled too, as if it never reached the air but travelled to her hearing through her bones and flesh. She sat up slowly and the trees leapt towards her with a flashing head pain, receded again. What place was this? Her improvised bed was near a fireplace, properly laid with bricks and mortar. Had a house stood here once, been burnt down? Maybe some of the Maoris had once built a European-style house here, with a fireplace. A copper sat in the fireplace, identical to the one she'd had in her wash-house at the farm. Two other coppers were fixed together with a small machine above them. There was a roof over them, a railway tarpaulin held up by manuka sticks. Behind William a hogshead lay fallen on its side, the dark wash of its contents seeping into the earth. Several other barrels, still standing, were linked by pipes running from one to the other.

William watched his wife take it all in.

'What's it for?' she asked when her eyes rested on him again, her voice unnaturally loud.

'For making whisky.'

Myra inclined her head. She hadn't heard him, William realised. Had he hit her that hard? He felt sick, swallowed bile as he watched her push her skirts aside and try to stand.

He helped her up and she gasped, holding herself. There was no blood on her dress – he prised her hand away to see – he hadn't hurt her that badly. She pulled away from him, though he could see the movement hurt her, and went to the fireplace.

'When this went missing you blamed the Maoris,' she said, touching the rim of the copper.

William gazed at the ground.

'I believed you. I said a terrible thing to Riha.'

There was real remorse in her voice. William wondered at her self-reproach. It was as unnatural as the volume. For five months, while she was large with child, she'd had to make do without it, boiling small garments in the preserving pan, thumping the laundry dolly on grey sheets, scrubbing his shirts with hard soap in cold water.

'Riha will have forgotten that by now,' William said, although he knew she wouldn't have. She loomed before him, formidable, twice the size of his wife.

'What is this?' Myra was asking again. She rested her hand on the stillhead.

William went to her, took her by the shoulders and said loudly, 'For making grog. It's a still.'

She was still quizzical, so he tried again, contorting his face with each syllable like a clown.

'Whis-kee.'

Her eyes lifted from his lips, registering dismay. 'Whisky? Why?'

He didn't answer her. Instead he put his hands on his hips, smiling a little and gazing over her shoulder into the gloom of the bush at the clearing's edge.

The river in her head was quietening now to a trickle. Myra watched her husband and saw suddenly how he must have been as a little boy: sly, cocky, bent on secret schemes. His father he spoke of with utter contempt, almost loathing, the old man who lived in a fine house in Auckland, with servants. She knew this only because William had told her.

Myra had never been invited there herself; she had spent the night before the wedding alone in the hotel. And the old lady, who'd come to their wedding with William's favourite sister, she was finely dressed. It was she who'd brought them their Bible and the teapot with the roses on it . . .

William caught her faraway look and hurried over to her. He took her hands and gazed at her earnestly as if he had some vital news, talking, pointing down the track and at the barrels and hogsheads around them. Perhaps he was explaining their various functions, she thought. She couldn't hear him. Her eyes rested on his animated face, the sweet lips and brow, and she remembered the life he had rescued her from in Sydney. She would forgive him, of course, how could she not? She had seen the alternative life, the life she would have led if he hadn't come to the Home that day. Her husband's rages were brief, easily survived. Had she stayed in Sydney she would have died, she would be dead by now, worn out by it all. She remembered when she first saw him, standing in the Home's porch, a good Samaritan. He had brought in a first fall, a girl large with child whom he said he'd found on the street. The girl was a stranger to him, he told Matron, but even so he'd pressed money into her hand.

She put her hands up to rest on his shoulders, offered her lips for a kiss. William stopped talking, bent his mouth to hers. One hand slipped behind her, ruched up her skirt handful over handful, until his rough palm slipped over her smooth skin, his fingers eased her legs apart. He was leading her backwards to the pile of sacking, dropping onto it, his trousers were unbuttoned and he was pulling her onto himself.

She was watching him, he noticed. There was a resistance in her, or was it apprehension? He hadn't seen her face like that since their wedding night. He used a hand to ease himself in. It was their first time like this, with her on top, and the first time since the birth of the child. No wonder he had hit her then, what would she expect? His abstinence had been unnatural. She was all he had to relieve him, there were no whores for miles and he hadn't wanted to insist, not so soon after the birth.

She moaned, he thought perhaps with pain. He'd make it quick then. She'd turned her face away. He reached up to her chin and brought her around to look at him again. How a woman's face changed in congress! Most women, he corrected himself. When he was sixteen, in Wellington, he'd had an old whore who'd made him think of the magician's assistant at side-shows, the woman cut in half, entirely removed from her lower portion. She'd gazed over his shoulder with unfocused fish eyes. He held Myra firmly by the hips and jogged her up and down. There was the moaning sound again, pleasure this time.

She had begun to make the journey with him, step by step in her heart, the very heart of her body, to want him there. The next time she had him her journey would be complete, she promised herself. She would be with him when he reached her very centre, just beneath her heart, the seat of her soul. He was grinning up at her. That even full mouth, his strong teeth. Dark hair curled in the bow of his breastbone: she dipped her finger in it, at the base of his throat, cupped the other hand behind his head. He cried out then; she saw his mouth open. It must have been a loud cry, loud enough to flush a bird from a nearby tree away into the dim forest. It flapped close over her head, the draught of its wings startling her as she stood up, bringing one leg stumblingly over his body for decency while he buttoned himself. She lifted her face to trace the bird's progress, but it had vanished.

William lay still on the sacking, the tin cup by his shoulder, its contents tinged pink. He was laughing now, she realised, after watching him for a moment. How odd it looked when you couldn't hear it. His head was tipped back, his red mouth open below her. She had a childish urge to drop in a spider or a slaterbug. Why was he laughing? Had he made her ridiculous, having her that way? He knew different ways of how men and women could be together. Sometimes he would take her from behind.

33

He was leaping to his feet now, taking her hand, kissing her cheek. As his mouth came close to her ear she heard a gust of his laughter, as distant as if she were standing on a windy railway platform while someone yelled from an open window in a passing train. He led her away across the clearing. There was a metal pipe that gleamed in the fallen leaves and bracken beside them. They followed its length along to where it dipped into a stream. She had to balance on the huge river stones as he pushed ahead, holding back toi-toi and raupo until they reached the water's edge, where he helped her to unlace her boots.

Lifting her skirts above her knees, Myra paddled out, squatted away from him. He could hear splashing in the clear shallow water. She was trying to wash the mud from her skirts, from when she'd fallen on the track. Perhaps when he got back to the house he would try to write it all down for her: the epiphany, his decision to dismantle the still. He couldn't shout it at her now, loud enough for her to hear. He would be forced to abridge it and he wanted her to have the details, the whole truth of his epiphany as far as he could remember it. He wasn't much good at explaining ordinary things, he thought; words were apt to freeze in his mouth, numbing his tongue and thickening his lips.

Lifting each foot out of the water step by step, like a grey heron, pointing toe first to submerge it again, she was picking her way back towards him. He saw how the colour that had flushed her face when they made love had drained away.

While she sat on the warm stones to lace her boots, he waded out to the iron contraption which sat above a small cascade. She watched him bend over it and wrench it free from its connecting pipe. The bush was silent; she couldn't hear his feet moving through the water. A dull pain glimmered deep in her head and Myra shook herself, hoping to dislodge it, but the motion had the opposite effect – it was like breathing on a fire. The pain leapt up and burned brighter. Panic flared with it, questions raced with the creaming river in front of her. Would her hearing return, she wondered, sooner or later? Perhaps William would be irritated by her deafness, perhaps he would see it as another instance of failure. A great pit opened in her stomach and she longed suddenly to be sitting beside her baby, watching the tiny face before she was lost to her for ever. For ever until she held her again in Heaven. What did God do with all the babies that died on earth? she wondered. Was there a kind of nursery where they were cared for by the angels, or were they fostered out among the women? If that were so, then she hoped whoever it was who took Alithea cared well for her, better than she had herself.

In the stream William wrestled still with the pump, lifting it in his arms and crossing towards her with his legs bowed by its weight. A fine drizzly rain had begun, which didn't so much fall as well about them, like smoke.

The long descent was protracted by William's insistence on bringing the copper back to the farm, though he had failed in this mission. On a ridge he had fumbled and dropped it. It rolled away, down the steep slope, banging and ringing like a bell. Then for the last part of the downward climb he'd had to carry Myra on his back, while she shivered and clung to him for warmth. A cold moon had risen early, bringing with it a sharp strong wind. As he carried her through the kahikatea, her skirts flapped and cracked behind him like a sail. The sound gladdened his heart for a moment, made him remember his youthful voyage to England in 1885, too long ago now. A notion of the outside world beyond this hideous, dark, endless solitude glowed softly, gold and inviting. He saw the lobby of a grand hotel, its thick carpet and glittering chandelier, the gleaming white bosom of a woman he could have for a night, a woman he'd never need to carry through mud on his aching back.

The photographer had left the door open. Myra pushed at his shoulders for him to put her down, her head full of a silent clamour. The baby was gone from her in the most profound sense, but still here, a little body requiring care until she was folded under the earth. There were dogs, thieves, strangers, demons . . .

In the kitchen William helped her find the lamp and held it over her into the parlour. The hoop and muslin, the flowered cross, the white candlesticks had gone with the photographer. The mother bent in the gloom, the smell of the picked ferns rising as she trampled the leaves underfoot. The child's face peeped from the wrapping – she'd been wrapped by the man. It was not how Myra would have left her: the head was bare. The eyes gleamed white, almost as if the eyelids had sprung open. Myra bent closer; William obliged by holding the lamp lower. No, the translucent lids were closed and her face – Myra's finger stroked again – the face was so very cold. She let her hand drop to the child's receiver to adjust it.

There was a tiny moan, a sound that chilled William's bones. It was the sound the child made at the end of a long crying bout in the early hours of the morning.

'William.' Her new loud voice grated on his nerves. He put the lamp on the mantelpiece and turned up the wick. All he wanted was to lay his head down and sleep, it pounded so. He wanted to think about what had happened last night, forget about the child. His wife was crying properly now, less like a child and more like a woman. Lord help him, he couldn't abide that noise.

'He's taken my shawl. The one I made with the wool your mother sent. And the brooch! My mother's brooch . . .' Myra was on her knees, looking under the chairs that held the child. There was no other furniture in the poor room, nowhere else for her to look.

'Quiet now, Myra. No more.' He pulled his wife to her feet, took up the lamp and led her, gulping and limp, to their bedroom.

CHAPTER 3

It was light at six. Myra had been up for an hour by the time her husband woke and felt for her. In the kitchen a bowl sat by the porridge pot with a spoon in it. Was he expected to get his own, then? He inclined his head to the sound of the axe outside and held the flat of his hand against the pot. It was warm, just. The fire was out. At the sight of the grey insides of the fire-box, rage blew open in him again and he slammed its door. What the devil was the matter with the woman? Why didn't she go and chop the wood before the fire went out, not afterwards? The axe chopped steadily, strong. William pressed his lips together, turned towards the door. The axe stopped and there was a tumbling noise as she filled the basket, the weighted tread of her foot on the boards behind him. He made a show of sitting at the table, took on the face of a man who's waited hours for his breakfast. The Maori woman at the door was vast – taller than him – his senior by twenty years. She wore a ruffled flannel nightgown in an alarming shade of pink. Riha.

'Morning,' she said. He sensed her disapproval and ignored it. He wasn't responsible for the baby's death. Riha fed the fire, blew the embers back to life.

'Where is she?' he asked. Riha flashed her eyes towards the parlour and he stood, would have gone there, but Riha's hand dropped hard, open-palmed on his shoulder.

'You leave her. Let her grieve.'

'Why did you come back?'

'My sister Poihaere saw you carrying it down. The kohue for doing the washing.' Riha made no effort to keep the scorn from her voice. She doled out his porridge, handed him the salt. 'But I'm not staying.'

'Saw me carrying what? Speak English.' William looked up at her for long enough to see her face harden with dislike for him. Then suddenly she shivered, looked around the room with her flashing eyes. Her large gestures reminded him of a Vaudeville artist, or a clown.

'What is it?' The rage had burst now. He couldn't hold it back. He crashed his spoon against the edge of the bowl. The air was suddenly heavy with Riha's loathing. She curled her lip, tapped the side of her head.

'Porangi,' she said. 'Little Myra in there. She hides her face from me. She doesn't answer when I speak to her.'

He said nothing, picked up his spoon again, shovelled down his lumpy porridge.

'Another thing,' said Riha, 'I should tell you. The gang has gone.'

'Good riddance,' said William. 'Useless mob of black bastards.'

'Don't you use language like that around me,' said Riha. She was coming towards him with the spoon and for a moment he thought she would strike him, but she leaned across the table and slid his bowl away. William waited. She didn't move.

'You're a bad man, Mr McQuiggan,' she said. 'I don't know what you've done to little Myra. She's gone dead in her heart, as dead as that poor baby.'

William left the room. The parlour door stood open, the chairs were gone. It occurred to him he'd sat on one of them while he ate his breakfast. His boots rang on the floorboards. There, through the window, outside, Myra waited for him, facing away down the valley. She was in her church clothes, her old-fashioned black bonnet, and the child was in her arms. William cursed his father. If he hadn't deserted him, expected the farm to support the young couple, if he'd kept paying William's allowance, he wouldn't be in this situation. He flung out of the house, caught the mare and brought her to his wife.

The drizzle of early evening had swollen to heavy rain during the night and much of the track was over two feet deep in mud. Behind him on the horse Myra sat hunched over the child, protecting it from the dripping leaves above. When he'd helped her up, William had met her eyes and wanted immediately to take to the hills, dig up a bottle. He'd seen the misery in them and he didn't want to. A woman's misery was different to a man's. A woman takes on a begging look, unlike a man. Misery makes a man angry and how angry he was, thought William, angrier all the time, with the man who had put them here: Justice Elisha McQuiggan, his own father, who in return for meeting William's debts – which the son had incurred despite his generous allowance – had bought the land and put the young couple on it. He had reserved capital for the purchase of further stock after the land was cleared; he had promised furniture and goods for the finished house. The house was finished and the furniture was not forthcoming. How hungry he was, William thought: he had the constant sense he was starving. The son of a widely respected judge, starving in this land of plenty! He had told his father so in his last letter, had used the very phrase, but the old man had replied that there would be no further assistance until the land was cleared. All of it, not just the narrow flats. How he knew the way things stood William had no idea. A spy perhaps, an informer, someone who came under the cover of night, or when William was on Pukekaroro with his still, or sleeping off a binge in the daylight hours in a darkened room. His father could never chastise him for the still. It was all he and Myra had to hold body and soul together. He would tell him that too, one day.

A drink. A blessed, sweet dram. How he needed one. The pain was worse than usual this morning – not in his strong legs which sucked and tore and stumbled through the thick mud, but in the bones of his skull, the tendons in his throat and tongue. The pain only ever struck him in the head.

'Wait a moment,' he said to Myra, without looking back at her, and he left the track for a moment, going out of her sight to drain the hip flask in his jacket pocket. Not much, though it warmed his stomach and softened his heart, enough for him to feel pity for the small dark figure when he returned, hunched in her ugly bonnet on the horse, the tiny wrapped corpse close under her cloak. Pity. It was all he felt for her now really, though he never would have dreamed, when he first laid eyes on Myra Hopkins, that she would engender that.

There was nothing to stop him going up to the still tonight, he thought, as he led the horse down the lower slopes of Pukekaroro, nothing at all. He hadn't taken the pledge, he hadn't told his wife about his vision. The experience was still locked away in his own head. He could forget it, break it down to tiny particles of memory, a broken mosaic devoid of meaning and resolve. Yes. It never happened. It was not an epiphany, but a dream brought on by the whisky. There was no need to form a loyalty to it, no need to feel this deadening guilt that took him now. He would go to the still tonight and before he drank he would pray. Yes. He would give God another chance.

Wide brown puddles lay in the Hakaru road. A beam of sunlight pierced the heavy clouds and the puddles winked and flashed like the new pennies she'd put on the baby's eyes. William struggled to keep his mind on the matter at hand. The child must be buried, the wife returned to the farm, then he could quench his thirst. The puddles broke, splashed around the horse's legs.

For the first time in the silent, jolting journey down from the farm Myra lifted her eyes from the child.

'You're going home now.' Her right hand pulled the cloth over the baby's face and she knew she would not look at her again.

They stopped outside a little wooden church set in a wide green churchyard. Except for at its periphery it was bare of trees, as if the vicar considered he would one day need all the ground for his departed. A young macrocarpa stood near the lychgate and William let the horse stand beside it. A small white cross topped the steeple, gleaming against the black roiling sky. Myra lifted her eyes to it and felt a kind of warmth, an engulfing sense of relief. Her husband had draped the old mare's rope over one of the fence palings, his mouth was moving and he was walking away.

'William!' she called, wanting to dismount. She held out the child, but her husband misunderstood, shook his head, backed off.

'You wait.' She read his lips. 'I'll get the priest.'

He had no need to. The Reverend's wife had seen them and came hurrying from the vicarage gate. She took the small parcel from the younger, icy hands. William helped his wife down from the horse.

'Mrs McQuiggan,' she said, 'come and dry off in the house.' She noticed how keenly the young woman watched her lips and was a little disconcerted. Myra nodded but waited still by the gate.

'No, no – this way.' Mrs Wayland took her arm and guided her further down the road to the vicarage.

William watched them for a moment before he trudged after them, wondering if the older lady would notice the bruising around his wife's eye. He'd only noticed it himself as she walked towards him then. The colour must have come up between home and Hakaru. Now, in the vicarage garden, Myra was touching a spot on either side of her bonnet, shaking her head. Mrs Wayland leaned towards her, touched her face. William saw her glance quickly in his direction before she turned, took her guest across the veranda and inside. He would count on the old lady's good breeding and his wife's shame: nothing would be said, which was just as well. He couldn't stomach a sermon from the priest.

He took his time traversing the space between the gate and front door, pretended not to have noticed that Reverend Wayland himself had come out to meet him and was standing on the front step. William bent to the roses growing on either side of the path, admired the grove of immature oaks on his right, lifted his gaze to a line of poplars showing their heads above the house roof. He reached the lower step and the priest's hand clasped his.

'Mr McQuiggan.'

'Good morning, Reverend.' William would not meet his eye. The priest's arm was rigid, unbending, keeping him on the bottom step.

'May I suggest that you call on Mr McNeill and procure a small white coffin. I do not provide them. Indeed, Mr McQuiggan, I am surprised that you did not build one yourself immediately after the child's passing.' The old man's eyes were rheumy, yellowing. His nose was spread across his face. As a young priest he'd sought out recalcitrant parishioners and fought them. He had not let go of William's hand: he strong-armed him still.

'God have mercy on you, you miserable sinner,' Reverend Wayland finished his speech, which he had prepared while he watched the still-maker dither in the garden. He released William, turned on his heel and walked inside. A lace curtain at the window of the front room twitched with Mrs Wayland's liver-spotted old hand. There was a flash of his wife, the white wrapped baby on her knee.

It was her fault the baby had died. If she'd looked after it properly it wouldn't have happened. If the baby had lived Myra would be none the wiser about the still, the copper would still be there, he wouldn't have lost control of it and had to stand there, helpless, while it bounced into a ravine on the journey home. If the baby had lived Myra would still have her hearing. This last thought so aggravated him, he kicked one of the fence palings, hard, as he passed the cemetery.

In the dim vicarage parlour Mrs Wayland lit a lamp. She set it on the occasional table beside Mrs McQuiggan and made a remark about the light, the way the thundery clouds made it seem as if it were five o'clock in the afternoon.

'And it's only eleven!' she finished. Mrs McQuiggan's mouth lifted minutely at the corners but her eyes gave no indication that she'd heard. Mrs Wayland sighed and took a pencil and piece of paper from the sideboard.

'Mr McQuiggan has gone to fetch a coffin.'

The notepaper was held out to her in the glow of the lamp. Myra narrowed her eyes and read as quickly as she could – 'McQuiggan' and 'coffin'. She nodded and the paper returned to Mrs Wayland's lap to be inscribed with a question. It was the one Myra knew she would ask. She had dreaded it since the child died.

'Is the child baptised?'

Myra shook her head, kept her eyes on the white-wrapped cocoon of the child.

'He wouldn't . . . my husband . . . he wouldn't bring us down for a christening. I should say . . . I shouldn't say he wouldn't because I'm sure he meant to, but he couldn't. He was busy, up in the hills and I . . . I . . . forgive me, Mrs Wayland . . . I did it myself, as best I could, when she was a few days old.'

Mrs Wayland lifted a hand in amazement. Myra saw her lips say, 'Yourself?' and nodded in reply. The priest's wife wrote on the piece of paper again.

'What did you do?'

'I knew the words. My father was a minister in Australia and I attended many baptisms.'

Mrs Wayland was looking at her strangely and Myra thought perhaps she disapproved.

'Forgive me,' she said again, 'the baby was ill and I thought she might die.' The baby's face filled her mind, the drowsy eyes opening with the first drops of cool water on her brow, her expression puzzled as she looked up from the crook of Myra's arm. As she'd knelt on the veranda boards, Myra had set down a saucer of water.

' . . . in the name of the Father, and of the Son and of the Holy Ghost,' she'd murmured, making the sign of the cross on the baby's translucent skin. 'We beseech thee to sanctify this Water to the mystical washing away of sin; and grant that this child may receive the fullness of thy grace . . .' She'd faltered then, realised she'd confused two different parts of the order. She'd held the baby close, felt the infant butt weakly for milk, but her breasts had been swollen, so sore she could scarcely bear the rub of her clothes. The movement of the baby had sent tendrils of pain through her, even into her groin. She'd felt suddenly hot and breathless and had rearranged herself to sit with the child on her knee.

The front door closed and the priest's footsteps sounded in the hall.

'I only knew some of the words,' Myra corrected herself. 'I said them, then the Lord's Prayer. I made the sign of the cross . . .'

Mrs Wayland glanced towards the door, then at her bereft little guest, who was silenced by her momentary distraction. The bruising around the eye, the deafness. The husband had struck her. Mrs Wayland quickly brought a finger to her lips to ensure Myra's continued silence, while at the same time offering up a prayer, asking for forgiveness in advance. She was going to lie to the Reverend.

Her husband's hands gripped the chair back behind her.

'So. How are we, ladies?' he asked, peering into Myra's face.

'Mrs McQuiggan has lost her hearing,' said Mrs Wayland. 'We hope only temporarily.'

'In that case,' said the old man, 'I might be frank. Mr McQuiggan is a wastrel, as I have long suspected. I've sent him to McNeill's.'

'I gathered as much,' said his wife.

'Will she let me take the child?' The priest came around to face Myra, a smile creasing his tough old face.

'I think so,' Mrs Wayland murmured.

Her husband bent, scooped up the little body into his arms. The mother made no protest. 'Was the child baptised?'

Forgive me, Lord Jesus, thought Mrs Wayland and nodded.

'I did not officiate myself. Where did they take her?'

Mrs Wayland took a deep breath. 'You remember when the young cleric was here, young Andrew?'

'I do indeed,' said her husband.

'And one day he went walking, up into the hills? Yes. Well, on that day he chanced to meet Mrs McQuiggan and she asked him to oblige her. Her husband was too busy with the breaking in of the farm to make the trip down here.'

Myra watched the old couple, heard their words only as a faint murmur. Possibly she was hearing more – it seemed every now and then as if the sound blew towards her, then retreated again.

Mrs Wayland's chest ached, her heart thumped too fast. Lying didn't agree with her, but she couldn't have borne it if her husband had turned the young woman away. If he suspected that the child had not received the sacrament – and look how he was gazing at her now, he suspected that very thing – he would do just that. It was a rule that most vicars in the new country had dispensed with, but her husband held to it still. He weighed the wisp of a child in his hands, gazed upon the pale little mother and pursed his lips.

'Andrew never mentioned such a meeting to me,' he said to his wife. 'It must have slipped his mind.'

Mrs Wayland suspected that at this point she should meet her husband's eyes. It would add to the veracity of her story. But she could not. Forgive me, Lord, she thought again, for my deception of this dear man.

'Perhaps in a little while you could send Mrs McQuiggan out to the lychgate. Join us in the churchyard as you would like, or not.' And Reverend Wayland went, taking the child with him.

'Where has the priest gone?' Myra asked. She would not turn her head for a last glimpse of the child.

'He will return soon,' wrote Mrs Wayland. As she wrote Myra suddenly wanted to reach out and pat the silvery top of her kind head but she kept her hands in her lap, just as she had when the priest had bent to her to take the little corpse away.

Mrs Wayland thought of her husband in the churchyard, digging the grave. An unpleasant task and doubly so in the rain, though Reverend Wayland, who many years ago had made a grim resolution to preserve an unrelenting optimism, maintained to his wife that grave-digging was easier in the rain than in drought. This summer had been a healthy one for his parishioners: the McQuiggan child was only the second death and the first one a drowning with the body unrecovered.

Myra nodded again, sensed a rattling in her ears, a sudden pain on the side that William had struck, answered by a twin pain on the side that had struck the ground when she fell. She lowered her head with it.

'What is the matter?' the old lady asked.

Myra heard her, as though the query had been called from another room, but heard her nevertheless.

'Shall I see if there is an object or . . .' Warm hands took her face, turned her head to the light.

'Your ear is bleeding,' came the diagnosis as Mrs Wayland turned Myra's head to look into the other ear. 'And the same on this side. A clot must've formed or some such . . . I will get you a piece of gauze and some drops.' The old lady left the room.

A trickle of blood ran down Myra's neck. She caught it with her finger and uncovered a worn patch on the rug with her toe. The room was hard-worked, faded, genteel. A silver-plated teapot had the black showing from years of polishing. There was the settle, two chairs, a painted firescreen, china figurines in pale colours, a fern frond made of kauri gum on the mantelpiece, an elaborate pink and gold vase of late summer roses from the garden, a clock in a glass dome with its workings exposed, a pewter jug, a picture of Queen Victoria and, above it, above that –

'Oh!' Myra stood, crossed the room to the black-framed daguerreotype. It was a child, older than her own, plump cheeked and pictured lace-gowned in his coffin. She reached up, touched the face. Above the coffin, which had been carefully balanced against a wall, was a steadying hand. An attempt had been made to paint it out. It looked ghostly, like the hand of God. Myra recognised the wide knuckles and blunt fingernails as belonging to the priest.

Mrs Wayland had returned. A small glass bottle glimmered in one hand and she clasped a wad of clean cloth in the other. She put the things down and wrote again on the paper.

'He was three years of age. He was my angel.'

Myra's tears welled; the old lady clasped her hand and drew her back to the settle. She wouldn't tell her about the two daughters she'd lost even younger, as babies: the girl was not containing her grief.

'Here.' She offered a handkerchief. 'I have six grown children with families of their own,' she said loudly. 'You will too.'

'Oh, I hope so,' whispered Myra. 'I would like seven. Seven to live.'

Mrs Wayland smiled, tipped Myra's head to one side and administered the soothing drops, a concoction of wine of opium, oil of anise and sweet almond.

McNeill's was a half-hour ride from St Stephen's and, although he was one of William's dedicated customers, the two men had scarcely exchanged a word. It was men like McNeill who reminded William that he was the son of a judge. They made his mouth clam up, shamed his slumming blood to sludge.

At first, opening the door to the still-maker who was unshaven and wild eyed, the carpenter thought McQuiggan was making an effort to be friendly. But it was out to the shed at the back of his tiny cottage that the man wanted to go. Four of the McNeill children trailed them.

'Back inside to your mother,' he snarled, cuffing them away.

There were two raw, unpainted coffins, the right size, on the shelf.

'Don't like making them.' McNeill's tone was doleful. 'But they're always filled one way or another.'

'I won't be back here again,' William said quickly.

The carpenter raised a sardonic, ginger eyebrow. 'You work out a way of stopping them coming, you work out a way of stopping them dying.' He slid the coffin into his arms. 'You'll have to wait while the paint dries.' He bent to a shelf under the bench, produced a bottle of McQuiggan's and offered the bottle to its maker.

William stuck his finger into a cobweb that masked the shed's smeary single window. It pulled away, revealing an alarming eye, a face, tufts of ill-kempt hair, a protruding tongue. One of the carpenter's children, not much more than a babe, held swaying on the shoulders of an older sibling. Such risk, such carelessness.

He stepped back, his hands folded around the narrow neck of the bottle, and laid the open neck against his lips. Sudden love rose in him for his own daughter, more than he ever felt for her in her short life, a jagged, violent wrenching that scraped at his bowels. The Scotsman looked at him suspiciously as he doubled over. He took the bottle from him, swigged at it himself.

'Nothing wrong with it.'

'It's my whisky, is it not?' William replied in his best city voice, straightened up. His hair brushed the tin roof: he was head and shoulders above McNeill. He took the bottle up again and drank. It burned, scorched his open gullet; something in him begged for the bottle to be laid aside but he drank as a penance. A softer man would hurl it out again. He resolved to keep it down, felt himself sway, his vision blacken and blur as the brush flew back and forth spreading white on the pale wood.

'Can't wait for that.' His lips felt swollen. 'The paint. Got the priest waiting for me.' He pictured them all sitting in that lace-curtained room, the priest murmuring a prayer as they waited for him. He despised them all. None of them had the courage to approach God as he had, to know the terror and awe of Him. He knew God as they never could. Their lisping, whining prayers were despicable.

McNeill gauged the level in the bottle: an amber inch where previously there were six.

'. . . take the raw one,' William went on, grabbing it from the shelf, tucking it under his arm and lurching for the door. But the carpenter had him by the back of his coat, his other hand palm up in front of his face. William caught a whiff from his mouth, the bad teeth only partly masked by the grog.

'Settle up now,' he was saying. 'The whisky as well.'

William dug deep, fished out two shillings and slapped them into his hand. Then somehow the door fell open ahead of him and he followed it, wiping moisture away from his eyes. McNeill's wife had come from the house, big with child, to shoo her brats away from his horse. She turned her face up to him as he took a clumsy mount. She was mixed blood, half her husband's age.

'Tell your wife Tui is sorry for her troubles,' she whispered.

He nodded, laid the coffin across his knees and turned the mare's head towards Hakaru.

Myra waited on the rough bench under the lychgate roof, holding Mrs Wayland's gauze against her ear. What delight it was to hear: quick, gusty winds whipped a tree above, its autumn leaves rattled, rain caught in its branches fell in heavy drops on the iron. The sound was full of rhythms and patterns, like a dance.

She had seen William arrive on his horse, watched quietly as he slid from the saddle, slipped in the mud and fell on his seat in a deep puddle before the gate. He'd looked surprised, then horrified, held his hand to his mouth for a moment and belched, loud as a barking dog. Then, white faced, he'd struggled to his feet and checked the coffin was undamaged. As he'd passed through the narrow passage between the bench seats of the gate, she'd held her breath, pushed her whole being backwards away from him. There was a sense of herself passing out of her body, through a gap between her shoulder blades, recoiling away from him. A vapour clung about him, the same as the one that had risen from the barrels and coppers at his bush camp.

Myra closed her eyes to his staggering back as he went to the vestry for the priest. Two years ago in Yarrabin, when she'd buried her father, she'd sat like this under a little gate roof that had cast a black, sharply defined shadow in the dust. She had been alone then too, her solitude piercing, but full of promise. There was a little money; she was the only beneficiary. In all her prayers, for all the bewildering months afterwards, she'd asked God to reveal a little of his plan for her.

God's plan, she could see now, was more of the same. Her father had been priest of a lonely parish. His wife had died four years after the birth of their only child. The old man – he was old even when Myra was born, wizened by the long roadless distances he daily traversed and by the hard souls of hard men and the unwelcoming land – never married again. There was a succession of housekeepers until Myra was thirteen, when her father deemed her old enough to run the household for him. For three years after that there were only the two of them, Myra and her father, a shy, silent man who'd made love to his wife only the once and found the experience too alarming to repeat. The father was surprised that his daughter even existed, that on the one regrettable time he had lain between his sad wife's rigid thighs he had created her. He'd looked on her always with astonishment, which prevented any understanding or intimacy between them. He never marvelled over her beauty or cleverness, because she possessed neither particularly, and neither did he furnish her with toys or playthings. Once, an elderly parishioner had given the lonely, pallid child a wooden doll. Poppet, Myra called it, remembering it as a name her mother had had for her. Poppet had sat upon her desk as she struggled with her lessons, given in an indifferent kind of way by her father. When the duties of the household took up all the hours God gave, he was as content as she was to give them away, though the child could scarcely read or write.

For years there was the old man and Myra, for two years there was Myra alone, for a year and a half there was Myra and William, for six weeks there had been three of them.

Reverend Wayland had donned his surplice in the vestry. The child was with him, laid on the little vestry altar like a sacrifice.

'At last,' he snapped at the younger man. He sniffed the air, glared ferociously. 'Have you no shame, you scoundrel?'

William tried to glare back but his eyes throbbed with the pressure. It was an infinite relief to close them, to lean against the wall of the church. He felt the coffin snatched from him, heard a clunk as it was opened. Quick, practised – there was no undertaker in the district – the priest laid the child inside.

'Your wife waits for you in the lychgate.' He would not look at him now, even when McQuiggan's legs gave way underneath him. The old man stood above him, his white robe glaring in the sudden sun. William's head ached. He stumbled upright and made his way, the path ahead blurring green and brown, to the lychgate. At his back he heard the quick hammer blows as the priest nailed the lid shut.

His fingers closed around her arm, he hauled her to her feet. Myra looked up at him, with that searching, wounded expression he so despised and he let go. Already, hurrying from St Stephen's in his robes, was the priest. Under one arm he carried the little box.

At the side gate between the churchyard and the vicarage Mrs Wayland joined them, drawing Myra behind William on the narrow path between the headstones. They followed him to the place where the old priest now waited, a man who reminded Myra of her father. She tried to take some comfort from that while the coffin was laid in the grave, but she could only think of the little blind face, eternally alone, on the other side of the lid. She would not do what she had heard of other mothers doing, young, heartbroken ones like herself, who fainted, fell to their knees, or into the grave. She held tightly to Mrs Wayland's hand, looked at the pale grain of wood in the box, saw how the gusty winds that had worried the trees above the lychgate were stronger now, flurrying the priest's skirts, lifting his hem to show his muddy boots. Currents of air as rapid as fists knocked at her aching ears. She would not look at William, who stood on the other side of the grave, nearest the priest. He was blubbering, wiping his large, square hand across his nose and mouth, openly mourning a child he had not cared for in life. It was because he was drunk, she realised: she had smelt it on him at the lychgate.

The priest squinted at the sky and decided to take up the Order of Service towards the end: a black tide of cloud was washing over the narrow isthmus from the west to the east and was almost upon them.

'Almighty God,' said Reverend Wayland, 'with whom do live the spirits of them that depart –'

William's eyes were on her face. She met them at last and didn't know them. They were blazing, blue, lambent, too bright with feeling – as if, she thought, as if he were enjoying this scene, the sensations it afforded him.

Mrs Wayland murmured beside her. They were at the Collect already. Myra joined her.

'. . . raise us from the death of sin, unto the life of righteousness . . .'

William's lips were still. He didn't know the words; he'd not attended a funeral service since childhood. His brothers and sisters survived, he'd told her – even poor Henry who was not right in the head and was never expected to. Both his mother and his father lived. He had no experience of death, though all his life, it seemed to Myra, he'd flirted with his own. Why else would he have run away to sea at fifteen, if not to tempt it? It was a curious thing, how those who were the liveliest were also the ones who risked all, who looked misery full in the face and defied it. How William had glittered and shone when she first met him, how he'd enveloped her. Her heart went out to him, wrapped around him in his grief. Until his father had put him on the farm, immediately after their marriage, he'd had no experience of real unhappiness. Perhaps that was why he was a man of so little faith. This thought occurred to Myra easily, the truth of it slipping across her mind like butter across a hot pan, but in its wake she was seared with guilt and pain: a man who knew no sadness, no suffering, had no need of God.

While the priest took up the shovel, smearing mud across his robe, Myra asked for forgiveness. At her own daughter's graveside she had committed a terrible blasphemy. She let her head droop onto Mrs Wayland's shoulder and that lady, fearing the young woman would faint, led her away, back to the house.

Scones and tea were set on a small, spindly legged table in front of the fire in the back parlour, next to the kitchen. Steam rose from the hems of each lady's dress and they said nothing to each other.

This is what she was doing while I waited in the lychgate, thought Myra, laying the fire, baking the scones. She felt she could weep again, this time with gratitude. There was no evidence of a servant to help. The back parlour was spartan, furnished with only a larger table and two hard chairs. It was the older part of the house and lacked a window, though the shape of it was still there in the plaster. Extra rooms adjoined the windowless wall.

Mrs Wayland closed her eyes and dozed a little, her cup in her lap. Myra took the opportunity to dab at her ears with the well-used gauze. There was no fresh blood and the pain had lessened. She cocked her head to the crackle and spit of manuka twigs in the grate.

When the old man came in at the back door he didn't join them.

'Mr McQuiggan declines our invitation.' He broke their pleasant silence. 'He waits for his wife by the cemetery and, given the man's mood – not to mention his state of health – I suggest she wastes no time.'

He passed through to the hall and Mrs Wayland stood as if to follow him. The little table jiggled, wavered on the uneven hearth. Myra put out a hand to steady it, her mouth full of warm crumbs. She was suddenly unable to swallow. Her new friend turned to her.

'Perhaps you had better go,' she said, though she didn't want to treat the younger woman coldly. 'It seems our husbands have had a disagreement.'

In Myra's mouth the crumbs formed a solid mass and glued themselves to her palate.

'My husband has no patience with intemperate men.' Mrs Wayland had passed into the kitchen and was lifting Myra's cloak from the drying rack above the stove.

'No,' mumbled Myra, taking a desperate sip of tea, washing the mouthful down. 'Neither did my father. I did not know about the effects of drink until I was seventeen years old. When I went to Sydney.' She wanted to tell this kind lady everything, how she came to be married to William at all and living here, miles from where she had grown up. But Mrs Wayland went on.

'Is he often drunk?'

'Who?' Myra pulled the cloak around her, shivered.

'Your husband.' There was a new tone in the older lady's voice, harder, as if she would judge her by William's shortcomings.

'I don't know,' Myra began. 'I –'

'You must know. Men change when they drink – their voices, their stance, their state of mind.'

'Yes,' Myra agreed quietly, 'you're right of course, Mrs Wayland. He – Mr McQuiggan – is sometimes greatly changed and I can tell the instant he comes inside that he . . . and on other occasions I suspect it, but he gives nothing of it away.'

'Why don't you ask him?'

Myra looked at the priest's wife in amazement and would have laughed, but she saw that the other lady meant it.

'You are frightened he will strike you?'

Myra shook her head. It wasn't that. How could she explain that when William returned from the hills it was as if he stood on an island in the centre of a noisome lake, or was surrounded by a moat of poisonous mud, a sulphurous ring – he was unapproachable. He would glower alone on the narrow veranda, refuse food and company. Then suddenly the barrier around him would break open, violently admit her. He would seek her out, want her and she would find herself wanting . . . Myra blushed, fumbled with the hook and eye at her neck.

'He did strike me,' she attempted, 'but only the once.'

'Had you aggravated him in any way?'

'I don't think so.' She didn't want to assume arrogance or self-righteousness.

'You must try to wean him away from the drink.' Mrs Wayland had taken her hands in her own. They were warm, dry, square-knuckled like her husband's. 'His still brings misery to the misguided souls of the parish.'

Myra's forehead burned and the breath caught in her throat. Would she faint with shame?

'Do you mind me speaking so frankly?' Mrs Wayland had dropped her voice and Myra had to strain to hear her. Beyond the little room, on the other side of the wall, a man's footfall sounded on the floorboards. She shook her head.

'You have been very kind. Goodbye, Mrs Wayland.'

The priest's garden was shaded now; the evening was coming. Myra hurried up the path, waving to Mrs Wayland, who called to her from the veranda, 'Come and see me whenever you can,' and dropping her hand only when she passed out of the vicarage gate to find William squatting against the fence, waiting, the mare cropping at a shrub that pushed its English leaves between the palings.

'I'm sorry, William,' she said, anticipating his anger. But he stood and embraced her.

The rage that the old man had aroused in William had abated, replaced as usual by this silent remorse. It was just as well Mrs Wayland had detained her. She leaned her head against his chest.

True to her word, Riha had left. Even before William lit the lamp the dark room gave up the gulf of her absence and something else. The smell of bread. There was a new loaf on the table, covered over with a clean cloth. William sat down to it while Myra brought him a plate and knife from the dresser. The stew she'd made for the gang the day before was gone.

'There's nothing else,' she murmured. 'Just the bread.'

William grunted. His head hung over the table, his mouth worked the bread without enjoyment. She decided not to tell him about the mutton and potatoes. Riha had made a fair exchange, her work this morning for the stew, though William would never think so. Myra brought him a bottle of beer from the safe.

'Take a candle and go to bed,' he said.

'Will you follow soon?' She wanted him beside her. The house creaked in the wind, the kahikatea closest to the house scraped its branches on the roof.

The moment passed when he might have answered her, when his throat shifted, swallowed, emptied his mouth. His lips pursed for another swig at the bottle.

Behind him, she bent and kissed his neck, though it was grimy above his collar.

'Goodnight then,' and she left the room.

In the bed she rubbed her feet on the icy sheets, chaffed her elbows through the flannel of her night-gown, willed her body to remember warmth. The February night the child came was stifling hot. Now it was April, she was dead and winter was coming.

Sleep now, Myra told herself. Her wet skirt and cloak hung over the door. Her candle, flickering in a saucer on the upturned tea-chest that held her brush and combs, cast a shadow with her clothes, a tall shadow like someone coming in at the door. Riha. William. Shorter now, her father.

Sleep now . . .

But sleep shifted sideways, left her with memory instead. It was memory brightened by exhaustion, the wizened face of a dying baby not her own, of another tired, young face hanging over it. For a moment she couldn't place the face, remember where she'd known her. The girl whimpered now, wiped a hand across her eyes. It was Tessie, the fall William had brought into the Home with her pains already well advanced. Myra had helped her onto the bed, pulled her poor shoes from her puffy feet and loosened her gown at her neck. While they waited for Matron, she'd bathed her hot face with a cool cloth and murmured soothing words until a movement at the door had caught her eye. Not Matron at all, but the good Samaritan, the tall, well-dressed man, watching her closely.

'You must go!' she'd whispered with alarm. 'You shouldn't have followed us up here!'

How strangely he had watched her. She had never been the object of such — what was it? — those extraordinary shining eyes: it was admiration. Later he said it was love, that love was what he felt as he'd watched her kindness for the strumpet. Such goodness in her chapped, soothing hands, such care and warmth in her tender words. He'd wanted it for himself. Matron had come in while they still stared at one another, the swollen girl panting and bleating between them, and she'd sent William away downstairs with Myra to show him out. Only the married staff helped labouring women, and the girl, like most first falls, had cried out in the most appalling way when her time came, like a rabbit caught in a trap.

Had she cried out, too? She knew she'd prayed silently and aloud, that Riha had rubbed her back and told her off for her skinny ribs.

After her baby had been born, Riha had wrapped her in the crocheted rug and had showed her the little fingers and toes, her little puku — too skinny, said Riha again — her tiny chin as big as a sixpence. She'd showed her some magic, how she could stroke the baby's cheek to make the little mouth open and how at that moment the child would nurse. The strength of the infant's jaws had astonished her; she'd expected a sensation that corresponded to the sweet, moist softness of the baby's lips. There had been something shocking in the hunger of the child, something bestial, sensual, the primitive way she'd tugged and pulled at her pale, ungiving breasts. She'd felt ashamed of the baby, sure Riha would tell her there was something wrong, but that lady had sat beside her on the bed, marvelling at the pink glow of one tiny heel and smiling gently. When the baby slept, Riha had tucked her into the bed, so that the little head was just beneath Myra's nose, a warm, furry dome with an exotic, strange scent lifting from it. It was the smell of her journey, of something brought from the other side, a hint of the world on either side of temporal life.

The longed-for warmth coursed suddenly through her. Hands and feet burned, legs and arms felt liquid, floating. Loose from the nape of her neck, her hair lay heavy on the pillow, falling away from her ears.

From the back room came the sound of William's boots striking the floor as he took to his feet. He was clumping across to the door now, opening it, his tread sounding hollow on the veranda. The door, ill-fitting in its frame, fell back against the outside wall. He was leaving the house, stepping out into the mud. Myra sensed him pulling away from her and the viscous, silent running-knot that connected them, she thought for ever, flowed out through the walls of the house to follow him as he began his ascent into the hills.

Exhaustion weighted her to the bed: she would not go after him in body. By now, striding against a wall of fatigue, he would be climbing the bush beside the granite face of Bald Rock, heading towards certain oblivion and bliss. She envied him it suddenly. There was no obvious escape for her, save sleep or death.

Sleep now . . .

She quietened her mind, abandoned herself to her only hope.

Heat. The shifting of small limbs against her.

Logic would not be useful now. She saw herself as a black-garbed child after her mother's death: innocent and rational, accepting, skipping in the Yarrabin dust. The memory was banished.

The little ghost nuzzled between her breasts. Myra breathed again the sweet nascent perfume of the tiny head, felt her soft sea-hair tickle her nose and drifted away, more comforted than she could ever be by a living being.

CHAPTER 4

Justice McQuiggan never allowed matches loose in the house. They were kept high in a locked cupboard in the kitchen, the key to the cupboard in the apron pocket of Gordie, the cook. At dusk a taper was lit for the maid who went from room to room lighting the lamps. At an early age Henry, the first-born and simple son, had displayed a fascination for fire and a disdain for sleep: the judge feared his family would burn in their beds.

So it was that William, when he attained the age when tobacco could have lent him an aspect of manliness, had to do without. There were compensations, however. His unsullied nose now afforded him many scents and smells other men may not have detected. In fact, he prided himself not only on that, but on all five of his senses.

His sight now, as he climbed the hill, was as keen as a cat's. Above him the moon was bright but waning, the night sky awash with stars. Dusk winds had blown away the thundery clouds of the afternoon. Where the bush had been cleared, he saw his way through the blackened stubble and stumps as easily as if it were daytime. When the trees closed overhead again, his progress was more deliberate but just as unerring.

In one dim place he found himself pausing and wondered why: it was where he had hit her. He stumbled to get away, his boots slipping on the slick of mud left by her fall. Cold clean air filled his heaving lungs, his brain throbbed. He pressed on, hating her for making him sad and fearful. Perhaps the rising was all her fault, perhaps she'd been praying for God to take him.

'Damn you to hell!' He ached with exhaustion and thirst. Something moved ahead of him on the track, he thought at first the drab wings of a night-bird. But it was a giant kauri moth, flapping towards him, drawn by the shimmer of his eyes and hair. He recoiled, closed his arms over his eyes until his father's face took the moth's place, a pale oblong forming in the gloom.

The spectre would vanish with the first swallow, William told himself. He uncovered his eyes, put one foot in front of the other, but the face remained, leading him on, looking back towards him with grey reproachful eyes, its narrow unsmiling mouth below its large, disproportionate nose. It was the way the old man was before a beating, the way his face set on the short journey from the house to the stables: unchanging, not flinching from the task, even as he lifted the riding crop down from the rack on the sun-warmed bricks, the other hand maintaining its hold on William's arm or collar or ear. And William, fear making his small body rigid, would rise on the balls of his feet and shake his agitated hands. Dust and tears would mix to a paste on his face while his father, silent, raised the crop. It was only then that his father's face would change, once the beating had begun. As he spun away from the welt of cracking leather, William would see the glint of his lower teeth exposed behind a fallen lip, would smell how the leather and horse dung of the stable was spiced by his father's close sweat, how his narrow grey eyes had almost folded themselves away below his brow. Later of course, as his weight and height approached and passed that of his father, he was able to break free and run – to the town, to the bays, over the hills – or on the fateful day when he was fifteen, all the way to England. Why the devil had he ever come back?

Regret and fury choked him now, until he stopped on the track again and threw back his head, his tight, hungry belly pushing his voice up through his chest, up out of his open, contorted mouth, roaring into the night. He remembered the child, remembered Myra sitting over it soon after it was born, telling him how it resembled him, he remembered her begging him to take it down to the church for a christening. He would write to his father, tell him of the birth of the child and the death of it, ask him to allow him to leave the farm. The blame for the child's death rested squarely on the grand-father's shoulders. William would point this out to the judge. The plan gave him hope, quietened his bellowing heart.

Another small climb, then he dropped down into the clearing. He'd reached the still. Something was wrong, was different to how he'd left it. He could smell a mineral pungency, upturned earth. Panic gripped him. Someone was here, hiding in the shadows. His trouser leg caught against a clod, which crumbled; his boot struck and caught in a long tree root, severed by the sharp edge of a spade.

Swiftly he moved out into the centre of his ground, where his eyes would be struck hardest by moonlight. Deposits of soil and leaf mould were all around him, ringing holes where the thieves had searched for his whisky. He was frantic now, moving from one cavity to the next, bile rising in his gorge and every vein in his body trembling with rage: here – he had buried half a dozen here, another half-dozen here. The bottles buried under the mare's punga: gone. Towards the stream now, before the first clump of toi-toi, there were a few there – or did he drink those bottles, or sell them? He couldn't remember. It was all gone, all of it, nearly a hundred pints.

The thieves had shared a bottle and begun another, leaving it half full and standing propped against the fireplace. He must've frightened them off, crashing through the bush and – his face burned with shame – roaring like a child. Who were they? Either McNeill taking revenge for an imagined slight or some Maoris from the pa. Poihaere had told Riha about the lost copper. Maybe she retraced his steps and found his set-up.

He sat on the muddy ground and drank the half bottle they had left him, cursed them. He could find out, use some of his father's money to bribe the information out of Riha. She wouldn't be able to stay away from Myra; he knew she'd be back. He'd watched her with his wife, seen how tender and solicitous she was, as if Myra were her daughter.

The bottle gleamed empty in the moonlight. He held it up to the sky, saw the splinter of moon smudge and blur in the flawed, cheap glass. On the night of his epiphany, the shining brittle threads had fetched him down to earth. Or had they? He remembered kicking them away, then only a tearing, warm sensation at the crown of his head, an anticipation of light, of mercy, of mortal release and then – nothing. He shook the last few golden drops into his mouth, pushed the rim against his gum hard enough to draw blood. It was obvious, he saw now. God had used glass to speak to him: He would know of his affection for it since infancy, the Venetian blue glass beads his mother owned, the stained glass windows of St Mary's in Parnell, the cut-glass tumblers he and his sisters drank from at the table on special occasions, the round, flat glass paperweight on his father's desk. You could hold that paperweight to your eye like a solid lens and see how the world blurred, how it melted at the periphery into oily, prismatic light. It was a favourite of the Lord's too, thought William, for hadn't He sent a vision of glass to Saint Paul, as he remembered from Sunday School? There was the verse that everybody knew: 'When I was a child, I spake as a child, I understood as a child, but when I became a man I put away childish things . . .' and St Paul goes on – William remembered it word for word, though he hadn't opened a Bible for years – 'For now we see through a glass, darkly, but then face to face: now I know in part; but then shall I know even as also I am known.'

The Lord's face, then, was obscured to Paul, though he had faith that one day they would see each other and he would know God as intimately as He knew him. William's mind moved on: that was only part of the message God had for him, for wasn't he a modern man? He had to take into account scientific explanations, of what was known at the end of this nineteenth century of the true nature of glass: that it is a slow-moving liquid, not the solid, inert material it appears to be. It retains its nascent character, oblique, secret. His lesson from the Lord was – it must be – that nothing is as it appears. Science must not be used to deny the Lord, to explain away his vision as a moment of – what? Insanity?

He turned the bottle, felt its dull glimmer touch his face. A question, monolithic and frightening, rose in his breast like a whale to the ocean's surface, spouted its brave curiosity a thousand airy miles. Was any man sane? Or was all mankind only as lucid as glass was inert? If he had lost his mind he had no real proof of it. He lifted the bottle to his open mouth again, though there was little point. It was dry as dust.

'You will have to show me, Father.' The half bottle burned inside him, made him braver. 'Show me, Father.' He rocked forward to his knees, lifted his face. His mouth trembled, his eyes filled. 'Forgive me. Show me. Are you there?'

The bush around him creaked and shifted. Night insects rasped and clicked, an owl hooted, another bird answered. He was surrounded by creatures who hid themselves in the daytime, animals he had no name for. They moved through the leaf mould under the trees, lived their unseen lives. His mind raced on. It was all to do with scale: what was fast, what was slow, large or small. He might be as invisible to God as those strange, flightless birds were to him, with their mournful calls, two-part calls.

'Show me,' he whispered again, though he felt hopeless. His eye fell on the cold, old ashes in the fireplace. It was a clue, a sign. They were scattered all over with fallen leaves, green blown from the trees. Green, the colour of life and innocence among the grey death of the ashes.

As William began his descent from the hills, Myra dreamed of Mr Beardsley and the journey with him from Yarrabin to Sydney. They had taken the train for the last part, Myra's tin box between them. Mr Beardsley had the window seat and never took his eyes from the passing world, the oceans of gums, the occasional lonely house. In the hottest part of the day a miasma of evaporating eucalyptus oil hung above the canopy like smoke. Every now and then Mr Beardsley would chew on his sandy moustache, which Myra took as a sign that he was about to renew his dampening speech. He had said the same to her in the dusty parlour of her father's house, again as they travelled by cart to Mudgee, and three times so far on the long rail journey. He scarcely altered it by a word, though he gave ever-lengthening pauses between significant phrases.

'It would have been better for you if you had notified us of your father's death more promptly. Most unfortunate, most . . . How a slip of a girl survived out there alone for as long as . . . Mrs Ardill has said she will take you. Good, clean, young. Stronger than you look, I'll wager.'

'Who is Mrs Ardill?' she asked once, while they sat on the platform at Katoomba.

'Very kind. Not strictly Anglican, you know, but they'll take you anyway.'

In her sleep, three years later, Myra tossed impatiently. His voice droned on, though in reality he had been silent as he carried her box from the station to Stanley Street. She had paused on the path, observed the three arches on the long porch, the three-storeyed building, its blank windows. The discreet sign above the door caught her keen eye. The words, once she comprehended them, squeezed the breath from her.

Home of Hope for Friendless and Fallen Women

Is this what Mr Beardsley had planned for her? The first part was right: she was indeed friendless. Her father had had no faithful parishioners to check on her, his congregations were mostly small and transient. Mr Beardsley had only found out about the death a year after the event. He was staggering ahead now, with the box. Behind him Myra thought she would be ill, her stomach cramped with fear. She was not fallen, she was sure of it, not like Mary Magdalene. She remembered Mark, where he has it that Christ cast out from Mary seven devils. Myra had no devils. She hurried to catch up with her benefactor to explain, to suggest that maybe he was mistaken, but a woman in a white cap and apron had opened the door to him and he had vanished into the dark hall.

Waking, Myra wondered if the woman who had opened the door on that long-ago day had been Mrs Ardill herself or one of the other nurses. She wondered whether, if it had been Mrs Ardill, she had seen her standing out there before she closed the door on her. For close the door she did, and Myra's face burned while she looked up and down Stanley Street. In the west the sun was beginning to slip behind the Blue Mountains. The low roofs of the city shone gold, the two-storey limestone terraces glowed yellow and white. Tears needled Myra's eyes: the sun sank over her home, the only home she'd ever known. Another priest would take it up, she supposed. She wondered if he would have children of his own, or worse, a lonely child, only one, as she had been. Mr Beardsley had locked the vicarage door after them with a heavy silver key, which he had then buried deep in his pocket.

There was a baby crying from inside the Home and another whimpering, higher pitched, from further down the street. Myra turned from the sunset to watch a group of boys playing outside one of the terraces. They had a puppy with a length of string tied around its neck, which they were endeavouring to teach to jump through a hoop. It was the puppy crying and yelping, while the boys tugged and yelled. Myra had just made up her mind to go to the little dog's rescue when the door opened again and Mr Beardsley, red faced and flustered, emerged at a trot.

'Miss Hopkins, please, please do follow me – this way.' As soon as he reached her, he turned away again, bobbing his head and bending at the waist, one arm executing wild sweeps in the direction of the Home's door. Myra halted her progress down the street. Nobody had ever addressed her as Miss Hopkins. Mr Beardsley, she realised, had never before addressed her as anything.

'I was bewildered to discover that you were not behind me' – Mr Beardsley took her elbow and steered her firmly past the iron gate – 'when I was in the very act of introducing you to Matron.'

'But Mr Beardsley,' began Myra, 'I think you – I hope you don't think I – you see, I'm not.'

'Shshsh!' Drops of saliva flew between the considerable gaps in Mr Beardsley's teeth and speckled Myra's face and the flock-wallpaper behind her.

'In here. Oh drat!'

Mr Beardsley dropped Myra's arm and heaved a huge sigh of exasperation before throwing himself dangerously into a narrow brocade chair with gilt arms. There was a coal fire in the little grate and a polished clock on the mantelpiece. Above a green velvet settee hung a lurid picture of Our Lord descending from Heaven, His arms out towards the multitudes of people who gazed up towards Him. She drew closer to the painting, looked up into the face of Jesus. He looked sad. Perhaps He was leaving rather than arriving, she thought, kneeling on the settee, reaching up a hand towards Him. Her father would have called such a painting idolatry.

A firm footfall sounded behind her; the parlour door clicked shut.

'Miss Hopkins, at last. I'm sorry, I was called away to attend a troublesome confinement. But I am with you now. I am matron here, Mrs Ardill.'

Myra felt herself blush for the second time in an hour. Confinement! How could the lady talk about such things in front of Mr Beardsley? That gentleman had lurched to his feet, playing his fingers along the rim of his hat as he held it against his stomach.

'Please be seated.' Mrs Ardill was head and shoulders above Mr Beardsley, broad shouldered and heavy boned. Looking into her face, Myra was reminded of the shiny white railway cups. Her skin looked glazed and hard, her tightly corseted body unforgiving. The lady caught her staring and, far from chastising her, smiled warmly. Large, well-shaped teeth showed yellow against her complexion.

'Curiosity! One of the many traits a nurse requires. Mr Beardsley is of the opinion that with training you would make a fine nurse.'

'Oh!' Myra thought she said, wanting to express her relief at finding she had been mistaken, but perhaps she made no sound at all because Mrs Ardill was sailing past her to a roll-top desk, hidden in the corner of the room by a silk screen. The screen was pushed aside, the roll-top flicked up and Mrs Ardill removed a piece of paper, which she handed to Myra.

'Perhaps you could acquaint yourself with these few rules. A quiet word if you will, Mr Beardsley.'

Myra took the paper. It was neatly headed 'Rules of Conduct for Attendants and Nurses of the Home of Hope for Friendless and Fallen Women'.

Myra feared her new employer would ask her to read the rules out loud. She could not – she could barely read the heading. What was the long word beginning with 'A'? If she could sound it out loud she may be able to work it out, but she dare not for Mr Beardsley and Mrs Ardill had not left the room for their quiet talk. They stood by the fire, heads inclined, murmuring. After her six months of isolation, Myra's ears were primed to pick up the slightest hint of possible communication from miles off. She understood every word. She kept her eyes on the paper, struggled to comprehend the first rule.

1. NURSES MUST BE OF GOOD CHARACTER.

'Seventeen, you said?' Mrs Ardill was saying.

'Yes. Raised and educated by her late father, a minister of our church –'

'. . . who has just recently died?'

'One year.'

'And in the meantime?'

'I beg your pardon?'

'Who can vouch for the girl's conduct since her loss?'

'Oh, Mrs Ardill!' Mr Beardsley's hoarse whisper gave away a little of his impatience. 'Have you not travelled beyond the Blue Mountains?'

'Why would I, Mr Beardsley?' The lady's tone was unperturbed. 'My work is here, in Sydney. The Lord has not called me inland.'

'The girl grew up in Yarrabin, miles from anywhere. Reverend Hopkins was . . . well, let us just say he was unsuccessful. He had no flock.'

Myra kept her head down, her heart panged for her father. A lifetime in service, but an unsuccessful one. Was he in Heaven, or did God deem him failed too?

2. WITHIN THE CONFINES OF THE HOME A
   NURSE WILL ONLY SPEAK WHEN
   ADDRESSED BY A SUPERIOR.

Perhaps she had the meaning of this one. She was to keep quiet, which was easy. Her father had kept her rigorously to the same rule; she would sometimes go for days without speaking. Sometimes she would sing a line or two of a hymn in order to check she still had a voice.

'So the girl was literally alone for the year? No company at all?'

'I don't think so, no.'

'You don't seem sure, Mr Beardsley.'

'I am fairly certain she was alone.'

'What did she eat, then?'

'There was a house cow for milk, an overgrown bed of vegetables, a few chickens.'

Myra would have liked to lift her head, to tell them that she mainly ate eggs and drank milk and that she had no liking for vegetables, but she had already taken to heart the second rule.

'You will find her less sophisticated than the city girls you are used to,' Mr Beardsley went on. 'Keep me abreast of developments.'

3. DUTIES BEGIN AT 5 AM SHARP AND END AT 8 PM, EXCLUDING NIGHT DUTIES WHEN NECESSARY.

4. NURSES WILL BE GRANTED TWO HALF DAYS OFF A MONTH, PROVIDED MATRON CAN SPARE THEM.

'Goodbye then.' Mr Beardsley had come to stand in front of her. 'Perhaps I will call one day.'

'Please do,' said Mrs Ardill. She had her hand out for the rule sheet. Myra handed it to her with an attempt at a smile. The rules numbered twelve and it had taxed her to read as far as the fifth.

Without any semblance of regret, her deliverer took his leave, and Mrs Ardill showed her up three flights of stairs to her room. On their ascent they met no one; the doors onto the landings and corridors were firmly closed.

'Everyone is at evening prayers,' Mrs Ardill told her. They had come to a tiny attic room with a narrow bed. There was a small chest of drawers with a candle stub on top of it, a tiny crucifix above the candle.

'Join us for a meal in the dining room at seven,' Mrs Ardill told her from the door. 'Mr Ardill will be there also.'

But Myra had no way of telling the time, and a leaden weariness filled her from head to foot the moment she was left alone. There was a window, smaller than her face, which looked west. She stood looking out until it grew dark, knowing she would never again see those open dusty plains of her childhood and imagining she would grow old attending Mrs Ardill's fallen women. She wasn't to know, not then on her first night, that within months she would meet William and he would take her thousands of miles away to New Zealand.

There was the smell of woodsmoke and he was calling her from outside, so loudly his voice was breaking.

'My-ra! My-ra!'

She slipped out of the warm bed, pulled her damp cloak around her shoulders and went to the window. There was a strange flickering light and in it her husband was leaping, waving his arms. He caught sight of her, gesticulated even more wildly.

'Get out of the house! It's on fire!'

She turned away, ran for the door that led to the kitchen and wrenched it open. Flames churned along the windowsill, engulfed the wall where the dish-pan hung on its nail: through the open door she could see the back porch was blazing.

'William!' Myra knew he couldn't hear her. Her only way out was back into the bedroom, through the window. He was opening it for her now; she could hear the scream of the weights inside the frame as he flung the lower half up, saw his wavering shape through the smoke while behind him the veranda post came alive, orange and red. He was pulling her through; sparks fell to her hair and scorched, fell to her damp cloak and smouldered. He had his arm around her, was hauling her down towards the stream that ran below the house. There was a tremendous clap as the fire reached the roof behind them, and a rushing sound as it took the first of the kahikatea. She clung to her husband, terrified.

'It won't burn more than the house and pine. There's been a lot of rain.'

They stood ankle deep in the stream, the icy water running over their feet taking away with it all sensation. William tore his eyes from the fire, watched the dark top of his wife's head tucked into his chest. He lifted her then, carried her across the stream to the horse track and sat her down. She looked up at him, dazed.

'Did it start in the kitchen?' she began, but her husband flung a hand out, suddenly. She flinched for the blow, but he just laid his hand heavily on her head. His hand slipped lower, he crouched before her, slipped his palm against her breast in the warmth of her nightgown. He lowered his face, pressed his lips against her neck and his weight pushed her down.

'No –' She brought her hands against his chest; there was mud at the back of her head. He circled her round, his arms passed between her gown and cloak, his face pressed into her breasts. Beyond him the fire raged, the iron of the roof fell in, crashed and boomed. Myra struggled, cried out, but he had pushed himself inside her, raised his body so that the smell of his burned hair filled her nostrils. There was another smell, on his shirt, of paraffin oil and she knew suddenly, while he pushed and sobbed, that he had set the fire.

He pulled away, stood up, struck at his weeping eyes with a grimy fist. Dear God, what had he done? It had come upon him all at once, desire and rage mixed together as combustible as paraffin. He swallowed it down: thick, elemental oil at the back of his throat.

He would have to leave Myra behind. He had thought he would take her with him but, now he had defiled her, he could not. He could not have her cowering around him at his father's house, recalling for him at every instance his lack of self-discipline, his capacity for evil. While he stared at her, she half rolled in the mud, her exposed white legs gleaming wet like a newborn lamb. She was a sacrifice he would have to make: a man does not need his conscience before him all the time, pleading for examination. It would be unendurable. It would distract him from his purpose.

From behind him there came the sound of hooves and the mare stood, the black silhouette of her between them and the burning house. Myra tasted blood, her tongue felt swollen. William had turned, splashed across the stream to the horse. His wife watched him pat the mare, soothe her with indistinct soft words, before flinging his leg over and catching hold of her bridle. Smoke from the house obscured him then; a dawn wind sprang up and wrapped him around in a grey cloud. She felt him pass close by, heard him click to the mare, turn her head, and go.

CHAPTER 5

There was a scow loading timber before the tavern in Mangawhai Harbour and the skipper let him aboard on the proviso he worked his passage to Auckland.

'Not having you aboard like a lump of ballast.' He had a mean little chin with a cluster of long ginger hairs sprouting from it. The poor beard flew up and down as he spoke. William met his eye.

'I'll work.'

The skipper nodded, muttered something, but his words didn't carry above the rattle and whine of the winch. He looked William over.

'You're a working man?'

William wondered what the skipper had seen in him. He was too thin now perhaps, from the deprivations of the farm. Under his red shirt he clenched his knotted muscles. He pulled his hands from his pockets and held them palm up so the skipper could see – how soft his skin had become – but the man had turned away, was shouting to the loader below. Kauri logs knocked against the hull and between them the skipper and the loader got another one hooked. It began its ascent. William turned his blackened hands over. Ash clogged his nails, an abrasion showed red and angry. He picked out a splinter.

'Hop to it!'

The skipper was bellowing at him and he ran to work with the three men rolling the logs onto the deck. The two older men wore heavy canvas gloves. When William joined them they looked him over once and were not to bother again for the rest of the journey. Only the younger man, a Maori, nodded and smiled. Head and shoulders above the others he worked hardest, swinging the logs on their chains into five pyramids on the deck, stacking them six up a side, pulling the hook from the bark. The larger load lay midships, the four smaller on either side of the two masts. A scent of ancient sap rose and mixed with the salt wind, which blew the sweat from the men in a sharp westerly across the isthmus. The Maori's hands were scraped raw but he worked on oblivious. The older men took the lower end of the logs, shouting now and then to the skipper to hold it steady. The kauri was roped down; the ship sat ever lower in the water.

They set sail around nine, after a poor meal. William ate nothing. The crew squatted in the stern out of the wind and ate biscuits and scraps of meat from a bone wrapped in cloth. Mutton, William supposed, though it smelt worse. The Maori sat apart and produced from his roll, surprisingly, a peach. It was brown and battered, as bruised as his hands, but he held it gently and ate it with relish. A bottle of cold tea was passed around, offered also to William. He drank thirstily, wishing for something stronger. It was not to be had, though the captain, when he emerged from his rank cabin, had a whisky odour about him.

All the way out to where it was breaking up beyond the heads, William stood in the bow, his back to the land. He felt the autumn sun on his face and all of a sudden the farm and Myra ceased to exist, as surely as if the devil himself had opened the flats – a great, green soggy rent in the paddocks – and swallowed them down to hell. It was as likely as his flight of two nights ago: it was entirely possible. He was utterly free of them, he was forgiven for his previous life, wiped clean of it. It was a question of polarities of existence, of weights on a scale, a question of faith.

An hour or so past the heads, the wind swung around to a vicious southerly and the captain worked them hard, tacking all the way down the coast to Auckland, never lifting a finger himself except to raise his flask to his lips. The heat drained from William's body, grey-green autumnal waves slopped over the decks, he ached from head to foot. Between them he and the Maori worked the boat, while the older men hunkered down, backs to the rain. Beyond Cape Rodney the main load shifted and William was sent to bring in one of the foresails. The bow was not so pleasant a place now, less so when the sheet snagged on the bowsprit and the captain yelled for him to go after it. He hung on the lurching limb of the ship, his legs wound around, groin hard in to the wood, the sea hissing below him, rearing up to slap him, falling away. It was like lying over a resisting woman. There was the crackle and roar of the fire at his back, the smell of mud, of the scorched cotton of her nightdress. He was inside her before he knew what he was doing, she was warm and soft, yielding after the first moment, his one flesh. Just as the stomach must welcome the opening of a mouth, the body sustaining itself, so must a wife sustain her husband. He would not pity her again. Pity leads to betrayal, to the bewildered turning on the sympathetic. It was the lesson he had learned as a boy, and later, all over again when he returned from England. It was as if his violation of her dated from that previous existence, before his epiphany, as if the fabric of time had been rent and his old, bad quiddity had flown in, even more sinful than it had been when he allowed it dominance.

The plunging spar jarred bile from his throat, the loosened sail struck against his body, heavy and wet, first from one side, then the other. He crawled backwards, his eyes closed to its sting.

In Mechanics Bay the scow waited to unload her logs into the booms. After the Brynderwyn mountains the land surrounding the harbour seemed low, lumpy and dull. Wet to the skin, William leaned his aching arms in the stern and took in the city of his birth, grey under the slow spitting sky. Tin-roofed wooden houses clung to the ridges that led away from the shambles on the shore. Further around from Mechanics Bay, out of sight now, was the solid respectable vein of Queen Street, which fed the rest of the city's ragged body. On previous returns, William had longed for Queen Street, the upper half of it, its bars and bawdy-houses, but now the odour of the marsh filled his nostrils. The place was just a swamp, with a series of volcanic mounds rising on the horizon. There was never a more ridiculous place to build a city. It invited failure, a drowning in mud or death from a cataclysm of boiling rock. No wonder he had never thrived here, he thought. Even without catastrophe, swamp-gas mixes with the salt air and depresses the inhabitants' spirits.

Late in the afternoon, a dinghy came alongside the scow, carrying a company clerk to consign the cargo. William seized his opportunity, making his escape before the work was finished: he jumped aboard the small boat as the clerk, a weasly youth, took his leave. The skipper yelled abuse after him, his words lost on the gritty wind sloughing across the jumble of timber yards. In the dinghy's bow, William turned his back on him and wished he had a hat to ward off the chill. Winter was coming to Auckland too, the third deadening season he would have spent on the farm. He felt something like relief, mixed through with trepidation: he had no money and his father's wrath would be incalculable. At the slip he helped the clerk pull the dinghy up before taking off across the yard, along Customs Street and up Jacob's Ladder towards the Supreme Court.

At the bottom of Symonds Street he almost collided with an errand boy running down the steep hill, propelled forward by his burden of a crate of apples. The child's eyes widened in alarm the moment they rested on William's face. William brought a hand to his hair, felt how it had frizzled and crisped in the fire. There was a burn on his forehead that hurt under the weight of his palm. He drew his shirt together and tried to close it over his vest. There were only two remaining buttons. The boy's gaping mouth annoyed him. He grabbed him by the arm.

'What are you gawping at?'

'You, Mister. You been in a war?'

William pulled the cap from the boy's head with his free hand, jammed it on his own head. Too small, but at least it went some way to hiding the burnt stubble.

'What day is it?' he asked suddenly. A smirk twisted the boy's lips.

'Friday.'

'Have you come from the court? Is Justice McQuiggan sitting?'

'No. Don't know. Give me back my cap, Mister.' The boy's skinny arms shifted under the crate: he wasn't strong enough to pull one out and make a lunge. William grabbed an apple in his wounded hand, bit into it and swallowed. The boy snivelled.

'I'll get in trouble.'

'Here.' William dug in his pocket, pulled out a coin. He dropped it down the boy's back and gave him a shove, sending him on his top-heavy way.

He wouldn't go to the court, then, but to the house. He retraced his steps and made his way along Beach Road, under the railway bridge and up the hill. On Parnell Road women stood gossiping in shop fronts and the Windsor Castle was full. Outside St John's a knot of snot-nosed kids gazed at William, who slowed his pace when he drew level with the churchyard. The McQuiggans' house was clearly visible from here, cream-coloured and grand on the ridge parallel to Parnell Road, above a narrow bushy gully. High on its western wall a dormer window, set beneath the green raked-iron gable, caught the sun uncovered by a shifting cloud. It was early evening, not dark enough yet for the

lamps to be lit. One of his sisters, or Henry, might be standing behind one of the second-storey panes, hidden by the
glare, watching his slow progress up the hill.

He eschewed the front door, went around to the lane and
looked over the gate. The door to the scullery stood open
and Henry sat on the back step holding one of the cats,
stroking it gently and whispering. It flicked its ears, its eyes
half wild. William watched, waited for it to scratch and leap
as they always did eventually, as they had all through
Henry's childhood. His brother's head was bowed and
William saw that he was beginning to go bald. Two years ago,
when William had last seen him, he had seemed ageless, his
unlined face a repository for his calm, happy disposition. He
looked up suddenly, though William had made no movement. His face was unchanged. He stared at him for a
moment, puzzled, his child-eyes wide, until William opened
the gate. A roar of delight frightened the cat away and Henry
was on his feet, wrapping his brother in his big arms.

'Will! Will!' he crowed, pulling the cap from William's
head, kissing his cheek, his ear and his neck, his bristly face
colliding with William's.

'Henry –' William made a grab for the cap.

Henry had taken his hands now and was skipping in a
circle on the path, his big tummy bobbing above his belt
until a movement on the step caught his eye. A brown skirt
fell against its wearer's legs. Abruptly, he stood still.

'See, Ellen! See who has come!'

'Don't excite him, William.'

'No, ma'am. I won't, ma'am. Don't give me the strap,
ma'am!' Having regained his cap, William flourished it,
bowed elaborately. Henry giggled.

Sour as ever, as the cats' milk congealing in the row of
saucers set out on the back porch, Ellen did not smile. She
would be thirty-four now, William thought, a mere two years
older than Henry, though she looked ten years his senior.
Her brown and silver hair, scraped back and rolled over her

ears, looked thin, old-fashioned. Fine lines had multiplied around her eyes and mouth.

'Father is inside.' Ellen stood back to let him pass. As he went by, with Henry close behind, William took one of her hands and gave it a clumsy squeeze. Ellen turned her cheek to him, as if she thought he might kiss her. When he didn't she was glad: he smelled rank.

'Perhaps you could wash before you go into him.' Her voice was quiet, cold. 'Have you no luggage?'

William shook his head.

'Henry will give you something. Dress in his room.' Ellen hurried him through the hall, gesturing quickly towards the front parlour as they passed its closed door. 'They are in there, Mother and Father together,' she whispered.

At the foot of the stairs she stopped, laid her hand on the carved newel.

'I'll send Mary up with some water.'

William nodded, took the steps two at a time. His brother followed, his heavy shoulders rolled over his thundering feet, his eyes concentrated on their echoing impact. He gave out a whoop.

'Shush, Henry!'

On the second landing Henry shoved past him, took William's upper arm and galloped off down the corridor, towing him after him. A long runner carpeted the kauri floor, glowing with oriental greens and reds. A stained-glass window glazed the light in a niche at the corridor's western end. Their father had had it made to his specifications when the house was built: the family crest, newly drafted by the judge himself – a navy shield with sentinel, at either side a lion rampant and a square-rigged schooner central, the whole thing presided over by a set of silver scales. The McQuiggan forebears had not the social standing to bequeath them one. As William passed over its puddle of colours cast on the gleaming rug, he heard the parlour door click open below.

'What the devil is going on?' came Justice McQuiggan's voice into the hall.

His brother wheeled to the left and flung open William's old bedroom door. Its orbit was loudly terminated by the manrobe. William listened hard. There was a clunk from downstairs as his father pushed the parlour door wide open and set a wedge against it. Then there was nothing. The judge must have returned to his chair.

'How long have you slept in here, old boy?' All Henry's belongings were here: his hordings of stones, shells, birds' eggs, pinecones, skeletons of karaka leaves, a battered wooden train thirty years old at least, a one-legged bear, three rimless bicycle wheels leaning against a wall. Discarded clothes were heaped up in piles, the burrowed bed a mound of blankets.

Beaming proudly, Henry stood among it all in the centre of the room. After trying for years to answer questions about time, he pretended now not to have heard them. A week ago, three months ago, a year? He hadn't a clue.

'Ellen wanted me to go in the room off the porch so I could have the cats. I'm not allowed the cats up here,' he offered. 'Mother insisted I have this room.'

William heard his mother insisting, her shade in Henry's voice.

'Mother did. Ellen closes my door. Whenever she walks past, she closes the door. I've seen her. Sometimes I'm in here even, and she closes the door. She shuts me in.'

William shook his head in sympathy, though Henry didn't seem perturbed, just bemused.

'Is there anything clean?' he asked, gesturing at the draped floor. Henry shrugged, his shoulders momentarily eclipsing the window behind him with its view of Parnell Road, the fall of the hill beyond with its clustered darkening roofs and tiny gardens, all falling away to the railway line that snaked to the port. William kicked aside a faggot of reeds tied together with a turkey-red handkerchief and two sticks lashed together which resembled a crucifix but was probably a sword. From the third drawer of the tallboy he lifted a pair of moleskins. Henry had long been dressed in workingmen's clothes.

'He's so hard on his trousers,' their mother had complained.

At the back, squashed and unworn, were a pair of his father's cast-offs, narrow broadcloths that would not have fitted Henry since his early twenties.

'These should be in a trouser-press,' William said. He shook them out. They would do, though they were crumpled and musty.

The door nudged open; a wisp of steam preceded the maid and the hot jug.

'Where's your wash-stand, Master Henry?' she asked in a strong Midlands accent. William hadn't seen her before. He had expected the previous maid, old Mary, her resentful heavy foot, her sour face. This one had reddish hair, small breasts, tiny uneven teeth.

'What's your name then?' he asked.

The young woman startled, the folded towel slipped on her forearm. Miss Ellen had not told her Henry had company.

'Your name?' repeated William, hardening his tone.

'Mary,' answered the girl, blushing.

With both hands, Henry was gesturing to his ewer and basin like a magician, as if he were revealing something marvellous. Quickly, Mary crossed the room, emptied the steaming water, then righted the jug and turned on her heel in the same instant. William smelt fear, felt a quickening in his blood. The girl stepped lightly towards the door.

'Aren't you going to leave me the towel, pretty Mary?' He moved towards her for it. The girl blushed again though the first colouring still tinged her cheeks, and offered the towel in an outstretched hand. How delicious it would be, he thought, to pull her in by that gleaming wrist and kiss her. The girl read his eyes, stepped backwards and caught her toe in her hem. She put a hand out to steady herself and dropped the towel.

'Did Ellen tell you not to bother with Henry's room?' He sharpened his tone. 'This used to be mine. I don't like seeing it like this. Pick up the towel.'

But Mary was dipping minutely, her back to him, and then she was gone, closing the door after her.

William ripped off his burned and filthy shirt and kicked it against one of Henry's piles. He added some cold water to the basin from Henry's ewer, though it smelt suspect, and submerged his head. He felt giddy, breathless, like a boy bowling a hoop the full descent of Parnell Rise. At long last his life would change: excitement thrummed in his veins, fast, insistent. With a loud sucking splash he broke free of the water, wildly flicking his head to spatter the back wall.

'Be with me tonight, Father,' he prayed.

Attentive, Henry handed him the soap.

Ellen had been listening for him at the first landing. William let her have the balustrade and she picked her way carefully downstairs beside him like an old woman.

'I haven't told them you are here,' said Ellen. 'Father has been unwell. I did not want you to –'

'Startle them,' finished William. The parlour piano was playing something sweet and sentimental. Blanche, William supposed. The three of them were in there. It would be better if he could see his father alone. His mother would pity him, she might have him weep. He would see the old man first, then her. He would tell her of his epiphany.

'You must admit that your appearance would have alarmed them. What on earth had you been doing? I think I should go ahead and announce you,' Ellen started on him as they reached the foot of the steps, her voice little more than a whisper. 'Surely you could have found a better shirt than Henry's regatta –' Henry interrupted her, thundering down the stairs, wet cheeks jiggling. He too had washed, though he had neglected to apply the towel to his dripping head.

'Come with me, Will,' he said kindly to William, tugging on his hand, leading him past the parlour door. 'Beach.'

'It is too late for that, Henry,' said Ellen firmly. She laid a hand on William's arm. But Henry was remembering a long-ago late-night walk with William down St George's Bay Road to Augusta Terrace, down the cliff steps to the beach. His full mouth drooped.

'Maybe later,' William told him. Ellen had already opened the door a crack and the music had stopped mid-phrase. She looked warningly at Henry. His shoulders slumped and he went out through the narrow passage beside the kitchen towards the garden and his cats.

'Why have you left the farm?' Twenty years of keeping his face sober and unintelligible at the bench had set the judge's face into two plains, long and ashen on either side of his grand nose. For as long as the son could remember, the father's beard had been encouraged to sprout in low-slung Dundreary whiskers along the line of his jaw. They shone now, white and combed, puffing out over his narrow black-clad shoulders. William resisted the impulse to greet his mother and youngest sister, to take in the room and see what had changed, what had remained the same, but found his father's eyes, which had been deep set in youth and were now even more so. In their sapphirine depths he read some-thing he had never seen there before: it was soft, disap-pointed, almost resigned. The old man sat close to Blanche, the better to hear her playing. She was smiling: William could feel reflected warmth from her welcoming face. She was the only one who had cried out with surprise when he had entered the room. A sharp gesture from their father had kept her at the piano. William wouldn't look at her yet; he would wait until his father broke his gaze.

From his chair Elisha took in the spectacle of William dressed in his brother's regatta shirt, blue on white. A suppu-rating red mark striped his forehead, tiny beads of pus at his hairline. A wound, or burn perhaps, protesting against a too vigorous wash. His hair was wet, combed. He looked pale and agitated as he had at other times of crisis. Elisha struggled to stand up.

'Please stay seated, Father.' William took a step into the room, then approached him properly, strode into the room in a manner he knew his father liked to see – confident, well-intentioned – and took his hand. His father closed his fingers, grasped him firmly, shook once, twice, let him go. His focus sat at a midpoint on William's chest.

'Your mother,' he said, almost inaudibly.

Hidden in the green wing chair, Alithea sat close to the fire. She was standing up now, turning in astonishment to her son. One hand grasped at the air above her silk-encased heart, the other lifted towards him.

'But whatever have you . . . what has happened? Where is Myra?'

At the sound of his wife's name, his mother's ruffled mauve gown dimmed to the grey of Myra's nightdress; her smooth silver hair darkened to the blue-black of Myra's, oily as a starling's wing. He remembered her as she was when he had had her in the bush, the day after the baby died: her lips full of blood, the white underside of her chin, her hands tense on his shoulders, her thighs astride his loins. The room was quiet. His father's disturbing eyes were still on him. The piano lid thudded dully on its strip of green felt.

'She is with the Waylands,' he said without realising that that was what he would say, though the sudden truth of it broke over him like a cold wave. He was in control of his own destiny suddenly: alert, clear, able to dismiss his father's misgivings, his mother's concern.

'Who are the Waylands?' Ellen drew a bentwood chair near her father's and sat beside him with her hands in her lap.

'Neighbours.'

'He is a priest,' the old man supplied.

'Do you know him, Father?' William matched his conversational tone. 'From the cathedral?' His father nodded abruptly and looked away, as if he regretted his remark. Of course, William realised, it was Wayland who kept him informed of the ratio of bush over burn-off, of the number of hours he laboured and how many he spent in the hills. Father must know about the still then, though the mails were not fast enough for him to know of the death of the child.

'Is Myra well?' His mother was looking at Blanche at the closed piano. In response to her unspoken command, the youngest sister stood, crossed the room swiftly and turned her mother's chair. She was as beautiful as ever, William thought, her sweetly rounded arms and narrow waist, her falling, unruly hair. Although her childhood freckles had faded away, it seemed her skin had retained a little of their colour, a gold-tinted ivory. She caught his eye now, smiled, her mouth quick and moist. In her white gown she glowed against the dark varnish of the fire surround.

'Why must you consider your response? Was she well when you left her?' asked the judge.

'Fairly well.' William hoped Blanche would direct him to a seat also, but she knew as well as he did that his father would want him to stand. 'We had the recent misfortune of losing a child. A girl. We named her Alithea.'

His mother drew in a quick breath, turned her face from him and groped behind her for her chair.

'Do not allow him to distress you, Mother.' Ellen's voice came low and insistent.

'Quiet, Ellen! Has your heart frozen over entirely? His child has died.' Their mother regained her chair and pushed her handwork to one side so that the bright threads hung from the arm. Pallid now at the northern windows, the last of the daylight fell on her face and drained her of colour. Her hair, pulled tightly against her head, so much took on the hue of her complexion that she appeared almost bald. It was the colour of water, the pure sheen of a fall from a pump, or a clear lick flung from the blade of an oar. Tears glistened in her grey eyes as she held her hand out to William, drawing him between herself and the old man. Her son interlaced his fingers in hers but couldn't look at her: he wouldn't be able to bear the anxiety he would see there.

Ellen pressed her lips together, turned to look at William with hatred. 'I only meant that first we should listen to his story before we decide what is true and what is not.'

An impulse of rage forced through William's chest and head so violently his face stung as it retreated. 'How dare you imply that I would lie about such a tragedy?'

'Quiet.' His father was standing now. 'We will go to my study. Send in Mary to make a fire.'

'I'll carry your wrap, Father.' Ellen pulled a tartan rug from the back of his chair. Irritably the old man snatched it away, laid it back in its place. He clicked his fingers for his stick. William squeezed his mother's hand and would have let it go, but she was pulling herself to her feet.

'But, Mr McQuiggan, I want to know –' she began.

'In good time.' Her husband had begun his slow progress towards the door.

'May I accompany you?'

There was no answer.

'Come and talk to me,' she whispered to her son. 'I'll wait for you here.'

William nodded and kissed his mother's cheek. The finely lined skin beneath his lips smelt of soap, a trace of lanolin.

In the dim, small room a cut-glass decanter full of glinting malt glowed in the tantalus on the sideboard. It was flanked by a decanter of brandy on one side, and ruby port on the other, but it was the scotch that filled William's mouth with saliva. His father was almost to a chair that stood before the cold grate.

'Shall I light the lamps?'

'Leave it for the maid.' Elisha sat now, rested his stick against the chair's back.

'May I then –' William gestured towards the sideboard.

'I suppose you must.' His voice was harder now, his old rage returning. 'You have become that kind of man.'

William took up the silver key that lay beside the tantalus and unlocked it. The grooved bar that held the decanters prisoner lifted and he sloshed whisky into the glass, a curl of it overtaking the rim and puddling on the polished tray. William steadied his hand and knocked it back. As the spirit's heat warmed his heart and flared briefly in his belly, he offered up a sudden ignoble prayer.

'Don't let my father see me, Lord. Have him look away while I pour another.' He sloshed in some more, turned back to the room with the glass in his fingers. Elisha's eyes met his and the corners of the old man's mouth lifted in a surprising smile. It was not altogether pleasant. A foreboding wrenched William's guts and his throat closed, sucking the moisture from his mouth. It was his boyhood response, one he thought he'd shaken off.

'The farm?' Elisha asked. 'Is it making progress?'

William shook his head, took a breath. He wouldn't sit, he decided. 'We had a fire. Everything was lost. We only just escaped.'

'Do you know how the fire started?'

'Myra has been forgetful since the child passed away. She left an oil lamp before an open window and a gust of wind came up after we had retired. We were woken by the smoke.'

'You were lucky, then.' Elisha held his hand out for William's glass, took a tiny sip and placed it on the small table at his elbow.

'William?'

The son lifted his eyes from the glass. Did his father want that one? Should he pour himself another? He was aware suddenly of the bones in his hands, hanging loosely at his sides.

'I asked you a question.'

'I'm sorry, Father. I didn't hear you.'

'Did you lose the barn?'

'No, only the house.'

'It may be possible to build another one quickly. How much stock are you carrying into the winter? I have not seen any of your accounts for several months.'

He had poured another; it had taken shape in his hand. The old man's eyes were on him, but he suddenly didn't care. It occurred to him that his father might die soon: his forehead gleamed dully, like a grey paste.

'The farm is a failure,' he said brutally, 'as well you knew it would be. I have no interest in farming, and no gift for it either. I do not come from peasant stock. It is not in me to delight in dirt nor empathise with beasts.'

His father's eyebrows, silver above that alarming blue, lifted and fell. 'Is it not, indeed?'

Would he rage now? William wondered. He was so eerily calm. Perhaps this failure was expected and his father had rehearsed what he would say on his inevitable return.

There was a knock and Mary entered, carrying a basket of twigs and a lit taper. She hurried to the hearth and peeped into the coal scuttle. It was full.

'Shall I do that?' William asked, setting down his glass. He could tell the girl's heart knocked at the sound of his voice. She was afraid. Perhaps there had been kitchen talk about him.

His father nodded and she set about lighting the lamps. Three of them flared and dimmed, one after another, as she turned down each wick. Gilt lettering on the spines of the judge's books sparkled, the stern face of Elisha's long-deceased mother loomed from a dark oil above the fireplace.

'Peasant stock,' repeated Elisha, softly. He spread his hands on his thighs, examined his bony knuckles.

Passing the maid on his way to the grate, William trod lightly, purposefully, on her hem and blew on her neck. Her panicked head spun to face him, but he had pulled away, was already in the act of kneeling at the hearth. Mary set the taper in a glass with a trembling, swift hand. At William's back the door opened and closed.

'Your mother is pleased with that maid,' said his father, in that same mild tone. 'She was in service at Home and knows her duties. I would thank you not to misuse her in any way.'

William's neck burned. The old man had seen his little trick. He stood, took the taper from the glass and bent to light the fire. The dry twigs ignited and he fed in some coal.

'I have heard that when a person survives a fire he will often feel apprehension in its proximity, even a tame, domestic fire such as this. You have not this affliction, obviously.'

'Perhaps only women are so inclined,' William said carelessly, though the words stuck in his throat. What was he doing? He was showing off like a child. He felt God recede to the edges of his existence. He should not have had the drink: it had coarsened him, loosened his tongue.

'I trust Myra was not hurt.'

'Myra wants only for me to succeed in life.'

His father sighed, almost imperceptibly. 'And how do you propose to do that?'

'May I sit down, Father?'

'Have you not the short answer?'

William shook his head. 'It will take some time.'

Elisha nodded, the glass at his elbow still untouched. William took the chair from the desk, brought it around before the fire to face the old man, its back to the whisky.

'Do you believe in God, Father?' Elisha started, his heavy eyelids flicked open. 'I take great offence at that enquiry. Shall we end this discussion before we begin?'

William made no reply. Panic twitched at his mouth. Seeing him, the judge continued in a quieter voice. 'There is surely no need to remind you that the Law comes from God, the Law which I uphold in every way. And I am a church warden of thirty years' standing.'

William heard the patient, paternal tone and loathed him for it. 'I experienced the power of God,' he announced.

The words hung between them. Elisha brought his right hand to his face, pressed his fingers against his eyes. William continued in a rush, impatient.

'I was alone, on Pukekaroro, near Bald Rock. It was very late at night. The Lord showed me how he will answer us.'

'The Lord answers me in every moment of my existence.'

'Father, I should not like us to argue just yet.'

Elisha crossed his arms, met William's eyes. William was to go on.

'He did not intend us to labour in the dark. To raise us above the animals He not only gave us souls but also the power of rational thought and logic. It is this we must apply to our instincts and desires, to all that makes us sensual, including our religion. He showed me indurate glass and reminded me of how it retains its secret, liquid nature. He showed me ash and then fire. The world unfolded before me and I heard His voice: All may be explained.'

His father nodded and William's heart leapt. There was belief in his face: his father believed him! There was a silence, which grew slowly more expectant.

'Is that all?' asked Elisha.

'I beg your pardon, Father?' William's head whirled with the memory of his epiphany. He could not explain the ascension, would not. It was a matter only for himself and his Creator, occasionally when God's love for him became so ferocious it ripped him from the clutches of desire and addiction.

'After the Lord showed you the glass and the ash, what happened then?' Elisha picked up his whisky, turned it in the palm of one hand.

'I came to Auckland on a scow.'

'Forgive me,' said the old man, 'but I am struggling to establish an order for these events. Did the epiphany occur before or after you lost the house?'

William considered his tone, combed it for sarcasm. There was none, but clearly his father did not believe him after all.

'That doesn't matter.'

'Of course it does. I know you very well, my son.'

'Not so well.' He was cold, deliberate. 'I am mostly a stranger to you now.'

His father's shoulders twitched in a rapid, despairing shrug. 'If that is what you would like to believe then so be it.'

'You must release me from our agreement, Father.'

'I cannot. You have not fulfilled its conditions, William.' The old man brought his stick around, hauled himself up with one hand on the arm of his chair. 'I will bring it out so that we may refresh our memories.'

'I remember it word for word.'

Behind him his son's voice sounded childish, petulant.

'I doubt that very much.' He halted his slow progress towards the desk and turned back instead to the chiffonier, where he locked the tantalus and dropped the key in his pocket before resuming his approach to his desk. He slid out a drawer and brought out two sheets of paper.

The piece of thick white bond William recognised as the document he and his father had drawn up together, in this very room, on the morning of his wedding. The other paper, thin and crackling, written over in a pale, spidery hand, was unfamiliar.

'Firstly, you were to make the farm a success. Secondly, you were not to leave the immediate vicinity of the land without my permission. Thirdly, you were to keep me informed of your progress. Fourth –'

'I know, Father, I know,' dared William. 'Can't you see all that has changed now?' He sprang to his feet in the same instant that Elisha thumped the paper to the desk.

'In the light of what, precisely?'

'In the light of God.'

'How glib. How foolish!' He raised his walking stick, away from his leg, and struck William weakly on his closest shoulder. 'You have not attended church for many years now. You have scarcely read the Bible. Where is your Doctrine?'

'I will find one – one that does not burden itself with tradition, with the expectations of foolish old men!'

Rage burned in the old man's cheeks. 'You talk to me of knowing God. His plan for you was plain to me when you were born. You were to make the most of yourself, of your position. You have had every opportunity.'

'God has only just made my fate known to me.'

'I will say this. Once. You are not to talk of this to your mother. Not at all.'

'If I wish to –' began William. His father held up his hand and continued.

'It is an error of the greatest magnitude to assume that God favours you in any way, above any other of his creatures. That way lies egotism, even madness.' Moving more quickly than he had for months the judge crossed the floor, his stick agitated, tapping. He left the room, leaving the door hanging open.

William didn't follow him. His belly ached with hunger, growled first with fury, then shame, then fury once more. Each passion came separately, neither tempering the other, inflicting a strange paralysis on him. Before his blurring eyes his hand rose, pushed the door shut and the last of his rage faded to indignation.

It was warm now. He fed the fire more coal, turned his backside to the flames. Beside him, on the desk, lay the two papers the judge had taken from his ledger. William picked up the unfamiliar one, folded the frail, finely milled paper and put it in his striped pocket. On his left sat the squat chiffonier bearing its sweet cargo: an ellipsoid of blessed oblivion, glittering in its crystal sheath.

CHAPTER 6

Silently, late on the afternoon of the fire, Riha had come. Myra sat hunched and aching at the place on the track where William had left her. Around noon it had occurred to her to go to the barn where she could shelter from the sharp wind. She had even stood to go there, then decided against it: her husband might come back for her and not think to look there. The chill of the damp worked its way up her spine, cramping her shoulders and making her head ache.

'Myra?'

At the sound of her name, she first thought a man stood behind her on the track. She recognised Riha's deep voice only in the same instant that her friend knelt and put her arms around her. Myra could not explain what had happened, she didn't know where to start. Should she tell her William had set the fire? That he had shown her the copper? The last time she had seen Riha, on the day of the funeral, she had been shamefully deaf, mute with grief. Riha squeezed her tight, then stood and crossed the stream. She made her way up to the burnt wreckage of the house. Nothing stood but the chimney and the cast-iron range, marking where the kitchen once was. She circled the ashes, ran into the grove of kahikatea to look up towards Bald Rock. There was no sign of the husband, no sense of him: his absence seemed final.

Myra followed her friend as far as the house site. It was colder away from the protection of the ti-tree. Spirals of ash rose and fell; a gust of wind carried the sound of Riha's pounding feet back from the barn and scooped a layer of fine soot, a wave of it rising and breaking against Myra's damp, nightgown-clad legs.

Riha came to her, pressed her cool cheek against hers.

'He's gone.'

'Yes.'

'He's taken the horse.'

Myra nodded, shivered with cold.

'You come with me.'

With Riha's arm across Myra's shoulder and hooked under her opposing arm, they splashed their way across the burn and on through the belt of ti-tree to the track. Riha turned them towards the east, to where the track met the end of Bald Rock Road. There were grey hairs at Riha's temple, deep crowsfeet at her eyes. She was dressed as she had been the day before, in the pink flannelette gown. Inside it her body moved deliberately, smoothly, lithe and square-shouldered. In her time on the farm Myra had met only two women from the pa, Riha and her sister Poihaere. Until she saw Poihaere she'd suspected all Maori women were giants, the same as this one she'd met one day while she was scrubbing shirts against a rock in the burn. Riha had come off the track, taken a shirt and worked beside her. Later Myra had given her bread and a cup of tea and Riha had told her about her sons and husband, how they had drowned while they were fishing. Aside from this one tragedy of her life Myra knew no more about her, even her age. Forty perhaps, fifty?

'Are you taking me to your home?' she asked now.

Riha shook her head. 'That's the other way. Too far.'

'To Mrs Wayland, then,' Myra murmured and took Riha's silence as assent. They pressed on over the uneven ground, roots and stones knocking against Myra's soft white feet. The trees crowded over them, thick bush on either side as they followed the stream, wider now as it began its descent off the McQuiggans' land. Night had begun to fall already here, though the sky before the green tunnel's mouth had been streaked with sunset, pink and gold. It was colder too, the damp of the earth rising to dampen their hems.

'But I would like to see where you live,' Myra said, suddenly fearful of Hakaru, of passing McNeill's house, of who might see her stumbling on her numb feet in her nightgown. She saw herself and Riha through a stranger's eyes: Riha's scowling, concerned face above hers; Myra's dirt, her abandonment.

They'd reached the top of Bald Rock Road, where it met the track that ran west to the McQuiggans' farm and on to the pa on the Otamatea River. Below them spread the plateau, shimmering under clear glassy air, a tableland cleared for grazing. Pockets of bush fuzzed the grooves and gullies of the land. They were too high up to discern any movement of man or beast. The church steeple rose in the near south-east, beside the darker patch that was the Waylands' garden.

'Take me to the pa,' Myra whispered, her small hands icy on Riha's arm.

'I live away from my people.' Riha wouldn't look at Myra.

'Take me there, then. To where you live.'

'You would not like it.'

'I would. Please, Riha.' Myra squeezed her friend's arm and Riha met her eyes.

'Mrs Wayland will have garments to cover you. I have nothing.'

Riha's English often had a Biblical tone, Myra observed carelessly. She felt irritated suddenly, no longer helpless. 'We will send for her.' Her blood quickened at the thought, a pulse of warmth accompanying her plan. 'And she would bring me a dress. I cannot show myself down there.'

'Who will we send?' Riha snorted, almost laughed. 'There is no one.'

'I will go to the pa myself and ask for a boy.'

'The way is hard –' began Riha.

'As difficult as the path to the still? I have been there.'

'That is another problem. There is hatred at the pa for your husband and his waipiro.'

'But not for me. They wouldn't know of my existence.'

'For you also. You are his wife.'

Myra's hands fell away from Riha's arm at the ferocity of her response. 'And you? Do they hate you also? Why do you live alone?'

'They are indifferent to me.'

Myra moved a few steps away, back down the track. 'We will go to your house. I will not go down to Hakaru. Would you go home and abandon me here?'

Riha sighed and shook her head; her shoulders drooped gloomily.

Hours after nightfall they reached the slab hut. It stood in a small clearing on the western face of a hill, above the pa. Myra dropped to her knees, crawled through the low door and curled up on the dirt floor, every bone and muscle thrumming with pain. Riha, she dimly perceived, was still angry: she gave out an ill-tempered grunt as she pushed into the hut after her and sat scowling, her fingers interlaced across her knees. It was too dark for Myra to see that she scowled, or that she had laid her big hands finger by finger across her round knees. She knew that she had not lain down: even and loud, Riha's breath issued from a point above her.

The interior of the hut was utterly dark, but for a softer grey patch where the opening was. Like the Black Hole of Calcutta. It was something her father used to say on winter evenings when she was tardy with the lamp-lighting. She wondered if Riha knew what it meant. Her father had never explained it to her.

'Black Hole of Calcutta,' she said experimentally. A few minutes went by and Riha said nothing.

'Did you go to school, Riha?' Myra had told her, soon after they met, that she had never had any real lessons, that her father had not been inspired to teach her. She remembered now Riha's pitying glance.

'Eh?' Riha was scuffling now, feeling for her mat.

'Did you go to the mission school?'

'Ae,' said Riha, which Myra took as 'eh' again, but it sounded affirmative. Riha moved backwards on her knees, unrolling the mat as she went. Its fibrous edge knocked against Myra's knee and elbow, and with her last vestiges of strength she rolled herself over to lie on top of it.

'I was clever at school.' Riha's whisper was louder than her voice at its lowest: mellifluous, richly toned. 'More clever than the boys.'

In the dark Myra smiled. There was a pause while Riha lay down, the sound of her tongue licking around her teeth, a swallow. Her stomach rumbled, groaned.

'"Even unto this present how we hunger and thirst",' murmured Myra, curling her body towards the warmth of her friend.

'. . . and are naked, and are buffeted, and have no certain dwelling place,' finished Riha, silently in her own head. Corinthians. She had a bad feeling about this, her houseguest. Poihaere would come with her food in the morning and take the news back with her to the pa: that there had been another fire and the still-maker's wife was in her nightgown in Riha's hut. These two separate facts would be linked together another way, to take another shape. They would come to mean what they did not mean. It occurred to her suddenly that perhaps William hadn't gone at all, that he was drinking himself blind in the hills. Poihaere was her only hope then: she could send her youngest son, Eruera, for Mrs Wayland, who would make the journey, if she came at all, in the company of the Reverend. Myra was painfully slow in the bush but they could meet them halfway, at Kaiwaka, if she set off at the same time as her nephew. Pakeha women often required carrying, sometimes for miles. She refused to carry Myra. On their way to the hut she had towed her behind her, hand in hand, relenting now and then to lift her over obstacles that the young woman's breath sobbed at: fallen trees, mounds of undergrowth and rot.

At dawn Riha rose, sleepless, to poke a fire to desultory life before the hut. Beside it she realised she could never put her trust in Poihaere's silence. She would have to take Myra all the way back to the Waylands' herself. She would have to rouse her now and make her promise to stay hidden in the hut during Poihaere's visit. It would be all right. Poihaere never ventured inside unless it was raining, which this morning it was not. A weak autumn sun wavered behind high cloud.

'Kia ora!' And there she was, her sister, approaching from the half light of the trees. Riha shifted her body slightly to cover the door, and Myra's pink feet, bloodied and bruised, fell into shadow behind her.

'Kia ora!' She did not ask her sister to sit down, but Poihaere did anyway, pushing the basket of food away from her.

Consciousness returned Myra to the pain in her feet. The exteriors stung and burned while the bones beat with a dull, aching pulse. She slipped them around behind her and knelt, dry-mouthed, longing for water. Outside Riha spoke in her own language, another woman answering.

Myra crawled forward and pushed her head through the opening, nudging up against Riha's arm. At the sight of her Poihaere shrieked and fell backwards, so startling Myra with the intensity of her response that she bumped her head on the top of the low opening. Riha reached behind to pat her hand, moved aside to let her out and offered her a swallow from a chipped china cup. Stretching her feet out, Myra settled beside her.

Tentatively she looked at Poihaere. She had never seen her so close before. The sister had never approached the McQuiggans' house, only ever going as far as the creek, and waiting there for half an hour or so, as if she thought Riha would cut her visit short. Younger than Riha, by as much as ten years perhaps, she had a sensual, sulky set to her mouth. Her eyes resembled her sister's, though a different, harder light shone from them.

'There was a fire,' Myra told her. 'Yesterday before dawn. Riha came.'

Poihaere took in the Pakeha's ragged, filthy gown, her matted hair, her damaged feet.

Her expression changed, her shoulders broadened. Eyes narrowed, she turned on her sister, shouting in Maori. Riha listened for a moment then also sprang to her feet, her louder voice overwhelming her sister's. Myra could discern none of it, could only watch while Poihaere spun the basket with an angry, rising foot. Extending her hands, Riha took a grasp of her sister's shoulders and pushed her away from the hut. Poihaere stumbled backwards, throwing a condescending glance at Myra who, eyes starting from her head, drew her aching feet away from the scuffle.

'It was Riha who burned your house,' Poihaere hissed in English, 'like she burned the pa.' Then she was turning, running. Riha ran a few steps after her as far as the track that led down the hill to the foot of the pa.

'Tonoa Eruera kia haere ki te tiki i a Mrs Wayland!' Riha yelled after her.

Poihaere did not reply. She disappeared among the trees, which shifted and swam suddenly, blurring Riha to a pink smudge against their green. The ground lifted away from Myra towards her.

'You didn't, Riha. Please tell me you didn't.'

As she stood, wobbling, Myra's face was tight with fear. Riha would come no further towards her, but put her hands on her hips, glowered. The insects and birds, which had fallen silent while the sisters shouted, resumed their noise tentatively at first, a few rasps and cries, before building to their giddy pitch. Myra knelt, tipped her face towards the sky, her eyes closed to the shining clouds that masked the sun.

'There's no need to pray,' spat Riha. 'You know the truth. Your husband set the fire. He soaked rags in the barn, away from the house, then laid them against the walls in the dark.'

'How do you know? Did you see him?'

'I found the paraffin oil tin in the barn. The one from the house.'

'But your sister said –'

Riha's expression forbade her to go on. Perhaps it would have been wiser to have swallowed her foolish shreds of pride and gone to Hakaru. She looked around at the fading fire, the iron roof of the hut. Two leaning hills held a blade of the flat brown river between them. It was a prison. Her eyes filled again, unwillingly. She had been born weak and stupid, as if she were of another species to Riha, that woman now helping her to sit again, examining her feet. Eighty black men were worth one white man, so the lesson in one of her school books had run. What was the equation for women, Myra wondered, and how had they worked it out for the men?

Behind the hut grew a horopito. Riha took some leaves, crushed them in her fingers and held them to the abrasions in Myra's toes and soles. Breathing in the sharp aroma lifting from Riha's hands, Myra tried to quiet her mind but it ran on, lifting the frayed corners of everything she had understood to be true, returning again and again to Poihaere's parting words. What had she meant by saying Riha had burned the pa? The leaves' exudence stung at her cuts as gentian violet had her childhood wounds, though surely they were never as painful as these.

Riha sucked in her bottom lip, stood and tore the flounce from her pink gown. With the cleanest side facing in, she bound the tiny battered feet. She spoke not a word through the whole process, though a wounded rage hung around her bowed head. Myra castigated herself. She knew the fire was her husband's work. She had smelt the spirit on his hair and clothes. A thought struck her then, knocked the breath from her. Had he always intended to wake her, to lift her from the house? Or had that been an after-thought?

Riha glanced up, suspecting she had hurt her, but did not stop her rapid binding. In her hands the young woman's feet felt hot, warmer than the skin on her narrow shin bones. Why had she ever agreed to bring her here? If Myra grew feverish before she reached the Waylands' she would be too sick to explain that her night in the hut had been her idea, not Riha's.

Myra watched her rescuer wash her hands in a tin of water, right the basket and dust it off. There was a piece of smoked eel and two small flat cakes, like fritters.

'Aruhe,' said Riha, holding out a piece.

She tried to follow the example of Riha, who bit and chewed vigorously, but the cake was bitter and tough. Instead she broke off a morsel of eel, found it pungent, muddy textured.

'You eat,' Riha muttered at her. The young woman's skin was translucent; a blue vein snaked at her temple. Ash smudged in borders around the cleaner patches below her eyes, where yesterday's tears had fallen. If only she could leave her here, thought Riha, and make the journey alone. If only Myra could walk the distance back, if only they had a horse. She started with the sudden logic and possibility of this idea. It would entail leaving Myra alone in the hut, but only for a short time. She regained her feet and Myra stared at her, sensing her departure.

'I am going to get a horse,' Riha announced, turning and making for the trees before Myra could ask why, or where from. She didn't take the same path her sister had. Instead she crossed the track and plunged off into the thick bush that covered a steep incline to the sea. A cliff stood between bush and sand. Riha scrambled down it, hand over hand among a belt of flax to where a pohutukawa sent sprawling limbs against the rocks. She dropped from one branch to another, disturbing a vast flock of gulls as she reached the sand. They took off, screaming to the sky, which hung low over the ebbing tide. The beach was deserted.

Riha made her way around the point at a slow jog. Above her sat the pa. She could hear voices, an old woman with a child answering. The ground between the pa and the mission station, which sat at the point's lowest side, was denuded of its trees. It would be difficult to secure the horse without being seen.

A small canoe was crossing the Otamatea River, making its way to Kakaraea. On the far muddy bank a small group of Maori awaited its arrival. The canoe held two men, one of Riha's people and the other easily distinguished by his black garb and shining blond head: the young priest from the mission station. His wife would be inside the school then, giving the lessons. Riha was unknown to her; her exile had been complete before the young couple took their position here.

The muddy turf that lay above the beach at the point held her rapid footprints. Keeping close into the walls of the mission station, dropping below its sills, Riha found a place behind the tank where she could watch the school-house in the next paddock. Near the gate, which was open and fallen from its top hinge, stood the sad old bow-backed mare that bore the youngest children down from the pa. As it cropped the winter grass, one baleful eye regarded Riha, blinked. Riha clicked her tongue and the horse lifted its head.

'Haere mai,' whispered Riha.

The children were chanting now, inside the school-house. The small chimney puffed smoke, the one small window was fogged. Riha remembered the smell of the room on winter days: damp wool, the close young bodies. They chanted their arithmetic, their massed voices rising and falling. She clicked to the horse again and this time it took a step towards her, closer to the gate. Moving as fast as she could without startling the beast, Riha pushed the gate wide enough to allow the horse to pass through and took hold of its leading rope.

At the fire Myra fell asleep and dreamed of William. He sat at a wide desk piled with books. Head bowed, he read with avid eyes, his full lips wet. She had never seen him read before, save the few letters he had received at the farm from his father. It seemed entirely right that he should read in the dream, and as if he had been doing so for days. He was unaware of her, so much so that she had no sense of her own presence in the dream save that of observer. Neither did she perceive any detail of the room he sat in. There was nothing except her husband, his square hands on the book at the desk, his quiet breath.

She slept on undisturbed until Riha's return with the broken horse, already sweat-flecked from its gallop along the beach. Riha had led it up into the bush along a creek bed and it was up to its hocks in mud. Wearily Myra stood. She had been mistaken in coming here, she knew now. It was not her discomfort that led her to this conclusion, nor the dismissal of any romantic notion of Riha's life. It was whatever the secret was, the burning of the pa, which would make Riha a suspect for the house fire.

The twelve-mile journey was made in silence; an urgency set in Riha's grim face as she led the horse. She wanted only to deliver Myra to her own people and set the mare home, towards the pa. She set Myra down by the churchyard gate and let her limp to the vicarage alone. Too exhausted to speak, the young woman paused on the veranda and lifted her hand in farewell before she knocked on the door. Mrs Wayland was never to know where Myra had spent the days on either side of the night that intervened between the loss of the house and her arrival in Hakaru.

CHAPTER 7

William woke to the sound of someone moving about in the room that was once his and was now Henry's. There was rustling of folding garments, dull knocks as objects were lifted and replaced, the whisk of a duster. Light entered his skull painfully, even before he opened his eyes. There was a woman beyond him, a basket at the door, brimming with dirty linen. She picked an object from the top of the tallboy and carried it with some distaste towards the wash-stand. Blanche, with Henry's greasy comb at arm's length.

'Good morning,' he managed.

'Hello, William.'

He detected the tiniest trace of uncharacteristic disapproval in her voice, though she turned her head to smile at him while she dunked Henry's comb up and down in the basin.

'Why are you – and not the maid, what's her name? – shouldn't she be –?'

'Because Father asked me,' Blanche said simply. She wiped the comb on the grey towel, then flung the towel towards the basket. 'Are you not more curious to know how you came to bed? You are lucky Henry is still so strong. Father is none the wiser, unless of course Henry boasts to him of how he carried you up the stairs.'

'Henry?' William's head throbbed. He shifted his legs in the bed, realised then that he still wore his trousers.

'Oh yes, you needn't worry. He is quite happy. Mother has let him have the room off the porch, so now he may sleep with his cats. You know how he loves them.'

'Mother knows?'

Blanche looked strangely at him. 'That you have returned? Of course she does.'

William shook his head, which cost him dearly and was wasted. With her back to him, Blanche was leaning over the wash-stand to slide up the lower window. 'I meant, know that I —' His mouth was dry, bitter. He trailed off.

'Drank all Father's whisky? No, not yet.'

'Did I?'

'Both the whisky and the port. You broke the lock on the tantalus. Ellen followed behind Henry with a basin in case you were ill.'

There was a burning in his chest as if he had taken a lungful of acrid smoke. Perhaps it was impossible: he would never be able to maintain the vigilance necessary to prevent these falls from grace. It was because he was so alone, even now in his boyhood bedroom, with his beloved sister. The night in the bush had set him apart from every man.

'And was I?'

'Yes,' said Blanche, shortly. 'You had not eaten. You never came to join us at dinner. Ellen went to fetch you and returned with the news that you had fallen asleep in the study. Henry carried you up while Father finished his pudding.'

'With Ellen,' thought William. Under the sweaty sheets his feet tingled with shame.

There was the thump of feet on the stairs, resounding now on the landing before taking the last flight. Henry hurried along the corridor and into the bedroom, knocking the basket over as he made his way in. At the sight of William in the bed, he gave out a loud coo and stood over him, a heavy hand on his brother's brow.

'Poor Will,' he said. 'Better now?'

'Yes, thank you, Henry.' Irritably William jerked his head, but Henry only exerted more pressure at his thumb and fingertips. William suffered the vice at his temples, moaned.

'Leave him alone,' said Blanche. 'You can help me carry some of these things downstairs.' But Henry shook his head vigorously.

'Mother should engage another maid,' William muttered. He was uncomfortable with Blanche waiting on him, like a servant or wife.

Blanche laughed, her own delighted, untarnished giggle, unchanged from girlhood. 'Why should she? Because you have come home?'

William closed his eyes.

'There are none to be had, Will. Didn't you know that?' She adopted her mother's tone, her light, no-nonsense voice: 'It's a national disgrace!' and giggled again. She was too good natured, William thought. He remembered their sweet kisses as children, how they had played innocently as man and wife. No wonder he was eternally disappointed in women. None could compare with this sister, her luminescence, her grace. She had lifted the laundry to her hip now; her foot-steps had departed along the hall. Henry settled himself on the bed at William's shoulder, his face puckered with concern.

'Mother and Ellen have gone to Queen Street to the outfitters,' he announced. 'Father says to tell you that he waits downstairs for you, at your earliest –' He searched for the word.

'Convenience?' William supplied.

'Immm.'

So Ellen was not at school. Of course, it was Saturday. He pictured her at Hugh Wright's, standing at his mother's shoulder, advising her not to outlay too much, that William did not deserve the best-quality shirts and trousers. If she had her way he would be dressed much the same as Henry, as a peasant. Ever since she had begun to contribute to the domestic expenses from her pitiful schoolmistress's wage, Ellen had regarded them as her responsibility, hounding the cook, examining the household accounts before they were shown to Father.

'Go away, Henry.' William rolled away from him towards the curtains, which Blanche had left open. The bed shifted under him as Henry stood, his face drooping, mouth quivering.

'Will?' he said, after some moments. William's eyes were clamped shut. 'What shall I tell Father?'

'Tell him I have gone out.'

Henry shook his head, his instincts telling him his father would be unbelieving: the old man had waited with the parlour door open all morning.

'Through the window,' said William. 'Tell him that.' He opened his eyes now, sat up.

'Will?' Henry put a hand out from the other side of the bed, laid it on his brother's shoulder. But William shook him off, rose to his feet. He needed to eat. A clean, cold breeze pushed through the open window, chilled his clammy drunkard's sweat.

'Off you go, Henry.' William pulled the wash-stand away from the wall and slid the window the rest of the way up. He slipped through, swinging one leg then the other over the sill. Before he departed, hurrying along the veranda roof on his bare feet, he leaned into the room and spoke again to his brother.

'There's a good lad.'

Henry watched him go, heard him slip down the corner post into the back yard. He sat down on the bed and held his fingers over his eyes, looking between them at his tidy room that had latterly contained his brother. Everything kept changing now. For a long time things had always been the same, just him and his father and mother, Blanche, and the occasional hard word from Ellen or the maid. He felt his eyes water and his nose prickle and hoped he wouldn't cry loud enough to bring Mary.

Mrs Gordon, the cook, had her back to him. She was making up a luncheon tray. For his father, William supposed. There was a bowl of thin soup, some finely cut bread and butter. On another plate rested a pink curl of ham, a sliced tomato. He took a step into the room. Gordon's broad back showed her to be oblivious to him. Swiftly, he slipped the ham away, as well as what remained on the table wrapped in butcher's paper. In the next second he took the bread and butter in a piece, before stepping out the back door, across the bricked yard and out into the lane, where a moment of doubt took him. Henry's regatta shirt was crumpled from its night on the floor and in the light of day the trousers were smudged and grubby. He was hatless, unshaven. He looked, he realised, like a tramp. But perhaps that would work in his favour: he was unrecognisable as the judge's son. He could have a few hours of freedom before he returned to face his father, who would no doubt strike him again. The feeble strokes were ignominious, shameful for both of them. He gulped the food and looked up at the house. There was a movement behind the glass of the bedroom window. Henry gazed down at him, pointing into the back yard.

Too late, William saw that his brother had been warning him – Gordie was on his trail. She sailed through the gate now, took him by the arm, her face thunderous.

'You come back inside with me, young man, and tell your father you stole his lunch.'

'I didn't really steal it, Gordie. I borrowed it. Anyway, you can make him another one.'

'Can I just?'

'Yes. In my opinion he should be served a nourishing broth. Rich ham and bread and butter – which were delicious, by the way – might not agree with him.'

Gordon let her hand drop, pursed her lips together to stop herself from smiling. She wondered how old young William was now. Would he be thirty yet? She had lost track. He had been a beautiful child and just then he had seemed like a boy again, with a wheedling, teasing tone to his voice, but his eyes – oh, those beautiful blue-black eyes – they looked right into a lady's heart, made a lady want to give him whatever he wanted. All those times she'd fetched him from the stables, brought him into the kitchen and patched him up. Did he remember? She supposed he never gave it a thought; he was never a boy for dwelling on things. Off he'd be, on his next adventure. She patted him on the arm.

'Off you go, then,' she said.

Saturday was a busy shopping day in town and William was grateful for the crowd. With any luck it would obscure him from his mother and sister, should he chance upon them. He paused under Slaney's awning on the corner of Vulcan Lane, looked longingly towards the Occidental, his old watering-hole. He hadn't raised a glass there for four years, since the day before he'd left for Australia. He leaned against a post, wondered if any of his old cronies remained. Father was more generous with his allowance in those days. How good it had felt to walk into the hotel with a pocket full of money and shout his fellow man. He could go there now if he were decently dressed, quench his thirst and settle his stomach.

A knot of men and women were gathering a short distance away, in the lane. Keeping his back to the post he stepped around to watch them. A man in a shining new bowler hat, just his head and shoulders, appeared over the top, raised on a soap-box. He waved a small dun-coloured book, opened it and began to declaim. There was something foreign about him, a light, attractive lilt in his voice. He was a little older than William, in his late thirties perhaps.

'"Beware the scribes,"' he read, '"which desire to walk in long robes and love greetings in the markets and the highest

110

seats in the synagogues —"' He looked up from his book at the eight or nine faces gathered. He had a broad, fair face. A blond beard glistened on his tanned skin.

Beside him a small boy dropped to his knee and began rolling marbles against the box.

'Beware the scribes! Why does Luke write that, people? Is not the parable an elegant plea for us all to form our own affection for God?' Another book was raised aloft, larger, with a black jacket. William took the corner now, moved closer. The Occidental loomed on the left, the boy's marbles rolled, sparkled and thudded against the preacher's box. Two women caught each other's eye and moved off through the small crowd, distributing tracts.

'The Lord lives, ladies and gentlemen. And here I have proof that He has come since the Resurrection and will come again. He came to the tribes of America and he will come to you. Believe it, people.'

William was close enough now to see a young, well-built Maori who stood directly behind the American. He held a coat, the preacher's, and gazed at him with shining, rapt eyes.

'He will come in his own way to each of us. That is the lesson I take from the Book of Nephi, written not by one of those poisonous scribes that Luke tells us about, ladies and gentlemen, but by a voyager, a pioneer. You, sir!' The preacher pointed a gloved finger in the direction of a silver-haired gentleman, his shoes worn down, the knees out of his trousers. He had the look of a man who has just spent his last penny in the public bar, but whose sense of dislocation was made permanent by a lifetime's hard drinking.

'How long have you abided in these parts? You, sir, are one of the venerable generation, almost passed, of true pioneers, men and women —' Here he smiled at the posses-sor of an extraordinary pair of leg-of-mutton sleeves so wide they concealed the upper half of her body entirely from William's side-on view. She nodded at the preacher, a tiny dip of her brim. '. . . who believed in what was possible.

111

Nephi sailed to Bountiful. You, old man, sailed to New Zealand when you were young and virile. Has the Lord appeared to you?'

A particularly loud thwack struck the box then, a marble thrown not rolled, momentarily putting the preacher off his stride. He gestured with one hand, an irritated shooing motion, and the Maori stepped forward, took the boy by one ear and inserted him into the crowd. There were about twenty circling the preacher now, William estimated, though some of the original listeners had drifted away and been replaced by new faces. The preacher's specimen of the true pioneer spoke up before he stumbled away.

'I've only been 'ere three weeks and I can't abide the place.'

A man laughed nearby. Another joined him, and another. The preacher ignored them and held up one hand, fingers outspread.

'I guarantee,' he shouted, 'that there is someone here today who has seen the Lord, who knows His face, who could stand here with me and tell you: If you seek, you will find. The Lord does not hide Himself!'

Suddenly the preacher loomed larger and William realised it was because he'd taken several running steps towards the box. Stepping down, the American spread his arms to embrace him. He was tall, the same height as William. They stood eye to eye.

'Your name, sir?' the preacher asked, his mouth close to William's ear.

'McQuiggan,' muttered William. The man smelt of cologne, his waistcoat was silk.

'Brother McQuiggan has seen the Lord! Alleluia! Let us raise our voices in song!'

William was only just aware of the crowd at his back moving away. Two voices, female, one a piercing and reedy soprano and the other lower, richer, began a hymn.

'The Spirit of God like a fire is burning –' they sang. The higher voice was not as tuneful as the lower and lay over it like a thin sprawling net. A male voice joined in, harmonising with the more resonant voice and the second woman's singing broke off, the two remaining voices escaping from her restraint like fat golden fish, swimming and soaring in the dusty, shimmering summer air. Perfectly matched, the male and female voices entwined together now, moving apart. It seemed to William that it was the most beautiful singing he had ever heard. His neck prickled; sweat slicked the hand the preacher held.

'The latter-day glory begins to come forth –'

The preacher turned him now to face the singers, the woman and the Maori, who stood before him smiling as they sang. The second woman stood behind them, pensive, her head turned away. The crowd was dispersed, save for the marble-rolling boy who stood under the Occidental's awning, his hands thrust deep in his pockets, his face at once curious and sneering.

'The visions and blessings of old are returning –' the duo sang on while the preacher whispered in William's ear.

'We should talk together. Come to my room.'

William lifted a hand to his hatless head, pressed down on his skull. His hair moved roughly under his palm; he was shaking his head. It was not what he had meant by coming forward – he did not want to listen to this man talking. William wanted to do the talking: he had much to tell him. The likelihood of the preacher's belief in his experience beckoned with all the warmth and promise of redemption. He would not consider him mad and conniving as his father did; nor fear him as did Myra.

'Everett Ridge.' The American was pumping his hand. 'This way, Brother.' He nodded curtly at the singers, who shut off their hymn. The Maori held out the coat, but the preacher gestured for him to carry it still and they made their way up the hill towards the Central Hotel.

As he strode between Everett and the man whose name he learned was Paora, suppressing his urge to begin his story now, on the street, before they even reached Everett's room, William glimpsed his mother and sister. They were on the corner of Victoria Street. His mother he saw only, in that fleeting moment before he recognised them, as a little old lady waiting with a hint of impatience in her stance. Ellen's head was down as she fussed over some coins she held in the palm of her hand. Then, in the same instant as her hat lifted to show her face, she gave out an ugly screech quickly suppressed. There was a flurry of skirts and Ellen was upon him. Her coach fare dropped and forgotten, she pushed between the preacher and her brother.

'William – you –' was all she managed. The brim of her hat dug into William's neck.

'Excuse me, ma'am!' Brother Ridge took a step away, into the street. Doubtless the woman was from some protection league or other, something Methodist or Anglican, and she counted the poor lunatic as her own. McQuiggley, or McQuiggan was it, was no lunatic, she was mistaken. Everett had seen something extraordinary, wild, chilling in the man's eyes when he'd embraced him in Vulcan Lane. It was hunger there, not madness: a spiritual hunger that Everett knew he could satisfy.

The old lady was shaking her head, holding a finger to her lips. 'Hush, Ellen,' she said to the younger woman before she addressed Everett's postulant directly. 'Come along. The outfitter is delivering your suit to the house this afternoon.'

Evidently his mother and sister had paid a visit to the library. A book bulged hard-edged in his mother's reticule. William gazed at its shape, wondered idly what it was. Tennyson? Keats?

'William!' His mother's voice had hardened slightly, but not so much that any individual not her child could detect it. William's heart missed a beat: his father would strike him and rant and rave, but his mother was by far the more affecting parent. By those pure, deliberate, self-righteous tones she could so easily fill him with deadening self-hatred. He felt it now, a ball of lead in his stomach, outweighing for a moment the devotion she had earned on the two or three occasions she had stood, in his boyhood, between her husband and son, saving him from a thrashing. Looking at her now in the street, at her pale, worried face, William resented her for not defending him more often.

A loud bang, the firing of a gun, issued from behind him. William jumped, as did the rest of the company, and spun to face Paora. The man had clapped his broad hands together and parted his arms expansively, a large grin breaking his face.

'Your mother and sister?' he asked. William nodded. 'You all come, then. All of you! Up to our room.' He pointed to the balcony above the hotel's main door. Its striped awning fluttered its fringes above the iron lace of the railing. 'You are fatigued, ma'am, from your shopping. We will sit up there and enjoy a cool lemonade.'

Ellen shook her head, but it was Alithea who answered.

'Thank you for your kind invitation, Mr —'

'Tohu,' supplied Paora.

'Mr Tohu. But we must return home straight away.'

Paora looked to Brother Everett, shrugged his shoulders. The preacher smiled broadly, stepped up the kerb and shook William's hand.

'You know where I am, Mr McQuiggan. Please call on me. Tomorrow?'

'But I should like us to speak now,' said William. He heard the childlike whine in his voice and despised himself for it. If only Mr Everett Ridge would insist that the women leave him alone. Ellen tightened her grip on his arm.

'Good day, sir,' she said firmly.

'Tomorrow?' Everett persisted. He had not relinquished his hold on William's hand. 'Nine-thirty in the morning.'

'Tomorrow,' William agreed.

Ellen had begun to march him off without a backward glance.

'Come along, Mother,' she hissed.

'Room 21,' the American called after them.

A cab waited a short distance down Queen Street. Ellen bundled William into it and helped their mother after him. Strangely dazed and elated at the same time, William watched the street and its people pass by. He longed suddenly to read the voyager's tale, the story of Nephi, the man who had seen the Lord. He felt the promise of his own redemption, the certainty of it. The day would arrive when he would look on Christ's face. The ascension made it inevitable. By failing to reach his destination he had actually, without understanding, played out God's design, which was to show him how weak he was, to remind him of his mortality. Of course he had been unable to make that stellar, monumental, final journey because he must wait for Christ to come to him in earthly form. Suddenly it all seemed obvious and simple and true. He couldn't wait to explain it to Brother Everett Ridge.

A little girl stood outside Webster's, her cheek bulging with Russian toffees, sucking intently while she dangled her hoop from one hand. William waved at her and she waved in return, her smile showing the brown shiny sweet.

Before the inevitable interview in the parlour, the five of them sat through an entirely silent meal. Henry was fed in the kitchen to ensure the atmosphere was not trivialised by any of his antics. Pinched and worried, across the table from William, Blanche avoided his eye. In her position by the door, Mary kept her eyes down, her hands clasped across her apron front. William regretted frightening her now. There would be no time for women. For a while at least, he must pretend that they did not exist for him. He could not trust himself around them: his vigour raged at their fragility; they made him a predator.

The cottage pie and vegetables, honest robust food, met his fasting stomach, which had been empty but for Gordon's ham, and filled it benignly. Thinking it wise not to abuse its hospitality with rich Spanish cream, he excused himself early from the table to wait in the parlour.

Before his father came in, William had been sitting close to the fire preparing his speech. He yielded the fireside chair to his father, offered the other to his mother.

'I will stand, thank you, William,' said his mother, softly. She stood in the lee of her husband's chair.

'I have but one request' – William took his opportunity while the old man was still settling himself with his rug – 'and that is that you allow me peace of mind to study this man's books. If you will not, then I will adjourn to an hotel.'

'An hotel!' Elisha coughed the words out, was racked with a genuine cough. 'How ridiculous! You have no money.'

'I will work, then. Take a position as a clerk.'

'No one will have you. You forget you interrupted your education by running away to sea.'

'A labourer, then. I'll work as I did in Australia.'

His father narrowed his eyes at him, as if he had forgotten that, or as if he had never been told. 'No son of mine will work with his hands in this city.'

'Really? Though you were happy for me to grub an existence in the north?'

'If you had persisted with the farm you may have become a gentleman in your own right.'

'I doubt it very much. You made a bad purchase; you were poorly advised. The Waikato perhaps, or Taranaki. But the land up north is clay.'

On the carved head of the stick his father's mottled hand clenched and released, clenched again. William doubted that he would lift it against him in the presence of his mother. His father took a deep breath, changed tack.

'How could you go into the town dressed as you were this morning? Are you truly out of your mind?'

William ignored him. 'If you will not reinstate my allowance I will go immediately to Brother Ridge and prevail

117

upon his hospitality. Good judgement dictates that I bide my time and acquaint myself with his truths before I commit myself to them.'

'It will not be necessary for you to commit yourself!' His father pulled himself upright, away from the chair back, his voice raised, sharp and quavering. From where she stood in the lee of the fire by his chair, Alithea took his hand, patted it. 'You will stay in this house and we will send for Myra.'

'No, that will not be –' William began, but his father would not be interrupted.

'I see now I was overly optimistic, my son. It had not occurred to me that you would be so incompetent, so incapable of assuming your new roles as husband and farmer. Myra will take her place at your side, but here, where we can assist you in learning your role as husband.' Elisha turned his attention on Alithea. 'You say you have met this man, my dear?'

'I have, but I did not speak to him directly.' Alithea regretted this now. She should have accepted the Maori's invitation, gone with them, and learned what it was the American had promised William.

'Of course you did not!' The old man redirected not only his attention but also his rage towards his wife. 'I should very much hope you did not!'

Alithea said nothing, though she patted his hand again, soothing, deflating his rage. Her silence and her touch were all he needed when these moods took him.

'What was his appearance?' Elisha dropped his voice. 'Describe him, Mrs McQuiggan.'

'A tall man, strongly built. He was well spoken and carried two books.'

'What were they?'

'I have no idea, Elisha.' She shook his hand now, rattled it impatiently against her skirts. 'I too carried a book. I doubt Mr Everett knows its title.'

'Mr Ridge,' corrected William gently, 'Everett Ridge. And he is an American. You could ask me my opinion of him, Father. May I sit down?' He edged towards the empty fireside chair.

'You may not!' his father snapped. 'You have no manners. How dare you leave the table before me? Was the meal not up to your usual standard?'

'Elisha –' murmured his wife.

'And to return to the subject of your wife –'

'. . . whom, may I remind you, you have never condescended to meet, Father – I will be frank. Too frank for you, perhaps, Mother. You will have to excuse me. I feel it would be beneficial for Myra and me to spend some lengthy time apart. We have been greatly at odds since our marriage.'

'But she will be distressed at the loss of the child. It is a terrible lesson in life.'

William pretended he had not heard her. 'I have misused her,' he went on, bravely, at the same level, though he would not meet his mother's eye. His father shot him a look of intense hatred, which William met head on. 'With your permission I will end our conversation now. Good night, Father.'

He woke early, washed, donned his stiff new clothes and walked briskly through the crisp air. He had weathered the storm with his father, and marvelled that the old man had not yet realised the document was missing. He had it, the folded rice-paper scripted to the edges with a spidery hand, in the breast pocket of his new jacket. The jacket was of the usual clumsy, box-like colonial cut, but of fine wool. He wore a soft lawn shirt beneath it. It was the garb – from the black boots to the trilby – of a city man: Mother then, at least, did not expect him to return to the farm.

On the Grafton footbridge he paused to gaze down the gully to the shifting harbour, glinting and sparkling in the autumn sunlight like broken glass. A ship was sailing in the channel, the dark three-crested shape of Rangitoto glowering above it. He could see some of the crew, tiny figures from this distance, high in the rigging. For once he did not envy them the voyage ahead, the foreign landfall they would make. No country on earth could be as rich and mysterious as the landscape he was about to share with Brother Everett. The American would be compelled by his account of the epiphany to accept him as one marked by God for greater things. In the telling of it he would not exaggerate, nor offer any interpretation of the events. He would finish the tale before it ended, because he had to. Full of anticipation, he hurried on down Symonds Street to Victoria Street.

At the Central Hotel one of the women was waiting for him downstairs. It was the smaller, brown-haired one, the one who had sung with dirge-like voice the day before. She smiled as he came in, showing small, broken teeth. Deep shadows showed under her eyes; her skin was sallow. She looked exhausted, unwell.

'Brother Ridge is waiting upstairs,' she said. 'We have the balcony suite.' Before she turned to lead him away, she took his hand briefly. 'I am Sister Ridge. We were not properly introduced yesterday.'

'William McQuiggan,' said William, to her back now.

'I know who you are,' Sister Ridge said lightly. 'Brother Ridge told us at breakfast yesterday that the Lord would lead you to us.'

'Me?' he asked, in surprise and awe.

'Someone like you.' There was a slight, almost mocking tone in her voice. They approached the first door of the landing, which stood ajar. The room beyond was filled with brilliant early autumn light.

'You seem greatly recovered from yesterday.' He saw her take note of his new clothes. 'Your family must value you immensely. Do they take very great care of you?'

He was startled by her question and would have been offended had he had time to think about it, but Paora loomed at the door and took his hat.

'Welcome, Brother!' Everett Ridge called from the balcony. The french doors stood open, their fine lace curtains lifting in the breeze, like the skirts of young girls at Shelly Beach picnics. William's heart ached slightly, irrelevantly, for the summer he'd missed in Auckland – the boating, the outings, the concerts – entombed as he had been in that muddy, godforsaken hole of a farm. But if he had not been there, high on his mountain, then God would not have spoken to him; he would not have stood as he did now on the brink of his vocation . . .

A hand was laid gently against his back between his shoulder blades, propelling him towards the balcony. It wasn't until he reached its threshold that he turned back to see who it was had touched him. It was the other, younger, fairer woman. She had his coat over her arm, though he didn't remember giving it to her, and was smiling warmly over his shoulder at the man beyond.

'Brother!' Everett's hand gripped one of his shoulders, the other vigorously pumped his hand. 'We will make ourselves comfortable here –' He gestured to two wicker chairs positioned for the sun, which angled mid-morning to the tiled floor.

Sister Ridge brought a cut-glass jug of water and two glasses. Behind her the younger woman carried an occasional table which she positioned carefully between the two men. She was tall, broad shouldered. Fine lines creased the corners of her large grey eyes. William judged her to be at least ten years younger than her companions. Her hair, golden and thick, was piled on top of her head, with ringlets falling at the side. It was an old-fashioned style, ornate, out of keeping with the black high-necked severity of her dress.

Casually, Brother Ridge stretched out a leg and rested his heel against a curlicue in the iron lace of the railing.

'We will be going, then,' said Sister Ridge, 'Sister Ridge and I.'

A second Sister Ridge, then, thought William. One must be Everett's sister – the darker one perhaps, the one he had initially supposed to be his wife.

'Brother Paora will come with us,' said the older woman now.

'Is that not what we arranged?' said Brother Everett. 'We need not repeat these intentions a thousand times over, my dear. We must merely act on them and reserve our deliberations for greater matters.' He would have gone on, but checked himself as her sad eyes met his. Perhaps he had set within him, after eight long years in the field, in a self-imposed exile, a mechanical switch connected to a time-spring. He was forgoing his preaching this morning though, to gather in McQuiggan. He nodded at the woman, dismissing her, and she turned back into the room as the younger woman hurried forward, bent and pressed her lips against the preacher's cheek. It was a swift embrace, at once wifely, confident and sensual.

'Goodbye, Sister. Which hymn will you sing today?'

'Ah, I think –' Her large eyes sparkled and she rested a hand on his shoulder. '"How Firm a Foundation, Ye Saints of the Lord".'

'One verse, Sister Ridge. One verse before you go,' Everett implored. The young woman was delighted to oblige. She straightened, took a deep breath and lifted her voice. It was a slow, simple hymn with a repetitive strain at the end.

'Who unto the Saviour, who unto the Saviour –' carolled the second Sister Ridge, her strong, pure voice warming them as much as the sunlight did. As she drew to a close, the bells of St Matthew's rang out matins from the crest of the hill above the hotel. The preacher and his wife caught each other's eye and smiled at the beauty and coincidence of the sound while she sang on.

'Who unto the Saviour –'

'Sister Lydia!' The older woman broke the rendition. Two coats lay across her arm. 'Brother Paora is waiting downstairs.'

Lydia's cheeks flushed; her beatific smile hardened. Everett himself flashed annoyance in the older Sister Ridge's direction. The singer squeezed her husband's shoulder, passed through the shadow cast by the awning and crossed the room, Sister Ridge following.

'Sister Eliza is a conscientious missionary,' Everett said softly, watching them go.

William poured himself a glass of water. His mouth was dry; the urgency of his tale pressed at the back of his throat.

'You passed a pleasant night?' the American was asking him now.

'I did. I looked forward to this opportunity to tell you of my experience, to unburden –' William faltered. 'No. That is not the correct word. I have no need to unburden myself of my knowledge of God.'

'I should hope not!' exclaimed Brother Ridge. He was reaching inside his jacket for a book, the black one that had nested there the day before, so William hurried on before he could open it.

'I need to – I must express – I do not know how to convey to you the violence of my experience.' He felt again that he could not continue, but Everett's gaze wrapped him around, soothed him as his wife's song had, as the warm sun did now on the tiles, the glittering prisms in the glass in his hand. He told the American of his ascension. He told, in a flat voice, of the whisky he had drunk, of the death of his child, of how he had returned immediately to the house and knelt in prayer with his wife. The memory of Myra brought tears to his eyes. He felt them quiver there and could not bring Ridge's attention to them by lifting his hand to strike them away, so they broke and the other man saw them anyway. He remembered Myra not as she was then, in the parlour with the photographer, but sentimentally, as she had been when she had opened the door of the Home of Hope to himself and the trollop. She had been so welcoming, so earnest and eager to please, an innocent from the outback. Her slow deliberate speech had pleased him and he had wanted to remove her from the low life she was surrounded by, the predicament of the fallen woman that she seemed scarcely to understand but had so much compassion for. He had wanted her for himself: her calm, her tenderness, her healing ministration. She had failed him in this, as she had in countless other ways.

Brother Ridge had spoken, his words missed by his distressed companion.

'I said, Brother, that I believe you must dismiss your experience. You were unwell from the drink; it had poisoned your mind. You stood not at the gates of Heaven, but in the arms of brute sensation.'

A sudden and terrible pain gripped William, bands of it across his chest. He felt himself struggle in a yawning, inimical chasm, solitary, isolated from every man. The American's voice reached him from far away, as if he stood at the top of the precipice and called to William at the bottom.

'It is not that we Saints don't believe in Revelations. Of course we do. But we also believe, as Brother Brigham taught us, that if we receive a vision from the Almighty then we should shut it up and make it as secret as the grave. The Lord has no confidence in those who reveal secrets, for he cannot safely reveal himself to them.' He leaned forward and touched William gently on the knee. 'Had your vision come to you following hours of prayer, as it did for our prophet, then I would be more inclined to believe you.'

'You are a saint?' faltered William.

'A Latter-day Saint, after the prophet Joseph Smith, who through the grace of God transcribed the *Book of Mormon* from the plates of Nephi, in the year 1830.'

'You are a Mormon, then?' The word seemed familiar to him – he recollected hearing it, or reading it. 'Is that not a faith of the Maori people?' he went on. 'It is not a white man's religion.'

Brother Ridge smiled. 'You know of us, then? The Latter-day Saints? It is true that we work among the natives of this country, and that many of them have full-heartedly embraced our Testament. Listen a moment. This is what Nephi told the Lamanites, from whom your Maoris are descended.' The American opened his volume, which William saw now was lettered in gold: *Book of Mormon*.

'"And then they shall rejoice,"' he began, '"for they shall know that it is a blessing unto them from the hand of God; and their scales of darkness shall begin to fall from their eyes; and many generations shall not pass away among them, save they shall be a white and delightsome people."'

'I am not acquainted with your doctrine,' muttered William, without comprehension.

'Ah!' Brother Ridge leaned towards him, placed a firm hand on his knee. 'Then I will lend you our books. The truth is there, Brother. You must study them, the teachings of President Brigham Young: our *Doctrine and Covenants*, the *Pearl of Great Price* –' Everett broke off. The man was weeping again, soundless, struggling to control his breath.

'Do not be so disheartened. Why are you weeping?'

'Because you do not believe me. I tell you I rose as surely as if I were making the final journey. I did not know then that the Lord had a plan for me, but I am sure in that knowledge now. I will prove it to you.'

Everett heard the despair in his voice, leaned back into his chair to debate his response, sipped at his water. The man gabbled on.

'I will prove it to you! The Lord spoke to me though I cannot translate it into words. It was not a delusion, an hallucination.'

Everett sighed irritably, cut him off. 'Eschew the drink, my friend. Take these books. We will meet again in a few days, when you are familiar with them.' Everett stood to show the New Zealander that the interview was at an end. William stumbled to his feet, gathered to his breast the three volumes the preacher offered him and made his way down into the street.

PART TWO

THE JUDGE'S HOUSE, 1899

CHAPTER 8

The winter passed, the summer came. William read the books, saw Brother Ridge almost daily. His father left him alone, instigated an allowance. There was a correspondence between the old man and the Waylands, who pleaded for Myra to remain with them until she was stronger. Elisha sent them money and told William nothing of it.

It wasn't until after New Year that the son confronted the father with the paper he had taken from his desk. He had joined Elisha on the western veranda, where his father, who had retired frail and unwell from the Bench at the end of the old year, was taking in the last of the day's sun. William was newly returned from the Gladstone Coffee Palace, where he had sat in a dark polished booth drinking tepid water with Brother Ridge and accepted an invitation so spectacular and magnanimous that it had entirely filled his mind ever since.

'I had no idea I would be quite so wealthy when you die, Father.' William knew his father would take offence at his approach, but he could think of no other. Or would not. He was distracted by the other matter, one that required funds within a matter of weeks.

'How long have you had the letter?' asked Elisha, glancing up at his son and away. He had prevented Alithea from cele-brating her son's birthday, a denial of maternal affection that had caused her to suffer and had not at all prevented William from entering his thirtieth year. Twenty-nine and still lacking entirely in occupation or friends, aside from this American, thought Elisha, quelling an exasperated sigh before he went on. 'Not since that first night when you inebriated your sorry self in my study? Perhaps you have. I did not notice it was gone until November, which should validate your suspicions about the state of my mind. I am old now, William.'

William nodded, agreeing with him. There was no self-pity in his father's voice: he was stating it plainly, as it was.

'It is of no account, at any rate. I have received the benefit from the actual will. The paper you have in your possession is only the letter John Farquhar wrote me many years ago, informing me of his intentions. It is useless.'

'Who was he exactly, Father?'

'Your mother's uncle. He refined the flashpoint of gunpowder while he was in the service in India, an innovation that proved useful there and elsewhere in the Empire. The Queen was very pleased with him. We are fortunate the British Parliament prevented him from squandering his fortune.'

'Why is that, Father?'

'Why, because we should not have received it otherwise.' Elisha looked into his son's face. There was something child-like in his expression. He was enjoying his father's uncharacteristic garrulousness, leaning slightly towards him. Elisha decided to humour his son, perhaps inspire him, though he was half the man old Farquhar was. 'He was a little like you, though his passion was for an eastern religion. He would have built a Brahmin university in Aberdeen but they would have none of it.'

'He had learned of this cult in India?'

'Indeed.'

'Surely he did not practise it.'

'I have no idea. He lived alone with a housekeeper. Your mother and her brothers were his sole beneficiaries.'

'You say I am like him. Did you meet him?'

'No. Mrs McQuiggan did, as a child, but she does not remember him.'

'Why do you say I am like him, then?' William persisted.

Elisha recoiled from the question, regretted having made the comparison.

'Do you mean he was a spiritual man?'

'He was a chemist.'

'I am not a chemist.'

'Oh, for Heaven's sake!' exclaimed Elisha. 'Go away!' He knew he should not speak to William this way, that Alithea would chide him for it. But William was already turning back to the side door, his face bemused.

'Yes, I have much to do.' he said, his mind racing. His future plans were falling into place.

'Ask your mother to come to me here.' Elisha addressed his son's retreating back.

His words were unheeded. William did not seek out his mother as he made his way through the body of the house, but hurried up to his room. It was just on dusk; the room still held its close warmth. He flung open the northern window and looked longingly up the harbour to the ships at anchor, the distant bristle of their masts at the wharves. His father telling him the story of the Scottish uncle was a sign from God, directly addressed to him. It was as Brother Brigham had taught: 'Blessed are they who obey when the Lord gives a direct commandment, but more blessed are they who obey without a direct commandment.'

God was working His purpose out: the old man was dying just in time. He had contracted two severe 'flus over the winter and had not recovered from the first when he encountered the second. It would not take long now. Pneumonic fluid filled his lungs, his memory was indeed fading, and although he was of the opinion that the letter was of no account, William reflected, it was of great importance to William's immediate future.

Downstairs, Alithea joined her husband who waited for her impatiently. She carried a walnut secretary with folding legs, which she set up before her chair.

'It is five o'clock, dearest,' she said, settling herself and opening the secretary. 'That was our agreed time. I am not late. You need not scowl so.' She took a fresh sheet of paper from the banded quine in the secretary's lid, spread it before her and took up pen and nib.

Dear Reverend and Mrs Wayland, began Elisha, before Alithea was ready, still mixing her ink. She dipped her pen and wrote to his dictation.

I am forever in your debt following your great kindness over these past months and never more so than for your unpleasant duty in informing me of my daughter-in-law's condition. Regrettably, I was unaware of it.

The steamer ticket accompanying this letter is for the immediate passage of Mrs McQuiggan to Auckland. To my mind, it is high time she was reunited with my son. I have had some worry and trouble in determining the extent of the help I could safely and judiciously place at his disposal. However, he is now greatly recovered from the nervous condition that beset him soon after his arrival in Auckland and ready and able to take up his role as husband and provider.

I trust that, despite her illness, Mrs McQuiggan will be strong enough to make the short voyage.

In eternal gratitude,
Yours sincerely,
Justice Elisha J. McQuiggan

William had thought he was the first to rise the following morning, which promised with its clear sky to be like the day before, hot and sunny. It was only seven-thirty when he reached the lane, but the stable door stood open and Blanche was there with Henry, who had been scrubbed up for a visit to town. As he helped her strap the pony between the shafts of the tilbury, Henry had his tongue out to aid his concentration. He was deft and swift and the pony stood patiently for him. She was a young grey mare, sturdily built.

'We can all squeeze in!' Blanche called when she saw him. 'Father says I have to be at the post office the moment it opens its doors.'

'Why is that?' William asked.

'I have a letter to post, which I am not allowed to show you.' Blanche climbed onto the seat beside him. William took the reins while Henry clambered up, hooked his arm around his brother's neck and kissed him warmly on the cheek.

'You should not tell me about the letter if you do not want me to see it. Who is it addressed to?' William ignored his brother, though he inclined his head slightly towards him with the kiss. Blanche shrugged, held her purse close to her body.

'If you will not tell me, then I will have to take it from you.' William kept his voice light: this was a game, he would find out what his father intended. It would have to do with either wife, finances, or his will and the lawyers.

Blanche giggled. 'Our wrestling days are over, Will. Besides, I'm much stronger than you are these days.'

'Oh, really?'

'Yes. You see, I don't waste my time sitting indoors reading tedious books. Look – even going into town you carry one!' Blanche poked the *Book of Mormon*, the lump it made in his jacket. 'Poor old William. You used to be such fun.'

'Ah. As you grow up, little Blanchette, you will come to realise that life is not all tennis parties and rambles, lemonade and laughter.'

'Oh, but it is, Will. It's summer, so why shouldn't it be? Father said Henry and I could take the tilbury to Epsom to visit Fanny Allcock after we've run the errands. Do you remember her? She was most perturbed to learn you had married and gone north so soon after your return. I had made a bargain with her you see, to tell her the moment you returned from Australia so that she could call on us. She wanted to know all about Myra of course, but I could tell her nothing, not ever having met her –'

Blanche chatted on while William pulled the horse into the side of the road, around the milkcart, its old nag standing disconsolately, facing uphill, halfway up Parnell Rise. There was nobody around, no one of any consequence at any rate: the milkman; a barrowman with his fruit barrow setting up near the church; the butcher stretching a striped length of canvas across his window; a servant girl making her way up to one of the big houses. The way was clear: he dropped the reins and made a lunge for his sister's purse. The envelope's corner protruded and it was easily withdrawn. Blanche laughed wildly, reaching for the letter now held aloft in William's hand, before she grabbed for the reins. The horse was startling, showing signs of wanting to bolt down the hill.

'I will take this, I think. Slow up a moment, my dear.' William was rising from his seat to descend to the road. The small cart rocked on its springs. 'I will take this to town and save you the bother. Turn your pretty head towards Epsom and drink tea with Fanny.' Though the pony's ears still flicked wildly and her trot was uneven, William stepped nimbly over his brother's legs to the running board and the macadam below.

'William!' Blanche's voice called after him, the carriage stopped but not turning. 'William!' There was a hint of annoyance now. He sauntered on, towards Beach Road, not looking back. Blanche would not be able to resist the temptation of going straight to visit her friend.

'Will!' Henry bellowed suddenly. William quickened his step and vanished from their view below the railway bridge. Blanche hushed her brother, embarrassed by his hoarse, dog-like shout, and began to execute the difficult turn in the steep, rutted road.

At the Gladstone, William took the window table with its view of Queen Street Wharf, the table that he and Brother Ridge had frequented each day through the summer, sometimes for two or three hours at a time. Everett still did not accept the fact that the Lord had a special plan for William, though he had complimented his friend on his emerging gift as a preacher and urged him on to greater heights. William had preached to the stevedores on the wharf, the quarrymen at Three Kings, drinkers leaving hotels – the hard men. Once he'd been struck by an angry fist; more than once he'd had to make a quick escape.

He ordered water from the waitress, who gave her customary sneer at the paucity of his request, and opened the envelope. He read the letter quickly without taking it in, screwed it into a ball and dropped it on the greasy floor. From the *Book of Mormon* he took a scrap of paper, one of the many he'd leafed between the pages in anticipation of thoughts and observations, and wrote his wife a note. For once he and his father were in accord. Myra should come to Auckland, where the McQuiggan family could take care of her. She had imposed on the Waylands for long enough, and if all went according to plan he would not be confronted by her on her arrival.

He visited then the new Northern Steamship Company offices and bought Myra's ticket with his own money, wondering idly as he did so what Blanche would buy with the shillings their father must have given her for her sister-in-law's fare. The letter safely deposited at the post office, he strode up Queen Street to the Colonial Bank, in time for his nine o'clock appointment with the manager.

On the hottest day of the summer, McNeill came for her in a cart, an arrangement made by the Reverend after William sent the steamer ticket.

'Thank you for your kindness.' High on the bench seat beside McNeill Myra wanted to cry, but she would not.

'I am glad you chose to come to us,' replied Mrs Wayland, reaching up and pressing her hand. Myra looked down into her dear face and was grateful she had never told her how she had waited all day after William had gone, hoping first for his return and then for Riha. Had the fire burned during the day, the smoke would have been visible for miles: they would have seen it from the pa. But it had burned itself out by sunrise. Myra remembered herself walking, her cold feet in the warm ashes, picking up twisted nails and two halves of a china plate. Something white like an upturned eye was uncovered by her scuffling: the Limoges brooch, cracked by the heat, its brass surrounds warped and soft. She'd tucked it into the sleeve of her nightdress, drawing the ribbon at the wrist tight to hold it there. She had it still, in the small bag at her feet.

'I very much enjoyed our Christmas,' Mrs Wayland was saying now in an undertone, as the door of the church flung open and the Reverend came down the steps. McNeill acknowledged his presence with a curt nod, his face hidden by his hat. Since Myra's arrival beside him, McNeill hadn't allowed himself even a sideways glance at her. He'd watched her come down the path from the vicarage in her ill-fitting dress, noted her advanced pregnancy and wondered how such a plain little bird had snared a man like McQuiggan. There had been rumours that he'd deserted her, cut his losses after the fire, taken a scow to Auckland and then steamed to America or Australia.

'Farewell, Mrs McQuiggan.' The old man stood beside his wife. 'Our thoughts and prayers will be with you.'

'Thank you, Reverend.' Myra's hands writhed damply in her lap. She was hot and uncomfortable in her black woollen dress. 'I do wish I could –' she burst out, before her hosts had taken a hand each, smoothed it in theirs.

'We know,' said Mrs Wayland, 'but you must go back to him, dear. I do believe he has reformed himself. And he has sent for you.'

Myra swallowed her tumultuous response, which was to remind her that it was her father-in-law, a man she had never met, who had insisted on her return. Hadn't William said so in his letter, a terse note that had accompanied the ticket, and which the old lady had helped her to read? The Reverend nodded at McNeill, disengaged his hand from Myra's and patted the horse's rump.

'Goodbye, my dear.' The old man took his wife's arm and they stepped away from the cart.

Twisted against her rigid belly, Myra waved farewell to her benefactors until they were out of sight. McNeill took the road from Hakaru to Mangawhai harbour, a steady curling downward incline from the foothills of the Brynderwyns. The ocean opened before them, narrowed and disappeared as they gained the flats. The passing farms were tired and brown, dotted with scraggy cattle and sheep. A skylark took an arching flight from a field beside them, sang clear and loud. As Myra tipped her head back to watch its ellipses, the baby inside her kicked once, twice, on either side of her body. She had swollen so quickly with this one: she was far bigger now than she had been with Alithea. Her mind drifted towards thoughts of the voyage to Auckland, to her reunion with William, to the terror of the birth, and quickly retreated. This time there would be no Riha to help her, no Riha to comfort her through the pains.

Despite the heat, Riha lay inside her stuffy hut. Fleas bit the back of her neck, a mosquito whined. This was the day Myra was leaving, on a steamer from the tamer east coast. If she'd left from this side, Riha thought, I would be able to watch her go from high on the hill. I would be able to send my love after her, to wish her well.

Life had returned to normal. After the fire, there were accusations, retributions from her own people and Pakeha. Poihaere stopped bringing her her food, a youth who had been falsely accused of taking the school horse confronted her and blacked her eye. Eruera had been apprehended by McNeill and another white man and beaten senseless. Another beating followed then for Riha, far worse than the one at the hands of the youth, from her brother-in-law, Eruera's father. He had broken one of her hands, bruised her legs and thighs with vicious kicks.

Riha had borne the assaults in silence. Nobody understood that it was grief that had set the first fire – and would never have set another. The day she burned the pa, her grief had swollen to active rage: the pa had contained the men who had accompanied her husband and sons that long-ago day to fish – men who had come back, who had defied the stormclouds boiling on the fierce blue-black horizon. The storm had blown in, progressing almost at the same pace as the men as they went towards it, strangely silent until it was almost upon them, when its pitch dropped suddenly to a level detectable by human ears. It was an unearthly screaming whine, the voice of the vast incalculable body of the cyclone behind it. By the time it reached the village where it lifted roofs and flattened the western palisades, it had already snatched Riha's husband and her sons from their flimsy canoe, hidden them from sight among the roaring waves, dismissed the shape of their faces and the ringing of their voices from the surface of the earth for ever.

Riha lost her mind as surely as she had lost her sons, set the fire and went willingly to her isolation in the slab hut in the hills. Her sanity returned to endure a permanent exile, a life so intolerably lonely that when, seventeen years later, she made friends with the equally isolated Pakeha lady on the nearby farm, she had been frightened by the violence of affection she had felt for her.

Goodbye, little pale bird, God protect you from your husband. Riha could scarcely remember his face, didn't want to. She remembered instead her visits to Myra over the summer, once she'd recovered from the beating. She had only gone a few times and never inside the house itself, even if it was raining. If Myra was not busy helping the old lady around the house or parish, they would sit together on the veranda or walk in the garden. For much of their time they were silent together. Riha liked it best when Myra worked beside her as she had done on the farm. She would bring out the mending, or side by side they would weed the garden. Myra's small strong wrists beside hers, her quiet, thoughtful face: they became as intimate to Riha as if they were part of her own body, her own breath and skin. Together they tended the roses and dahlias, the jasmine and lobelia, the exotic flowers that grew in the vicarage garden. Sometimes, at the end of a day, back in her hut, Riha's mind teemed with observations of her friend, her grey eyes the colour of rain, her padded knuckles, her pale, kind mouth: small disconnected pictures that brought with them a broad, insistent comfort.

McNeill brought the cart to a stop before the Mangawhai Hotel. McQuiggan's wife had only a small bag, he noticed: she could make the rest of the way on her own. The steamer was tethered to the end of the wharf. Smoke puffed from its green funnel and a sail was set on the aftermast: its departure was imminent.

'Goodbye, then,' said Myra, 'and thank you.'

McNeill's only response was a terse nod. Once the woman had struggled down from the bench and gathered up her bag, he turned away towards the public bar.

Myra wobbled down the narrow plank onto the deck. As she went she had a picture in her mind of herself as a fat beetle, balancing precariously on a narrow stem or blade. It was a childlike notion, like a nursery rhyme, and made her smile. A crewman appeared from the quarterdeck, motioned her towards the windowless cabin. Inside was a family of three young sisters, each a copy of the others, in varying sizes, identical down to their dresses. They gazed at her mournfully as she opened the door. A strong odour of seasickness permeated the tiny dark room and she wondered briefly why they did not come outside and walk about, take in the fresh air, while the ship was paused. She retreated, closing the door, and found a seat on a pile of sails on the deck.

I should have suggested to those poor girls that they come outside, she thought a while later, chastising herself, just as the little ship gave a tremendous lurch and pulled away from the wharf towards the bar. Was she selfish, she wondered – was that why she had lost her husband? It welled in her then: her timidity, her lack of faith in her own conclusions. She would go back to the cabin now, she decided, and bring them out here with her to see the colour restored to their cheeks. She half stood, propelled by her resolve, but her big belly and the shifting deck conspired against her and she plumped down again immediately. It was safest to remain on her cushion of sails, though a wave topped the deck rail and drenched one side of her dress. The ship was breaching the heads now and rocking about. The crew ran around on deck, hoisted a jib; the funnel belched black smoke. Myra closed her eyes and didn't open them until they were through.

On the other side of the breakers beyond the bar, it was calm enough to stand, though not to walk. The motion of the sea made her knees tremble. She rested her belly below the rail, braced her elbows against it and wondered how it would be to make this voyage with William beside her, his steadying arm around her shoulders, his fine blue eyes creased against the glare. He had been solicitous on the voyage from Sydney to Auckland, overly so sometimes. He treated her then, before they were married, as though she were made of glass.

A tiny tremor, a tenderness, tugged at her heart. She wondered at it. Over the summer she had begun to think she would never see him again, that perhaps the Waylands would keep her, that the old lady would allow Riha to attend her during the birth and that she and the child would live happily in Hakaru. She had tried not to think of William, shying away from the terrible conflicting welter of emotions that arose at the idea of him, blowing up from her chest to her throat to choke the air from her. When he came to her, unbidden even now on her voyage to join him, she could not picture his face. In isolation she had his hair, the curls above his wide brow, his sharp chiselled nose, even his ears – but she could not arrive at a memory of his collective features. He was all in pieces. Memory sprang from her body, bringing her his coarse-haired flanks, the smell of his sweat, the warmth and weight of him. When he had taken her in the bush she had given him that sudden caress, the length of her fingers against the flesh of his neck, scooping the firm curve to his shoulder. She had wanted him.

Another memory intruded: of William hurrying her away from the falling sparks, of how he had brought his hand hard against the scorching fabric of her gown, of how he had forced himself onto her while she wavered on a knife edge of hysteria and fear, as if the time in the bush had meant nothing, as if he scarcely remembered it . . . or worse, that he did remember and was punishing her for disporting herself before him, showing him her animal self, her savage instinct.

Breast speckled brown on cream following behind a curved black beak, a young mollymawk flew along the rail of the boat, so close Myra could have reached out and touched it. The steamer was approaching a large flock of terns – multitudinous, black and white, bobbing on the chop. Beyond the terns a gannet dived in an exhilarating fall, its brilliant yellow head and white form slipping between two shades of blue. The sea was beautiful suddenly: yielding, inhabited, soft; the warm gusts that tugged at her dress and hair were clean and slaking. Opening her mouth, she drew in a draught of salt air and tipped her head back to the cloud-scudded sky. She would give thanks, she decided, for her life and the life inside her, that they had survived the fire and the absence of William. Both hands lifted to her stomach, over the stifling wool dress, to lie against her swelling sides.

There were two. Barely discernible, the little skulls were capped beneath the pressure of her palms, beneath her skin, within her flesh. As if they sensed her touch they slipped away, subterranean, liquid, as did her certainty. Perhaps she had been mistaken. Oh, please, God, let me be mistaken, she prayed. She'd learned enough from her time at the Home to know that twins came from long and difficult births, that more than other babies they refused their chance at life, or took away their mother's.

Guide me, Father. Protect me, thought Myra, though she knew that He did not care a jot: she was not forgiven. He would hold her and her kind accountable through all eternity.

Laborious Bible-reading had filled hours on the lonely farm, more than it ever filled in Yarrabin. She had read without real understanding, stumbling over words and meaning. Soon after Alithea's birth she chose St Paul's letter to the Thessalonians. St Paul had been a great favourite of her father's. Perhaps she chose to read it as a way of drawing close to his memory, which was proving more and more elusive. Upon sinners would come, St Paul thundered, 'sudden destruction, as travail upon a woman with child, and they shall not escape'. Her spine ran cold with the remembered words; fear brought bile to her throat while her mind raced for a foothold, a place to cling above the yawning chasm of panic.

She was strong, she told herself, rested from her months with the Waylands. The twins would come in Auckland and William's mother would see that she was properly attended. That's right. Yes. Her heart slowed. It paid at times to forget about God and concentrate on the practicalities. Her relations with Him, she knew, consisted of a series of desertions. So far His far outnumbered hers and were of a far greater magnitude.

She swallowed, realised she needed to sit down now. The deck was lurching under her feet, which had begun to ache.

The waistband of her dress had ridden high, billowing out the front of her bodice. She pushed it flat, though for comfort pulled the waistband still higher, which puffed the bodice out again. It was a futile exercise. She turned carefully and reached for the rail beside the cabin door.

The three sisters clung to one another, more mournful than before. They were only a few years younger than Myra and, despite their temporary pallor, their faces shone with a kind of freedom, of hills daily traversed, of sun and wholesome food. They wore fine, white summer dresses, now uniformly smudged with saltblack from the deck rail. The older one nodded at Myra as she came in, groping for a place on the opposing bench.

If only she could sleep. She wanted to hold inside herself the promise of that first moment, with the sea and warm wind and God and his creatures. The twins belonged to that, not to the moment afterwards when she remembered the Home. She closed her eyes, willed her ethereal self alone on the deck with her hair lifting around her face, her feet bracing with the buck of the boat as she stood firmly enough to balance the three of them.

CHAPTER 9

Myra scarcely remembered Auckland, though it was only two years since she was last here, for her wedding. That first night, exhausted from the voyage, she had slept alone at the hotel, her terror fighting her weariness, until after a protracted fit of weeping she had fallen asleep behind the locked door. The following morning she and William had been married and he had joined her at the hotel until affairs were settled for the farm at Pukekaroro. Everything had happened around her, and sometimes to her, and was made bearable only by the new sensation that her soul had vacated her body, and herself with it, and observed events from a distance. William had been pale and quiet for days after the wedding, in a state that she had not yet learned to recognise as abject rage. He went out during the day, leaving in the morning with a semblance of courtesy, or concern for her well-being, and returning with none at all.

She looked for the hotel now, as the two-wheeled gig rolled along Quay Street, and tried to remember its name. Morrison's was it? The Royal Mail? But it was further up the hill, behind them. She had never before driven along this eastern road. Progress had come to the port, and new buildings rose around the main gully of the town. The city was wet, rain slicked, though the sun shone brilliantly once more and drew steam from the puddles.

Outside a large brick building, a wide dray was hauled up, blocking the way. The severe-looking woman who held the reins clicked her tongue in annoyance. Ellen. The older sister. She wore a princess-style summer dress and a white bonnet. Both the dress, which was white with broad stripes in a soft pink, and the lacy high-crowned bonnet, were too young for her, thought Myra. It was as if she were dressed in the borrowed garb of a younger sister. When Ellen had first approached her as she came off the boat, Myra had thought her to be little more than a girl, until she looked into her face. Ellen had recognised Myra immediately, from her mother's description: dark haired, small, fine boned and heavy with child, and had taken her arm as she came away from the gangplank.

'Mrs McQuiggan?' she had enquired, leading her towards the waiting pony and carriage. Myra had nodded, nauseous, Queen Street Wharf rocking mysteriously beneath her feet.

'William is indisposed, otherwise he would have come himself.'

Myra had said nothing to that; wondered what had indisposed him but didn't ask.

The dray shifted forward slightly now, but a man at the horses' heads shouted, stopped them from moving on. The women saw that the dray was being loaded. Four men had emerged from a wide, low doorway. What was it they were lugging out? Myra wondered. What was it that filled the sacks? She distracted herself with anything rather than meet Ellen's critical eye. Slowly she read the letters below the building's cornice: The Northern Roller Mill.

'How are you?' Ellen asked now. 'Did you sleep at all during the voyage?'

Myra shook her head. The benches were too narrow. She had only dozed a little in a sunny corner of the deck, her back propped against the cabin wall, while the boat anchored at Orewa. 'You must be very tired,' Ellen said then, kindly.

Myra sneaked a look at her, saw how in profile she resembled her brother – the same straight, sharp-edged nose, the full pouting lips.

The men were emerging from the mill again, this time with a handcart. One of them looked up and saw Ellen and Myra waiting. Another carriage rumbled behind them.

'Give us here –' said the man, coming towards them and taking the pony's bridle. He led her around the dray, the wheels of the carriage knocking and banging in the deep ruts at the side of the road. The wheels sucked and tore at the mud with the sound of ripping cloth. The women clung on until Ellen took up the slack in the reins.

'Is my husband at the house?' Myra ventured as they took the corner into Beach Road.

'He is,' said Ellen shortly, not volunteering anything more.

William is all I have, Myra thought. I will be brave. I will hold my head up. A rapid tight pain flared across her belly, taking her so much by surprise that she almost called out. Her hands moved, involuntarily, from her lap.

Ellen's eye was caught by the flash of white, lifting above the handrail. It seemed William's dowdy little wife was close to tears. It was a mystery to her, now that she had met Myra, what her brother had seen in her. Before he'd left for Australia, he'd squired many of the local beauties to dances and summer parties, girls like empty-headed Fanny. This woman was entirely different. If Ellen had ever given any thought to the type of woman her brother might marry, which she had not, she would not have predicted Myra. Her sister-in-law's complexion was so pale it was almost blue. Her hands were small and chapped. There was a stillness in her offset by occasional flurries of anxiety, like a bird cupped between two hands. When she'd disembarked she'd carried only a small portmanteau, a bag not large enough to carry even one other dress. The dress she wore was heavy, unseasonal, the bodice puffed out pigeon-style at her skinny chest and the old-fashioned detachable sleeve closest to Ellen had begun to come away from the mancheron at the shoulder.

Like William, she must've lost everything in the fire. New dresses would have to be bought. Ellen sighed at the expense of it all. Now her father was retired, it seemed it had fallen to her to exercise all care and caution in the government of the family finances.

The trilby wound now into Augusta Terrace and up St George's Bay Road. At the stables, which stood in a lane opposite a fine large house, a thick-set, simple-looking man in his middle years bounded from a stool by the door to take the pony's bridle. A young grey cat, which had been sitting on his shoulder, wound itself around his neck. A servant, Myra supposed. He was roughly dressed in a smeary shirt and pants.

The simpleton helped her down from her seat and Myra followed Ellen through the gate, down the shell path and up the broad wooden steps to the back porch of the house. A shining, well-equipped kitchen opened up on their right, with a narrow passage ahead that led past the scullery into the wider hall. A broad-backed, grim-countenanced woman in a white apron was making pies at the kitchen table, fitting pastry lids over the steaming contents. She did not look up as Myra glanced in admiringly. There was a large black cast-iron range; a vast rack of pearly white plates above the sink; a muslin-wrapped ham hanging; a pantry bursting with provisions; a wide, scrubbed flagged floor. It could not have resembled any less the kitchen Myra had laboured in on the farm, with its old-fashioned colonial oven and worm-eaten boards.

'Come along.' Ellen was already in the hall, standing at the bottom of a flight of stairs and jiggling Myra's bag in one hand. 'I will take you up to William.'

Myra hurried her steps. It was cooler in the house, and as she climbed the stairs behind her sister-in-law she lifted her hair away from the nape of her neck and longed to take off her tight, itchy dress in one of the airy rooms they passed, longed to lie down and sleep. She could sleep for a week.

'This way.' Ellen led her off the second landing, down a hall. The second door on the right stood a little ajar, showing an indoor bathroom with a gleaming marble tub. The corridor smelt clean; the carpet beneath them was freshly beaten, brightly coloured. Myra had never before been inside a house so beautifully kept.

Pausing before the last door on the left, Ellen proceeded to unlock it with a large key that hung from the chatelaine at her waist.

'Why –' began Myra, but stopped, pressed her lips together.

'He has not been well,' Ellen whispered. 'Father has had the doctor to him.' She turned the door handle, stood aside to admit Myra into the room. 'I will lock it again. My room is just next door. I'll go there and sort out a change of clothes for you, something loose. A tea gown, perhaps?' Ellen had blushed, Myra noticed, with the reference to her condition, but she was hurrying on. 'Knock on the wall, or call out. I'll come and unlock the door.'

Myra remained motionless. Why was her husband a prisoner? What had he done? She stared dumbly at Ellen.

'You will be all right. It's perfectly safe.' Ellen took hold of Myra's shoulder and firmly pushed her through the door.

It was a corner room, large, with tall windows facing north and west, which had curtains drawn across them. The curtains were of a deep garnet and cast a rich red light. Below the western window was an orderly desk, with papers and books. A tallboy with a bottle of Macassar and combs stood in one corner beside an ornate wash-stand, with a dish of soap. A drift of sandalwood rose from the soap, scenting the room. In the bed, dark framed by his hair, which was longer now, his face looming white against a raft of pillows, was William. She could not tell from where she stood whether his eyes were open or closed. Stranded on the square of carpet her courage deserted her and she turned to knock on the door immediately, to call Ellen back.

'Myra?' His voice was strange, feeble and cracked, like that of an old man.

Her heart rose with pity for him and she crossed the room to embrace him, as fast as her big belly allowed – but stopped short when she read his expression of disgust. His lips were cracked and dry, his eyes feverish, bright.

'Ah. Look at you! So this is why the old man's had me bailed up.'

She said nothing, took the chair from the desk and turned it, sat down. He watched her, his eyes on her belly. Self-consciously she crossed her hands over it, bowed her head.

William sighed, irritably. 'You have no concern for your husband, obviously.'

'I can see. You are sick.'

'I am not, though the doctor would make me so.' Sweat glazed his forehead, he licked his lips. 'Laudanum. Enough to stun a bullock. To prevent me from taking a ship that sails tomorrow.'

'But you must not!' she managed in a whisper.

'I will,' he responded, loudly, 'and you will help me.'

'I cannot go anywhere. Look at me!' Hateful tears welled. William did as she asked and gazed at her. Through his eyes she saw her ugly dress, her swollen stomach, her puffy, weary face.

'Come here,' he invited, surprisingly, patting the bed beside him. 'Let me explain.'

Another pain, the same as the one she had endured in the trilby, flashed across her belly, extended itself to anguish her back and ribs. As its grip loosened, she longed to lie down, her head on one of her husband's pillows, close her eyes. She climbed onto the bed and William stared into her face. She was cow-like, imploring. He had forgotten her little hands, how red they were at the knuckles, how straight her thin lips over her uneven teeth. But you knew she was no beauty, his conscience told him, that is not why you married her. At this moment he could scarcely remember why he had. Tears trembled in her eyes but did not fall. He heaved a great patient sigh and laid a hand on one of her knees.

'You are unwell? Aside from the child?'

'Just very tired.'

But he had looked away even as she answered, was nodding distractedly. He sighed, licked his dry lips again. 'I sail tomorrow, on the *Moana*, without fail. Father will have to let me go. I have paid for my ticket, first class, a two-berth stateroom.'

He was proud of this, she could tell. 'Did he –' She trailed off, took a deep breath. She would persist with the question. 'Did he give you the fare for your ticket?'

William shook his head; wondered how much he should tell her, how much she would be able to understand. 'My mother inherited a fortune some time ago now and the old man kept it a secret. I borrowed the funds necessary for my voyage from the Colonial Bank. I had a copy of the benefactor's letter of intent with me, but as it happened the name McQuiggan was enough to secure the loan. I still have my allowance, in any case.'

'Where?' Myra whispered. She felt as though she could hardly breathe, the air of his room hurt her throat.

'Why, in town of course. On Queen Street –'

'No. I mean where are you going?' One of William's hands lay along the top sheet. How clean his nails were, how soft his skin had become in his months of city living. She rested her rough, small hand on top of his, felt the smooth ends of his fingertips.

'Clear across the Pacific!' He laughed, deep in his chest, his voice suddenly loud. 'Across the Pacific to San Francisco, then a train to Utah, where I shall make a home for us in Salt Lake City.'

Myra stared at him, bewildered. Not only was his voice louder, but there was an odd tone to it, a new, important tone she hadn't heard in it before, the rise and fall of the sermoniser. 'Why have you . . . Salt Lake City? I have never heard –'

He pulled his hand away from hers, straightened his legs under the bedclothes so that she was perched on a narrow strip of mattress. 'Quiet. You will have to trust me. I can't explain now. I have a pounding head from the damned laudanum. They gave it to me two days ago, you know. Dr Pollock and poor Henry who only manhandled me because the old man stood by and forced him to. Have you met Father?'

Myra shook her head. She let her feet slip to the ground, stood unsteadily. She hoped she wouldn't see the judge just yet, not until she'd washed, tidied her hair.

There was a glass jug of water on the bedside table, a beaded cover set over its mouth. A beaker stood beside it. Myra poured herself a drink, holding the cool tatting in the palm of her hand. While she drank she examined it. It was exquisitely worked: birds and flowers in the weave, each bead a different colour: sugary red and yellow, a deep green, a lilac. The water slid down her throat and she found herself speaking almost as soon as the last was swallowed.

'Will you come back from America, William?'

'I don't know.' He had never seen her drink so thirstily before. She was still absorbed in the little cloth in her hand, letting the beaded fringe fall at either side of her wrist.

'Will you send for me, then?'

As he considered his reply, his wife gave a gasp and a hand shot out to cup the hammock of her belly.

'Listen to me, Myra, you will be cared for here. My father wouldn't allow his daughter-in-law to wander the streets. You will be perfectly all right.'

'But it isn't only myself – there will be –'

William cut her off. 'Forgive me if I am unable to consider your condition right now. It is a complete surprise to me.'

'It should not be.' Her voice was so quiet he wondered if he had heard her correctly. She was looking directly at him now, whatever pain that had seized her passed. Their eyes locked and he saw, as rapid as a bird's wing, a flare of anger in her moist eyes. It pleased him, relieved some of his burden of guilt. She only pretended to timidity; her real nature was the one he had married.

'Please excuse me, William.'

She moved away towards the door, praying that he would stay in his bed, but from behind her came the rustle of the bedclothes laid aside, the soft impact of his bare feet on the wooden floor. Panicked, she rapped on the door but his legs were rasping into trousers and then he was at her shoulder as she lifted her hand, knocked again. From outside in the hall, Ellen's footsteps sounded with the rattle of the key. His back to the door, William laid a finger across his lips and glared at his wife as the door swung open. He put his foot against the door, reached out one of his strong hands, grabbing for Ellen's shoulder or neck or any part of her that he could thrust away. His sister and wife were pushing against him, crying out in the stuffy, airless hall for him to return to his room.

'Henry!' It was Ellen yelling. 'Hen – ry!'

He shoved Myra away from him and ran for the top of the stairs. In his pocket was his ticket and a bank order for a hundred pounds.

One of the women moaned behind him – a sudden bestial noise that reminded him of a nightmarish night on the dreary farm. He turned once, for long enough to glimpse Ellen kneeling beside Myra, who lay on the ground. There was a sickly sweet smell and the shine of something liquid on the runner, a pool spreading out from under his wife's skirt in the same way as the whisky had spread from the fallen barrel at his ransacked still.

He took the steps three at a time, hurdled the banister for the last few to drop to the hall, his headache thrumming with the beat of his pulse and the urgency of his escape. The front door stood open and a figure was kneeling on the veranda, polishing the brass tread of the step. Mary. She looked up at him, aghast, and William realised the servants had been told of his incarceration, his so-called illness.

'Sir! Sir! Justice McQuiggan!' Mary was standing, her voice raised now. Hysterically, thought William. She put out her blackened hands to stop him, smudging his white shirt. He looked down at her filthy fingers, his bare feet, his state of undress.

He couldn't go, of course. Not right away. Everett and the three missionaries had decided to spend their last night in New Zealand aboard ship. It had been arranged that William would meet them at the wharf in the morning. He couldn't depend on Everett to furnish him with a change of clothes. He would go tomorrow, as planned. Mary read a decision in his face and a small triumphant smile pulled at her lips just as a heavy pair of arms clamped around William's waist from behind.

'Come inside, Will.' Henry's breath was hot on his shoulder. 'Father says you're to come inside.'

Mary laughed then, quickly. To William's ears it was sharp and cruel, mocking. He aimed a swift kick with a bare foot, his toes furled to a prehensile fist, hard enough to bruise her thigh.

'You're a damned lunatic, Master McQuiggan,' Mary hissed. 'They should put you in the asylum.' Fearless and making a show of ignoring him, she was kneeling again to her task.

In the hall Henry kept a grip on his brother while they listened to the commotion upstairs: hurrying feet, Alithea's voice calling to Blanche to be quick. A moment later that sister came hurrying down the stairs, struggling to fit her hat over her springy hair, her face stricken.

'Where are you going?' William asked her, blocking her way.

'Where do you think? Excuse me, William.'

Henry gurgled, enjoying the game. He let go of his brother now and did as he did, spreading his arms from one wall to the other to halt their sister's progress.

'Where are you going?' he asked, completing his imitation.

Blanche adopted the tone of voice all the women in the family used, except Ellen, when they spoke to Henry. Her voice went up in pitch, she slowed her words. 'To get the doctor for Myra. Let me past please.'

'Is Myra sick?' asked Henry, his slow face creased with worry. Disconsolately, William let his arm fall, let his sister pass. Blanche jammed a pin into her hat and hurried off, past Mary and out through the front gate.

'Shift yourself.' It was Gordon, carrying a pail of steaming water. 'There's another pot in the kitchen. Go and get it and bring it up.'

The cook made her way up the stairs, shifting the heavy bucket from one cramping hand to another. As she went, an exhausted, tearing cry came from the hall upstairs, and Ellen's and Alithea's voices murmured on either side of it, their heavily weighted feet supporting Myra into one of the bedrooms. William listened attentively: he was damned if he'd allow them to put her into his room. He still had much to organise.

'Go and get the water, Henry,' he said, giving his brother a shove.

'Don't you go outside again, Will.' Henry was waggling his finger at him. He was enjoying his role as his brother's keeper.

'Oh, shut up,' said William, turning away. Passing Gordie on the way, he went up to his room, which thankfully wasn't occupied by his wife. They had put her in Ellen's room next door. He sorted out clothes, books, papers, his papers, made neat piles on his bed. When he had finished, he ventured out into the hall, his ears blocked to the moans and thumps that issued from Ellen's room, and climbed the narrow treads of the ladder into the attic. He passed Mary's room and Gordon's, which was slightly larger, before he came to the part where the boxes were kept. There were two leather suit-cases and a heavy trunk. William chose the former and lugged them down to his room one at a time. On his return for the second case, he detoured into the maid's room, which was windowless and smelt of must. There was a narrow bed, a chair with two black stockings over its back and a candle-stick, the same as it had been for old Mary. He put the suit-case down and sat on the bed. The thin mattress sagged with his weight. What did Mary dream of? he wondered. What does she hope for? Her pillow, a layer of sad feathers, sagged in his hand. He put it on his lap. The slip was fresh and laun-dered, crisp with starch, a narrow frill of drawn-thread-work standing at its edges. It cheered him slightly, to see that she appreciated the fine linen enough to pilfer from the family press. She took her little luxury . . .

He would have kissed her, nothing more. He could not have gone further – Henry was in the room. Though how he would have liked to – to have slipped his hand up her smooth thigh, to cup her warm rump in his palm. She had that sweet, fresh milkiness of English girls, the moisture. Myra's shanks were thin and sinewy; she had a dark mole above her left knee. Her childhood under the Yarrabin sun had left her desiccated somehow, two shades darker than the Manchester maid. He remembered her pure, dry smell.

Ah yes, and if someone had come to the foot of the ladder they would have heard his sigh – it was explosive with resig-nation. He would only have kissed the maid. His eye fell on the black handprints against the white of his shirt. She had no need to be frightened of him, nor to challenge him. On the step, when she pushed him back, her face was contorted with spite. He lifted the pillow and ground it gently against the impression of her hands, her fingers on his chest – and the warmth the pillow left in his lap slithered to his balls and prick, and one hand, his left, abandoned the pillow to unbutton his pants.

Afterwards he took out a handkerchief and turned the starched pillow to wipe the underside dry. He moved his trembling hand quickly, pulling away the glutinous white threads of his vapid climax and folding them into his handkerchief. Nausea wallowed in the pit of his stomach – though it was only a little sin, he told himself, perhaps I must commit the venial sins in order not to breach the mortal ones. I will not castigate myself, he thought. We will put this behind us, my Lord. As he stood hurriedly, the sick feeling dissipated. He stuffed the handkerchief into his pocket, took up his suitcase and made his way down the ladder.

CHAPTER 10

She left her body and sat on the slipper chair at Ellen's duchesse. It would have been better to leave the room entirely but that didn't seem to be possible. It was enough of an achievement to have moved this far away and to observe herself being helped out of the black dress by Ellen and Mrs McQuiggan. Both women's faces were intent on the unfastening of her hooks and eyes, the detachment of her bodice, the lifting of her mancherons and the unlacing of her boots. Ellen slipped the soiled chemise from her shoulders, pulled it down and tied it loosely around her belly and hips to cover her.

Myra wanted to die of shame. It was so much worse than it had been with Riha, who for the days preceding the birth had kept her quiet and rested. It seemed exhaustion from her voyage had left her with no control at all. One moment she was racked with unbearable pain, the next so spent that her eyes closed to all around her and she slept. For a whole ten minutes at a time, she would leave them and dream with each falling away of walking among the tall whistling kahikateas on the farm, towards the house. It was cool evening, William waited for her inside and she went to join him with her heart full of gladness. Each fractured dream brought her no closer to him, though her legs moved beneath her; at the edges of her vision the trees flicked by.

'Myra?' It was Ellen, patting her hand, and coming through the door was the big woman Myra had seen in the kitchen. She bore a square of oilcloth that the three women, bending on either side of the bed, worked beneath her under the bottom sheet. Pain runnelled her back as they lifted her, laid her down, but she had gone beyond feeling it, sitting as she was at Ellen's duchesse running an ivory comb through her fingers. A flash caught her eye in the gap at the door: William coming down the hall, a comical pair of black hand-prints on the breast of his lawn shirt. His face was grey but his eyes blazed with intent. A few moments later, she sensed him above her, moving about in the roof.

The black dress was gone, sloughed off like the skin of a seal and hooked over the arm of the cook, who was leaving the room. Mrs McQuiggan and Ellen were encouraging her to sit up a little in the bed to allow them to slip her into a clean nightgown. First one arm, then the other, then over her head, heavy on the stem of her neck. They rolled up the gown firmly, under her armpits, covered her with a sheet.

'Leave her be, now. Let her rest between the pains,' said her mother-in-law. 'The doctor will come soon.'

Sleep, dreamless this time, drew her back into herself, a momentary lapse in concentration. The rush that woke her kept her in the centre of it, a fiery-walled prison that allowed no escape. She lurched up in the bed, terrified, a lick of sweat slicked from her chest to her belly. The room was peopled by virtual strangers; there was the smell of manure from a dirty shoe which she realised in the next instant was actually rising from the sheet below her. Her mouth opened and she cried out not in a high-pitched scream, as she had dreaded she would, but in a low, guttural push in the base of her throat that somehow forced her legs apart, had her push with the centre of her being, her face straining forward, blood thrum-ming in her ears and fingertips.

'Oh, my God!' Ellen's voice was only just audible but trumpeted her horror.

'Stop it,' said Mrs McQuiggan behind Myra's head, and Myra hoped briefly, for as long as she could spare it a thought, that she wasn't speaking to her because she couldn't stop it, not with every ounce of her will. 'Help me with these pillows. We must keep her lying on her side. Fetch some others from another room.'

And Ellen hurried out, admitting as she did so the younger sister and a thin grey-haired man with a top hat and bag. He did not look at his patient at all, but crossed straight to the duchesse where Myra's escapee self no longer sat. From the bag he took a small glass bottle with a stopper and a wad of gauze.

The contraction was lessening, the ebbing pain taking with it the need for consciousness. She watched the doctor with half-closed eyes as he came towards her, his eyes on the ether-soaked wad, and then on her mouth and nose, before he brought her face against the cotton and by doing so obliterated the polarity of her recent consciousness, taking her to the brink of a sudden destruction far beyond St Paul's, beyond death, beyond Heaven and hell.

Blanche was sent to rouse him at near three o'clock in the morning. The supper tray Gordon had brought up for him earlier was untouched and if Blanche wondered why he lay fully clothed on his bed, she didn't ask him. He heard first the rustle of her silk skirts before he turned his sleepless head on the pillow to see her. Her face above the lamp she carried was dreamy, soft, the white skin under her eyes pale blue with exhaustion. She was beautiful. The gas lamps burned in the hall behind her to light his way out of the house.

'Father would like to see you downstairs,' she said firmly. 'Right now. He's very insistent.'

'Tell him I am asleep, drugged.'

'He knows the laudanum has worn off. He has spoken to the doctor . . . who was here earlier, you know.'

'Has he gone?'

Blanche nodded, a strange little smile on her face. He felt the blood leave his head and fought a sensation of falling forward. He was a father again. He would be expected to gaze at the child, to speak to Myra. He had thought – well, he hadn't thought about it at all, but he supposed he had hoped, or presumed – that the labour would take a day or two at least, as it had the last time, that Myra would have given him time to get away.

'Show me what you want for me, Lord! First one thing and then another. I am not ready.' He had dropped to his knees, hard, resounding on the wooden floor. 'I will go to Salt Lake, as You directed, tomorrow. I will –'

Blanche knelt swiftly beside him, tugged at his hand. 'Stop it, William,' she said quietly, alarmed. Tears were gathering in the corners of her brother's eyes, his voice squeaked with emotion.

'William – hush. Thank the Lord, don't berate Him. It's a miracle. Come and look. Hush now, Will. Stand up.'

He did as he was told, held her hand. Blanche took the towel from the rack, wiped his face and led him downstairs, where she left him at the parlour door.

A small fire had been lit in the grate, despite the warmth of the night and the late hour. In order to observe him as he came in, his parents' opposing chairs had been angled away from the fire. Pulling at his stiff butterfly collar and necktie, he nodded at them, finding suddenly that he couldn't speak. His father beckoned to him, waved the same hand towards his mother, and William saw that she held not one, but two infants, one in each of her crooked arms, swaddled in white shawls, their tiny faces simian, asleep, the colour of molluscs. One of them was considerably bigger than the other. The smaller twin was almost wizened, its skin darker, the two of them utterly still. He struggled to contain his breathing.

'Girls,' said his mother. 'Myra is asleep now. You can see her in the morning.'

He nodded again, tearing his eyes away from his daughters to the fire. 'She . . . um –' He cleared his throat. 'She is all right?'

'Fairly so.'

'And they – will they both live?'

'The doctor thinks one of them at least.' His mother glanced down at the larger one.

'Here –'

He saw that his mother wanted him to take one of the babies. 'Oh no, I –'

'Ellen has retired in Blanche's room and I hope Blanche herself has now done the same. I would like you to hold her while I stand with the other.'

William bent to lift the daughter that would be named Joy, so sowing the seeds of one of the stories his daughters would tell. It would run along the lines of how, on the eve of his departure to America, Joy and Dora were born, and how the only one he held was Joy. The story went no further, but ended there on a nonsensical, triumphal note. Throughout her childhood, Joy would believe that she was somehow special in his eyes. The small truth of the story was enough to fire the whole fiction.

In his arms the baby was as light as ash; her tiny nostrils flared and narrowed with each inaudible breath. He guessed her eyes were blue, and although her head was covered by cloth he knew her to be hairless. There was something repulsive about her and he recoiled from her, held her at arm's length as his mother stood, rearranged herself and took the child from him.

'Goodnight, William. Congratulations.' His mother lifted her face to kiss him. He felt her lips press firmly against his cheek and then she was moving away. She paused at the door.

'William, could you –' His father was looking at him.

'Oh, of course.' He hurried across the room, opened it for her to pass through. 'I'm sorry, Mother.'

She met his eyes. 'Yes, my dear,' she said softly, 'I do believe you are,' and she was gone.

There was a moment when he could have followed her – he even took a step. Still and silent in the room behind him, his father was not going to call him back, but something compelled him to turn, cross purposefully, manfully, to his mother's chair – though the old man's gaze appeared to remain on the closed door – and sit down. His father would have him think ill of himself, William thought: he would have him hold as little faith in himself as he did. He would show his father that he possessed self-respect and a destiny beyond the old man's dreams.

Elisha's hands were crossed peacefully in his lap as he gazed into the fire. His face contained some of the peculiar dreaming calm that Blanche's had, and William realised with a start that the old man was touched by the birth of the twins, made tender by it. It was because he was not responsible for them, he thought – not really, only as much as a grandfather is. They were his own shackle and iron.

He stood suddenly and crossed the room. It was over-warm: long, heavy maroon drapes dulled the air. William parted them and gazed out into the dark. Somewhere far below the parlour windows, concealed, the green-hulled *Moana* lay clinking at her moorings, the long necks and attenuated heads of her latticed derricks gleaming in the moonlight like graceful, fabulous sea beasts. Everything would change now. He returned to his chair.

'Shall we pray, Father?' Prayer by its nature was at once conversant and distant, a chance for his father to eavesdrop on his intimacy with God, to witness the power of his faith.

'Hear our prayer, Lord Jesus.' He closed his eyes, bowed his head. 'Bless all those who travel on the oceans, particularly those aboard the *Moana*. She sails tomorrow at noon. Give me the strength, Father, to be one of her passengers, to leave my wife and daughters, to make a new life in America.' From under lowered lids he glanced at his father, who was leaning back in his chair, his eyes closed. A collection of crooked yellow teeth broke wetly above his lower lip. Could he have fallen asleep so quickly?

'Father?' he said, uncertainly.

Elisha's eyes flew open. 'Are you speaking to me or to your celestial one, who I begin to perceive, is entirely fictional? Why should God single you out above all men, absolve you from your responsibilities? You indulge yourself in childlike fantasy, the primitive religiosity of the savage.'

William reeled out of his chair. 'You may practise your tepid, modern Anglicanism all you like, Father, but do not expect me to. It is the jaded faith of the Old World. I am one of the men God has chosen to lead us into the new century and He is sending me to America so that I may do so. He is not merely a set of rules and some sobering stories. He is terrible. His will itself is savage. Had the Lord shown himself to you as a young man you would have taken the same path.'

'Do not presume –' Elisha reached for his stick.

William stepped away from its projected range. 'I have no choice. Goodnight, Father.'

'William –'

'Goodnight.'

'We will talk in the morning –'

'I think not. Goodnight, Father.' William kept his repetitions level, in the way he and Elisha spoke to Henry during one of his excited talking jags: soft voiced, deep, a burring threat concealed in the soothing tone. Righteously, he tried to suppress the feeling of satisfaction that rose with the knowledge of how his father would detest being so addressed. He made for the door and closed it behind him before he leapt lightly, quietly, up the stairs and along the hall to his room.

Side by side at the foot of his bed, neatly packed, sat his suitcases. William used one of them to hold his door slightly ajar, the better to hear his father's weary progress, shortly afterwards, to his bedroom across the hall.

The house fell silent. Downstairs, in his room off the porch, a cat rose and fell on Henry's sleeping belly, another curled in the crook of his plump knees and the kitten Myra had seen in the stables was tucked under his chin. The last of the gas lamps in the hall dimmed in their sconces as Mary closed them off one by one on her way to bed in the attic. An hour or so later she stirred, turned her pillow, became vaguely aware of something unpleasant under her cheek and turned the pillow once more, sleeping still.

In her bedroom, the one that had once belonged to her married daughters, Alithea simmered in her heavy flannel nightgown and wished she'd worn a lighter one. On her way to bed, she had looked in on Myra in Ellen's room. The young woman slept the sleep of the dead, pale and limp. Earlier they had washed her, wrapped her with the binder, unrolled her gown over her hips and moved her to the clean side of the bed. There had been no need for the roller towel that Alithea had tied to the footpost for Myra to pull on, a necessity in her day. After the chloroform took hold, the doctor had dismissed Ellen and herself from the room. They had sat outside in the hall on chairs brought from the bedrooms. The poor child, thought Alithea, as Myra's frightened, anxious face filled her mind. It had been a blessed relief when the chloroform worked its little death. Eventually they had answered a sharp rap on the bedroom door, hurried in and wrapped the babies warmly in flannel receivers. The babies were still and drugged, but so perfectly formed and tiny her heart found room for them immediately.

Among her soft rugs and pillows, Alithea slept heavily until after eight, when she woke suddenly from a dream about William. She had entered a vast wooden church – it was perhaps St Mary's Cathedral on the hill above their house. A buttressed roof arched sepulchral above her head. Row after row of empty pews shone towards the altar, a gleam of gold on the green and white embroidered cloths. There was the scent of spring flowers and furniture polish and the coloured glass in the windows glowed, their little flames of refracted light licking the walls. There was a sense of well-being and calm until, quite suddenly, she became aware of a swinging object above her head: it was William, at first only the soles of his shoes and then, when she craned her neck back further, she could see his knees, and then his tongue, venal and black, protruding from his swollen, down-turned face. He was hanged by his neck from a beam.

She sat up, heart pumping, pulled on her dressing-gown and rushed down the hall towards his empty room.

CHAPTER 11

A steward in a white jacket and black trousers showed him to his stateroom on the upper deck. It seemed more like a hotel room than a ship's cabin, with a deep, wide bed and a narrower bunk above it, a wardrobe, chest of drawers and bureau. A small padded suite was gathered around a polished occasional table and a connecting door led through to his lavatory. The floor was polished wood, with a small thick Brussels carpet. Someone, a woman, a passenger on the first leg from Sydney, had left the cabin the night before and the room still held a hint of her perfume. He sniffed a little at the air.

A note waited for him, folded on top of the chest of drawers. 'Brother William,' it read, 'We are making the Music Saloon our own. Do come and join us at your convenience.'

William longed suddenly to join his friend and hurried along the upper deck. A sign above an open door announced the Music Saloon. He would have found the room anyway, if he had only followed the sound that issued from it. It was the same voices in harmony that he had heard that day in Vulcan Lane.

'Hail our patriarch's glad reign, spreading over sea and main –'

Cast by an immense stained-glass dome in its ceiling, coloured patches of light lit here and there upon the lounges and easy chairs. The room was panelled with a blond, tinted wood, interrupted now and then by rich hangings of a delicate blue. On either side of a large ornate upright piano stood Sister Lydia and Brother Paora, while Sister Eliza plied the keys. She was no better a pianist than she was singer, her timing dragging behind the others. There was a lengthy pause while she found her place to begin another verse. Resignedly, as if out of habit, her vocalists watched her hesitant fingers.

'Sons of Michael, 'tis his chariot rolls its burning wheels along!' they resumed, with some relief.

Brother Everett stood from his place at a small table spread with papers and warmly shook William's hand. Lydia and Paora smiled in greeting, their voices booming louder and Sister Eliza, sensing an arrival, lifted her hands away from the keyboard and swivelled around to see who it was. The singers carried on regardless, unaccompanied.

'We will go up on deck shortly,' Brother Everett was saying, 'to farewell Auckland and watch the dear green hills disappear. You are well set up, Brother William?'

'I have a stateroom in one of the deck-houses which –' William wondered if the singers would cease now in deference to his conversation. Folding his arms across his chest he waited pointedly for them to stop. Sister Eliza kept her head bowed, not meeting his eye, and something in her quiet mien reminded him of Myra. Perhaps if she had not got herself with child again he would have brought her with him. He would have abstained from her of course, installed her in another cabin some distance away from his. He longed to experience the eternal marriage of the Saints, what Brother Brigham called the 'foundation for worlds, for angels and for Gods', but he could not, not until she understood, not until she had read the books he had, and they could kneel together in the temple at Salt Lake.

In full voice and braking rallentando, the Brother and Sister were on the final words of the hymn ' . . . the ancient one doth reign in his Father's house again!' Paora's voice reverberated off the sycamore panelling, Lydia's swept up an octave suddenly so that she could warble her highest, most dramatic vibrato on the simple closing notes. Giving them all his attention, Brother Everett smiled indulgently and Paora ended with a deep, delighted flourish, his laughter growing from the final note.

Watching them, William envied the American's good strong teeth, his clear benign brow. By contrast, he was still mired in the after-effects of the laudanum: dry mouthed, his responses slowed. Paora swept around the piano to Everett's sister and gallantly offered her his arm. She looked up at him wanly.

'To the deck, Sister,' he asked her, 'to promenade?'

'We will all go,' Brother Everett announced, shrugging on his coat. It was a summer jacket, light gabardine, an elegant American cut. William envied him that, as well as his beautiful wife who was at his side, helping him, her hands lingering lovingly on his shoulders. Everett took her arm and William followed after them.

A large crowd had gathered on the wharf to see the ship off. It seemed a scarcely smaller crowd milled about onboard. The passengers leaned against the rails, calling down to their well-wishers, or walked singly or in twos or stood in groups to talk. Three boys chased one another wildly towards the stern, whooping and yelling. Streamers, thousands of them, linked the first- and second-class decks with the earthbound, myriad tenuous connections soon to be broken.

William allowed the others to get ahead, leaned his elbows on the white rails and looked out towards the Gladstone Coffee Palace and the Customhouse beyond. Impatience burned in the back of his throat like bile. The view was flat, like a page in a book he had read again and again but failed to get the meaning of. Suddenly a figure, painfully familiar, emerged from the coffee palace corner door and hurried across Quay Street. Henry had come to see him off, but in a great hurry evidently. He was hastily dressed and favouring one of his legs, which he must have injured on his downhill run, or so William thought until he saw that his boots were on the wrong feet. At the neck of the wharf he paused by the *Weekly News* man and gazed towards the ship.

William imagined their mother waking, saw her colour- less hair, loose and thin, flying behind her as she hurried down to Henry's room off the porch, waking him from his characteristically deep sleep and sending him off after his brother with little or no assistance in dressing. His vision went no further than that, though he could have presumed with no extra effort that she had stood then at the parlour window, watching Henry's lumpy, clumsy form flicker between the immature trees of the street down the hill to Augusta Terrace. Later she would regret not waking Ellen, who might have stood a chance of bringing William back.

From the deck of the ship, William could see that Henry's intended farewell did not spring from his own heart. His poor brother looked terrified, his unshaven face swinging wildly up and down, his panicked eyes blindly sweeping the length of the decks. Grey whiskers glinted in his stubble; his hands repeatedly grasped the air in front of his belly and passers-by gave him a wide berth. William raised a hand, thought the better of it and dropped it. If Henry saw him he would bellow, would howl at him to come down. An unpleasant memory, fifteen years old, uncoiled and stuck in William's mind: there had been an embarrassing scene on the deck of the schooner on which he had sailed to England when he was fifteen. Almost twenty, stubborn and fiendishly strong, Henry would not let go of him. William had needed assistance to fight him off the ship and ever since then, in the absence of a more recent misdemeanour, Elisha had liked to lecture William on the negative effect his absconding had had on his brother. It had brought real trauma to Henry's life, in the father's opinion, and made him even less likely to realise any kind of mental maturity.

'What has caught your eye, Mr McQuiggan?' It was Sister Eliza, moving towards him, though she had obviously been watching him for some time. Behind her, flanked on one side by the lifeboats, stood Brothers Everett and Paora in conversation with one of the liveried crewmen. 'Or should I ask, who?' Lifting his elbows from the rail, William straightened and smiled at her. The warm, gusty air of the promenade had touched her cheeks, bringing a hint of youth, or animation. 'My brother Henry,' he said. 'He is down there in the crowd.'

'Which one is he?' She leaned eagerly over the rail.

'If he observes me pointing him out he will become over-excited.'

'Ah. So you will not?'

'No.'

'That is very stiff of you. I would like to see your brother. Is he like you?'

'Not at all.' William disliked her prying tone. The man talking to Everett and Paora, he realised now, was the captain. He was shaking Brother Everett's hand and walking on, hailed by another group of passengers.

'You are still a mystery to me, Mr McQuiggan. Brother Everett tells me you have a wife.'

'I do so wish you could find it in your heart to address me as Brother, Sister Eliza. I have proven enough of my commitment to deserve that.'

Paora and Everett were making their way back to them. Below their feet the rumble and thump of the ship's engines grew louder, the smoke stack's exhalations more energetic. The sister hurried her words.

'Wait until you have visited Utah. I was born there and have had no choice. Life there is better for men than it is for women, so you may well enjoy it. But wait until you have seen it and been among us for a time before you make your decision to join us or no. It is a place of great desolation.'

'I do not think your brother would approve of your advice, madam.' William felt a pulse of strong dislike for the woman.

'My brother?' She seemed startled. 'Who –'

But Everett was behind her, urging William to walk on with them and make the acquaintance of other passengers. As he took William's arm and moved him away, William noticed with some surprise that Sister Eliza was blushing. It was not an innocent feminine blush, but an indignant reddening, perhaps even of anger, as if she were suppressing a violent response.

'I find ship life is very often conducive to the proselytiser's success,' said Everett. 'Captain Carey, just now, was telling us how glad he is to have us aboard.'

Paora gave a gurgling, deep-throated giggle, which to William's ears sounded warm and benign, though strangely childish. 'Anything to raise the tone, he said. He's a character, all right.' He shook his head and William envied the man's happiness. A deep contentment shone around him, lending him conviviality and grace. Sister Lydia, too, had a little of it. It was their new American faith, he thought. If the Maori can have it, then I can too.

'Where is Sister Lydia?' he asked.

'She has returned to the Music Saloon,' replied Everett, 'to make sure we maintain our hold on it, at least for the first part of our voyage.'

They had reached the bow, where a young man leaned against the mast smoking a pipe. Brother Everett gave a signal to Paora, nodding his head abruptly to his left, and the Maori moved away to a large group at the port rail. They were mostly young and as fashionably dressed as the young man with the pipe: a party of theatrical people, perhaps. Brother Paora took up a gap in their circle and introduced himself to the man beside him.

'Good morning, sir!' Everett greeted the young man at the mast, who was now engaged in the lighting of his tobacco.

His fashionable Piccadilly collar, stiff and six inches high at least, challenged him – he could not bend his head to the flame. He succeeded at last; in his cupped hands the small bowl flared and glowed.

'Mr Everett Ridge,' Everett held out his hand, which the young man ignored. Pointedly, he rounded his shoulder on them and went to join his friends at the rail. Undeterred, the American followed him.

'I wonder if I could have a moment of your time, sir!'

The ship gave three loud blasts of its horn, a signal that it was reversing away from the wharf. William decided to return to the Music Saloon himself. Thicker, even darker smoke pumped from the stack and gusted over the sheds on Central Wharf. Briefly he paused at the rail and looked into the crowd as it slipped past, searching for Henry. The ship's departure coaxed from the upturned faces a welter of emotion: fixed grins or smiling benevolence; faces solemn and inscrutable or collapsed in grief. For a moment William despised them all. They were the weak, the frightened, the trapped, the stay-at-homes.

Striking up on the lower deck a brass band in Union livery began the hymn for those at sea: 'Eternal Father, Strong to Save, Whose Arm Doth Bind the Restless Wave'. The slow strains of the tune lifted to William's ears and his heart gave an inadvertent pulse of regret. He hardened himself against it, reminded himself that there was nothing he was leaving that he could not later regain, and hastened on towards the Music Saloon. Henry must have gone and he had long wanted to have Sister Lydia all to himself.

She had her back to him and was playing the piano. It was Bach, he read over her shoulder. The two threads of music wove together in perfect accord, a magical entwining of independence and harmony. He stood behind her, watching her white hands moving over the keys. The scent that rose from her glossy hair had the purity of water, the healthy warmth of a young animal. She wore a grey jacket, tightly cut, with wide revers that showed its silken lilac lining. The chemisette that frothed at her neck was white, goffered, spotless – out of her missionary garb Sister Lydia was a woman of style. Racing and flickering over the keys her right hand was ringless, but the left one bore a heavy shining wedding band, fairly new, undimmed by time.

The piece finished and he clapped.

'Thank you, Brother,' she smiled at him.

'What is it called?'

'"Solfreggio", which is usually a song. Bach wrote this one for the piano. Beautiful, isn't it?'

He strolled away to sit in the nearest easy chair. An elderly lady was picking her way into the room with her stick, her gaze now and then fixing on the destination of her chosen chair.

'Did you learn as a child?' he asked her.

'Oh yes. Many of us do. Music was very important to the Prophet and to Brother Brigham, of course. It remains so to us.'

'I should like to hear you accompany yourself and Brother Paora, rather than Sister Eliza.'

'Eliza enjoys her part,' she responded with loyal vehemence, 'and she is not well. She has gone to her cabin to lie down.'

'A sudden affliction?' William asked dryly. 'I spoke to her on the deck just now and she seemed in good health.'

'She is prone to sudden neuralgia. It bothers her here.' Sister Lydia lifted a hand to her temples as she stood to carry her music back to the rack. 'I have asked her to leave her door ajar, so that I might hear her if she calls for me.' She gestured towards the two doors at the aft end of the saloon, one of which stood open.

'Ah. So the other is occupied by Brother Everett and yourself?' William asked. She faced him squarely.

'We share the two rooms, yes. The Ladies' Boudoir and the Stateroom.'

There was something defiant in her attitude, which puzzled him. She turned back to the rack, her fingers drifting over the sheets of music, then ranging over an adjoining shelf that held fat albums of songs. Having selected one, she sat herself in an armchair a distance away from William. Their exchange was obviously at an end. She bent intently over the pages and one of her hands ghosted a melody on the open book.

William debated rising and sitting near her again. The creamy, serious planes of her face retained the intensity of her final response and his curiosity was aroused. Suddenly she lifted her head, her eyes half closed as if she were listening, though he had heard nothing. He had seen Myra listen in the same manner on the farm, after the child was born. A faint, querulous voice called again from the cabin end.

'Lydia —'

She rose, laying the book to one side and hurried out, the stiffened hem of her long pleated skirt moving like an accordion at her ankles. The door closed firmly after her and the truth of her circumstances struck William so forcibly that he gained his feet without knowing it.

When the little tug left, the *Moana* blew its horn again, one long brassy note as it turned into the Rangitoto Channel to steam into the gulf. Its mournful importance was heard all over the small city as it lay baking under the noon sun. In Ellen's bedroom on the second floor of the judge's house, Myra began to stir. Her babies lay side by side in a crib beside the bed. She leaned out and picked one out, marvelling at her, despite the discomfort of the binder and the tearing pain below it. There was a jug of fresh water and a glass on the bedside table. She lay the child on her lap and drank deeply, her heart swelling with a secret, vibrant pride. The baby's eyes opened, focused dimly on the shining glass as it lowered from her mother's lips. Myra met her daughter's eyes for the first time and tears prickled at her own.

'Hello, dear,' she said. She would call this one Joy and the other one Dora, the names of two of the sisters on the little steamer from Mangawhai. She liked the names for their gentle simplicity. They were strong and modern.

Replacing Joy in the cradle, she lifted Dora and noticed that she was heavier than her sister. Her little cheeks were much rounder, her wrists and fingers chubby. With dreaming hands she unwrapped the receiver to reveal an embroidered Viyella gown, the neck of which was ornate with handmade lace. It was old but fine and smelt slightly of camphor.

'Perhaps your father wore this,' she whispered to Dora, whose eyes remained sealed shut. 'Was it Papa's, do you think?' Myra stared at the baby, wondering for a moment if she could detect any resemblance to the child born on the farm, but found to her astonishment that she had no recollection of the earlier face.

She lifted the tiny girl to her shoulder and sniffed deeply at her head, behind the miniature ear. William will come soon, she thought, to see his daughters. She remembered his stricken face at the Hakaru graveyard, how he'd tipped it beseechingly to the billowing, tumultuous sky, the anger and grief in him. If he sat there, on the slipper chair, with one or other of his infants in his arms, surely his mourning would end as entirely as hers had: he would be mended.

CHAPTER 12

For the first three days of the voyage, William stayed in his cabin, making use of the small bureau. He had his meals sent up to him and ate hurriedly at the small table, more out of a sense of duty to himself than with any relish. The rest of the time he pored over his books and pondered Everett's moral predicament. Brother Ridge was surely a man of principle: there would be a clue, an explanation, William was sure, somewhere in the Bible, or the *Book of Mormon*, or the *Doctrine and Covenants*. He worked from one to the other, washed about by opposing dictums.

Everett visited him twice on the first day, but William called out for him to go away. Paora, too, pounded on his door to no avail.

Joseph Smith's revelation given to him by the Lord in 1831: '. . . if any man espouse a virgin and desire to espouse another, and the first gave her consent and if he espouse the second, and they are virgins and have vowed to no other man, then he is justified . . . ' In the *Book of Mormon* Jacob has it that David and Solomon had 'many wives and concubines which thing was abominable before me, saith the Lord'. But Brother Brigham maintained that plural marriage was 'the most holy and important doctrine ever revealed to man on Earth'. In the second book of Chronicles, Rehoboam had eighteen wives and was a wise man who provided for his family and whom God rewarded.

'And he desired many wives,' William read over and over again, though the book at his elbow, open at Mosiah, thundered against the concupiscence of King Noah who caused his people to sin by the wickedness of his own example. Was it more sinful to desire wives rather than mistresses? As he read the words of the Prophet and the stories of David and Solomon and Rehoboam and imagined their lives, he gave each patriarch Everett's face, and wondered if he could ever look into his friend's eyes again. His bowels churned with poisonous excitement, a dread, an impending sense of the entirely alien, a thrilling, foreign morality. If only the Lord would speak to him, tell him either that Brother Everett was a sinner, or that He walked beside him.

Periodically he longed for a drink and the knowledge of the ship's proximitous store of wines and spirits, available for a price from the steward who brought him his meals, brought him out in a cold sweat. Unwillingly he anticipated the whisky burn on his lower lip, the sweet slip down his throat, the spreading warmth and ensuing oblivion and struggled to resist his yearning for it.

At noon on the third day, he fell to his knees at the foot of the bed, despairing, the books spread on the firm mattress before him. There was no answer. Had he turned away from God since leaving the farm? Had he negated his own true experience of Him? He emptied his mind, prayed now for the Lord to take him. He would avoid this dilemma; he would travel towards the light pure in heart, guiltless and free; he would escape all this; he would not accept false prophesy.

It was hopeless. The Lord would not hear him.

That evening Everett put his mouth to the keyhole.

'I think I know what is disturbing you,' he whispered. 'Could you not admit me so that we may discuss it?'

William hauled himself up from his aching knees and turned the key on his side of the door.

'I married Lydia in Mexico three years ago, before we began our mission. She is my second wife.' Everett began talking with his first step into the room. 'Eliza is eight years my senior and I married her ten years ago. There are many of us who view the Everlasting Covenant with the same disgust as you do, Brother.'

'It is not —' began William, but his three days of silence had furred his throat.

'Disgust? Indeed it is. More than that, in my observation of the monogamists. Speculation, which arouses disgust and titillates the mind. It is an inflaming cocktail of the two sensations.'

'I am not in the slightest aroused,' William responded dryly. Everett looked at his friend's crumpled, slept-in clothes, his unshaven chin, his despairing demeanour.

'No. I don't believe you are.' He sat on the bed, his fingers interlinked between his knees.

'I have been praying for guidance,' William said, moving the books away, closing them and setting them on the bureau. 'The Lord has not heard me.'

'I came to marry Lydia only after long hours of prayer. Eliza and I knelt together to receive the word.'

'Eliza too?' William was incredulous. 'It seems odd to me that a wife should wish to share her husband.'

An impulse, tense and unreadable, tightened the muscles around Everett's mouth for a moment. 'Perhaps my wife prayed for a different answer,' he said briefly, 'though she did not hear it.'

'Does she regret —' began William, but Everett made an impatient movement with his hand and stood again.

'I do not know. Perhaps she will be happier when we have returned to Salt Lake and she is among her own kind. Frankly, I am surprised that you are so tardy in realising our circumstances. Since the days of Joseph Smith we have been persecuted for our Covenant.' Everett paced the length of the cabin. William shook his head slowly.

'I had not realised. You had never explained, Brother.'

'I had not judged the time to be right. It is irrelevant though, to what I have come to tell you.' Everett was before him, taking his hands. 'Do not allow this matter to injure your affection for the faith. There are many men in the church who think as you do, who will not receive the fullness of exaltation. Voyage with us. Let us enjoy our time together on the ship. You may leave us in San Francisco, should you so desire.'

'No, I won't be leaving you there. I will take Sister Eliza's advice,' William said dully.

'Ah.' Everett smiled. 'Sister Eliza is a very earnest adviser. What did she tell you?'

'Almost exactly as you have, but to delay my decision until I have been among you for a time, in Salt Lake.'

'I would not even think of contradicting my dear wife,' Everett said softly. 'She is a most sensible mentor. I often use her as such myself.'

William drew breath to ask a further question, though which of the many that teemed in his brain he did not know. How did a man with two wives arrange his private life? If one of his women was his solemn mentor then did the other share his bed? Or did they both, and if so, singly or together? And where were the children of these unions?

None of the questions could be asked, not with any degree of decency, and besides, Everett, anticipating the likely nature of William's queries, intercepted him.

'It's twilight, Brother. Walk with me before we dine in the Grand Saloon.' He picked up William's jacket from where it squared against the back of a chair and held it out to him. 'Let this matter rest for a while,' he continued. 'Let God guide you to the right answer in His own time.'

Silently, William took his coat and followed Everett out into the dusk. Four days into the voyage the rush and anticipation of departure had dissipated. The wide uncluttered spaces of the first-class decks were dotted with drifting, promenading couples. In the north-east Venus shone low and bright, set into a sky of deep, light-suffused blue. Towards the horizon, in the ship's trajectory, lay a thick layer of dark cloud that mimicked in pitch the spreading night in the west. Slowing his pace to an amble, Everett bent their path towards the rails. Beside them their long shadows flickered along the boards of the deck, melted around steamer chairs and ventilators.

It was wonderful to be outside again. William swung his arms. Ten months of indolence had left him out of condition: he hadn't done any real work since the clearing on the farm last April. There was no longer any sense of muscles pulling across his chest; his body felt flabby, its tendons and bones softly connected.

'I have never asked you,' said Everett, watching him, 'what your occupation was before you took up the farm.'

William folded his arms across his chest. 'My father intended me for the law, but I was a poor scholar.'

'So, instead?' prompted Everett.

'I have worked here and there,' he said vaguely. White water streamed at the hull. Part of his dreaming mind fixed on a particle of foam, watched it fling away from the ship in a diagonal. The sea was glassy, darkening under the evening sky. Everett waited for him to continue. He cleared his throat.

'In Australia, where I spent some time, I worked as a carpenter.'

'Ah!' Everett brightened. 'Like the Lord and Brother Brigham. I have long held the opinion that the practical occupations employ the hands and conscious mind while allowing the soul to progress towards glory and salvation. Was that your experience?'

'No,' William answered truthfully, 'not at all. I was surrounded by men of low character who drank and caroused and took up with women who matched the men in their appetites. It was a time of bewilderment and confusion.'

'I suspect you have had many times like that,' Everett said gently. 'Shall we walk on?' He had laid his hand on one of

William's arms, which was still tensed across his body. William shook it off in a sudden fit of pique. Everett was his contemporary, possibly even slightly his junior, and William wanted suddenly to impress upon him the value of lessons learned in the world of men.

'You are right, I have. But they have been of some benefit to me. You saw for yourself how I preached among the workers and labourers. I speak their language.'

Everett pursed his lips. He disliked the competitive tone in William's voice. 'As I do, Brother. I am not in contest with you. I also suspect you were not a carpenter for very long. I think you are a man like me, a man of independent wealth.'

'How do you come to that conclusion?'

'It is obvious. We both travel first class. Brother Paora, I must tell you, travels because of his colour in second class. We have had some trouble with the stewards over his dining with us in the Grand Saloon.'

William was not interested in Paora just now; before Everett finished speaking, he resumed his progress along the deck.

'The others will be glad to see you. The women particularly were worried about your well-being.' Everett was behind him, touching him again, lightly laying his hand in the small of his back to propel him through an open door that led to a companionway. 'These stairs will take us to the Grand Saloon, directly below the Music Saloon.' Voices rose from the space below, among them the crying of an infant.

'We eat early, with the other families, even though we do not have our children with us.'

'Children?' The question William had earlier repressed had been answered.

'I have a son waiting in Salt Lake, a fine boy of six. Eliza longs to see him.'

They took the stairs, which were wide and thickly carpeted, descending to the main deck.

'It is lucky for you that you are childless,' continued Everett. 'It is one thing to leave a wife, but another to leave a son – though in my case my son is well cared for.'

They had reached a wide shining vestibule. Two tall parlour palms stood sentinel at either side of the saloon doors, their fronds shifting in the gentle breeze of the overhead fans.

'It has pained me to think of him these past three years, much less to speak of him.' Everett was talking fast, as though he wished to finish his confidence before they reached the group that waited for them. In the far corner of the room, the full width of the ship away, Brother Paora was standing and waving to get their attention. Like the music room, the saloon was lit by a large stained-glass dome. The same pale wood and carved pilasters decorated the walls, and the chairs were upholstered in a delicate blue moquette. For a moment William was oblivious to his surroundings. He shrugged in his jacket against a proud, prickling sensation that ran along his shoulders: in the last half hour Everett had laid his soul bare to him, told him of his son and wives. He felt privileged, honoured by his friend's confidence.

Eliza watched her husband and the New Zealander make their way towards them, as did many of the younger female diners. They were, after all, two fine men in the prime of life, almost of a height, one fair, one dark. She noted the spring and vitality in her husband's step, the way the softly glowing table lamps cast up a golden sheen to his hair and face. Behind him, William was pale from his self-imposed exile, all lean chin and hungry eye. She wondered how much Everett had told him. There had been a scene after William had disappeared and bailed himself up in his cabin. Her husband had been angry with her.

'I saw you talking to him at the rail,' he had accused her that night in his stateroom. Even though it was the largest cabin on the ship, with the three of them in it it seemed crowded. A muslin sleeve of one of Lydia's dresses protruded from a hastily closed wardrobe. They had given Eliza the only chair. 'You must have said something then.'

As always, Lydia had stepped in and saved her. Her sister-wife loathed her for it, though she prayed the Lord would forgive her mean-spiritedness.

'No. He came to me as we were leaving the wharf. He seemed his usual self – charming, but ill at ease.'

Everett gave her a hard look, which glimmered at the edges with unwilling amusement. 'Charming, eh?'

'In his own way,' she had said, coolly.

Sister Eliza had pulled herself upright with a quick, tight breath.

'I do not think he is charming at all, but rather strange. We were only talking about his brother, who was down in the crowd. He would not point him out to me. There was nothing in our conversation that may have disconcerted him – nothing that I remember.' As soon as Eliza had spoken, she recalled her words of advice – but they had been deliberate, well meditated upon, and she did not regret them in the least. No doubt her husband would, if he knew of them.

The men were joining them now at the table. Slapping William's shoulder and imitating his long mournful face, Paora bellowed with laughter. Suppressing a smile, Lydia nudged him.

'I do not see the joke, Brother,' said William tersely. He pulled out his chair and sat down. Immediately behind the table rose a little stage, set into the forward end wall. Two narrow steps led up to it on either side and its carved arch was draped with a thick deep-blue curtain, spangled with silver moons and stars. From behind the curtain issued soft bangs and thumps, as though someone were preparing for an item.

'We may be in for another turn from Mrs Myers,' Sister Lydia said quietly to her husband as he sat down beside her. He grimaced, looked around the table.

'Not for some time yet, I hope. We will return to the Music Saloon once we have eaten.'

A plump woman in an elaborately collared pale-green gown emerged from the stage door on the port side and hurried to sit with a grey-haired man of long-suffering demeanour at a centre table.

'She must have been setting up her music stand,' said Paora, wiggling his eyebrows. Lydia giggled.

'Not all of us are as gifted as yourselves.' Eliza's reprimand had the younger woman blush violently, and William remembered her earlier loyalty and concern in the music room. Scowling, Eliza scanned the menu.

'The beef and Yorkshire pudding,' Paora advised her. 'I had that last night and it's very good.'

'Sister Eliza would be better dining only on the fish,' the other wife said from his other side. 'Beef is too rich for a bad sailor.'

'Truly, Sister Lydia, I do not think you have spent enough time in my company on this voyage to know my state of health.'

'I was only –' began Lydia, looking to her husband. He remained staring fixedly at his bill of fare, though a muscle twitched in his cheek with irritation. Lydia sighed. After a moment he laid down his card.

'You did well not to respond, my dear. It would be beneficial to our general mood, Eliza, if you could exercise the same degree of self-control.'

'And you were ill on the voyage out, three years ago. Do you not remember? You could neither eat nor sleep,' Lydia chimed in, hard on Everett's heels.

'It was not the sea making me ill,' whispered Eliza quietly. William did not know if she intended her sister-wife to hear her or not. If the other woman had heard she did not respond, choosing instead to smile brightly at the steward who had come to take their order.

After the soup and fish course, William ate hugely of what Paora had recommended and ordered cabinet pudding to follow, while beside him Sister Eliza picked at a Welsh rarebit and took frequent sips of water.

In three weeks she would be with Matthias, she told herself. It would be easier then to turn her gaze from her husband and Lydia and their painfully obvious happiness. She remembered Matthias as he was when they had left: his flat brown hair, like hers; his father's smooth olive skin; his own plump knees and high querying voice. Now she knew, had known for a year or more, that she had made a mistake in going to New Zealand. She should have stayed with her child and let the others go on the mission alone. How foolish she had been in the early days of her husband's second marriage, how racked with jealousy. Now she was beyond that, beyond embarrassment and shame, either for them or for herself. She wanted to sit Matthias on her knee and hear his voice, feel the warmth of his sweet whispering breath in her ear.

Paora and Everett were discussing the travel arrangements to Salt Lake, the many trains from California to Utah. Between them, Lydia sat as deep in thought as her sister-wife, her mind set on the same child though she longed for one of her own. She was young and healthy and loved her husband dearly. Why, then, had she and Everett not been blessed? It was her husband's belief and comfort that the Lord had not wanted them to start a family during the mission, but that He would send them many children on their return. After the wedding in Mexico, the trio had travelled to Los Angeles and taken a steamer. Some days, particularly early in the mission when Lydia had suspected Eliza was becoming unhinged with jealousy and longing, Eliza had talked of nothing but Matthias. It was as if she thought that by imagining the routine of his day, his playmates in the family he had been placed with, his toys and distractions, she might have him with her, the shade of him. Now she hardly mentioned him. No matter, thought Lydia: she herself could be mother if the woman who bore him had forgotten him. He was hers in part anyway: he was her husband's son.

Eliza felt Lydia's eyes upon her and looked across the table. Did she detect antagonism in the younger wife's face? Her water glass halted before her lips as she searched Lydia's eyes. Surely not, she must have imagined it. Sister Lydia would never relinquish her high moral ground for a moment: she was the wife who had her husband's well-being always in the forefront of her mind and to that end acquiesced to his senior wife in myriad small ways. Though not in the largest way, thought Eliza. Her husband had promised her that young Miss Allred, as she was then, would be his spiritual wife, and Eliza had taken that to mean only . . . Oh, but she was sick of it. It had occupied her silent mind for far too long now, the treadmill of it turning at various speeds, forwards or backwards, and she was none the wiser. The law said plural marriages were wrong, which was why they and many others were forced to travel to Mexico for their solemnisation, but hadn't the Prophet written that plural marriage was 'the thread which runs from the beginning to the end of the holy Gospel of Salvation' and that it was 'from eternity to eternity?'

Lydia, who had ceased chewing for a moment, resumed, swallowed and smiled at her. Breaking her gaze, Eliza put down her glass and, avoiding the querying glance of her husband, excused herself from the table.

William watched her go, her small quick steps beneath her long skirts carrying her the length of the saloon. As always, her head was bowed and he noticed that the hand that was not engaged in holding her skirts away from her hurrying feet was clenched in a fist at her side. The clash of plate against plate drew his attention back to the table. Brother Everett had pushed his half-finished meal away from him and had lifted his hand to his eyes. His remaining wife stroked his arm, a momentary, comforting caress.

The approaching bad weather that William had seen from the deck enveloped the ship just after eight. The *Moana*, which had seemed so vast and dependable when she was tethered at the wharf, was now a tiny expendable speck. Towering waves rose above her smoke stack; she shuddered up their flanks and fell giddily down their slick, retreating backs.

Leaning against her closed cabin door, Sister Eliza surveyed her apartment, the so-called 'Ladies' Boudoir' with its gold toilet fittings, leather writing desk and wide bed. It was wasted on her, she thought – another extravagance of her husband's. Why should he want her so close to him? If he would deprive her of love, then so he should in other ways, to be consistent. She struggled against the list of the ship to lift her trunk down from the luggage rack. Tucked deep in one corner, under her winter dress, wrapped in a napkin, was a small bottle labelled 'chlorodyne'. For a moment, while she unstoppered it and drank deeply – one, two, three draughts – the world narrowed to contain only herself, her shaking hands, and the promised oblivion from the brown phial. It had been her comfort and stay when Everett and Lydia had been on the other side of a closed door as husband and wife and, later, during the long months when they had been in the South Island among the Maoris. It was necessary for Eliza to stay behind in Auckland, Everett had said. The Saints in New Zealand adhered to the Woodruff Manifesto and did not make plural marriages.

The sweet liquor coated her mouth, the taste of peppermint, liquorice and treacle; the spirit, chloroform, ether and morphine dulled her mind and heart. As she replaced the trunk, she caught a glimpse of herself in the mirror, her pale, lined and angry face, her lank hair falling from its pins. No wonder Everett was captivated by his younger wife: he was, after all, only a man, with all the desires and needs of his kind.

As she balanced on the edge of the bed to unbutton her boots, the ship heaved and fell and the violence of the motion filled her with joy. Perhaps the Lord would see fit to have the ship swallowed by the sea: perhaps He had decided to take them all tonight. By virtue of the lifeboats there would be some survivors but she, Eliza, would be grateful for the weight of waterlogged skirts, the elemental filling of her lungs. Sealed as she was to Everett for ever, he would join her again in Heaven, as would Matthias when his time came. In the meantime the Lord would have her as His servant, His angel, and she could watch her child from the clouds.

Fully clothed, she lay back on her bed, closed her eyes and pictured the little ship rolling in the tumescent sea and prayed for a monolithic wave, freakish, ferocious – a watery saviour to end her suffering.

The steward responsible for co-ordinating entertainment in the Grand Saloon introduced Mrs Myers as a classically trained singer who, though she preferred to sing lieder, would favour the assembled company with some light opera. Haltingly, he read from a small card which Mrs Myers had pressed into his hand in the wings. She nodded encouragingly at him when he finished and swept on to take her place at the music stand. Unaccompanied, she launched into a song from *The Mikado*.

'A wandering minstrel, I –' she trilled, waving her hands in gestures suggestive of rags and tatters, ballads, songs and snatches, and lullabies. As she embarked on the third verse, a large wave caught the ship broadside and the music stand skittered across the stage and crashed onto the floor below. Mrs Myers continued undaunted, for she knew the song off by heart, and moved closer to the edge of the stage, her arms spread expansively. Perspiration glazed her brow and her face set in a desperate expression, her voice straining louder to retain her escaping audience. Stewards hurried from table to table, dampening the tablecloths and flipping up the fiddles at the edges to prevent laden plates from taking the same gravitous course. Everett seized the opportunity afforded by the commotion to stand and offer his wife his arm.

'We will retire to the Music Saloon. Please accompany us, Brother William.'

Many of the diners were likewise vacating their tables, leaning into one another against the motion of the ship. They bottle-necked at the door to the vestibule. The chief steward moved among them, comforting the paler and more apprehensive.

'A spot of heavy weather,' he repeated. 'Nothing to worry about.'

Paora led the others away from the companionway, which was crowded with diners arriving and those leaving, and through an external door to the lee side of the ship. The gale outside was wild and exhilarating – they bent into the wind and moved in single file against the saloon walls to the midships stairs, shouting to one another to take care. There were drops of rain now and again: the dark sky was low and thick, the earlier star obscured.

The Music Saloon steward had turned on the lights. He sat on his stool beside the switch that controlled the electric fans, watching with wry amusement a group gathered at the piano. Seated at the keyboard was a young man William recognised as the pipe-smoker from their day of departure. In a pleasant light tenor he was singing a music-hall song, much to the amusement of his companions who passed between them a silver flask. One of the ladies, flushed and giggly, reclined in an easy chair and held aloft a wine glass. Bowing excessively, an older gentleman replenished it for her and she licked her carmine lips. William watched them with an edge of envy and nostalgia. There was a time in his life, not so very long ago, when he would have joined a group such as this and ingratiated himself with the ladies. He would have perceived them as he had the gale outside, exciting and dangerous, the infinite possibilities of their fates whirling around them. This evening he was determined to see them only as sinners; to pity their dark, deluded lives.

'We have had some trouble with this lot –' began Everett quietly in his ear. He broke off as the singer, joined by the men of the group, entered a rousing chorus. The words 'bloomers' and 'ankles' and 'snowy bosom' met Brother Everett's now-enraged ears. A few swift strides bore him to the piano where he flicked its lid shut. The musician only just withdrew his hands in time.

'There are ladies present.' Everett glared at him, then sniffed the air. 'Have you been smoking in here? Please confine that revolting practice to the adjoining room, which is designed for that purpose.'

'Listen, Mister. This is a big ship. You and your wowser friends have got a lot of other places to go.' The young man opened the piano and the gentleman who had previously filled the lady's glass staggered against the rocking floor to stand protectively by his friend. Below his unnaturally black hair, his eyes were luridly bloodshot. The piano gave out a few teasing notes.

'Mr Everett Ridge is a God-fearing Yankee,' the young man extemporised, 'with lots of money in the bankee –' The woman on the chair was seized by a fit of laughter.

'Percy!' she gasped. 'You'll be the death of us all.'

Percy brought his left hand up to the keys to give his song a rollicking bass and continued.

'Too many wives'd give a man a tumour – maybe that's why he has no sense of humour –'

Everett grabbed the man by the collar and threw him backwards off the piano stool. His companion, almost in the same moment, brought the wine bottle up in an arc, red wine flowing from its neck, and connected it soundly with Everett's head, while another of their party vaulted over a settee to front up to William and Paora, his fists raised. Paora closed his hands over the fists, pushed them down, while William, misreading the Maori's pacifist intentions, clocked their threatener's jaw with dislocating force.

'Brother William!' Lydia reached up to restrain him from a second blow and pushed past him to reach her husband, who lay prostrate beside his provoker on the Brussels rug. She was interrupted in her progress by the reclining actress, whose hilarity had given way to hysteria and who now rose to her feet to block Sister Lydia's way. The other women of the party, five of them, backed into the lee of the wall, while the remaining men began a rowdy and violent assault on Paora and William, who were outnumbered. William saw Paora fall and was knocked to the ground himself a moment later. A pair of highly polished boots – Percy's – delivered a bruising kick to his stomach. Above the fracas came the frantic tones of the steward's voice, pleading for them all to stop. Another voice, that of the Smoking Room steward, joined his, and blearily, through puffy eyes, William watched their black-trousered legs push against those of his assailants. A sharp pain flashed in the fine bones of his right hand and travelled the length of his arm as he forced himself to sit up to see Paora, his colour making him an easy suspect, being frog-marched by the two stewards out onto the deck. His collar had come unpinned and hung from one shoulder. William took a step towards him and would have gone to his assistance but his knees, on which he had heavily landed during the fight, complained fiercely. Instead he fell into the nearest easy chair and held a handkerchief to the blood gathering on his cheek.

The Music Saloon steward returned and approached Everett, who was sitting up now with Lydia hovering beside him. The theatrical party was dispersing, the man who had wielded the wine bottle assisting the musician, the others escorting their women. There was an uncomfortable, thick silence while they left, none of either party meeting the eyes of the others. The last of them struggled with the door against the gale, which now howled around the ship, closing it finally with a bang, and their footsteps died away along the alleyway.

Sister Lydia began helping her husband to his feet. He was groggy, unbalanced, and she would have taken him immediately to his stateroom to attend to his wounds but the steward stopped them.

'The captain is on his way – my mate is fetching him,' he said. He was a man of fifty or so, grey haired, with a nicotine-stained moustache. 'Here –' He pulled the stool away from the piano and guided Everett to it. 'Perhaps, Mrs Ridge, could you away to your berth? What the captain will have to say is not for ladies' ears.'

'It's quite all right, thank you,' Lydia responded frostily. 'I want to speak to the captain myself.'

At the news of the brawl, Captain Carey hurried from the bridge to the upper deck. Tension of this sort sometimes erupted among his crew, occasionally among the stewards, but rarely among the passengers, still less among those in first class. He would have to speak firmly to the American. In the Music Saloon the steward was sweeping up soil and broken pieces of ceramic from a fallen aspidistra. A wicker chair was turned on its side with a broken leg. The New Zealander, whom Carey gathered was a recent convert, slumped in a chair clutching a blood-soaked handkerchief. His wounds appeared worse than his companion's, but the woman with them, Mrs Ridge, paid no attention to him. She had brought her husband a glass of water, which he irritably pushed away. His upper lip was swollen on one side almost to his nostrils. The captain stood before him.

'The Music Saloon is for the use of all passengers, sir. If you disapprove of our Percy Barrett then kindly shift yourself elsewhere –'

'Our Percy Barrett?' interrupted Lydia. Her eyes were flashing and her hands rose almost to her hips before she remembered her manners and dropped them.

'He's our star passenger. He and the rest of the Australian Williamsons. They're off to San Francisco with *The Two Little Vagabonds.* Marvellous show. Seen it myself and it's capital. We're honoured to have them aboard. I understand you struck the first blow.'

Everett said nothing, hung his head like a chastised child.

'Not very Christian of you, sir, if you don't mind me saying so. Do you require the ship's doctor? Either you or your friend?'

'There are no broken bones,' Lydia replied for her husband. 'I will take care of him.'

'Goodnight then, sir. Madam.'

'Goodnight, Captain,' said Lydia, looking now towards William. He longed for her to come to him, to lay her cool hands on his hot brow. He wondered if she had seen him in the thick of the fight. He had lain about him with great effect until three men had set upon him at once. He had smelt drink on their breath, tobacco in their clothes and it may as well have been the stink of sulphur. Any curiosity about them had dissipated. He knew their lives, their facile need to impress one another with their grubby wits, the morality of their women. William himself had once sampled one of their kind – in Christchurch, an actress, a pretty little thing from the chorus line of a travelling opera. She had given him the pox.

'Go to bed, Brother,' Lydia called over her shoulder. 'We will see you tomorrow.' She walked with her arm around her husband's waist and the door of their stateroom closed after them.

William craned his head around and deduced from the sudden pain that jabbed him in the base of his skull that he'd also jarred his neck. The steward returned to his chair and took up a newspaper, the room now set to rights. He would wait a while, William decided, letting his head rest gently against the back of his chair and closing his eyes. Blood thumped at his temples, roused by the curl and thump of his fists, his outrage at the assault of his friend. What would Myra do if she were here? he wondered. Would she be tender and solicitous, or would she quiver and weep? No doubt she would fail him again as she had on so many occasions since their marriage: her placid, sure exterior cracking, breaking apart to reveal her quaking, tremulous heart. Her voice, though quiet and sweet like his mother's, had grown steadily more tentative and hesitant. Even as he would push her away in fury or disappointment she would cling to him. How completely she had deceived him: she had executed a neat reversal of the roles he had intended them to play. He felt his old rage returning, churning his stomach.

If he had not injured his knees he would have fallen to prayer for comfort. Instead he tipped his face towards the swaying ceiling and opened his eyes. Just inches away, casting a soft shadow over him from the flickering overhead lights, was a pale and hollow-eyed face, framed with lank dark hair. He startled, went to push it away. It wasn't real, it was the knock on the head bringing him visions of Myra –

'Are you all right? What has happened? I was asleep.' It was Eliza, quiet in her stockinged feet, bending over him.

He looked away. Rain lashed at the portholes, streaking the glass. Beyond it was the endless dark of the ocean and the night. William shrugged, gestured towards the steward on his stool. He didn't want to talk about it in front of him.

'You must sleep like the dead,' he said finally. Sister Eliza's hair was in disarray, her black dress crumpled.

'I do. Yes. It is such a blessed escape, isn't it? Sleep, I mean. Though death would be a greater one.' The sister spoke quickly, words tumbling over one another, as if she were drunk, thought William, or drugged.

'You are not yourself, Sister. What was it that woke you?'

She made an attempt to smooth her hair.

'Raised voices?' he persisted. 'The plant falling?' He gestured to the plant stand, empty of its pot. Eliza shook her head.

'My husband and sister-wife,' she whispered, nervous of the steward's hearing, 'going to their room. I had taken a sleeping draught but the walls are thin. I had hoped to sleep for longer. What is the time?'

William pulled his watch from his fob pocket. 'Just on ten,' he said, tired now. He would retire to the privacy of his room. The voyage, now that he and Brother Everett had made enemies of the Australians, stretched interminably before him. As he hauled himself out of his chair, the ship gave a shudder, her bow lifted, the floor of the Music Saloon lifted towards the north and Eliza lost her balance and fell against him. She smelt strangely of grass, or hay: the damp of a poorly roofed barn. He held her thin shoulders for a moment, until she groped away from him and held on to the back of a settee that slid, as she reached it, to the full extent of its leg rope, some six to eight inches, and she lurched forward with it, catching her foot in the hem of her dress. She would have fallen but for William's quick response: one lunging step around the sliding arm to catch her. He pulled her down onto a two-seater behind them as the ship bucked, rose, slid interminably. He felt suddenly nauseous, his skin prickling against the contact with Sister Eliza's hands, which remained spread against his chest, her forehead below his shoulder. The lights dimmed so that the ship could employ all the force of its engines to hold course in the gale. The elderly steward, although undisturbed by the weather, gave his newspaper an irritated crack now that he could not perceive it in the gloom, and folded it away back to its hiding place between his cabinet and the wall. Above the saloon roof, the wind screamed and choked in the lattice of the derricks, flipped and whistled in the wires of the attenuated masts.

William brought his hands to the woman's wrists, pushed her back against the cushion in the opposing corner of the settee and remembered Everett's words about her in the deckhouse cabin. She could not have seemed any less like a sensible mentor. As he moved her away, her eyes flashed at him, their dull green enlivened by alarm before they closed and remained so, her head rolling from side to side with the motion of the ship. In the brown light her complexion was ghostly, devoid of its usual liverish yellow. It improved her, thought William, watching her. Behind them the steward stood and made his way to the internal stairs at the aft end of the cabin, which led eventually to the crew's water-closet. He walked easily, seemingly able to predict the force and direction of the ship's roll.

'Sister Eliza?' whispered William, thinking she had perhaps fainted with fear until he saw how her hand, clutching the polished talon of the wooden arm, betrayed consciousness. 'Shall we pray?' he asked.

Above the stiff neck of her gown her throat moved as if in savage, silent laughter. Her face remained impassive.

'Sister?'

'Pray for what, Brother?' The sarcasm weighing her final word was wounding. She paused to lick her dry lips. William felt his nausea rise again, quelled it.

'For release? To rise to the Lord without any further distraction? A distraction is all this is, after all. A design of God's, or Satan's, to throw us about and alarm the furniture.'

William was appalled. 'How may you confuse the will of God with that of Satan?'

'God and Satan are equally occupied in the testing of our resolve –' She moved her throat in the same odd manner again and sat up sharply, her hand over her mouth. William turned away from her, disgusted. He could not bear it if she were ill. He wondered now if he would be able to make his way out to the deckhouse, but a palm, smooth and damp, slid over his lap to his clenched knuckles and stung his grazed skin.

'Yes. Let us kneel down.' She was pulling with her other hand at his wrist to draw him down to his knees. Pain with the teeth of a bow-saw ran the length of his thigh, resisting his forward slide. She arranged her skirt and knelt before him, looking up into his face. He couldn't meet her eye.

'I have never confused the will of the Lord with the mischief of the devil,' he said quietly. 'I am not interested in your theorising. The Church has them set well apart.'

'I am sorry you are perturbed. I did not intend you to be so. Pray with me.'

There was such vulnerability in her that he glanced at her against his will and saw that she had bowed her head. He had seen it bowed so often, he realised, knew how the grey flecks shone on either side of her fierce parting, how the odd silver hair threaded the dark brown. He knelt on the flaming agony of his kneecaps, his left surely worse than his right, but found he couldn't do as she did and bow his head. His nose was quite possibly broken – gravity drew fresh blood to the ridges of his face.

'Dear Lord,' she began, so softly he could barely hear her, 'If you should see fit to take us now, Brother William and myself, then do not hesitate. Spare the other poor creatures of this ship, from the men who labour around us to the men who lie in bed, and take us in their stead –'

'But I do not want to die!' William stood, realised how loudly he had cried out against the wailing of the storm. Rage, black and ungovernable, closed around him in a sudden punishing fist and he saw one of his hands reach out for Sister Eliza's shoulder. He shook it, dragged it up, pulled her towards him and she cried out, thinly, like a bird.

'But you must! Do you not understand what you did that night in the bush, the story you related to Brother Everett? You had poisoned yourself with drink so that you might die.'

'You misunderstand, Sister Eliza.'

At the far end of the saloon, beyond the piano, the door to Everett's stateroom silently opened. The light had been extinguished some time ago. Brother Ridge watched the two figures standing close together and saw how the woman's arm stole around the man's waist and how her head leaned softly against his chest as if it were returning to a place it knew well. Neither his wife nor Brother William made any attempt to pull away from each other: they had not seen him.

'I did not want that, and you must not want that either,' came William's voice. It was tight, higher than usual.

Brother Everett closed his door, though another one opened simultaneously in his mind. Through that portal lay a revelation – not a true one of course, but the type that showed a practical course of action, a marrying of temporal needs. A man required this instinct: it was exercised in the conduct of business and church affairs, it was a divine test of intelligence, an invitation to aid God's plan. He returned to his bed, giving thanks for this generous removal of his guilt and daily blame. Groundwork would have to be laid, he told himself. He would have to take it slowly and, with God willing, he would succeed.

CHAPTER 13

Late summer was warm and damp and it seemed to continue so, from the confines of the house, through autumn until the winter came in earnest. Myra absorbed herself in her babies and the goings-on of the house, and the days drifted by, not unpleasantly, with little to distinguish one from another. Slowly she returned to the peace of mind she had known with the Waylands. She did not long for William at all. In fact, if Myra had had a confessional nature, which she did not, believing her thoughts and feelings to be of no interest to anyone else, she might have remarked that she was relieved that he had gone. As it was, with no need or experience of intimate conversation, she did not value or examine her own private thoughts. She did not think of the future, only of the present. The idea of William executing his days on the other side of the world, miles away from her and her children, gave her a sort of strange, barely acknowledged comfort. There had been no letter from him, and if Ellen's calculations were right, gleaned from an atlas and a ruler and a visit to the Union Company's office, he had been in Salt Lake for some five months. The details of the time of his departure were still hazy to Myra. He had told her he wanted to leave the moment she had seen him, but until the twins were three days old it wasn't that she knew he had carried out his plan. Since the birth she had asked for him repeatedly. 'He is out,' answered her mother-in-law or Ellen.

It was Mary the maid who had told her in the end, and with a puzzling degree of vehemence.

'He's on the ship that went at the beginning of the week,' she had said one stifling February day during Myra's lying-in, 'to America.' Her voice was muffled, coming as it did from under the bed as she retrieved the chamber pot. 'He's been gone for days!'

Myra had a sense of herself going out to meet this news and bringing it back at arm's length, turning it this way and that, the perplexing shape of it. He has left me. The words formed chiming in her mind. He has left me again. For the next few days she kept silent, her heart longing to dwell on him, but her mind knowing it mustn't. The two impulses cancelled each other out and left her numb and dry. When she slept she had a peculiar, childlike recurring dream of herself as a tiny figure trapped in a bone china cup, the walls around her circling smooth, white and unyielding.

Then, one afternoon towards the end of her time, she was roused from a dozing, semi-conscious state by Blanche and her mother-in-law, their consternation over her hair and rumpled bed. They set her to rights against the pillows and tucked the covers tight over her tender breasts, to make her ready for her father-in-law, who waited on a chair in the hall.

'How are you, Mrs McQuiggan?' He deemed it necessary to address the young woman formally on this their first meeting. Here she was, his son's wife, the mother of his grandchildren, and he was only just making her acquaintance. On his way up the stairs, supported by Henry, he had suddenly been seized by a curiosity as strong as any he had felt for many years. What calibre of person was this young woman? An Australian, who had been dependent on charity when she made William's acquaintance, in a Home of some sort. The child of a vicar. He had gleaned only one or two of the facts, had half-listened to their telling. Since William's return from Australia, he had imagined her to be somehow the female counterpart of his son, her nature equal parts sensuality and instinct, unpredictable and wearying. In the two weeks that had passed since the birth of the twins, his impression had been modified. Alithea had spoken highly of the young woman, her fortitude during the confinement and her almost pathetic gratitude for the family's hospitality since.

She was not much to look at. He surprised himself with the observation and supposed it occurred to him only because he had always assumed William would be drawn to beauty to match his own. The room was hot, airless, with the same peculiar cloying smell of the lying-in room he remembered from the birth of his own children. His daughter-in-law was examining her hands, which clasped and released each other in her lap as they had done since wife and daughter had left them alone.

'Congratulations,' he tried, in as gentle a voice as he knew. 'You have done very well.'

'Perhaps if I had had sons William would not have left.' The words slipped out before she realised she had even thought them. If her body didn't ache so, its young vitality forced to founder in the stale sheets, then perhaps she would have more reserve. For days she had wanted to get up, to walk down the hall and go out into the garden. From the window she had seen a young magnolia in the garden below, cool and glossy leafed, and there was a rose bed full of heavy summer blooms, petals spiralling away from the heads in the hot northerly wind. She had lain for so long in this upper-storey room that she felt she had come away loose from the earth.

She censured herself. The old man was seating himself at the duchesse, turning his chair to face her.

'I should not concern myself with that idea if I were you.' Elisha sat with his stick between his knees, long purplish fingers curling around the carved ivory head. 'William would have left in any case. He was blind with intent. You must have seen him so yourself, at other times.'

At first Myra wondered if she had properly heard him. He was looking at her directly and she forced herself to meet his eyes. He returned a kind though critical gaze. Suddenly she realised, with tremendous relief, that William's father could see the patterns, the light and shade of her husband's behaviour. She was not the only creature on God's earth who struggled to understand him.

'How long was your association with my son before you made the voyage to Auckland?' he asked, and Myra knew from his deliberating tones that the question was most likely one of a list he had prepared. William did not look like his father at all, she thought. He was big-boned, like his mother. Justice McQuiggan looked as if he had never been very tall and was now even less so. He was stooped and crumbling.

'Two weeks,' she answered, remembering that it could well have been the next day had it been possible. A tremendous, magical, frightening haste had engulfed them from the moment they met. She had given him some money from her tiny reserve and he had bought tickets on the next available ship.

On that first day, when Matron had sent her from the room to show William to the door, she had found herself answering his questions. She had gone with him right to the gate, where the light of the summer day had seemed to fall glittering upon them. He was a working man – she saw the knocks and abrasions on his hands, but he was richly dressed, his hair shining.

'And so you are a recent arrival in Sydney?' he had asked her, all curiosity and health, opening the gate so that it stood between them. At his shoulder the honeysuckle hedge thrummed with bees.

'I am, yes. Nearly a year.'

'A whole year! And do you enjoy the confines of those walls?' His questions leapt about, like flames in a wind, baffling and entrancing her.

'I – I have never thought about it.'

'Where did you live before?'

'In Yarrabin.'

The young man raised an eyebrow comically and laughed. 'You Australians have such names for places! And your father. Where is he?'

'At rest,' she said, simply. She gave a nervous glance up towards the windows, the three levels of arched eyes that gave out onto the street. The young man brought a caressing hand to the front of his waistcoat. It was startlingly modern: Myra had never seen one like it before. It was bright yellow, collarless and edged all around the front with russia braid. He was close enough, the thickness of the gate away, for her to breathe in the scent that rose from his clothes. They were new and clean, the body beneath them warm and vital, with a scent of its own that seemed to draw her closer to him, to make her want to lay her head on his chest.

'Come with me,' he had said suddenly, reaching behind her and tugging on the bow of her apron. Myra had laughed, astonished and thrilled by his temerity. He took her laugh for encouragement and tugged a second time. The bow flew open and Myra, her heart pounding, was lifting the starched white apron over her head.

They had gone off down the street together, the apron left hooked over the gate-post, and Myra had returned that evening only to gather up her few belongings while William waited in the hall below with Matron, who was irate and accusatory. Myra supposed now that there must have been a small scandal, one contained within the walls of the Home, but she couldn't have helped herself if she had tried. Perhaps it was all the months alone in the house after her father died that had taught her to please herself. And how she pleased herself, carrying her little box down the Home's stairs – and she pleased William too.

They had taken separate rooms in the same boarding house and lingered together wherever its damp surrounds allowed them – over meals in the dust-laden dining room, in halls and stairwells. The intensity with which she longed to touch him seemed no longer comforting but terrible, as if he would burn her. He seemed to know that, though how he could when she could scarcely meet his eyes she didn't know. He would caress her lightly on the hand, and once, burningly outside her bedroom door, on her throat. She was a girl who'd scarcely made a friend in her lonely eighteen years and now she had a young man who took her to dine in hotels and, on both Saturdays before they steamed, for a carriage ride to the Parramatta River and a wide yellow beach. Even when he was ready each morning to leave the boarding house in his work clothes, his finery stripped away, she was filled with an urgent, secret desire. She had no idea how to satisfy it. It was something shameful, of that she was certain. She wanted him closer than he would allow her.

'Myra?' The old man had been speaking and she had not heard a word of it.

'I'm sorry, Mr McQuiggan,' she murmured. Her legs shifted restlessly in the bed.

'It was a personal question and I had no right to ask it.' He sounded querulous, crabby, as if his irritation were not with himself but with her. The stick shifted to lie against the chair beside him.

'Please repeat it,' she implored. She could not bear his discomfort.

'I would like to know if you accepted his proposal of marriage before or after you knew of his wealth.' The question reached her ears sibilant, voiceless, and she was perturbed by it.

'Before, I think. It was not like that. I knew . . . I could see, of course, that he was not a poor man. But I was −' She wished she could arrange her thoughts. 'I had no need of his money. I had a little of my own.'

The old man nodded. 'From your father?'

'Yes.'

Mr McQuiggan went on with a question so startling that she felt the breath catch in her throat.

'How long had you been at the farm before the child was born?'

'Almost a year and a half.'

He relaxed visibly then. It appeared that the girl had fallen for William, but had maintained her Christian principle and he in turn had fallen for her, for whatever reason. There was a stillness in her, a quiet peace. Perhaps that was what his son had wanted, as a balm to his own internal clangour.

'I will leave you to rest.' Mr McQuiggan stood. 'Forgive me for my prying. Your marriage was another event in William's life from which he excluded me. I admit my response at the time of your nuptials was not a positive one, but I am encouraged now, Mrs McQuiggan.'

It was soon after his visit to Myra that Elisha's wife and daughters noticed a new calm in him, and soon after that that they felt something in him give way, a release of the tension that must have previously sustained him. He made one last mysterious excursion out of the house, then gave up on the daily assault of the stairs, took to his bed and prepared to die. At first, with the doctor's help, Blanche and Alithea managed his care.

While the rain fell steadily in the sedate chill of August, there was a visitor, a man who came to see Myra on two consecutive days. By this time, the middle of winter, the stronger and more curious of the twins was already trying to sit up, beaming as she did so at whoever watched her, whether it was her mother, grandmother or one of her aunts. Her Uncle Henry made Dora frown, as if she sensed the anxiety of the supervising adult. He was delighted with the little creatures, more so than with his cats who would have fallen entirely from his favour had he been allowed to hold the infants. As it was, the cats still suffered his vice-like embraces and he could only gaze at his nieces, while either Blanche or his mother hovered nearby. The twins had brilliant, clear-blue eyes ringed with black lashes, like William. When Henry was with them, it was as if two small versions of his brother fixed him with critical attention. He loved them, their little plump hands spread on a rug or coverlet or grasping for a proffered toy. Joy took his eye more often than Dora, being smaller and quieter and less given to crying. More often than the other she was left propped in her perambulator while her sister was passed from hip to hip. Joy was easier for Henry to concentrate on, to take in the small details of her fingernails, the fair whorls of her hair.

On the morning of the first visit, Henry blundered into the morning room on the eastern side of the house. It was, in Alithea's opinion, entirely misnamed because it lacked a northern window. On winter days such as this, the sun – if there was one – was so low it could scarcely penetrate the glass. By noon it had gone from the cool wall, arcing low in the north towards the west. Mary had lit a fire and Blanche and his mother had recently, prior to Henry's arrival, been engrossed in their handiwork. Abandoned, Alithea's arrascene trailed threads of silk and wool from its circular frame down the pedestal of its stand, the needle jabbed in for safe-keeping at the top. Blanche sat on a stool, her painting on its small easel ignored while she watched Myra lift the screaming baby from the pram. Alithea rocked the remaining child vigorously, though she did not require it.

'Henry's cloth!' said Alithea quickly, and Blanche rose to take the faded grey square from the back of a bentwood, set against the wall. She spread it in a captain's chair, reserved especially for her brother.

'Shall I put it closer to the fire?' she asked him. 'Are you cold, Henry?'

He shook his head and went to stand by his mother to watch Joy who gazed up at him, her fingers in her mouth, a prodigious dribble soaking into the frill of her gown.

'This child should wear a bib,' remarked Alithea, abruptly ending her rocking, though the pram continued to reverberate on its springs.

'Yes, they both should,' said Myra, sitting now and placing her baby on her lap.

'Are they getting their teeth?' asked Blanche. Henry bent his face to peer into Joy's mouth, but he could only see her wet plump lips against her hand.

'You were a dreadful dribbler, I remember,' Alithea said. Blanche giggled.

'I was not, Mother! Don't say such things!'

'Well, you were – though you won't remember.'

'I'm sure Henry dribbled more than I did,' said Blanche playfully, squeezing her brother's shoulder. She didn't observe, as Myra did, the pained, startled expression on her mother's face. The older lady shifted slightly, inside her clothes, away from her son, before returning to her chair.

'Henry was a lovely baby,' she said stiffly, taking up her needle. And he had been, for Henry's problems all stemmed from a single careless moment. If she had not allowed Ellen to hold him when he was only a few weeks old, then the child would not have dropped him and the baby would not have caught his head on the edge of a wooden chair as he fell. There had been several occasions, as Ellen grew up and Henry failed to, that the mother had given vent to her frustrations as vitriol and blame, laying the responsibility for the boy's condition squarely on the little girl's drooping shoulders. She wondered again, as she had so many times, whether Ellen remembered those turgid scenes. They had continued until she was about nine, when Alithea had found the resolve never to mention it again, not to anyone. Henry was what he was. There he was now, sitting on his chair and edging it closer and closer to the fire, his boots extended, and she knew that as surely as night follows day she would soon be compelled to warn him to go no further. She peered at the china clock on the mantelpiece above him, a mass of pink roses and gilt leaves, the object's function almost overawed by its ornament. If her eyes did not fail her it was nearly midday, when the twins would be taken to the kitchen to be fed and Ellen would return from the gabled, turreted school at the top of Parnell Rise for luncheon.

Carefully watching her mother-in-law, Myra saw her gaze shift to the clock. Perhaps the old lady was tired. She would take the twins early, then.

'Say goodbye to Grandmother,' she told Dora, standing with the child against her. Dora lunged sideways, extending her round fist towards the old lady. The women smiled and Myra drew the baby close again and kissed her, before she laid her in the perambulator, opposite her sister.

As she manoeuvred the grand, bulky conveyance – which had been a surprising present from severe Ellen – out into the hallway, there was a loud knock on the front door, followed by an insistent ring. The twins' heads swivelled in the direction of the noise and Myra wondered if she should open the door or wait for Mary. Mary had very sure ideas about her role and inadvertently, once or twice, Myra had infringed upon them.

There was no reciprocal sound of footsteps from the dark reaches of the hall and the knocking renewed. Myra could see the shape of a man through the double frosted lights. His right hand still knocking, he was lifting his other to ring the bell.

'For pity's sake!' Alithea had arrived beside her. 'Mr McQuiggan is asleep!'

Myra pushed past the pram and opened the door to someone who was familiar to her, his red face and small features, his pale watery eyes, though she could not think for a moment where from. Was it Sydney? Or more recent than that, the farm? The package under his arm, it was a picture perhaps.

'Mr Baxter!'

He bowed slightly and held up the flat brown-wrapped parcel. 'I have something for you.' Behind him, his overcoat and hat dripped rainwater from the veranda hook.

'Who is it, Myra?' Alithea called from behind her. 'If it's a tradesman tell him to go around to the back.'

'No – it's –' Myra opened the door wider to show Alithea. 'Do come in,' she added, feeling that now she had taken a step into the hall she would have to admit him. How would she explain him to her mother-in-law? No word had passed between them about the other child, its birth or death, its brief existence.

Mr Baxter saved her. 'I'm a photographer, ma'am,' he said. 'Professional. Mostly scenic and occasionally domestic. I took a picture for Mrs McQuiggan a year or so back and thought she would be liking it.'

Dora gave out a loud shout, which visibly startled her grandmother and drew the photographer's eye unwillingly to the pram. Joy regarded him steadily but Dora, hungry and cross, took a deep breath to power a longer, louder wail. Alithea cast her attention up the stairs in the direction of her husband's room.

'Take him down to the kitchen and conduct the business there,' she said, hurriedly, helping to turn the pram towards the back of the house.

At the kitchen table Gordon was mashing kumara and apple together for the twins' midday meal. Her usually stern countenance softened as the black snout of the pram breached the kitchen with Myra behind, but froze again at the sight of the man. She nodded at him, curtly.

'This is Mr Baxter,' said Myra. 'He is a photographer.' She pushed the twins across the flagged floor towards Gordon. Dora craned her head around for the cook, whom she already loved above all others owing to her customary proximity to food. She waved her arms, entrancing Joy, who took hold of one and rubbed her wet gums along the woollen sleeve. One rounded spoonful hovered towards the babies and both little mouths opened.

'Shall I –?' asked Mr Baxter. He motioned towards a cleared spot on the table and drew closer to it with his parcel. Myra nodded.

'What is it?' asked the cook, leaning to see, as Mr Baxter laid the photograph on the table and began to unwrap it. Myra heard the crackling of the brown paper pushed away from string, the liquid enthusiasm of Dora's mastication, the other daughter's increasing whimpers for the spoon, and watched the rain falling beyond the kitchen window in a torrent. The sky was uniformly silver, diffused with the light of a pallid winter sun miles in the heavens above the tight cloud.

'There!' announced Mr Baxter.

At first glance it appeared as though the child floated in space. The white shawl gleamed in the centre of the picture; the dark room about it melted away to black.

Then she made out the shape of the chair legs, the shel-lacked forms connecting with a darker floor. The two candles glowed crookedly either side of the child's head, a tiny sphere which was only a shade darker than her wraps. Shadows darkened her starveling face at the temples, in her skinny cheeks, while two translucent eyelids returned the captured flicker of the flames. The weightless hands, minute, their grip on temporal life weakened and gone for ever, lay softly against each other on the resisting weave of the shawl. The parlour of the house Pukekaroro enveloped Myra with its memory, a whirl of that day. She recalled how William had made her kneel with him, what had passed between them in the bush, the return to find the child and – 'My comforter!' she said suddenly. 'You took it. By mistake, I'm sure Mr Baxter. The white shawl I made myself, the one in the picture.'

Though it did not seem possible, the photographer's hue deepened to a more intense red. He straightened, adopted a business-like tone.

'Would you be wanting to purchase the picture, ma'am?'

Myra's heart sank. She had no money of her own.

'Perhaps I could speak to Mr McQuiggan. Is he at home?'

'Yes, but he is unwell and would not –' Myra stopped, confused. Mr Baxter had meant her husband, of course, not the old man who lay dying upstairs. Gordon was looking at her strangely, as if she thought she had lied on purpose. Myra turned away from the picture and engaged the photographer's eye.

'My comforter,' she persisted. 'Do you have it with you in town?' He would not resist her question a second time.

'Yes, yes I do,' he said finally. 'It is in my trunk – a little soiled, though, I regret to say. I did intend to return it to you, but I have not passed through Kaiwaka this past year. I chanced to meet the old priest who gave you refuge after the fire and he told me of your whereabouts.'

'Did Reverend Wayland tell you about the fire?' asked Myra, surprised.

'It was all about the north: a rumour that your husband had set the fire himself, not the Maori woman who took the blame.'

Gordon replaced the plate and spoon on the table with a bang and stood heavily. Her face burning, Myra bent and wiped at the twins' kumara-smeared mouths with a corner of a tea-towel. At the range, Gordon briefly laid her hand against the back of an enamelled saucepan of milk. She lifted it from the hotplate and filled two feeding bottles, firmly stirring a spoonful of sugar into each.

'Perhaps, Mr Baxter, you could return tomorrow with the young lady's shawl,' she said, as she made her way back to the twins, 'and we will pay you for your picture then. It would be, ah . . .' she searched for the word, 'inconvenient for you if this was a wasted journey.'

The photographer nodded. 'You're right of course, ma'am.' He made a half-formed lunge towards the picture to wrap it again, but Gordon had not finished.

'Leave the picture. Save yourself the bother of carting it about.' She and Myra took a child each onto their laps. The little girls reached eagerly for their bottles and sucked noisily, and Myra, glancing up at the photographer saw that he was blushing again.

'Tomorrow then,' he said, shifting himself towards the door.

Myra smiled at him, feeling sorry for his discomfort. He looked away from Gordon, to Myra's kindness and away again, and hurried out.

His knock the following morning interrupted Ellen at her task of setting the dining-room table for breakfast. She was sorting the napkin rings. Her own and Blanche's were silver, engraved with their names for their babyhood christenings; Alithea's was pewter and from her father's family; Myra she gave the carved wooden one, inlaid with paua shell, that was reserved for family guests. Amelia and Sophie had taken their christening rings to their marital homes in Wellington, William's lay fallow and blackened at the back of the drawer and Henry's one was kept in the kitchen since he most often dined in there. The compartment in the drawer that held the rings had been empty for years and gave Ellen a heavy heart, the sense that her most companionable and intimate years were over.

The man she opened the door to was the photographer Gordie had told them about the previous evening, the man returning with the dead child's shawl. Gordie had encouraged Myra to show the family the photograph and Myra had done so, after much urging, later, in the parlour. Ellen had privately thought it macabre and old-fashioned; Alithea had exclaimed at its beauty.

She led him down to the kitchen where Myra was once again feeding the twins. Folded clumsily into a piece of black photographer's cloth and draped over the man's arm was the shawl. Myra stood hurriedly and reached for it as Mr Baxter held it out to her. She unfolded it and held it up. A mouse, she thought at first, must have made a nest in Mr Baxter's trunk and gnawed a hole in its centre. The fringes had become middle-aged, streaked here and there with grey. Then she saw that the hole was a tear, that it had caught on something – the wire hoops he used to make the canopy perhaps, or the rough edge of another child's cradle.

'Will you be able to mend it?' Mr Baxter had a frog in his throat. He cleared it noisily, which brought on a louder fit of coughing. Gordie turned heavily from the bench, where she worked at the porridge and scrambled eggs, with a glass of water in her hand. After a moment, when his fit had eased, he took it from her, his eyes streaming, and drank in vast gulps, the skin of his thick neck moving up and down in its small soft collar.

'You poor man!' said Ellen. He required a handkerchief and groped for one.

'Excuse me,' Mr Baxter managed at last. 'That'll be two pounds five shillings and I'll be on my way.'

Gordie opened a cocoa tin on the dresser. The photograph was divested of its brown paper and stood propped behind a fat salt-pig and the cocoa tin, which was now rattled for its contents.

'Don't you be saying a word, Miss Ellen,' warned Gordie, as she prised the lid open, took out the notes and coins from the housekeeping money and counted them into Mr Baxter's plump, damp hand. His free hand wiped at his continuously streaming nose.

'I'm sorry about the state of the shawl, ma'am,' he said from under his handkerchief.

'So am I,' replied Myra stiffly, taking up the spoon though the twins' mouths were closed. Wide eyed they stared at Mr Baxter, who for the moment was more interesting than their porridge bowl.

'At least he returned it.' Ellen's voice took on its habitual lecturing tone. 'Although what you will do with it I don't know. Perhaps you could give it to Henry for a bed for his cats.'

This last remark had a new coquettish lilt, which was at odds with the Ellen Myra had come to know. She shook her head and waved the spoon before Dora's eye to catch her attention. More quickly than her mother anticipated, the baby's fist rose from under her long bib and knocked the spoon away. A dob of porridge flew against Myra's dress, the same pink and white striped one that Ellen had worn on the day of her arrival. Ellen had made her a gift of it and Myra thought it the prettiest thing she had ever owned. She scraped at its bodice now, exasperated, with the handle of the spoon.

'I will show you out,' said Ellen, a small, slightly mocking smile on her lips, which Myra felt sure was directed at her. It seemed sometimes as though the pram and dress had been bestowed from a great height as charitable donations. Often Myra sensed in the older woman the same disappointment she had engendered in her husband, though less intense. In the months since William's departure, Myra had sometimes wondered whether Ellen held her accountable, as if her brother's disappearance were fuelled more by a desire to escape his wife than to travel to America.

The photographer tucked his money into his trouser pocket.

'I trust you are not superstitious,' Ellen said to him now, in that same new voice. 'It will not matter to you if you leave by the back door, since that is the closest?'

'I am not acquainted with that superstition,' the photographer said. 'What is that?' They had passed out into the narrow passage that led to the porch and Henry's room.

'The one that dictates that if a person enters a house by one door and leaves by another, then that person will never return.'

Mr Baxter gave a quizzical, phlegm-ridden laugh, which Gordie and Myra heard from the kitchen, before two sets of footsteps sounded hollow on the back steps. The servery opened and Mary's face appeared.

'Mrs Gordon!' she hissed. 'Mrs McQuiggan and Miss Blanche have been seated at the table for a good ten minutes!'

At the range, the cook heaved a sigh and filled the porridge bowls for the women of the family. She set a tray for the old man, though it seemed pointless. It would return untouched, not out of petulance and turmoil as it had done with the young master, but because Justice McQuiggan no longer had an appetite.

CHAPTER 14

After breakfast Mrs McQuiggan went to sit with her husband and wait for the arrival of Dr Pollock. His visits had been daily for the past three months and he made no secret of how astonished he was at the duration of the old man's lingering. The patient scarcely spoke and certainly never complained, his reserve being the greater part of the fortitude that kept his heart pumping in his skeletal frame.

'You're a tough old Scot,' he said to McQuiggan gruffly. 'You'll go on for ever.'

Today Elisha gave a response to that notion. He shook his head. The doctor returned to a theme he regularly took up on his visits.

'I do wish you would allow me to appoint a nurse, if not for your own sake, for the benefit of your wife and daughters. It is not as if you cannot afford it.'

Elisha turned his face towards the light of the window.

How translucent his forehead had become, thought Alithea, lifting her hand to its cool upper reaches. He was a man who had always been pale; he had spent most of his life indoors and now what little colour he had had dwindled away with the rest of him.

'Our daughter-in-law Myra is a nurse,' remarked Alithea, as if she had only just remembered.

'A proper nurse?' asked Pollock, surprised.

'I don't know about "proper",' answered Alithea. 'She worked in a home for women, for —' A tiny pinkness heated her cheeks. Her embarrassment was not so much due to having to mention such a thing to a man — he was after all a doctor and must have tended some disreputable women in his long and distinguished career — but rose more from her desire not to allow him to form the mistaken idea that William's wife had come to the Home by her own transgression.

'Quite,' answered the doctor, shortly. He thought for a moment before he went on. 'If you think the young lady would be willing then I can see no harm in trying her.'

Alithea stood, full of resolve. 'I will go downstairs, then, and arrange for her to come to you here.'

Dr Pollock felt the time that elapsed between the lady's departure and Myra's arrival to be inexplicably long. He took his patient's pulse, examined the whites of his eyes and the pallid texture of his tongue. He offered the judge a sip of water, which he declined. The old man kept his eyes closed and his silent mouth set in a straight line.

'There is no use in willing yourself to die,' Pollock told him, bending over the bed. Elisha's dry lips parted a little and the doctor thought that perhaps he would have responded, but his mouth closed again in the same instant as the bedroom door opened and Myra came in. She had been draped in one of the cook's aprons, spotlessly white and vast, the ribbons passed twice around her waist. Her eyes were puffy as though she had been crying. Inwardly, Pollock groaned. Not only an unwilling, begrutten nurse, but very likely an incapable one. The judge's wife, however, as he had learned during their long association, was not a woman to be crossed. Not only should he accept her decision, he should forswear to enquire after the cause of the young woman's tears.

'I understand you were trained in Australia as a nurse?' he rapped out, turning his back on Myra to look out the window, a view that took in the construction site of the house next door, which was abandoned because of the weather. A large dog snuffled among sodden paper and food scraps left by the workmen. Beyond that, higher on the hill, was the intersection of St Stephen's Avenue and Parnell Road, pitted with puddles and carriage ruts and slick with mud. The white bell tower and steeple of St Mary's Cathedral rose above the brown and red of closely clustered roofs, glimmering in the rain.

'Speak up now, I cannot hear you.' He glanced around quickly at Myra and saw that she was shaking her head.

'My duties were confined to the care of new mothers,' she whispered. 'In truth I was little more than a maid.'

'Oh? And why was that?' The doctor extended a finger to squash a spider that had made its nest in the corner of the sill.

'I was not in the establishment long enough to be given other responsibilities, and –' Myra stopped now, red with shame.

'And what?' Pollock's ill-temper, which formed the greater part of his nature, now bubbled over. The spider had been a fat one and made a nasty mess on his hand. 'Hurry up, I haven't got all day.'

'And . . . I can scarcely read and write, sir. I – I have improved since, with my Bible reading at Pukekaroro, but Matron gave me a medical text to read and when she saw that I could not . . .'

She trailed off. Dr Pollock was splashing water from the ewer to the basin and energetically washing his hands.

'In that case,' he said, 'I shall tell you your duties rather than write them down. You must not allow a draught to strike upon the patient. If fresh air is required please lower the upper sash only. Govern the light with the curtains during the day; you will require artificial light only in the night hours. Justice McQuiggan feels the cold. Ensure he is well covered at all times. And surely it is not necessary to remind you, even given your limited experience, of the necessity for cleanliness and quiet. I will take away the chamber pot and replace it with a slipper pan –'

It was as if the doctor had somehow shrunk to a proportion small enough to climb inside her ear and hammer directly upon her eardrums. She ceased to listen to his words; there was only the rhythmical clangour of speech, a pulse that she realised suddenly was her own, her blood surging with fear and disbelief. Was she to be removed from the care of her babies for the sake of the old man, or was she expected to take care of all three? She had scarcely seen William's father since that March day when he had visited during her lying-in.

'For pity's sake! Come with me.' The doctor had taken her upper arm and was escorting her from the sickroom to the corridor, closing the door after him. At Myra's back stood her own room, the room that was once William's and briefly Henry's. It was larger than Ellen's and deemed by Alithea to be more suitable for the mother and twins. She longed now to run to it, to fling herself onto the bed, to take refuge from the severe man before her.

'Will you stop crying!' He kept his voice low. 'What on earth is the matter with you? This man is your father-in-law, is he not? I tell you, he is three times the man his son is and –'

Myra wiped her eyes on the corner of her apron and looked directly at the doctor. He was no different to her limited memory of him at the birth six months ago: brusque and overworked, any artificial kindness long abandoned in favour of greater concentration on his cases, which were multitudinous and often unpaid.

'And it will not be for long,' the doctor finished.

'It is just that I am concerned for the care of my babies,' Myra managed, keeping her voice as steady as she could. 'I am happy to repay my father-in-law's kindness in this way, but I don't see how –' Alithea's harsh words in the kitchen returned to her, her irritation once she had detected Myra's unspoken reticence. It had been less of a request and more of an order to join the doctor upstairs, and Myra had wondered briefly if her mother-in-law was punishing her for not helping more around the house. She had wanted to wail at her, to point out to her that she did more than either of the sisters in the kitchen and always helped Mary with the weekly wash. Nobody would expect the same help from Ellen – most of her working hours were spent at the school. Blanche seemed still to find time to go out and about in her little carriage, though when she was home she answered to her father's needs. Elisha's parsimony made no allowance for a paid nurse.

The children had cried when Myra left them, as if they sensed that her constant attention was soon to be rationed.

A floorboard creaked at the top of the stairs and Mary appeared with Elisha's tray bearing a bowl of broth and a piece of soft white bread.

'There are other women in the house to help you with the twins.' The doctor made no effort to keep the exasperation from his voice. 'Mrs Gordon, I understand, is very capable. You are to try to maintain a bright countenance and leave your own worries at the sickroom door. Good day, Mrs McQuiggan. I will visit tomorrow at the same time.'

He turned and went off down the stairs with Mary before Myra could respond. She took the tray into the old man. She would have to touch him now: to take hold of his shoulders to prop him up. She took a deep breath and willed her hands away from her sides. A sour, unpleasant smell was released from the bed as she moved him. He was so light she could support his weight on one arm while she arranged the pillows at his back. As she gently settled him against them his eyes fluttered and opened and he looked at her but through her, his eyes glassed and unfocused like those of a feeding newborn, as if he had no recollection of who she was and no curiosity either. Myra loaded the spoon, held it to his lips, and realised the doctor had been right: it would not be long. The old man was present in body but not in spirit. He had almost departed.

She returned the spoon to the bowl, tapped half of the broth away and offered it again, smaller, but as she did so the old man did what his grandchild had done earlier: he lifted a hand and knocked it away. Its cargo landed with a soft plop on the white sheet folded over at his waist. For a moment Myra sat in stunned silence before she gathered her wits and scraped at it with the edge of the spoon, which only served to worsen it. She would have to change his linen. There were other smears and patches: hurriedly spot-cleaned relics of other meals and uneasy sleep. She replaced the bowl and spoon on the tray and laid it outside the bedroom door on her way to the linen press, which stood between Blanche's and Alithea's rooms at the other end of the corridor. As she hurried back with the sheets, pillowslips and a fresh bolster case, she wondered suddenly what William would make of the situation, what his opinion would be of his wife thrown into this intimate contact with his father. Whether he had an opinion at all would depend on his other distractions, she knew: on the degree of his 'blind intent'. She treasured that phrase, rolled it around in her mind often, applied it to her memory of certain events, of her husband's passions and dreams. For the first weeks after their long-ago talk, she had hoped the old man would seek her out, to explain a little more of his son to her, but he never had. In the intervening months he had seemed to avoid the women altogether, excepting for periods in the evening with Alithea in the parlour. Before he adjourned willingly and permanently to his bed, he had lain long hours on the chaise longue in his study. Myra had not wanted to contrive a meeting with him. She could have – she could have intercepted him on one of his slow progressions and asked the question that nagged at her whenever she thought of her husband – but she shied from the idea of confronting Mr McQuiggan with it, of forcing an opinion from him when he more than likely would not want to give it.

Elisha gave no sign of having registered her re-entry to the room. He had fallen asleep, his head lolled slightly to one side. She took hold of the eiderdown at the foot of the bed to slide it down and lay it over the slipper chair. It had not moved five inches before it was arrested by the blue grip of the old man's hand. His eyes were open.

'What are you doing?'

'It's all right,' she said firmly, tugging at it again and securing its release.

'Who is that?'

'Myra.'

'My dear girl. Where is Blanche?' The old man heard his own voice and thought it sounded as though it had struggled up through sand. He had come back then, back into the room, forcing enough of a presence to ask questions. He had hoped for a longer absence. There was a moment always, when he took himself out and away from this room to the rooms of the past and to the memory of a body innocent of pain, when his concerted will was washed away by a slow grey tide that bore off the pictures from his mind, lulling him towards soft death. Every time he welcomed the prospect of oblivion, but the tide would ebb and he would find himself returned to the contemplation of his wife and daughter and the torment of his bones. He wondered now why he pondered so much on his immediate surroundings and so little on God, whose face he would no doubt look upon very soon.

Leaving the eiderdown over a chair, Myra brought him a glass of water.

'She went out after breakfast.'

His body rose up against him and insisted on taking a sip, enough to allow him speech. A tiny, almost mischievous smile twitched at the moistened corners of his mouth.

'They have made you nurse, Myra?'

'Yes,' she answered shortly, replacing the glass and returning to the foot of the bed. There was a way of changing the lower sheet on a bed without disturbing the patient. At the Home she had always done it with the assistance of another nurse and so long ago now that she couldn't remember . . .

Her father-in-law's nightshirt was revealed to be most unpleasant, with the odour of the chamber pot. Myra wondered what Mrs McQuiggan and Blanche could have been thinking of, to leave him like this.

'I said it wasn't worth the bother of employing a nurse,' he was whispering, watching her face, 'because no sooner would she be engaged than she would needs be dismissed.'

'Are you warm?' she asked him, replacing the upper sheet for a moment. He nodded. 'I'll be back soon.' She took up the jug from the washstand.

All the way down the hall she trained her ears to the floor below for sound of the twins. There was none. Perhaps Blanche had set the pram outside, under a tree. The house had fallen silent. She passed through the small passage at the end of the hall to the bathroom. The room was warm and damp: someone, Alithea perhaps, had bathed recently. Fixed above the bath was a geyser, which she regarded with nervous apprehension. Ellen, impatiently, had shown her how to use it, how to fine-tune the little wheel that brought in the gas, how to hold a match to the aperture that held the pilot light and to wait a moment before slowly opening the tap, thus avoiding a cascade of boiling droplets from the vent at the top. She had avoided its use even after the lesson, bathing the babies downstairs in the kitchen and herself too, if she rose early enough. She felt ashamed, stupid – a modern, well-equipped bathroom and she did not avail herself of it. She took a deep breath and opened the spigot into the jug. It half filled with hot water before the supply spluttered and stopped. Half a jug would have to be enough.

'Please, God,' she prayed, hurrying back. 'Please don't let me be ashamed. I must not blush or fumble. It's the body you gave him, Lord.'

This last thought cheered her a little, calmed her agitated heart. She paused for a moment, her hand on the door knob, the jug steaming in the other, and took a deep breath.

The judge had departed again, this time with closed eyes, which she found less alarming than the earlier unfocused trance. Quickly she sponged him down while he gave the impression of absence. He was easier to undress than the heavy youthful female bodies at the Home. William's father's skin was papery, inoffensively dry, and the task did not seem nearly so onerous once she had lifted away his nightshirt. His drawers she left for the last moment, worrying while she took flannel and soap to the rest of him that he would open his eyes to look at her. She had never before nursed a man, of course, and the prospect of tending to the parts of him that made him male was intimidating. She had never even seen William, not at close proximity. He had liked to look at her – he used to ask her sometimes if he could do so, while they lay in the bed together on the farm, or when she took her bath – but he himself had been bashful. In the end she took her cue from her patient and vacated her conscious mind from the situation, focused herself only on her busy hands, easing a towel under his hips, bathing and drying him and fetching a clean nightshirt from his tall-boy. It was coming back to her now, her small training. She rolled the clean sheet towards the middle of the bed, rolled the dirty one away on the other side, rolled his passive body to the clean one while she changed the pillowslips. When he was comfortable again she took up his comb and straightened his sparse hair.

Elisha opened his eyes and looked up at her intent face above her gentle, busy wrists. 'Thank you, my dear,' he said, and noted with pleasure how his gratitude pinkened her cheeks. She bobbed her head and went to replace the comb but Elisha lifted a hand from the bed and would have caught at her clothes to halt her if he had had the strength to do so. There was a question he wanted to ask suddenly, one that would bear heavily on what would unfold after he had died.

'Do you miss him, Myra?'

Alarm flashed in the young woman's eyes before a more guarded expression came into them, as if she would hide from him her progression from truth to falsehood.

'You need not lie to me, my dear.' He patted at her apron now, the apron one of Gordon's and the dress he remembered both his daughters wearing. Yes, first it was Blanche's, then it was Ellen's, and now it had been passed on to plain, kind Myra.

'No,' she whispered. 'I have thought of him, wondered about his well-being or . . . otherwise.'

'You don't think he is dead?'

Was there a hopeful tone in the old man's voice Myra wondered, or was she imagining it? How could a father wish for such a thing for his own child – a premature death?

'You must not regard me so sternly,' he was saying now. 'It is just that I have wondered myself, more than once, why it is that we have not had even one letter.'

Myra went on her way with the comb and began to bundle up the dirty linen and damp towel.

'There has been no letter?' Elisha persisted, and Myra shook her head, humiliated. Her husband held her in such poor regard that he could not spare the time to write.

'And would you, should he return, be so quick as to trust him again with your future?'

Myra stared at him, incredulous. 'Are you suggesting that we should live apart?'

The old man scowled at her. 'I mean your spiritual future.'

'I have never entrusted him with that,' Myra answered simply. 'I will return as soon as I have taken these downstairs.' She was at the door, the bundle in her arms.

'There is no need. Spend a while with your infants,' her father-in-law said, and Myra realised as she went out that he was comforted by her, her ministrations and confessions both.

The time before she began to nurse the old man and the time after seemed divided entirely, with almost nothing in common. The twins, though cosseted and treasured during the day by Blanche and Mrs Gordon and their grandmother, returned at night to the sleeping patterns of their early infancy, disturbed by their mother when she rose at intervals through the night to light a candle and tiptoe across the corridor to check on her patient. On her return, Myra would be compelled to spend anxious hours trying to settle them again until, more often than not, she resorted to removing them from their cot and placing them in the bed with her, one on either side. Quietly she would sing to them, from the meagre store of nursery rhymes gleaned from her own sad mother, until they slept, fretful and hot. She would lie awake between them, listening for noises of disturbance from Ellen's room next door. There had been none so far, but even so, Myra would lie sleepless and worried, each day bringing with it new depths of exhaustion. Her work was not particularly taxing — the old man weighed less than she did, and the provision of the slipper pan and invalid cup and various other utensils sent by Dr Pollock made her duties lighter. Sometimes she would drift off in the nurse's chair by the window and be taken by strange shifting dreams of babies' mouths and an old man's stringy neck, a jumble of beseeching anatomy.

Alithea had grown silent and reserved in her company, which was infrequent as the younger Mrs McQuiggan would most often take her meals in the kitchen or upstairs with her patient. Alithea's reticence bewildered Myra, as her mother-in-law was aware, but she could find no recourse for explanation. At times her gratitude for Myra's stoicism overwhelmed her, when she saw her lithe, quick body descend the stairs laden with tray or clanking pail, her face set with quiet, accepting duty. It was right, Alithea deemed, that Myra's talents should be used in this way: the younger woman need not worry about becoming a burden on the family and meanwhile Alithea could play her part as doting grandmother. Excepting for the rare occasion that the twins were taken for a walk in their high-wheeled carriage by Blanche, which given the muddy macadam of the winter streets was a challenge, they would spend the morning with her in the morning room. Alithea adhered rigidly to this rule; it assuaged a niggle in her conscience, a niggle that rose from the blue shadows under Myra's dark eyes. Her care of the children would not have been nearly so easy if it were not for Henry, who lay on the rug with them and allowed them to clamber on him as they learned to crawl and who engrossed himself in building towers of their wooden blocks. Rounding her plump white fist, Dora would strike them down with loud exactitude and wild giggles would issue from all three, Henry's wheezing gurgle beneath the sweet laughter of the babies. Sometimes, with emerging teeth or lack of sleep, the twins were fractious and their grandmother would end by having to call for Mary early. They did not like Mary and would squall as they were handed over, and she in turn did not like them because she was only ever given them in an irritable mood.

A second part of the routine decreed that for an hour in the afternoon Mrs McQuiggan would relieve Myra and sit at her husband's bedside. His silence in her company encouraged her own with Myra, by making it seem natural and owing. Elisha obviously reserved his conversation for the younger woman, she thought. She had heard them talking, once or twice, as she came to the sickroom door. She quelled any thoughts of jealousy – good heavens, she was nearly sixty years old and intimacy was most certainly a pleasure of the past – and had Mary bring up her arrascene so the time would not be wasted, though she found herself meditating on aspects of the young woman she found distasteful: her left-handedness, for example; her poor complexion; her inaudible voice. After a time these thoughts would become circular and repetitive and she would upbraid herself for being uncharitable, and her mind would drift towards her impending widowhood and the change that would bring to the lives of her daughters. In the full month since the regime had started, she had hardly seen Ellen. Work days at the school had grown mysteriously longer and on several evenings her eldest daughter had stepped out to the theatre, to public lectures or bridge parties in the company of Mr Clement Baxter. Sunday last he had accompanied the sisters and mother to Holy Communion at Saint Mary's and Alithea had thought him not at all handsome and rather dull, though his photograph of the lost child was becoming. She needed to remind herself that Ellen was, after all, nearly forty and that Mr Baxter might be the best she could do.

On the last night of September, only hours before he died, Elisha had a lucid spell. He woke while Myra took his pulse, something she had learned to do under the scowling tutelage of Dr Pollock. The two bones of his forearm were clearly distinguishable one from the other; the thin vein throbbed faintly between them.

Justice McQuiggan had not spoken at all for two days. He had kept his eyes closed and appeared to be in a deep sleep, though Myra found she could rouse him to swallow water or tepid thin soup. In truth his conscious mind returned to him infuriatingly often, though briefly: enough for his soul to rage at it for release. On each reappearance it took on the shackles of weighty, bitter guilt, a remorse the judge believed, before his sickness, that he had dismissed fifteen years ago, when William first absconded to England. Waking fully now he applied a reluctant logic to the situation. He would unload it, he decided: his conscience would expire to be followed shortly after by his temporal self.

'What time is it?' His sudden question, unheralded by any change in his immobile face, gave Myra such a start that she almost dropped his wrist.

'Nine o'clock,' she replied softly. 'I am about to go to bed myself.'

'Stay a moment.' He concentrated all his energies into the hand Myra had replaced on the coverlet and gestured towards her chair.

'I whipped him severely, you know.'

She had not quite sat down. She lifted herself from the chair and returned to his side, seized with a strange apprehensive gratitude. William's father would speak at long last about his son, and Myra feared what she would learn. The old man's eyes were open, staring in their sightless way at the ceiling rose above the bed.

'It began when he was scarcely old enough to discriminate between right and wrong. God forgive me.' The child's tearful, swollen face loomed before him, eyes deep with the father's betrayal. 'Following his punishment he was expected to meditate alone on his sins, and though I suspected he did nothing but seethe with unthinking resentment, I took no action.'

In the hope he would continue Myra waited for a moment before she responded, but he did not. 'You should have comforted him, perhaps.' She straightened the edge of his sheet.

'I could not have!' he said. 'It would have been immoral for me to go to him and apologise for meting out only what he had deserved.'

'No, not to apologise,' Myra said hastily, 'not that. I meant to offer solace.'

'He has too great a need for that, even now.'

'For comfort?' she whispered.

The old man gave no response. The son he pictured now was older than the tear-streaked child and ruined, irresponsible. His eyes closed again, his mouth drooped. His nurse put out the sickroom lamp and closed the door after her.

Sluggishly, in the recesses of his brain, the final sparks of cognition extinguished themselves. He had made his confession but he had compromised it by a dearth of tenderness. He would go to Judgement with his burden still, though lighter.

Plumed horses, a polished black hearse with wide glass windows, a full muster of mourners rich and poor, the most sumptuous of ecclesiastical embroidery and the best organist in the diocese – Justice McQuiggan gathered them all to St Mary's on the hill above his house. From the time she was told of his death to a moment many weeks after the funeral, Alithea maintained her public face, even in her most private moments, and Myra, who sat now in the family pew, dazed and quiet, thought only of William and what he didn't know. A stiff norwester blew the clouds away outside the wooden walls. In the ploughed field over the road, newly planted lettuces ruffled their infant leaves in the first warmth of spring. Where William was it was autumn, but her image of him had him striding in a hot white light. Was it a desert, she wondered, where he was? The 'Lake' in its name made her think of water, but the 'Salt' before it somehow cancelled that out and had her believe it was an arid place. She had looked often at the map in William's childhood atlas in his room and compared the continent of her homeland with the one that held Salt Lake, which was so much further inland than Yarrabin was in its corresponding giant palm that it seemed quite possible that the Lord could decide to close that massive hand to the fist it already resembled, the thumb defined by the east coast, Jacksonville to Boston. It was oddly comforting to think of William somehow folded over into the care of the Lord, he and all those other earnest seekers of Him that America must hold.

Henry sat between Myra and his mother and held their hands. There had been talk of leaving him at home with the twins, but he was brought at the last minute with only just enough time to dress him before the carriage arrived. Tears wet his big cheeks and his gaze remained fixed on the gold crucifix on the altar. An elderly canon, a life-long friend of Elisha's, read the funeral service. During the 23rd Psalm, Ellen and Blanche remained seated while Henry sang lustily, his voice occasionally breaking into bellows and sobs. With great dignity Alithea also sang and at the psalm's end she turned to her son with the large man's handkerchief she had tucked into her reticule for the purpose, and dabbed at his face. Elsewhere in the congregation sat Mrs Gordon and Mary, and near the doors Mr Clement Baxter.

After the funeral, the family gathered on the street beside the hearse, waiting for the pall-bearers to slide the coffin in once more and begin the journey to Cemetery Gully. Blanche appeared to know everyone who milled around them and hailed friends more as though she were at a wedding or christening, Alithea noted critically, though she supposed Blanche had had a long time to accustom herself to the notion of her father's death. As the youngest of the six surviving children, she must always have seen him as old and frail. Between them Ellen and Mr Baxter took over the care of Henry, Ellen holding him firmly by one arm though he gave no sign of wanting to leave her side. He bent his head and stared at his shuffling feet.

Myra was leaning towards her, talking in the new hushed voice she seemed now to use all the time. She had always had a quiet voice; now it had diminished almost to a whisper.

'I'm sorry, Myra, you will have to repeat yourself.'

'I will go home now to Dora and Joy and help Mary with the wake.'

'Of course.' Alithea nodded and saw that the maid hovered at Myra's side. The two young women turned away for the house in St George's Bay. Alithea did not approve of this new friendship particularly – it too much blurred the distinction between the family and staff – but it was in some ways inevitable. Not only were they of an age, but her daughter-in-law herself straddled the line. She was, Alithea believed, one of nature's servants: there was a sensitive, yet oxen part of her character that would willingly shoulder a burden. Perhaps that, she thought now, watching them depart, was why William had chosen her as his wife.

With Myra gone there would be room in the carriage for Gordie. Of all the servants she was the one most affected by Elisha's death: she had been with the family for over thirty years. By contrast, Alithea noted, Mary had a spring in her step: she'd had a half day, almost, and she was young enough for the mortality of a man the age of Justice McQuiggan not to resonate on her own. She was, also, the only one in the entire household who had any inkling of Alithea's plan, having one day come across her employer quietly packing a box of sterling and pewter in the dining room. They were objects not often used: the silver grape scissors and second bread fork, an unpolished cruet stand and teapot. Mary sensed change, and change was what she craved.

Mary described the scene now as she and the young Mrs McQuiggan rounded the corner onto the crest of the rise. There was a new shop being added to the row on the bend and two of the carpenters paused to watch them. Mary, Myra supposed. She was beautiful and fresh, animated somehow, as if there were an imminent excitement to look forward to.

'And I reckon,' she was saying, 'that Mrs McQ is going to go back Home. She'll sell up and go.'

'Is she from England, then?' asked Myra uncertainly. Mary squawked, as if Myra had said something foolish.

'Scotland! Can't you tell? Born there. Came out when she was three. Gordie told me.'

The cook was Gordie in Mary's conversation but never to her face.

'She'll never sell up. Why should she?'

'To go Home,' Mary repeated, louder, as if Myra were deaf. 'Ooo!' She shook her shoulders like a dog coming out of the water. 'I wonder what will happen! Maybe I could go with her, though I've only just got here, really. McQuiggans' and round here is all I know. Maybe I could go to Wellington. Ask Mrs McQ if she'd send me down there, to one of her daughters –'

'You don't have to stay in service,' Myra said mildly, though she wished the maid would be quiet. The future banged unpredictably around her, unseen, suddenly as unformed as it had been when she left the Waylands'. Mary had stopped, staring at her as though she were insulted.

'That's what I'm trained for,' she said in the same deliberate voice she had used before. 'I did five years 'fore I came here.'

'Come on,' said Myra. Ahead of Mary she had turned into the lane behind the house. Suddenly she needed to see her babies, to cradle them in her arms. In their company, the recipient of their love and trust, she felt she could look after them, and inadvertently herself, no matter what fate brought.

'You'd better find that husband of yours. If you want to keep him, that is.'

There was something in the maid's tone that made Myra spin around to face her. 'What did William do?' she asked, so quietly it scarcely reached her own ears and she wondered if she had only thought it.

'Can't hear you.' Mary picked up her feet and passed her. 'What did you say?'

Myra struggled for the resolve to say it again. 'Did he – William – do – did he –'

Looking at her pityingly, Mary rested one hand on the gate. Her other hand rose briefly to pat Myra on the shoulder before she clicked the catch open. 'Of course. He's the sort. Wanted to, at any rate.'

A flicker of feeling – loyalty, or love – rose from the cold bed of Myra's horror. She did not recognise it for what it was and it was short lived, doused almost immediately by an icy curiosity.

'Were you not frightened?'

'Me? Not at all,' lied Mary, the shell path crunching beneath her feet, though while they climbed the steps to the back porch she remembered him in his bedroom, when he'd stood on her hem, and then in the study when he'd blown on her neck while the old man looked on. 'Does he scare you, then?'

Myra shifted uncomfortably in her new mourning dress. It was stiff bombazine, and now and then she grew convinced there were pins left behind in one of the side seams.

'Does he?' Mary was looking into her face and must see the answer, Myra thought, though she didn't want her to.

The mourners returned from the interment to the drawing room where, laid out in a buffet, were hot savouries and a cold collation of lamb cutlets, chicken creams, cucumber salad and a mayonnaise of eggs, which had been laboured over the day before by Gordie and Mary with Mrs Beeton's method lying open on the kitchen table. There were whisky and sherry and a heavy boiled fruitcake to follow. The room filled with doctors and lawyers, men of commerce and a lesser number of affluent merchants.

Their wives regarded Myra curiously. This was the first time they had had an opportunity to scrutinise William's wife, the woman who had married the boy many of them had hoped would come courting their daughters. The christening of the twins had been, due to Elisha's illness and William's absence, a private affair and the wedding, preceding the baptisms by two years, had been even quieter. On first learning of William's wedding, many of the ladies had experienced a mild pulse of regret: the judge's dashing son, a man of independent wealth, the rumours of his wild spirit only serving then to increase his mystery and allure. Now they gave thanks, in the light of the gossip since he had disappeared, that he had not become a member of their families.

Myra felt their eyes on her and wondered what each matron made of William and how much they knew of his recent past: his shameful still at Pukekaroro, his desertion and his drinking, the fire. His catalogue of sins was full and well beyond, Myra finally came to see, what lay within the bounds of most people's idea of temporal transgression. Fearing what she might say in response to any casual enquiries, she volunteered early to sit by Henry at the buffet table, a duty Blanche was begrudgingly fulfilling, while he filled his capacious mouth with savouries and eggs. Blanche had made no attempt to limit his intake and so Myra did not either. As his sister moved off, Myra took up a pair of tongs in order to serve him whatever he desired. Nobody joined them at the table and her limited vision of the black-clad shoulders and chests of the men around her, the undersides of their jaws and conceal- ment of their expressions, gave her the sensation of occupy- ing a lower plane in the crowded room, like a child. The talk of the men centred mainly on the booming economy and the parliamentary antics of someone called King Dick, whom she gathered was not a real king, but the prime minister. The world leaned in through the walls and across the table, and Myra realised suddenly that Mary had been right, that every- thing would change, that she would be out in the world again, and possibly alone.

Blanche reappeared, holding by the hand a young woman of about twenty-five or -six, a little older than Myra. She had a smooth, plump, open face, with freckles and deep-set eyes.

'Myra, this is Fanny,' announced Blanche, 'my friend from Epsom.'

Fanny smiled, showing a crowded mouth that evidently saw a lot of tooth-powder. 'Hello, Mrs McQuiggan,' she said.

'You sit here,' Blanche said, pulling out the chair beside Myra for her friend and adding in a whisper, 'Nature calls!'

Myra thought Blanche's remark curious, though Fanny gurgled with amusement as Blanche departed.

'I've been wanting to meet you for ages!' Her conversa- tion rose seamlessly from her mirth. 'Simply ages. We're all dying to know where William is and what he's doing. I expect you'll be joining him now the children are old enough to travel.'

Myra took between her pincers a savoury and dropped it on Henry's plate.

'He's a character, your husband. Very different to the other fellows around here. Do anything for a lark.'

Fanny had made a mistake, Myra concluded: she had confused her husband with someone else.

'A bit of a daredevil all right,' Fanny concluded, staring at a distant point above Myra's shoulder. Myra turned her head to see that the women had gathered at the far end of the room at the fireside. Mrs McQuiggan was there, and Ellen, and three sombre ladies of Mrs McQuiggan's generation. Myra didn't know whether they were friends or relatives and they were obscured now at any rate by Mr Clement Baxter, who was bringing Ellen a glass of sherry. It was five o'clock and though it was still light outside, the curtains had been drawn and the room lit by candles on the table and a single gas-lamp on the chiffonier. Above the lamp hung a vast oil, a mountain snow-capped and reflected in a still, placid green lake, the lake itself absorbing the colour of the heavy bush around it. Figures, hunters perhaps, were tiny on the far shore below the mountain. The height of the perspective gave the painting a sense of expanse, of enlightenment, as if the viewer herself looked down from the effulgent sky. Myra wondered if it was a place in New Zealand, the South Island perhaps, which she had never seen, or Scotland.

Alithea, briefly regarding the painting herself from her chair at the fireside, wondered whether it was that Oregon landscape, which had been a great favourite with William when he was a boy, that had planted the seed of America in his mind. She dismissed the thought, focused instead on the peace in the streaming clouds behind the mountain and prayed for strength. In a moment she would stand, have Mr Baxter ring a glass, and she would make her speech. It was not often done, even in the colonies, for women to speak at functions, weddings or parties, still less wakes. It did seem quintessentially colonial though, crass even, to announce her intentions so soon after Elisha's death, but it was best to accept, she assured herself, even at this late stage, that that was how things were done here. Fast, with little or no regard for time or dignified contemplation.

Fanny was rattling on and Myra realised she had not been listening. Something about a boat, and Motutapu Island in the Gulf and William – 'drunk as a lord,' laughed Fanny – sailing the mulleter in a high sea while Fanny – and her brother, she added hastily – disposed of their picnic lunches in the rushing tide. She had been his friend, Myra realised: there was a warmth in her account of him that was missing in his late father's two cold, brief pronouncements. She did not marvel at how the girl could describe herself in such a state and think it humorous, as the senior Mrs McQuiggan would have done, but felt a returning warmth, almost gratitude. Beside her the chomping of the heavy jaws halted. Henry was paying close attention to Fanny's story.

'Walked down to St George's Bay, me and William would,' he said suddenly, 'and round through the port at night. Ships and the moon. Dark and windy . . .' Lost in this recollection, Henry gazed at his plate as if he were remembering many such excursions, when in truth there had been only one and so long ago – soon after William's return from England at the age of sixteen – that the episode glowed in his mind more like a dream than a memory. He'd forgotten how frightened he had been of the sound of the wind howling in the schooners' rigging, so frightened that on Queen Street Wharf he had held tightly to William's hand. He did remember, though, with pride, how later on, when they had met a group of young men who passed a whisky bottle between them and taunted him, William had rolled up his fists and knocked one of them down.

Ellen was leaning across the table towards them.

'Mother would like you to take Henry into the garden, Myra. She is going to make a speech and he might interrupt her.'

Myra stood and whispered in Henry's ear, 'Let's go and feed the cats.'

He pushed his chair away from the table, which had all its leaves extended and stood poorly balanced on its spindly legs. The china and glass knocked together and several pairs of eyes were turned on them, though nothing fell. As Myra hurried with him through the door, glad of escape, at her back came the ringing of a crystal glass.

There was to be no escape from the reading of the will, a week later. Ellen fetched her from the kitchen where she had been put to work by Gordie, shelling peas.

'Mr Ryde wants you too,' she said tersely, and Myra wiped her hands and followed her down the hall to Elisha's study, which had not been used at all since his final illness. Mary had given it a perfunctory dusting and lit the fire and now old Mr Ryde sat behind the streaky desk, a glass paper-weight gleaming dully at his elbow.

Myra sat between her mother-in-law and Blanche while Ellen, who had refused a chair, stood behind them. The will was as everybody expected, with provision made for the widow and unmarried daughters. Mr Ryde read with frequent sips of water to ease his dry throat, until he came to a new, fresher piece of paper leafed between the others in the sheaf he held in his hand. He glanced up at this point at Myra, inadvertently catching the steely eye of Mrs McQuiggan, and wondered how much the widow knew of this recent addendum. He cleared his throat and began:

This is the first Codicil to the last Will of me Elisha Henry McQuiggan of Auckland in New Zealand (Judge) which Will bears the date of eighteenth day of March 1899.

I hereby revoke the provision in my Will which deals with the residue of my estate previously bequeathed to my son William Farquhar McQuiggan. The residue of my estate previously left to my said son shall be, upon my death, bequeathed to my daughter-in-law, Myra McQuiggan. In the event of her renewed association with my son, she is to discharge any debts incurred by him and in his name and he shall continue to receive his allowance administered by the Colonial Bank of Auckland. It is my solemn request that my son be kept in ignorance of Myra's inheritance. He is to be told he was entirely disinherited, barring the aforementioned remittance. I believe this arrangement will encourage my son to shoulder the true burden of his responsibilities while providing my daughter-in-law and grandchildren with the necessities of life.

This will was made before me, etcetera, etcetera.

Alithea had turned her head to stare at her, as had Blanche on her other side. Ellen moved swiftly to the corner of the desk.

'May I see that?' she asked. 'The date of the codicil?'

'The eighteenth of March,' supplied the lawyer, handing her a sheaf of paper. 'I think it is a fair will, most thoughtfully considered.' He did not much care for this sharp-eyed daughter. The newest beneficiary stared still at her knees, draped in the mourning dress that was made of a coarser, cheaper stuff than the other three. Mrs McQuiggan had today interrupted her black silk with an old-fashioned white lace cap, though it had black ribbons that draped behind her shoulders. He had heard, as had most of Auckland's society, of her odd decision to have the young woman nurse the judge on his death-bed. Suspicion then was predictable, though he had not expected it in such a brazen form. The school teacher ran her eye over the page and replaced it on the desk.

'Did you know about this, Mother?' she demanded.

Alithea shook her head.

'Blanche?'

'Of course not!' the younger sister exclaimed. 'Father would not confide in me about such a thing.'

'Myra?'

She had not thought Ellen would include her in her questioning.

'No,' she whispered, struggling to comprehend the meaning of the will. She suddenly had become William's keeper, should he need that – or her – again. Its immediate meaning, she clearly perceived, was a ferocious jealousy from Ellen and an ever-deeper silence from her mother-in-law. The lawyer stood, gathered up the papers.

'A word, Mrs McQuiggan,' he said, offering his client's bewildered widow his arm and escorting her out of the study. Once in the corridor he spoke quietly as they made their way towards the front door.

'You must see the sense of this alteration,' he said, going on before Alithea could reply. 'I too had to be persuaded of its worth at first. I advised him otherwise but he was adamant. He had the highest opinion of that young woman's character.'

'Yes, obviously,' said Alithea.

'Do you not?' Mr Ryde felt it necessary to ask. Perhaps the McQuiggan women would contest the will.

'I think . . .' began Alithea, forced to formalise her conflicting opinions of Myra, 'she is kind and responsible, though I suspect . . . stupid is too strong a word. She is naïve, unworldly. Not at all capable of administering such a large sum. May I ask, by the way, how much there is for her?'

'Not so much,' replied the lawyer. Mrs McQuiggan opened the door and they went out onto the veranda. At the gate a plethora of new hydrangea blooms nodded their green heads, not yet bleached to their purple and pink.

'In effect, Justice McQuiggan has divided the money: a third for William and two-thirds for his wife. Don't concern yourself unduly, Mrs McQuiggan. Perhaps I could institute an allowance for the young lady also, and administer the balance as a trust.'

This made sense to Alithea, as she was sure it would have done to Elisha. It was how he would have liked things to be arranged, she assured herself. She would go inside now and explain it to her daughters and Myra, and get Mary to bring them all a cup of tea before she finished sorting the furnishings and ornaments from the morning room. There was so much to be done in so little time. This afternoon she would sit at her secretary and compose a letter to her son, care of the American in Salt Lake City. She struggled to remember the man's name and it came to her: Ridge. She would address it to Mr Ridge and hope it found him.

Chapter 15

21 St George's Bay Road,
Parnell,
Auckland,
New Zealand.
October 8th, 1899.

My Dear Son,
I have long wanted to write to you but have desisted for lack of an address. I trust I have correctly remembered the name of your companion and that Salt Lake City is not such a large place that this letter will not find you.

I have some sad news which I must come to straight away. Your dear father died last month, a long-awaited release after his protracted illness. As you are well aware, Father was most disappointed with your decision to leave New Zealand and this is reflected in his will. He made provision for your allowance to continue as before, but I regret to tell you that excepting for that you have been entirely disinherited. This will come as hard news to you, I know, but neither you nor I can do anything about it.

By the time you receive this letter Blanche and I will be in Edinburgh. At the end of the week following this one we board the steamer. This house will be sold and I shall use the proceeds to buy another house in Scotland. Ellen has decided to stay in the colony. She has conceived an affection for a photographer, Mr Clement Baxter, and I expect they will be married, though they have as yet made no announcement.

What to do with Henry continues to be of great concern to your sisters and myself. As of your last departure he is subject to an even greater fear and loathing of ships. He will therefore have to be left behind in New Zealand but we have not yet decided on who will care for him. I should not like to further burden Myra, who has already been of invaluable service to us. She was your father's nurse for the last few months of his life and earned his gratitude for her tenderness and practicality.

My dear William, as I write this I have before me the photograph you had taken in a studio in Sydney, five years ago now. It is a strange quirk of nature that a mother may not change her opinion of a son as readily as does a father. I think of you many times in a single day and wonder how you are faring. Please write to me as soon as you may, care of your Aunt Elspeth in Edinburgh. I am very wearied by the events of the past months and long to be surrounded by what is familiar to me. You may think this odd, if you remember that I came first to this country when I was little more than an infant, but that is how it is: I am a Scot and you, my dear boy, are a New Zealander. Now that your father has departed it falls to me to advise you on your future: of course you must return home to your family. You must begin to make the necessary arrangements as soon as possible.

I will close this letter now, with the hope that you are not burdened by the gravity of my news nor the weight of my intent for your future.

Ever my dear son William.
Your affectionate mother,
Alithea McQuiggan

A full year and a half after receipt of his mother's letter, William was still a house guest in a twin-turreted mansion on Temple Street, Salt Lake City. He had not set pen to paper in reply. Many times, in the quiet of a winter Saturday or warm summer evening, in the peace of his ground-floor room, he had gone so far as to lay out a piece of fresh paper and take up a fresh nib, but he didn't know where to begin. The longer he left it the more difficult it became, and now, on a Saturday morning in May 1901, as he waited for Brother Everett's knock, it was close to impossible. His mind was crowded with scenes and events, from his journey across California and into Utah by train, to the violent, eerie landscape that surrounded the new city and its surprisingly verdant gardens, to his envy and delight in Everett's fine mansion, to his admiration of the Mormons and their seemingly universally sunny dispositions. Since his arrival in Salt Lake he had had to accustom himself to the knowledge that his friend was not only the possessor of a great fortune in copper but also a respected Elder.

He could have begun his letter simply, by telling his mother about his work, describing how every morning he left Everett Ridge's regal rooms to drop down to the town, through the thick coal-laden blanket of smog that Salt Lake laid over itself morning and night, to work as a carpenter on sites around South Street and State, alongside Italians and Slavs and Celestials, and how he returned in the evenings to his host. He would have had to explain that it was Everett's idea that he seek work almost immediately they arrived. Work, Brother Everett maintained, was a part of his religion and therefore must be a part of William's. Alithea would understand that: it was close to what she believed herself. She would agree also with Everett's insistence that her son find work independently, without any interference or help from him. William could describe how the job had come about, from an introduction one Sunday morning at the Tabernacle – and the Tabernacle itself would have to be described, or a picture sent of its strange wide, domed roof, the shining oval expanse. How could he find the words to describe faithfully the joyous singing that took place within its walls; the fresh, practical notion of God that these people adhered to; how he himself, William McQuiggan, had stood and spoken in the assembly building, which was a little like a wooden New Zealand church? He could tell his mother how every particle in his body and mind longed for his baptism in the grand temple, the interior of which was unknown to him: he could only begin to imagine its glorious beauty . . .

Salt Lake Temple rose now in his mind's eye. He could only describe its exterior: the six gothic turrets in triplicate at either end of the nave walls, the body of the building rising between the turrets like a castle keep. It was topped with battlements as if, among the temple's excess of ornate spires and minarets, the builders had made provision for cannon- and gun-fire. What would it have been to help build the temple, he wondered, to have been one of the men who laid the silvery stone, spread the mortar, walked the length and breadth of the clerestory walls before the roof was raised? It would have been to see as far as the Angel Moroni who topped the central spire, cast in glorious gold and twelve feet tall, facing east and blowing puff-cheeked on his trumpet . . . He laid his pen aside, overwhelmed, and lay on his back on his bed.

Better perhaps just to tell his mother that the work he'd found suited him. He was mainly out of doors, in the hot dry sun of the summer or the bracing icy chill of winter or in the clean, warming spring. He could boast a little, tell his mother he had learned fast – though his mother would not like the idea of her son as tradesman. Within two weeks on the job he was promoted from labourer to hammer-hand. The clothes he had brought with him from New Zealand had grown tight around his shoulders and chest and he had gladly replaced them at a good tailor in Main Street, as well as picking up a good set of working clothes off the peg at ZCMI. The little he earned he kept for evenings at the Salt Lake Theatre and Saturday outings to Saltair, the resort on the lake shore: Everett had not invited him to contribute to his keep and William's offer to do so had been refused. There was a new tone in their friendship, at least William supposed it to be new. It was as if, in every possible way, the American considered himself superior and all attempts by William to prove himself his equal fell on deaf ears.

William remembered how the word in his mother's letter had affected him the first time he read it. Disinherited. Entirely disinherited.

He rose from the bed and took up his pen once more. If he were to write to anyone, it should be to Brother Ridge, to explain point by point, without the interruptions and distractions of conversation, what he thought of that man's treatment of his wife, of poor Eliza, of the deception that surrounded the child. He swung his arms and paced the room. It was spartan, though comfortable, the bed softened by a quilt worked by the senior wife and given to him soon after their arrival. Above the bed-head hung a picture in bright oils of Alma in the waters of Mormon baptising some of the two hundred and four who followed him there. Wet, opaque white robes clung to the thighs of a woman in the foreground; her face was transfused with grace.

Heavily, William sat on his bed, tried to ignore the picture – he looked at it too much – and opened the bedside drawer to extract the letter from his mother. He would draw some comfort from it now perhaps. He had not on its arrival. Then, at the time he had received it, the winter before last, he had only just begun to feel himself out into the extremities of his body again, to abandon the tightly wrapped kernel he had retreated into since Eliza's embrace on the ship. At that moment, in the rocking, sliding cabin, he had not known that a woman could plumb such depths of despair or anticipate her willing demise as keenly as he had once done his own. Her thin clinging arms had set up unpleasant resonances in his memory, questions about Myra's happiness or otherwise. For the remainder of the voyage he had ensured they were never alone together and avoided her gaze whenever they met in the company of the others. At night in Salt Lake, no matter how cold he was, he took the quilt from the bed and hooked it over the back of his chair. He would not sleep under it.

His mother's letter did not mention Myra except in passing. Of invaluable service, she had been, attending the old man. He went on to the end then, remembered how angry he'd been the first time he'd read it. It wasn't that his family had used his wife as an unpaid nurse that had enraged him, though it rankled as he read the letter this second time, it was his mother's demand that he go back to New Zealand. Why would he, when she wouldn't be there herself? If it were Myra that she meant by the word 'family', then he would send for her when he was set up. He couldn't send for her to join him now, not until he had his own house. His eye fell on the words 'allowance' and 'continue' and he felt a little softening, a sudden gladness. Reading was often like this for him: a word here, a phrase there, leaping out at him and making its meaning clear. Dogged following of sentences left to right down a page frequently left him with no meaning at all.

He would go to the bank tomorrow, he decided, and arrange a transfer of funds. The paper of the letter, softened first by its long keeping in the drawer, flopped in his hand like a bandage as he crossed back to the desk. He folded the fresh paper in half and scrawled a note to himself, one word: 'bank'. It was foolish to think he could ever write to his mother. How, for instance, would he be able to describe the household he had become part of? It would be impossible for his mother to understand; it would be as if he spoke in tongues.

During their absence from Salt Lake City Brother Everett had had the house altered and the wives had claimed their respective territories immediately upon their return. But for the kitchen, William's room and the second-floor parlour, and the room that was Everett's own, the house may as well have been divided entirely in two. Each woman kept to her own apartment: a small third-floor bedroom and adjoining sitting room, Lydia's on the north side and Eliza's on south, separated by the nursery. In a single momentous concession to his senior wife, Everett had had the door that gave from Lydia's room into the children's quarters locked and the key put away. His younger wife had wept at this, his first perceived unkindness to her, though Everett assured her that if they remained faithful to their covenants a time would come when it would be necessary for the key to be returned.

On the floor below the women's apartments there was a sewing room, which was the one sphere of possible contact for the two wives, but Lydia avoided it. On her single foray Eliza had impressed upon her that Matthias's needs came well before those of a childless sister-wife's and that she was not welcome. She and the boy made it their daily practice to spend the afternoon there, while Eliza taught him his letters and Gospel. The mornings Eliza sat alone, at the sewing machine or reading.

In the evenings, unless there was company, Everett, Paora and William ate alone in the male province of the dining room. The women never entered that part of the house to dine, though William considered they must have done to decorate it. It was overstuffed, the curtains pink and floral, the centrepiece lilac glass, the mantelpiece laden with ornament and baubles. The high cream walls were hung with cross-stitched representations of Bible scenes and homilies gleaned from the prophets.

William hardly saw either of the sister-wives. He presumed that his friend did, that he was an active husband to them both. Occasionally Matthias would join the men at the table. He was seven years old and as solemn a child as William had ever met, though he'd not taken an interest in any before. From the little he remembered of his own childhood, he was sure children were generally more light-hearted than this one, even children whose fathers relied on the whip as his own father had done. He wondered if Everett beat the boy for misdoings. It was unlikely: not only was the child frail and myopic, he had a quiet dignity and confidence about him unknown to the beaten child. Perhaps it was because he had no siblings and no play-fellows either, as far as William could make out. Eliza kept him to herself.

One Sunday evening, a week before his final disagreement with Everett, William had attempted to engage the son in conversation.

'Will you be a missionary when you grow up?' he asked, as one of the maids brought in the baked chicken and greens.

'If I am chosen,' the child answered gravely, and William saw how much he resembled the mother. Everett's paternity was scarcely detectable: there was Eliza's colouring, her slight build, even a little of her stoop. From being so much in her company, Matthias had absorbed some of her more obvious mannerisms. He put his head to one side to answer, he brought his fingers to his lips while he thought.

'But I may refuse,' the boy continued, surprisingly.

Everett was drawn in now. 'And why would that be?' he asked, brusquely waving away the maid and her dish of chard. The child speared his chicken with his fork and left it wavering there.

'If I am by then a father,' said Matthias, the eyes behind his spectacles suddenly belligerent, 'if I had a boy, or even a girl, I would not leave them alone for three years.'

'You were not alone,' his father corrected him, 'and sometimes God's will conflicts with the desires of one's family and friends.'

'When you left me' – Matthias took up his fork – 'I was three years old and even though you told me how long you would be gone I had no comprehension of what you meant.'

Paora laughed and the boy looked at him disapprovingly. 'I did not intend to be humorous.'

'You are such a little fella to know such long words.'

'Mamma is a good teacher. She would like to teach you, Mister.'

It took William a moment to realise that the child addressed him. After his first question he had concentrated entirely on his meal. Mormon food appealed to him, hearty, generously apportioned as it was.

'Pardon?' he asked.

'You must address our guest as Brother McQuiggan, not Mister!' the child's father admonished.

'Mamma says you are working so hard you have not had enough time to study our scripture. She says she will help you, if you like.'

'Did your mother tell you to say this?' asked Everett, with the tone of a man surprised. His son narrowed his eyes at him.

'No. But Mamma will always do as you want.'

In the rosy evening light that slanted through the dining-room windows, William saw that his friend was blushing.

'I did ask her, that is true,' Everett said, 'but so long ago – it was while we were at sea – I thought she had forgotten.'

'She had not,' Matthias said, before applying himself to his chicken as intently as he had his conversation. William too kept his eyes on his plate, perturbed at this turn of events. He worshipped at the Assembly, he had attended the Tabernacle twice weekly since his arrival, he had studied many hours alone in his room, finding himself alternately filled with glory and envy as he read – in his piecemeal way – Joseph Smith's revelations. How he envied the Prophet of this thriving church! If only God had chosen to wait, to reveal Himself to him after he'd been properly baptised a Mormon, then he would be taken seriously, his epiphany combed for further meaning. The time that had elapsed since his near brush with God had only served to brighten and extend his memory of it. If only the Lord had actually spoken to him – if only He had provided him with as many real words as He had Joseph Smith – a dialogue he could have written down on his return to the farm.

At night, as he drifted to sleep in his narrow bed, he would return himself to Pukekaroro to search for the Voice and its inchoate urgings. Without a doubt it was the Lord who had shown him the ashes and put the idea of the fire in his mind. It had always been God's plan for him to leave the farm and come to Salt Lake. He would like to discuss this with his host, but Everett seemed to sense whenever this was on his mind and prevented any mention of it.

'Brother William?' Everett had paused, his fork halfway to his mouth.

'I'm sorry, Brother?'

'Do you agree?'

'With what?'

'To undertake further studies under the tuition of my wife. When we were first married, Sister Eliza – partly by dint of her seniority – was better versed in the Scriptures than I. I have overtaken her now of course, but I am too busy with my work to do you justice. Sister Eliza is the next best tutor to myself.'

He was nodding, William realised too late, as he absorbed his friend's advice. Brother Everett dropped his fork and clapped his hands together. 'It is decided, then. Tomorrow morning you will begin, before you leave for work.'

'But I leave for work at seven!' William protested.

'Eliza is an early riser. You will join her in the sewing room at five.'

Brother Ridge was a man few people had dared to cross. Accorded to the priesthood at the age of twelve, he had been successful at healing fevers and casting out devils, whenever he was called upon to do so. There was a beneficent authority about him and although William demurred, suggesting that perhaps Brother Paora could undertake the task, Everett was not to be moved.

Everett had not spent any time with William for weeks, not away from the table. He had lost interest in having William at his side at the theatre or sharing a pew at the Tabernacle. The New Zealander was sullen and terse these days. Paora too could be wordless, but his silence sprang from delight: his eyes would shine, his face crease with fond smiles as he was greeted by his many friends. Affectionately, he would take their hands as they approached him. Brother Everett loved him all the more for his serenity, while William's silence was the very reason Everett had tired of him: that and his guest's compulsion to return again and again to his alcohol-induced false epiphany in the New Zealand bush. Further, Everett's light remarks and expressions of joy while in William's company were met now by a turbulent, jealous eye, the mouth below falsely set with a smile. The idea that had spawned itself at sea, flaring across Everett's brain like phosphorus as he had closed the cabin door on the touching figures, as he had stood breathing into the warm darkness that carried Lydia's scent, had burned on, casting off any slag of doubt until it solidified into an elemental, definitive form. The night before the scripture lessons began Everett paid a discreet visit to his senior wife. He waited until eight-thirty, when he was sure Matthias would have been dismissed to the nursery, before he tapped lightly on the door. Later, he knew when he went in to Lydia he could just turn the handle and enter. Sister Lydia enjoyed the surprise of his coming upon her; Sister Eliza made it perfectly clear that she did not.

'Come in.' She had arranged a footstool before her and removed her boots. To Everett they seemed, as they always had, to be child's boots, neatly side by side, tiny, the lapsing laces and scuffed toes before the fall of her skirt. Her stockinged feet rested on the pouffe, her hands clasped on her lap: she was the calmest and happiest he had seen her since his second marriage – though the increase in her contentment, Brother Ridge could not help but be painfully aware, was directly proportional to the decrease in Sister Lydia's. Such delight and yes, revenge, she mined from the child, now that she was certain he would survive, he thought. At first it was as if she were frightened to love him, to feel natural maternal affection. The separation, during which she was absolved of all responsibility for Matthias's continued existence, had transformed the previous reluctance to the present strenuous, morbid love.

He took her hand briefly, lightly squeezing her fingers, before he sat down and saw the small, slightly mocking smile on her lips.

'You should have come earlier and bid Matthias good-night.'

'Sister Lydia played and sang for us in the parlour. It was most pleasant.'

'Had you company?' she asked curiously. She pictured them there, the three adoring men around the woman at the piano.

He shook his head and began to arrange his thoughts, how he would explain his intentions, and once he started she listened carefully, her sardonic smile softened to a certain wryness, her head bowed, her fingers at her temples.

'It is in accordance with the Scriptures. It will not be for the purposes of fornication nor from lowliness of heart. You must trust me.'

'But it is not the truth. Matthias is our son – and I have been your physical wife.' Sister Eliza wondered why, if the seat of emotion were the heart, it was her stomach that burned and roiled.

He bears no resemblance to me: the phrase was at his lips but he did not shape them around it. 'How strong is your regard for Brother William?' he asked her suddenly, instead.

'"Thy desire shall be to thy husband,"' she quoted. The discomfort of her stomach transferred itself to her back and shoulders.

'". . . and he shall rule over thee,"' finished Everett. He came to stand behind her and laid one open hand on her head. 'It is God's will that you do this for me. If you are to perpetrate happiness and contentment in this world and the next, then it is your only course of action.'

'But Matthias!' she whispered, and he knew without bending to her face that she was weeping.

'We will come to an arrangement. You were able to leave him before, and you shall do so again.'

'Oh . . .' Her exhalation came in a gust, tearful and sighing but, he thought, acquiescent. He withdrew his hand and would have turned away, bid her goodnight and left the room, but she took hold of his arm, looked up into his face.

'Will you take a third wife?'

'If she will bear me children. The Great Physician will lead me to her, if it is to be.'

'I think –' began Eliza, but her husband, bending to pick up his Bible from where he had laid it on the arm of his chair, interrupted her.

'I am not interested in your opinion, on this or any other matter.' It was the phrase she was later to parrot to William. 'You are a sensible woman. You are required to join your fate to his.'

'But forgive me, Everett, I still do not see how I am to persuade him.'

'I do not think he will take much persuading.' He told her then of the last part of his plan, which as he outlined the story she was to tell him, seemed to be dictated by the Lord himself, a parable to effect His will.

'Is it not an unlikely tale?' she asked, when he had finished.

'Brother William is a man of the world. It will not seem so to him.'

'But a Mormon girl and a Catholic –'

'Hush, Eliza. Tell the story to him as I have told you. There will be a week of early morning scripture lessons, as arranged with Brother William this evening. Then, a week from today, I will take him to see the smelter and seek his opinion on the matter. Not a word of this to Sister Lydia.'

'Why not?' Her voice was harsh. It grated on Everett's nerves, reminded him of her outbursts on the ship and on countless occasions during their mission. He had had a taste of life without her in New Zealand, leaving her in Auckland while he and Lydia journeyed with Paora to be among his people. Soon, for him at any rate, her emotionalism would be a trial of the past.

'This is all for her, then? To take me out of the way? And what of my son?'

'I will make arrangements for Matthias,' he repeated carefully and, not wanting to debate the topic further, which in his opinion distressed her unduly, he took his leave.

As he took the stairs at five the following morning, William passed a maid returning with the ashes from the parlour fire, her apron smudged and the brush and pail clanking. She was young, her face dark in the pre-dawn shadows. She was what they call here 'coloured', William thought, though they spelt it without the 'u'. She was possibly a quadroon, not dark enough for a mulatto, her limbs long and lithe, her mouth soft and full. He met her eyes and she startled away, hurrying down into the gloom of the lobby.

He wished now, as he went along the glossy hall towards the sewing room at the end, that Paora had spoken up at the table. He could have volunteered, as his fellow countryman, to bend with him over the closely written pages, to submit him to exhaustive questioning before he recommended him to Brother Ridge for baptism. But Brother Paora, being neither black nor mulatto nor quadroon but Maori and difficult for the Americans to classify, was nonetheless coloured and unable to hold office in the church.

The sewing room was dark, excepting for the light shed by a candle glowing between the windows. It served to brighten the room not at all: the grey dawn had found the narrow interstice between the heavy drapes and entered the room to strike a balance with the single flame, which resulted in general amorphousness. There was the shape of a high-backed chair beside that of a pedestal table which held the candle; at the chair's extreme right were the blurred knobs and edges of the treadle machine. On the other side of the candle, just the blind shape of her, sat Eliza.

William took the empty chair, his heart pounding. He could find no words to greet her, having seen her only at family prayers and on Sundays for many months. In each instance they were in the company of others and Eliza had kept silent. By contrast Sister Lydia had grown ever more voluble and high coloured, her vocal prayer a naked clamorous plea for a child of her own. Brother Everett too would pray for that blessing and his testament at meetings would return to it again and again.

'It is customary for us always to greet one another,' Sister Eliza said softly, after a moment. 'We are exhorted to as children.'

'Forgive me,' William returned her tone. There was the scent of something flowery in his nostrils, too sweet for lavender water. Violets perhaps, or gardenia. He looked around in the gloom for a vase but there was none. Sister Eliza wore perfume.

'You have treated me very coldly for so very long that I am surprised you agreed to this arrangement.' Not a hint of coquetry affected this statement, though William would not have traced it if it had. He was only mildly astonished that Sister Eliza had taken up the theme so directly.

'You know very well why I kept my distance,' he whispered. 'Let us not discuss what passed between us that night.' He saw her lips part against her teeth, more a grimace than a smile.

'What did pass between us, indeed?' she asked. 'I was not aware that anything had, save the love of the Redeemer.' She reached now for the volume that lay beside the candlestick and he saw how her wrists below the cuffs were plumper and how a new ring set with a dark gem caught the light. The observations were mechanical: the conscious part of him sank to his boots with humiliation and rose again with a flicker of his old rage. She had placed him in an invidious position. She had pretended to forget.

'Sister —' he began, but she was too quick for him.

'You must not embarrass me, Mr McQuiggan.'

'Brother!' The word broke angrily into the quiet.

'So it seems. You have decided then to proceed with baptism?'

He nodded, which she perceived though she was not looking at him.

'My husband tells me you would rather have enjoyed Brother Paora's attention. It must seem illogical to you, to be counselled by a mere woman.'

'Yes. But you have been sealed. You are destined for the Celestial Kingdom, for the upper tier of Heaven, and I would know you there.'

She made no response, though the instant he ceased speaking a sudden irregularity skipped in her even breath.

'Sister?'

'I was sealed in marriage to know only my husband for all eternity.'

She was twisting his words, loading them with intention.

'What is your wife's name?' she asked him suddenly in a lighter tone, twisting her body towards him. 'Mary, is it?'

'Myra.'

'Her religion?'

'She has none.'

Eliza was regarding him curiously as if waiting for him to elaborate, but when he didn't she said, 'Is she an evil woman, then?'

He shook his head, almost laughed. 'Not at all.'

'So you did not marry her to bring her to virtue?'

'I married her out of pity.' He remembered the afternoon of their meeting not as Myra did, but with an overlay of her tears and trembling since. 'But not because she was lost or fallen. She grew up with a notion of God because her father was a minister among the Protestants, but He has no real presence in her life. She prays silently, if at all, and does not consider His will before she acts.'

'Harsh words from a loving husband.'

'I am not –' began William, his mind continuing for a moment too far along this honest path. Sister Eliza rose suddenly and crossed the room to a sideboard where a glass jug of barley water and two tumblers sat on a small tray. Before her appointment with William, even before the workers in the house rose wearily to their duties at dawn, she had gone to the kitchen to fetch it herself. She poured a glass for him and one for herself, the simple shining duality of the cut glass reflected in the polished mahogany, her clasping hand setting the water shimmering below the gilded rims.

'I have not written to her.' William's voice was soft and thick behind her, but she made no response.

I am not interested in his confession, she told herself, and was about to bring him his drink when he spoke again.

'And you, Sister Eliza, are you a loving wife?' He watched her shoulders tense, a long crease forming in the fabric of her dress.

'If you persist with such questions, I will call for my husband to bring the bottle of oil from his medicine cabinet and cast the devil from you that rouses your impertinence.' She was struggling not to raise her voice.

'I don't think that will be necessary. Besides, if you do that we will have to tell him how you pressed against me in the Music Saloon of the ship.'

She spun towards him then, her eyes wet with tears. 'You misuse me, Brother William. I am only doing what my husband bids me. My efforts are not out of kindness to you, but obedience.'

'You keep to some part of your marriage vows, then.'

'We pledge to the Law of Obedience and the Law of Sacrifice. It is beyond anything you could imagine.'

'I can but try, Sister Eliza. Just as I try to imagine the Temple. Its interior, I mean. Is it decorated as an ordinary church, with a crucifix and cloths? What happens there?'

She turned back to the dresser and took up the glasses, shaking her head slightly, as if William were a persistent and irritating child. The movement enraged him. He pressed his feet into the floor and gripped the edge of his seat, knowing he must concentrate on staying there, on not rising and crossing the room. If he drew close to her now, while she denied him, he . . . He did not know what he would do. His arms ached to hold her too tightly, enough to hurt her. He would strike her, or shake the knowledge from her.

'It is not only you who is denied entry. It is everyone who is not baptised.'

'How can I know God is there until I see Him?' William cried. 'Tell me, Sister, have you seen him there? His body? His face? I have felt Him close. He took me, that night, in the bush in New Zealand. He drew me towards Him, but it was as if He were testing me, He would not let me see His face –'

'That is enough, Brother William! You must not speak so. It is a heresy. Why would God single you out then, when you were not a Saint nor even knew of our existence?'

'I took it as a sign from Him, that my life was about to change and I was destined for a new life here –'

'Hush! Let us begin.' Sister Eliza took the glasses across to the table between the chairs and bent at the waist to set them down. In the candlelight her face was blotched, as if she had coloured and blanched quickly with his interrogation and the red had not had time to fade into her pallor. She sat, turned her face into the shadows. 'You are familiar with our *Doctrine and Covenants*?'

'I am.' He took a sip of the barley and it slid cool and mildly sweet down his dry throat.

'You are familiar with the Prophet's Revelation?'

'Which one?' he asked lightly. 'There are so many.'

'The Revelation given through Joseph Smith, where the Lord gives us to understand that all covenants, contracts, bonds, obligations, oaths and vows made outside our church are meaningless. Where were you married?'

'In the Church of England.'

'Then you are free of her. Remember what the Redeemer told Joseph Smith: "The great and abominable church is the whore of all the earth." '

The quotation reverberated in a kind of inadvertent memory, though the hours he had spent alone with his book before him had very often been wasted. He would feel himself drift out to embrace the words on the page, to hover above the paragraphs before dissipating in the quiet air of the room. Some time later he would come back to himself, to find his concentration fixed on the angle of his thumb on the arm of his chair, or a mark on the window's joinery, as if the centre of his being had come to rest in the grain of the wood or smirch on the paint. The journey between was stimulated by the few lines actually read: '. . . the sun shall be darkened and the moon shall be turned to blood . . .', 'The Father has a body of flesh and bones as tangible as a man's . . .' Sometimes it seemed as if he took flight from the room altogether. He would gaze up, through the pane to the formal garden, its irrigated rows and patterns, to the blue, distant Wasatch mountains beyond.

Sister Eliza had once more lifted the volume from the table between them and opened it on her lap. She turned the pages hurriedly, coming at last to a section much worked over and marked.

' "Behold, mine house is a house of order, saith the Lord God, and not a house of confusion," ' she read.

'Amen,' supplied William. He watched her finger move down the print, saw how she narrowed her eyes and bent her head closer to read. The hand that guided her wore the new ring and was otherwise unadorned. What he had first thought was a wide bracelet, of mother of pearl perhaps, he saw now was a band of coarse white cotton, the sleeve of an under-garment that had slipped below her silk cuff. Was it a hair-shirt, he wondered, a garment she wore for penance?

' ". . . if a man marry him a wife in the world, and he marry her not by me nor by my word, and he covenant with her so long as he is in the world and she with him, their covenant and marriage are not of force when they are dead . . ." William? What will happen to you if you are not sealed in the Everlasting Covenant?' Eliza's tone was rigidly academic; she betrayed no concern as to his eventual fate. Would that be hell, William wondered, or the lowest tier of Heaven? Perhaps he would ascend unsealed to the second level, as long as he abstained from drink and lechery and telling false-hoods for the remainder of his natural life.

'I don't know,' he answered.

'You will remain singly, as an angel, in service to those of us who achieve the full glory of exaltation.'

'An angel?' William found that he was smiling. 'Then that will not be so bad.'

She drew herself up then, correcting her stoop, and met his eye. 'I am not in the least interested in your opinion, on this or any other matter.' It was a masculine statement, thought William, one that sat uneasily on her.

'But you are,' he said softly. 'You have shown me that.'

'Perhaps it should be Sister Lydia guiding you thus.' Footsteps passed the closed door into the hall and she lowered her voice to a level even below his, a whisper.

'Why so?' he asked.

'She is easily led. She would grant you a respect you do not deserve.'

'In your opinion,' he rejoined, unable to help himself.

Sister Eliza pressed her lips together against her response, but it escaped anyway. 'In the opinion of any person of virtue. When we first met, you were an adulterer maddened by drink.'

William recoiled as if she had stabbed him with a pin. 'On the second count you are right, on the other quite wrong.'

Satan stirreth them up that he may lead their souls to destruction . . . The phrase entered his mind, though Sister Eliza was not reading from that revelation. It was another passage she was intent upon.

'". . . if a man receiveth a wife in the new and everlasting covenant, and if she be with another man, and I have not appointed unto her by the holy anointing, she hath committed adultery and shall be destroyed."' She closed the book, leaving her finger to mark the place, and brought her other hand to her eyes.

'You are unwell?' William asked.

She shook her head, turned her face away from him. Gently William took the book from her, slipping it away with his own finger between her chosen pages.

'Perhaps we should read from *Pearl of Great Price*?' he suggested. 'You are distressed by this Revelation.' He laid the book aside and watched her for a moment. She was perfectly still. 'We will finish for today, then.' He stood.

'Tomorrow?' The single word was whispered, pleading. He turned to look at her and saw that beyond the chink in the curtains the sun had fully risen. He would be late for work, he realised, observing in the same moment that Eliza was weeping again. Perhaps she is mad, he thought suddenly, perhaps she has lost her mind.

She stood now too, taking advantage of his pause, and came to stand before him.

'It is that Revelation, the one we have been studying, that most interests newcomers to the church.' She took his hand and, closing her eyes, quoted from memory: '". . . if any man espouse a virgin, and desire to espouse another, and the first give her consent, and if he espouse the second, and they are virgins and have vowed to no other man, then is he justified . . . and if he have ten virgins given unto him by this law, he cannot commit adultery, for they belong to him . . ."'

His body betrayed him. He felt his heart convulse and throb within his breast, his arms ached to enclose her, he wanted her, though she did not attract him or rouse him fully, not as Sister Lydia had done, nor Myra during their courting. She opened her eyes, saw the want in his face and took a step towards him. He wrenched his hand free and stepped clumsily away from her, spinning towards the door.

'Tomorrow morning at the same time.' She attempted a rapid, no-nonsense tone, though William heard again the pleading note. He nodded abruptly and left the room.

On his return passage through the house, he thought he caught a glimpse of the other wife, the soft whisper of her skirts vanishing around a corner, her fair regal head, the shadow of it, held high against the dark varnished panelling. He was seized suddenly by a desire to catch up with her, to gaze upon her fair skin and sparkling eyes, but he remembered then how Sister Lydia had changed. She was no longer the lighthearted young wife he had come to know aboard the *Moana*. Her longing for a child obsessed her and she made no effort to draw her conversation away from it. On the rare occasions they had met and talked, she had embarrassed him. Her concern was an intimate one, which he thought should be reserved only for her conversation with her husband.

He went that morning to work without breakfast, as he did the following morning and every morning for the rest of the week.

CHAPTER 16

Over the following days, Sister Eliza's manner was subdued and distant. She abandoned the Revelation concerning eternal marriage and the plurality of wives and they concentrated instead on Nephi and Alma and Ether and the other stories in the *Book of Mormon.* William found he was able to drift as he had in his private studies. He could sit on the shore of the lake with Saltair at his back, the green water before him thick with the larvae of brine-flies, a scene he took from an excursion he'd made late last summer, when the last of the season's dance music issued from the open windows of the wooden rococo palace and families picnicked around him. A distance away, shimmering in the haze at the far reach of the pebbly beach, was a cluster of bathing sheds. Wheels and shafts resting in the mud, they discharged only a hardy few into the olive-coloured, reflective waters. The air was heavy and dull and the lake appeared to steam, especially at the foot of the brown island that floated in melancholy, arid beauty a short distance from the shore. The rock was closer in late summer than at any other time, the unrelentingly blue skies drew back an ebbing, slow, solar tide. It seemed to William that this was a place God had made many millions of years ago, at the beginning of Creation, and then cast aside, deciding in His wisdom to leave it incomplete.

Ancient and raw, given form but kept void: His spirit had moved upon the face of the waters and gathered it together in one place, whereupon He had enclosed it with such harsh grandeur that no man could forget here His terrible will. Perhaps, thought William, when Brother Brigham had come upon this place, the voice he had heard was strident, God as Creator: Behold! Even my unfinished work is beautiful.

Sister Eliza maintained the demeanour of a reticent and slightly disappointed tutor, the tears and rage and intimacy of their first lesson dismissed from the light, forgotten. She never once met his eyes and for their subsequent sessions moved her chair to the treadle table, lighting a lamp on the sideboard and eschewing the candle altogether. Neither did William scent gardenias in the room, as he had on his first visit.

On Friday night he learned at dinner that Sister Eliza was ill and had taken to her bed at noon. As he climbed the stairs on Saturday's dawn, late for their appointed time and aching in the shins from where a floor joist had struck him at the site the day before, he doubted whether she would be there to meet him. He hoped not – then he may descend to the kitchen and eat a cooked breakfast with the servants. It being a Saturday, he would be able to eat again later in the dining room with Everett and Paora. Such an appetite compelled him at table now, more than any had as an adolescent or younger man. The cloth-wrapped meal he took to work from Everett's larder filled his hungrier workmates with envy: white bread, ham and cheese, cold chicken, pickles and fresh tomatoes in season. William gave no impression of actually enjoying his meal – he bolted it as he believed a hard man should. The quality of his food was the only aspect of him that roused the curiosity of the others. None betrayed any interest in the origins of another: Serbs and Czechs spoke their own tangled and intersecting tongues, the Celestials kept to themselves.

But Sister Eliza waited for him. He knew she was there by the fuzz of light beneath the door, and that she was not alone by the soft, whispered singing that brushed against him, like a cobweb, as he opened the door and went in. It was a cradle-song she was singing, by its cadences and lulls intended to comfort, but in Sister Eliza's high tuneless voice it took on an eerie, haunting edge. She sat in a wicker chair by the sill. The child, Matthias, was wrapped in a quilt and held on her lap. He was too big for her embrace now: his head hung away from her shoulder and his thin white legs lay bare against her robe, which William saw was a teagown perhaps, or a peignoir: the child's body hid its defining characteristics. Her hair too was undressed, falling on either side of her face in thin wisps. She had not lit the lamp, but opened wide the curtains to admit the grey dawn.

'You should not have come,' William said.

'My husband tells me he is driving with you out to the smelter this morning.' She was studying her child's face, the open, bloodless breathing.

'Why is the child not in his bed?' he asked.

'He had been crying for me. I had not the heart to replace him. He has always been a sickly child, much as his mother was.'

'Not at all,' William demurred. He sat in his customary place in the high-backed chair by the table. 'You have hidden strengths, I believe, Sister Eliza.'

'He is my sister's child.' She spoke as if he had not, not lifting her eyes from the child, plucking at the wrapping, rearranging a dangling, sleep-heavy arm. A white scurf peeled at the corners of Matthias's mouth. Milk perhaps, or a powder. 'My sister passed away soon after the confinement and her husband was killed not long after that in an accident. He came to us by the Grace of God.' Odd tendons and muscles pulled at her face, distorting it as if she made a supreme effort not to weep. He wished she had not chosen to confide in him. It made no difference to him whose loins Matthias had sprung from. How black his fingernails were, he noted, turning his hands over. Bruising and abrasions from his working

266

week scattered the skin on their backs. He curled his nails into his fist, looking up at her as he did so. Perhaps he would bathe later. She regarded him quizzically.

'Are you not surprised by this?'

William shrugged. 'It is common enough all over the world for orphaned nephews to be taken in by their aunts –'

'Yes, yes of course.' She was insistent, impatient. 'What is unusual in this case – curiously so, I would have thought – is my husband's desire to deceive those closest to us: not only yourself, Brother, but my sister-wife also.'

'She believes the child is yours?'

She nodded, and as she did so another tress came free from her head, falling over her eyes. She did not brush it away, but left it there as if she were grateful for the small privacy it allowed her. William felt the ground shift under him in the way it had on the *Moana*, when he had realised Everett's relationship with the women who accompanied him. This time, he was sure, there would be no doctrine or revelation in which to root his duplicity. He stood, planting his feet.

'Why are you telling me this?' he asked. 'Surely there are many people in Salt Lake who know the truth of the child's origins?'

'It has been kept a secret – and it must remain so. You must promise not to tell a soul.' He shook his head and alarm flashed in her eyes. 'Brother William –'

'No – no. It is not that I will not keep your secret. It's just that I wonder at the concealment of such a thing in this place. It seems to me that every man's business is common knowledge.'

'Some of my sister's story is known. I will tell it to you, but I must have your promise you will not repeat it. To anyone.'

'You have it.'

'My sister –' began Eliza, wearily, trailing off as if she could not go on. She took a deep breath, the child rising and falling with it on her breast. 'My younger sister married outside the church, a man from the town of Mercur.' Her final word carried the weight of a moral judgement or curse, much as a priest would pronounce Sodom or Gomorrah.

'A Catholic,' she continued, hushed. 'An Italian. It was a terrible scandal. He was a poor man, a farmer, and she was always impulsive, a little unbalanced perhaps, in the light of what happened. There had been signs of it before her . . . elopement.' Sister Eliza stumbled over the word as if it were one she had not often used. 'She was a lovely girl, full of life. They met once, on the street, and soon after, one night, she vanished. There was no word from her for years.'

'Until the child,' William prompted. The story absorbed him suddenly: there was the sister, a Mormon girl, clean of heart and spirit and destined by birth for a celestial purity beyond any the lustful, idolatrous Roman could perceive.

'Sometimes I think it was for the best. She could never have endured to live as I do –' A small dry cough choked her throat.

William looked to the sideboard for the customary barley water – he would bring her a drink – but there was none.

'With Sister Lydia watching my every move.'

He was baffled by the sudden swing away from the sister's story, which was beginning to redeem his friend and benefactor. He had made a sudden and hasty judgement, that Brother Everett was a liar, but he was beginning to see, until Sister Eliza changed the subject, scarcely drawing breath, that there were reasons for Everett's silence. He sat again, heavily.

'My husband eludes me, save for messages sent with Paora, otherwise I would ask him if he counsels her as he did me.' She paused, watching his hands roll between his knees, as he did himself, right over left, left over right, the black of his nails forgotten.

'You have become less of a conversationalist than ever, Brother William.' A thread of pale humour trailed this remark, which escaped William entirely. 'Are you not curious to know how a Mormon husband must chide his wife and bring her back into accord?'

He shook his head at her. He wanted to know no more. It pained and confused him. There was a clock, he noticed, a plain brass unwound clock on the sill, which previously had been hidden by the curtain. It stood on a silver tray, and on the tray lay the key.

'You may find yourself in the same situation one day. You are still young, Brother: you could marry again.'

He had crossed the room and picked up the key, which was as ornate as the clock was bare.

'On the voyage to New Zealand my husband advised me to fast, which I confess I found easy, having begun to do so already, inadvertently, from the sea-sickness. He spoke to me also of the fallacy of romantic love, and how it would be better if I revered him only as my means to come to God. We would pray also, for hours, the three of us in Everett's stateroom. The Lord gave comfort and strength to my husband and sister-wife – before my eyes they would fill with His light – but He turned His back on me, shamed me with tears and fainting fits.'

He began to wind the clock, steadying the casing with his left hand and bending to the key hole.

'Listen carefully to what my husband tells you today.'

Keeping his back to her, he feigned interest in the clock and the shrubs and flower-beds taking shape in the dawn garden beyond. Close to the house a breeze ruffled a pile of cuttings from a topiary.

'William?'

Grudgingly he turned to face her and saw she was making preparation to stand with the child and would require his assistance. It was a task he could fulfil with ease, he realised, feeling as though he had failed her in some unaccountable way. The same disappointment chilled her face to remote inscrutability as it had when he had failed to understand or quote sections from the Scriptures. She lifted the child to a sitting position and William bent to slip an arm between the child's back and her breast. Her breath was warm on his ear and neck.

'There would be no sin in it,' she whispered.

The child weighed lighter than he had expected and he employed too much lift, his left arm catching Sister Eliza under the jaw as he straightened with Matthias in his arms. It was not a hard blow, though the shock of it made her cry out and lunge away from him. The child's eyes peeled open and focused myopically on the man who embraced him. There was no spark of recognition and his bony frame flew into panic. The frail legs kicked, and from between the pale dry lips scraped a voiceless exhalation of despair. Eliza struggled to her feet, extending her arms, her peignoir falling open to reveal a strange undergarment of yellowed white, innocent of any frill or ribbon. It rose high at her neck, but its little row of buttons had come undone, and it gaped at her breast. Even as William's eyes registered the pale swelling of her flesh, he had torn his eyes away from her.

'You will wear this yourself, after you are married,' she murmured. 'The devout do not remove them even when they bathe.'

William held the child still. She made no attempt to draw her gown together.

'Are you not curious to see? You must have wondered why the Saints who work alongside you on the building sites never remove their shirts, even on hot summer days.'

'I thought . . . I thought it was modesty. Neither do I remove –' He looked at her finally, saw the ill-fitting long-johns bagging at her ankles. Embroidered over each breast was a Masonic compass and square, and there were other strange symbols he did not recognise at her navel and knee.

'It is not only modesty that keeps us in our garments. It is for protection.'

'From what?' William swallowed. His throat was coated in dust: she had revealed to him a skin more intimate than flesh.

'From fire. Or bullets.' Her eyes met his, as if she challenged him to believe it. He drew in his breath, adopted a stern tone.

'Shall I tell your husband you have shown yourself to me?'

'I do not think, under the circumstances, that he will disapprove.' She pulled her outer gown closed and fastened the tie at her waist, before holding out her arms for the child, who whimpered now as William stepped forward and lowered him into her embrace. As their faces passed close, Eliza lifted her lips to his cheek and he thought for an instant that she would kiss him.

'My husband has a proposal for you,' she whispered. 'There is no sin in it.'

They were the same words she had used earlier. He stared at her, uncomprehending.

'If you would be so kind as to open the door for us,' she said aloud, walking ahead of him towards it, the drugged child in her arms as limp as a corpse.

'Sister Eliza, you must not think I –'

'Shshsh.' Her admonition was as soft as the door rasping away from the hall rug, and he did not know if it was intended for him or the child. As soon as she had gone he hurried away himself, down to the safety of his ground-floor room. He re-read his mother's long-ago letter and gazed out the window, trying not to think about Eliza, or the garments, or Eliza's sister, or the child. He thought instead of the Temple, of the lake, of how he must go to the bank to arrange his finances.

There was a rapid, light knock and Everett stood before him. His face shone from his bath and there was the smell of cologne. They were to drive to the smelter in Everett's pride and joy – a White Steam Stanhope, built that very year, with solid rubber tyres and a cerise-coloured fringe above. William followed him out, down the passage towards the open door.

The horseless carriage passed first the mile-wide tailings pond before going on towards the smelter towers on the shores of the lake. The dull brown hills rolled away to the east, growing ever larger until they terminated at the skyline in snow-covered crags. A stiff wind was blowing, billowing the Stanhope's canopy over their heads and ruffling scum on the pond's surface. Above the roar of the engine Everett kept up a steady patter, explaining the complicated proprietorship of the enterprise. His father had had four wives and twelve sons and his money had been in coal, which enterprise Everett and five of his brothers had inherited. Together they had extended operations into copper and alloys, which provided a tithe of great magnitude for the church. William kept his face away, only glancing at Everett to discover in which direction he was pointing. A brown ribbon of land on the other side of the pond sprouted scrappy sagebrush. It was bordered by the railway line and beyond that, beneath a blanket of salt haze, lay the lake, which shared the same poisonous hue as the ponds. The Ridges had changed the landscape for ever, thought William. Surely even after Judgement Day, the blackened towers of the copper smelter would stand as they did now, in the shadow of a bare and ancient hill. William turned his gaze back to the tailings pond, which was behind them now. It was bronze and green, devoid of life.

'We bring in the ore by train,' Everett yelled. 'That's the crusher there – the part of the smelter closest to the lake. Need the water to make the slurry –'

William scarcely listened. Indicating which parts of the smelter were used for what stage of production, Everett's soft hand flailed before his nose. The cloth-capped driver maintained his anonymous back, and were it not for the Stanhope's roof, William would have tipped his face towards the sky. He was not interested in the American's industry, he would prove himself to be as indifferent to Everett as that man had shown himself to him. Early in his stay, he had learned not to contribute to discussions at his host's table when there were guests. Inevitably they were men of Everett's standing – captains of industry with interests in mines or railways, cottonwood milling or construction. The vicissitudes of William's spirit or the difficulties of his working day, which he had once or twice related in what he had hoped was a manly, vigorous style would earn him either pitying glances or worse, no acknowledgement that he had spoken at all. Now, under the flapping canopy, he wished himself a thousand miles away.

'Shall we walk a little?' invited Everett.

William came back to himself, realised they had come to the high blackened smelter gates. There was no one about save for the distant figure of a watchman. Overhead the sun hid behind a low mantle of grey cloud, but the dry air gave no hint of rain. They stepped down from the steam car, the engine of which sent one last white plume into the windless atmosphere as they walked away.

'We make blister copper here,' announced Everett, 'some of the purest in the world –' He had stridden too far ahead, he realised, towards the furnace chimneys, leaving William behind. His guest looked pale, distracted, almost as he had on the day they first met. His own desire for Lydia's happiness, this convoluted plan, the story of Eliza's sister – perhaps it would all prove too much for the New Zealander.

They reached the main doors of the smelter. Although it was a new building, only five years old, already the low step was scuffed and paintless from the feet of the hundred workers who came each morning by train.

'We could go in if you like,' Brother Everett offered, 'though it being a rest day you will have no experience of how it really is, the terrific heat and noise.'

William shook his head. 'I am not particularly curious,' he said coldly.

'Ah . . .' Everett strove for tolerance. He swivelled his body to stand parallel to William so that he might take in the same view. There was the rubble disrupted by the smelter's construction, a pile of grey rock between the wide doors and the lake, green and still.

'Why have you deceived me for so long?' William burst out. 'The woman you call your wife is so in name only and Matthias is not your son.' To his surprise Everett nodded calmly, as if he knew that William had found him out, as if he had known all along it would only be a matter of time before he did.

'Do you love me, William?' Everett asked, 'as your Brother in Christ?'

William nodded abruptly. 'Yes, of course, but I –'

'I am only a man, no better or worse than yourself,' Everett continued, 'and I have made my share of mistakes. Eliza has told you of her sister?'

'Yes.'

'It is an indication of her fondness for you that she has. Not even Sister Lydia knows the truth of the child's birth.' His listener had folded his arms across his chest and was glowering into the middle distance. 'Do you think me a happy man, Brother?'

William pondered. 'You give the impression of being so,' he said at last.

'I am not – at least, not completely. I must speak frankly to you. My marriage to Eliza, as I gather she has told you, is purely spiritual.'

William looked towards the distant Stanhope. It was the only vertical object above a foot high in a vast brown expanse. The driver had propped his Scriptures on the steering shaft and his head was bent to it. 'It is no business of mine.'

'It may not be, but you are in a position to be empathetic. You never speak of your New Zealand wife. Quite obviously she has no place in your affections now.'

He allowed a pause for William to contribute to their discussion, to refute this. He said nothing.

'And your marriage, like mine, is devoid of children.'

'I have twin daughters,' William told him suddenly, though he had not thought of the babies for many months.

'But you never –' began Everett, alarmed. This could destroy his plan. 'What are their names?' he continued falsely, buying time to think.

'I don't know. They were born the night before we left Auckland.'

Rage spread through Everett's breast, burned into the base of his throat. 'To leave a wife and new-born infants is hardly the action of a Christian!'

'I intend sending for them when I am ready, when I am settled.' Sullenly, William scuffed his heel on the ground, back and forth. It was just like Everett to turn his defeat into victory. Instead of being the willing recipient of the American's envy, he was now being chastised by him.

He could not accuse this man of hypocrisy, Everett realised. It made no difference anyway, the existence of the twins. He made a rapid calculation – they would be two years old, quite strong enough to travel, but the father had not sent for them.

'Leave them be,' he muttered. 'After all this time it is better if your wife finds her own way in the world. She is a simple girl, I presume, as so many of your countrywomen are. She would be unhappy here. Did you leave her provided for?'

William considered and supposed she was. 'She will have a roof over her head at least.'

'The Lord intends Eliza for you, as your physical wife. I have prayed for guidance on this matter and He has answered me, as surely as He did when He directed me to take the mission to New –' Everett gulped, stumbled back a step: William had spun him around, roughly grabbing his shoulder.

'You would not lie to me?'

Everett glared at the offending hand and William removed it. 'I believe the Lord gave me Eliza in keeping for you. I have looked after her, preserved her chastity on your behalf. I tell you, she has been to me only a spiritual wife, such as the many our Prophet took to secure their entry to Heaven. That was why he was persecuted by people of prurient mind who had no understanding of God's love for –'

'Enough!' Saliva flew from William's mouth. He lifted a hand as though to strike out and Everett, light on his feet, stepped out of his reach. 'I will not marry Eliza. I have no regard for her, and no need either.'

'It is not natural for a man of your youth and vitality to live alone –'

'I do not live alone!' William was shouting. 'I live with God –'

'Whom you would disobey!' Everett was shouting now, lifting his voice to match the other. 'Eliza is your natural wife, she will guide and care for you –'

There was the crunch of uneven footsteps on the gravel and an elderly man, the watchman they had seen from the automobile, came around the corner and looked at them curiously.

'You it is, sir!' he said. He was Japanese, poorly dressed, a battered hat pulled over his eyes. On either side of his body hung hands distorted with arthritis, the knuckles swollen and battered from a lifetime in the employ of Everett and Everett's father before him. William saw the grind of his lost days, realised how many people Everett held in his hand: the so-called 'helpers with the work' in the house, whom an outsider would recognise as servants; the slum-dwellers, like this old man, who worked at the smelter. It was not pity or compassion that rose in him at the spectacle of their sorry lives, but jealousy. Had fate smiled on him, had he been born here as Everett rather than to the small wealth of his own father, then he could have had this control, these riches, this power, this complacent relationship with God.

'Everything is all right?' the old man asked their silent faces. Everett gave his characteristic impatient shooing motion, and the old man did as he was told, dropping his gaze and moving off in the direction he came from. William had the sense of his leaning against the wall around the corner, listening. He wanted to leave. He would not travel back to the city with Everett Ridge. All his love for the man had turned to hatred; the curiosity and passion he had nurtured for his faith twisted to a bitter, violent sense of deception. He noticed suddenly how Everett was dressed: a shining new derby on his head, a freshly brushed duster over a tan Norfolk suit. He would not follow him for fear of ruining his natty clothes, and if he did, he would not be able to catch him.

As he had as a child in Judge's Bay, William leapt from rock to rock in the rubble, rounding the point on the firm mud at the lake's edge before he came up onto the shingle to run beside the railway line. The earth was flat around him, airborne salt grazed his lungs, his legs pounded beneath him, carrying him away from the man who would tie him to a woman who would burden him with her misery and confound him with her religion. And all the time, while he ran, he felt her breath on his cheek as he had when he had lifted the child, and heard her voice, 'There would be no sin in it', over and over again, growing thin and pleading.

There would be no sin in it.

CHAPTER 17

The post office had forwarded the letter to her cottage in Ponsonby and Myra had kept it, these past six months, on the mantelpiece above the range, tucked behind a cheap lumpen blue china boy. The heat of the chimney had cracked his glaze and turned the letter yellow and thin; the ink had faded on its outer folds to an illegible ashen grey. It did not matter: she had no desire to read it again after the first time. The merest glimpse of its dog-eared corners, as she went about sweeping the kitchen floor, or stirring pots or tending her daughters, was enough to remind her of the calamity and anguish of its lines.

As she understood them, the facts were that her husband had left Salt Lake because of the unreasonable and immoral expectations of his friends there. She wondered if Salt Lake were such a small place that he couldn't have found alternative lodgings and continued. He was a carpenter now, he wrote, like the Lord. He made no request for money nor any mention of return to Auckland, which Myra, as she had hesitantly opened the envelope, had thought he would. Her first response, on reaching the letter's close, was relief – relief that he would not be coming back, that she would not have to resume her life at his side.

He had begun the letter in Utah and resolved early in its first paragraph to post it in Colorado, but it seemed that once he had started a correspondence unattended for two and a half years, he could not bear to let it go. There were passages added in Kansas and Missouri, which she knew only by the state names written in block capitals at the head of a new page. The Colorado mountains and the plains of Kansas had flickered past his railway carriage window, unacknowledged and entirely undescribed.

Her relief at his continued distance from her, as she tucked the letter behind the china boy, was tempered a little by disappointment. She had searched the letter for a name other than that of the Father and the Son and the prophets of the strange American church. Halting and careful, she studied it line by line for a hint of intimacy, or temporal friendship with herself or any other, but there was none. Neither did he seem to have any idea of his destination, at least not until the very end when in one mysterious sentence he announced: 'The Lord is sending me to Chicago! Alleluia!' This last, with his name scrawled below, was written in lead pencil.

More regularly there were letters from Mrs McQuiggan in Edinburgh, the first bemoaning the fickleness and ingratitude of Mary, who had left her within days of their disembarking. Scotland, the maid had hissed as a parting shot to her disgruntled employer, was even bleaker and more barbaric than New Zealand and she was removing home to Manchester. Mary's treacherous act had far-reaching consequences in Alithea's correspondence: the weather was inclement; her relatives uninterested in her discourses on New Zealand; shop assistants terse and frequently – her ear not attuned to their brogue – incomprehensible. Neither could she cheer her heart by prayer: having accustomed herself to the incense and excesses of the Church of England, she found her new Presbyterian place of worship – though by its denomination the faith of her fathers – stark and bare, and its minister, she complained, too concerned with Satan and the fires of hell. Further, she never once refrained from the opportunity to expound upon her sense of betrayal at Blanche's hands, that sense deepened by Mary's subsequent desertion: a mere week before the date of their departure, Blanche had decided to stay in Auckland and live with Myra and the twins.

Blanche did not tell her mother, in her sparser though more cheerful correspondence, that she and Myra had ceased to go to church altogether. There had been no actual decision to abstain. It was just that after the move to Ponsonby they made no effort to acquaint themselves with the local parish, though the young vicar came calling on his rounds and admired the two little girls.

It was Blanche's idea to have a birthday tea on the occasion of the twins turning three. It would not have occurred to Myra – birthday teas were never a feature of her own childhood. But she liked the idea and was up at five, hunkered down at the firedoor to boil the kettle for a breakfast cup and prepare the birthday treats. Ellen and Clement were expected and they would bring with them Henry, and Fanny from Epsom would come in her buggy. Blanche had also invited the persistent vicar, whom she had met at Curran Street Beach only the day before.

The kitchen was at the back of the cottage, below street level. The front door, dark green below the lacy gable and striped veranda awning, opened into a hall well lit by the northern sun that streamed through its glass. There was a little-used parlour to the left, with Blanche's room beyond that. On the right of the hall was the twins' room, with Myra's adjoining. Between the parlour door and Blanche's room, a dim stairwell led down the southern face of the ridge that the house straddled, to a narrow passage and the back door. The kitchen lay off this to the right – cool and dark in the summer but arctic and gloomy in the winter. No matter what the season, a coal-oil lamp was always needed for work at the back of the room. There was no other source of light aside from a narrow double-hung window that gave out onto the garden, and there was no separate scullery. The floor before the sink was of tamped earth and the floorboards of the remainder of the room were poorly fitted and too close to the earth of the footings. It hadn't occurred to Myra, when she bought the house, that the kitchen might not be a pleasant place in which to spend most of her waking hours.

A pound of butter, three-quarters of a pound of castor sugar – Myra measured the ingredients into her scales, the scales she still thought of as belonging to Mrs Gordon, though Mrs Gordon had left them behind gladly, and the copy of Mrs Beeton's as well, when she departed to her widowed brother's in Dunedin. From the spindly tree outside, Myra took a lemon and grated its rind into the mixture, and 'with the hand beat it up to a very light cream' as Mrs Beeton instructed. One, two, three, four – in went the eggs. It was easier to concentrate and make a success of it without the distractions of the twins, though the kitchen door stood open to admit the sound of their first waking, stumbling steps on the floor upstairs and to allow the escape of the mounting heat. Too late she realised, after the addition of the flour, that the recipe called for three or four round tins and she had only two. 'Before beginning, read the recipe through to the end,' Gordie had exhorted her often enough, especially once it was known that Myra would soon be fending for herself once more. On the farm she had baked and stewed by trial and error with a lot of the latter, and Gordie had known that once young Mrs McQuiggan and Miss Blanche moved to the new house Miss Blanche would be unlikely to shift herself to help with the culinaries. Neither would they be able to afford a cook, even if one were to be had.

Myra filled the two tins she had and slipped them into the range, then stared glumly into the bowl, which was over half full. If she waited for the other cakes to bake, then filled them again, the fire would need to burn for three hours and would have to be tended for that time. It would be roasting hot and stuffy and the twins would trail around after Blanche rather than herself, their mother, on their birthday morning.

There was a footfall on the boards above and she cocked her head to listen. It was Blanche, too heavy for one of the twins, and now she was coming down the stairs.

'Morning!' Blanche called out as she went out the back door to the privvy, which sat at the end of the asphalt path. The asphalt was breaking up already, though the man from Samuel Vaille had insisted it was freshly laid.

'Morning,' Myra murmured, and lifted her head to watch Blanche go down the garden. The honey-coloured batter in the bowl between her two hands filled her heart with disproportionate despair. If only she could throw it out, down the dunny from which Blanche was now emerging and knotting her dressing-gown at her waist, or into the weeds at the back fence. It would be an act of such infinitesimal consequence that it would trouble no one at all, as neither should it herself.

Blanche came in, leaving the back door standing open.

'Is that tea?' she gestured at the enamel tea pot on the oilcloth.

'It'll be cold by now,' Myra responded dolefully, unable to fathom this new meanness in her. She felt it as a physical sensation, a zinging green speck of rot in her once-generous heart. The old man had left her with a hundred and fifty pounds a year and her mother-in-law, in the light of Blanche's staying in the colony, had paid for the cheap little house outright. There was more money than there had ever been before, and half a bowl of Mrs Beeton's farinaceous preparation was nothing, nothing at all.

'Is that the gift from Mother?' Blanche asked, sipping her tea and pointing at the brown-paper parcel on the dresser. The tea was tepid, but nothing could induce her on this languid January morning to fill the kettle and thus be compelled to remain in this hot, uncomfortable room for as long as it took to boil. Her sister-in-law, she noticed suddenly, had a wide-eyed and panicked aspect.

'What?' she asked. 'What's wrong? Has there been another letter from William?'

Myra shook her head and laughed. That was an idea. Imagine if that were the case. Imagine if he'd remembered the girls' birthday and sent them his best wishes. 'I've made too much mixture and I'm going to throw it away,' she announced, carrying the bowl past Blanche towards the open door.

'Not the bowl as well!' Blanche murmured, pulling an astonished clown face, wide-open mouth and popping eyes. Myra laughed again and decided in that moment the cakes would bake alone, without the rock cakes and other things she had intended. She and the twins would walk to the bakery at Three Lamps and buy the rest: iced finger buns and fly cemeteries.

'It's a terrible waste,' Blanche added, in a fair imitation of Myra herself. Myra coloured slightly. It was true she had said that a lot lately, over Dora's lost boots and Joy's uneaten porridge, and in the ladieswear department of Smith and Caughey's when Blanche had persuaded her to buy a bathing dress.

'Go on,' said Blanche, smiling, patting her on the shoulder. 'Get rid of it and then let's wake the twins.'

Dora and Joy woke in their wide bed to their mother opening the curtains and their aunt leaning over them to lift Joy and turn her right way up from her upside-down position on the hot, rumpled sheets. Mumma had a parcel wrapped in brown paper under her arm and another curious knobbly one in her hand. Auntie had an odd lump under her dressing-gown.

Dora opened them while Joy watched, even though their mother had firmly placed one of the parcels in the smaller girl's hand. Immediately she gave it to her sister. Wasn't that the same as opening it herself only quicker? With her usual determined, set jaw, Dora slipped away the string to reveal two finely knitted singlets of Ayrshire wool. Straightaway she cast them aside for the other gifts of Myra's: a board-book and Blanche's doll. The singlets being all that was left to her, Joy picked one of them up and pulled it over her head.

An indulgent smile creased the aunt's face, but Myra wished that Joy would grab and squeal. It was hardly something a mother should tell a child to do, but she could not bring herself to praise Joy for her generosity and perpetual placid tolerance of overbearing Dora. It was as if, she thought now, as Dora reclaimed the second singlet and pulled it over her own head to lie like her sister's in a bulky collar, one child had inherited the father's nature and one her own. The transposal from each adult to individual child seemed complete, entire, with none of one spilling over into the other. Myra did not waste time dwelling on this, for weren't their natures decided at birth by God, or nature, and there was nothing she could do about it? She loved Dora constantly, as she had loved William until the day of the fire, but her feelings for Joy swung from an irritable empathy to comfort from her emerging, biddable companionship.

Their aunt was lifting them one by one to the rag-rug on the floor, removing the singlets and evenly distributing the toys, and Myra saw as she lifted them free of the bed that the sheets were wet. Her exasperated tongue-clicking brought an expression of disgust to Blanche's face and a guilty, sad cast to Joy's, though Dora was more likely the culprit.

'Not again!' said Blanche. 'I will go and dress,' and she left the room, as Myra started to remove the little nightgowns and strip the bed.

By their appearance, the cakes were perfectly judged, though she would not know that for certain until they were cut. She left them on a wire rack to cool and hurried through the morning's chores and the preparation of lunch. Even while Blanche was still nibbling at her sandwich and turning the pages of the newspaper, Myra had filled the sink and begun the dishes. Then there was the girls' hair to be brushed, their boots to be found, faces to be washed and clean pinafores to be put on before they could emerge blinking into the sun at the front of the house with an hour to spare before the guests arrived. If Blanche had helped she wouldn't be in such a rush, she thought, as she took a small hand in each of hers and headed up the steep street towards Ponsonby Road. But Blanche never did help, at least not with the hard work. She might rinse an occasional cup or handwash her own silk stockings, but she never cooked or undertook the heavy laundry. To be fair, thought Myra, as she hurried up the hill, Blanche was hardly ever home. She had a strong sense that Alithea would disapprove of her youngest daughter's way of life, if she knew about it. Blanche had taken up smoking, and one or two of her gentlemen friends owned motorcars and took her touring . . . Myra lifted her head to look around and took a deep breath. Why was her heart hammering so, as if she were nervous, or in dread of something? There is nothing to worry you, she told herself: it is just the family and Fanny and the vicar coming.

The grocer's horse and cart were in the middle of the street and the grocer's boy was delivering a sack of flour to the Middletons at number seven. Dora and Joy pulled towards the horse, but their mother's arms stiffened and kept them to the dusty path.

'You can pat him if we see him on the way home,' she told them, but Dora wailed.

'He'll be gone by then!'

'The next horse, then,' she said. 'If he's one we know,' she added at the top of the hill, to stop Dora pulling ahead to see if the butcher's nag or any other was in sight. They turned left and hurried along towards the baker at Three Lamps, but not before Dora had consoled herself by scooping up a handful of stones and hard clay that she carried close-fisted all the way, even while her mother bought the treats for her tea.

Emerging from the shop door, which was crowded with children intent on pennyworth packets of broken biscuits, Myra cast her eye down the street towards the Club Hotel at the corner and the legendary three-headed lamp-post that stood outside it. Leaning up against its column was what appeared at first glance to be a sack of wheat, or potatoes, or coal. In the instant the sack moved of its own accord and showed itself to be a person, Myra realised who it was, and taking Dora's hot hand once again into her own and holding out the little finger of the hand that carried the string bag of buns to Joy, she ran as fast as her heavy skirt would allow her and the little girls could keep up. The woman was standing now, her sackcloth shawl drawn closer over her shoulders, the gown below it faded to dusky pink.

'Riha!'

The woman had taken one step out into the street as if she would cross Jervois Road towards St Mary's Bay, but at the sound of Myra's voice she turned, her mouth open in alarm.

'Riha!' Myra called again, pulling past a tram now, which had concealed her from Riha's view and Riha, seeing who it was who called her, ran across Ponsonby Road with no concern for traffic on hoof or wheel, her arms extended. Tears, huge and brimming in her wide brown eyes, had broken and run down her dusty, travel-worn cheeks even before she had drawn Myra in, holding her tight against her breast.

Joy retrieved the bag of buns that had dropped from her mother's hand and tugged at the strange lady's skirt while her sister, enraged by the sudden run and engulfing of her mother, yelled 'Mumma!' and launched herself kicking and scratching at the four legs. The embrace ended, and Myra's nostrils filled with the odour of Riha's stale sweat and the street that had been her bed these past nights, for however long. She stared at her friend and saw that her hair, which only four years ago had been a thick fall to her waist with a

glint of silver here and there, was cut short and hung in grey-
ing hanks away from her neck. Riha kept her heavy hands
clasped on Myra's shoulders, and her dear, loving smile, as
she looked down into the little girls' faces, one thunderous
and the other perplexed, had lost – as far as Myra could see
– a good many of its teeth.

'Who are you?' demanded Dora.

Riha pulled her gown to her knees and squatted before
her. The eyes that regarded her were the father's, distant, as
blue and cold as moons.

'My name is Riha.'

'This is Dora and Joy,' said Myra, proudly.

'It's our birthday,' Joy supplied, surprisingly, drawing
Riha's eye away from her sister. The new person looked at
her and she thought perhaps it was a man, although he wore
a funny pink dress.

'We are three old.' Dora put out a hand and drew Riha's
face back to her.

'No wonder your mother grew such a big puku – there
were two of you!' Riha said and Myra blushed. Riha
extended a finger to pry open Dora's fist and Dora emptied
her treasure into the palm of Riha's hand.

'Can you tell I'm not Joy?' demanded Dora. Myra could
see where Dora was headed and she sighed. The child would
want the list now, the same as her mother gave it when the
small insistent voice asked the question of her.

'Well, you are bigger,' she would begin.

'Else?' Dora would ask.

'Your hair is a little darker.'

'Else?'

'Joy has a pointier chin.'

'Else?'

'Your eyes are not as round.'

'Else?'

And the game would go on until Myra became aware of
Joy, watchful and confounded, unable to understand why her

sister wanted their differences and not what made them the same. Going to her sister now, Joy slipped an arm around her waist and Dora wriggled irritably in her grasp. They stared as one dual-faced creature at Riha, breathing together. Riha was very brown and perhaps very old and there was a smell of smoke and something else not very pleasant, the sort of smell that upset Auntie Blanche.

'Can you tell I'm not Joy?' repeated Dora, wriggling again.

'You are exactly the same,' said Riha, 'except you've got whiskers.'

Dora giggled. 'Have not!'

'Come home with us, Riha,' Myra said suddenly. 'We live close by. Come with us.'

Riha looked embarrassed, then; her face clouded as she stood.

'You can have a bath and something to eat,' insisted Myra. She wanted to give Riha some comfort, to see her clean and fed. Perhaps she could give her the fare for the steamer home. She remembered her kindness now as a kind of dream, the only warmth at Pukekaroro before her spell with the Waylands.

'Is your husband there? At your house?'

Myra shook her head, her cheeks pinkening again. 'He's in America,' she whispered, 'and even if he was at home you would be welcome.'

At this Riha snorted, but she was smiling as she scooped up Joy and took Dora's hand. They began the walk back to Summer Street.

'You're carrying Joy 'cause she's smaller'n me,' announced Dora.

'That's true,' said Riha. 'You're so heavy my arms would break off.'

'I am not,' Dora giggled again. She began to skip, scuffing her boots in the dirt, and Mumma either didn't notice or didn't mind, engrossed as she was in talking to the strange lady. It was a lady, she decided, even though she was so tall and her voice was so deep. Mumma was a lady and so was Auntie Blanche, though they were like little fine-boned cats or something and this lady was big and strong like the grocer's horse. Neither did Mumma notice the Middleton boy from over the road go by, a big boy of thirty or ten, or something like that, and he stared at Mumma's friend, his head craning over his shoulder even after he had passed them.

There was a name that kept going back and forth from Mumma to Riha, and Joy watched their lips form it, a word that usually meant something important or startling to Mumma. If ever this word was said at Summer Street and she and Dora looked as if they were listening, it was swallowed back and there was a moment of hollow quiet. She leaned her head into Riha's chest and listened uncomprehendingly to her mother and the rumbling, subterranean responses. There was talk of Grandmother in Scotland and the old grandfather who had died when they were babies, even though Mumma looked after him.

'So you are rich now, eh?' asked Riha.

'As I will ever be,' Myra said, 'though William does not know.'

'He intends to stay in America?'

'He is looking for God. Sometimes Blanche reads to me from the newspaper all the things that happen there, and truly, Riha, it seems such a large and wonderful place that perhaps God is there and William will find him. There is proof that Jesus Christ was there, in America, and William went to the place He visited – at least I think he did, but it was before – I mean, it was after He was crucified but a long time before William . . .' She trailed off, confused, aware that she knew nothing about it and wished she knew more. It suddenly seemed adventurous and clever, what William had done. A strange, newly discovered part of herself laid claim to his actions as her own experience, her own past, which she wanted Riha to perceive as exciting. For a moment she possessed him and in her mind's eye they stood side by side with the twins before them, as if they posed for one of Clement's studio photographs.

'My nephew wants to fight in South Africa with the Ninth Contingent,' Riha told her. 'We came to Auckland together but he got away from me as quickly as he could.'

'Oh, but they won't have him –' began Myra, but she closed her mouth on it, remembering in the same instant the birthday tea. How would she explain Riha to her guests? Would they disapprove of her, or worse, pity her? Blanche may even be wary of her. She'd told her once she was frightened of the natives, the way they stared if she passed a group of them on the street. She suspected them all of savage and brute intent.

'Won't? What are you saying?' Riha asked. They had reached the top of the steep street, the little houses built close, their gleaming iron roofs stepping one after the other down the hill, infant fruit trees struggling in the dusty back yards of the newest of them. Oliphant Street crossed at the bottom with its own tight lineal cluster of cottages. Beyond that were the villas and cottages of the southern slopes of Herne Bay and then the land opened up to roll away through field and gully and swamp to the harbour, bright and shifting in the confines of the low, bush-covered hills of its marshy upper reaches.

'Down here,' said Myra. 'You can walk now.' She looked at Joy.

'I'll carry her,' insisted Riha as Dora howled suddenly, startling them both, and hauled on her mother's skirts. Myra tugged at her waistband, smoothed her blouse at her waist.

'He's gone! I told you he would be gone!'

'For pity's sake! Who has gone?' asked Myra, bending to her.

'The horse! The nice old horse!'

Joy began to weep on Riha's shoulder, the sudden silent tears that always wrenched her mother's heart. Dora looked up at her.

'We've got the lady instead,' she said. 'She's strong and brown just like him. You can pat her.'

Riha threw back her head and laughed then, a kind of laughter none of them had heard before, not even Myra. It was raucous and wild, but somehow wounded and sad, like a child's rollicking rhyme made up by an elder to obscure and soften tragedy and loss.

For most of Myra's absence, Blanche had been before the mirror dressing her hair in a new way that she had invented that very morning: an elaborate back-combed and twisted chignon that required more hairpins than usual. Now in white muslin, her rolled hair shining, she was laying a cloth over the small table on the veranda. At the sight of Riha carrying Joy, and the child's tear-stained and dusty face, and Myra all flushed with her lank hair falling from under her hat, Blanche's mouth dropped open – like the tail-board of a cart, thought Myra – and closed again. She hurried down the step and opened the gate for them.

'This is Blanche, my sister-in-law.' Nerves constricted Myra's throat. It was the first time she had brought a friend home, though Blanche by contrast had plenty of visitors – brave, modern young women who, like herself, attended the business school in Queen Street. Riha was Myra's only friend and Blanche would pity her for it.

'And this is Riha –'

'How –' began Blanche, but Myra went on.

'. . . who was very kind to me on the farm and after William . . . after the fire,' she finished lamely.

Riha nodded and smiled. 'Pleased to meet you, Miss McQuiggan,' she said, but Blanche would not meet her eye.

'You're not going to take her inside!' she hissed at Myra, who at that moment had taken the Maori woman's arm and was escorting her up the path with Dora trailing behind. 'Everyone will be here soon. Ellen and Clement and Fanny –'

'It will be all right,' Myra said to her. 'Please, Blanche, don't –'

'Don't what?' Blanche raised her voice and stamped a foot on the hollow veranda as Myra ushered Riha ahead of her through the door. 'Don't what?' She was louder still. 'What do you think you're doing, Myra?'

Lifting her arms to her aunt, Dora launched into the tale about the grocer's horse and the dropped buns. Blanche was momentarily distracted, so Myra seized her opportunity: she led Riha down the narrow stairs and out the back door to the wash-house where the tub stood in a narrow lean-to, fed by the miraculous endless supply of city water.

Thin-lipped, with red spots burning in her cheeks, Blanche sat on a wicker chair on the veranda watching Myra fly back and forth with trays of cakes and buns, plates, cups, saucers and an organdie cloth to save it all from the flies. Incredulous, she watched her hurry from her room down the stairs, trailing a dress shirt left behind by William and an old and yellowing petticoat which she recognised as once having belonged to herself. Standing, she thought to call her back, to say she had given the petticoat to Myra and not to a charity case, and that she would have it back if Myra was so much as thinking of giving it to Riha, but there was the click of the gate and Henry's excited hellos and Ellen's restraining murmur and Clement's heavy foot on the step.

Riha soaked in the cold tub. The warmth of the day ensured she was only partly chilled. She scrubbed herself with the hard soap and watched the shifting patterns of light cast by a leafy tree into the water from just beyond the window. The leaves scraped on the glass in the hot northerly that had strengthened during their walk along Ponsonby Road. Tick tick went the leaves, as rhythmically as a clock, while the upper branches of the same tree scraped mournfully against the angled tin roof.

Eventually she raised herself, sending water cascading over the edge of the bath to the pitch floor, and reached for the towel. It lay on a stool just inside the door, with a fine white shirt with mother-of-pearl buttons and no collar, a man's one perhaps, and a cotton skirt that was probably a petticoat, Riha thought as she held it up to examine it. It had a frill around the bottom and tapes at the waist which, when she hauled it on, could only just be tied, leaving a gaping V-shaped hole where the cloth would not come together. She would go to the kitchen, she decided, as she pulled the shirt on, one arm banging resoundingly against the pressed zinc that lined one wall, and sit there until the others the sister-in-law had talked about were gone. The shirt-tails hung low enough to conceal the gap and the frill of the petticoat reached decently enough to mid-calf. Closing her eyes for a moment to better enjoy the clean, sweet sensation of the new clothes, she thanked the Lord for leading her back to Myra and asked Him to look after Eruera since she no longer was. She hooked her damp, pink dress up from the floor, swirled it around in the bathwater a few times and wrung it out. Outside she spread the garment on the tree that had entertained her during her bath and made her way through the blowy, hot afternoon yard towards the back door. She had seen the kitchen there, off to the right, as she and Myra had come down the stairs.

A fuchsia grew at the back step and Riha bent to it. She had never seen flowers like these before, like tiny women with billowy skirts and dainty feet. Just as she cupped one of them in her hand to admire it closely, a tremendous gust blew down the stairs from the front and the back door slammed shut in her face. She picked one of the blooms, cupping its pink and purple form in her hand and sat down on the step, her back against the warm wood. She would have remained there happily if she had not heard the twins, one of them at first and then the other joining in, calling her from inside.

'Lady! Come and see what Uncle Clement brung us!' Their four little hands tapped on the door and she heard them leaping to reach the catch. 'Can't open the door! Come round to the front, please, come and see –' And they ran, their steps quick and light, up the stairway to the hall and veranda beyond.

The side path was cool and dark – ferns grew between Myra's house and the house next door – and when she emerged it was out of a dim green tunnel that opened out beside the veranda.

Hearing the rustling of the leaves, Ellen turned to see a tall white-garbed figure, a Maori, materialise a foot away from her elbow. Of its own accord her cup leapt upwards, her fingers still attached, and scalding tea washed down her hand. Myra rushed towards her bearing a napkin, pushing past Henry who was absorbed in the twins' picture book.

'I'm sorry, Ellen – oh dear – Ellen, this is Riha and I –'

'Are you all right, my dear?' Clement leaned forward out of his chair to see who it was had startled his wife. With an air of martyred stoicism, with which Clement was familiar and oh so weary of, Ellen was wrapping the cloth around her hand and gazing, astonished, at the giantess in the fernery.

'Ah!' The vicar, who had been engaged in conversation with Blanche, his young face animated with more than concern for her mortal soul, came forward with his hands clasped. 'Are you lost, Wahine? How may I help you?' He spoke slowly, over-articulating, hoping the poor woman spoke English – and that she hadn't stolen anything.

'No –' Myra's laughter was strained. 'No, please! This is Riha, who –'

'. . . was very kind to me after the fire,' Blanche finished for her, imitative and loud, and so maliciously that the vicar blushed to his roots on her behalf.

'And who possibly set the fire herself, as I remember it.' Ponderous and stern, Clement narrowed his eyes over his teacup at the woman, who had not budged from the veranda rail. Myra was a poor judge of character. Any fool could see that from the man she chose to marry, Clement's own brother-in-law as he was now.

'I had nothing to do with that fire, Mister, and I don't believe you and I have ever been introduced.' Riha's voice was soft and clear, unchallenged by any distraction from the group on the veranda. Even the twins were quiet.

'On the contrary, I –' began Clement, but he cut himself off, the regions of his face unaffected by his rash reddening enough to match those that were.

'This is Mr Baxter,' Myra said quickly, looking desperately from closed face to closed face. Henry held the book to his chest and looked apprehensive. Since he had gone to live with Ellen he was apprehensive a lot, Myra thought – more than before. At the judge's house he would have said something true and ingenuous at this point, but he would not open his mouth now for fear of reprisal.

'I am Reverend Sanderson.' The vicar leapt down the stairs and rounded the corner to Riha. 'Our sincerest apologies for misreading the situation. Please join us –' He was making strange ducking motions with his head and gesturing with his long, thin black arm towards the table and chairs.

Riha, dignified and silent, climbed the steps and sat in the chair Sanderson had vacated. Her hair dripped down her neck and she gazed steadily at Myra, who was pouring her a cup of tea.

'See our picture. It's a photograph!' The twins were at her knee, the smaller one trying to clamber onto her lap. Ellen's heart pained as she watched them: they were never as demonstrative with her, though she had no need to be reminded of the fickle affections of children, she told herself sternly. Until her marriage had she not witnessed every day the spite of the vengeful infant, the heartbreak of the rejected? Joy, happily roosting, turned the wooden frame over and gazed at the image.

'They're twins, like us,' Dora supplied.

Riha took in the two pairs of little brown feet balancing on the photographer's hinged box, the two tins of tobacco between them, the sturdy Maori bodies, the pipes protruding from each mouth. They had been encouraged by the photographer to adapt manly postures: hands in pockets, chests puffed out. One boy hooked a thumb through his braces, the other clutched a beer bottle. They were diminutive, sad-eyed clowns. Then, suddenly, she recognised in the blurred background the meeting house of her own people, the simple unadorned one they had managed to build after the fire, and saw that the boys were Wiremu and Pai, who were now almost young men. The picture, Riha estimated, was made five or six years ago.

Dora and Joy were watching her sombre face for her response. She could find no verbal one but laid the picture face down on the table among the tea things. Immediately Ellen swooped on it and picked it up, wiping the glass with her napkin.

'I don't think —' began Myra and hesitated before she went on, 'it is entirely suitable for . . . the tobacco tins and so on —'

'It is intended to amuse,' Clement said dryly. 'That photograph has been very popular as a postcard.' Myra said nothing. She was aware that her friend was made uncomfortable by it, though she did not know why.

'What is it you don't like? The pipes?'

'The boys are a little young to be —'

Clement snorted. 'They're not really smoking. Although I have seen children smoking at the pas. All Maoris smoke. They love it.'

'I don't,' Riha said quietly. 'I cannot abide it.'

'Good for you!' enthused Reverend Sanderson, waving his arms again and looking pointedly at Blanche. 'You are an example to us all.'

At this Clement withdrew his pipe and pouch from his pocket, knocked the residue of ash free on the arm of his chair and packed the bowl with fresh tobacco. Riha shifted her gaze from the constricting collar on the vicar's neck to Clement's thick white hands, busy holding a flame to his pipe. She sighed heavily and yawned and wished she had stayed in the sun in the back garden.

'And so – ah – Rua, is it?' Clement's question was accompanied by puffs of smoke.

'Riha,' Myra said, but he was not listening.

'What brings you to Auckland?'

'I came with my nephew and two other young men from Otamatea. They are enlisting for the Ninth Contingent to the Boer War.'

'Are they as black as you are?' Clement left the pipe hooked over his lip while he rolled up his pouch. 'If they are, the army won't take 'em. Only mulattos and quadroons.' He chuckled a little. 'Better tell the lad to hop off home to the kumara patch. More use up there all round.'

'How very short-sighted!' exclaimed the vicar, and when Clement fixed him with a belligerent stare he hurried on, 'Of the authorities, I mean. Why, Maori warriors are fiercesome strategists and could easily win the war for us.' He smiled indulgently at Riha.

'Tosh!' exclaimed Clement. 'Don't you go underestimating De Wit. Granted, he's as cunning as a Maori but he's twenty times more civilised. Our natives barely understand the mechanics of a rifle.'

'My understanding was that the British South Africans would not have them – that their exclusion had nothing to do with our chaps,' interrupted Sanderson, 'and although I'm sure you do not intend to do so, Mr Baxter, you are offending our guest. Besides, the ladies do not appreciate talk of the war. I myself occasionally mention it in my sermons, but only in passing, in deference to my female parishioners.'

'Very sensitive of you, I'm sure, Reverend Sanderson,' muttered Clement. His pipe had gone out and he applied himself with vigour to the lighting of it.

Riha did not know which of the men she disliked more, the obsequious priest or the boorish photographer. She looked from one to the other, deliberating.

'Are you tired, Riha? Would you like to lie down?' Myra was beside her, whispering in her ear.

Riha nodded and rose to her feet.

'Come with me.' And Myra, not meeting the eyes of any of her guests, led her friend down the hall towards her bedroom, where Riha lay down on her soft bed and fell asleep even before Myra had finished drawing the curtains. An hour later she woke briefly to the sound of carriage wheels and a woman's voice calling out her apologies for arriving so late.

'Fanny! Fanny!' came the excited cries of the children.

For a moment Riha forgot where she was. Her sleepy eyes took in the pale oak bedstead, the chest of drawers with its mirror and silver-backed brush and comb, and a blue dressing-gown on a hook behind the door. Then her body remembered the soft warmth of the bed beneath it and she rolled over, closing her ears to the children's exclamations outside, the booming voice of Clement and those of the murmuring women.

The afternoon post came while they still sat among the crumbs of the birthday tea. The Reverend Sanderson, who had stayed for too long, taking into account his unwritten sermon that required inspiration and completion for communion the following morning, was just about to leave when the liveried postman came perspiring to the gate with one long envelope. In the spirit of the party, which was considerably lighter now that Myra's peculiar guest was no longer a part of it, Blanche tripped down the steps and took the letter from him. The vicar, she knew, was admiring her lithe, agile step and she turned her head prettily to examine the postmark.

'Oh Myra! How strange! We were only this morning saying – look!' and she opened her mouth to announce the sender. Myra caught her eye, shook her head and pushed past the Reverend, who was standing frozen in admiration at the crest of the steps. She took the letter from her sister-in-law and hurried inside, down to the kitchen where it joined its precursor behind the blue china boy. As she pushed it firmly between the first letter and the chimney wall, her fingers lingered – if she read it now Ellen might come and read it over her shoulder, and faster than she could herself, with unsettling comments and head-shaking. She could not bear her disapproval, which Ellen always directed at Myra herself, as if she were to blame for William's unhappy obsession and the rewriting of his father's will. She turned and hovered a moment, the letter flaring at her back, before she forced herself back out the door and up the stairs. Her feet clattered loudly on the wooden treads and she had the sensation of somehow not belonging to her legs, as if her upper half swung backwards, away from her, as she came out into the light of the veranda.

'Was that a letter from William?' demanded Ellen. Nodding, Myra passed down the steps and out into the garden where the twins were beheading yellow marigolds. Dora was inducing Joy to lie down on the grass, the better to decorate her with them. As Joy obliged, the blooms fell from the bib of her pinafore, where they had been tucked in a gleaming row, and she screwed her eyes shut against the bright sun streaming from the west, low over the Waitakere Range. Myra turned her face to the sun too, and saw how close the mountains were today, how it was clear enough to see the faint ridges in their fuzzed flanks. Days would go by without her ever lifting her head to gaze at them and now she wondered why she did not: they gave her such pleasure. Without them the sea would rise up – the sea of the wild black sand coast, blue and eternal – to meet the falling sky. They held the world at bay, a shield on the western stretch of the isthmus. She took a deep breath, tipped her head back and rubbed at her neck. A second letter. A wind to blow the world open, glassy and disruptive, to bring the presence of William returned, the sense of him among her pots and spoons and walking beside her on her errands, the echo of his voice under the twins' prattle.

'Will you not share it with us?' asked Ellen. 'It is the second letter, is it not?'

Myra nodded again, her hand still at her neck.

'Where was it from? Where is he?' Ellen was leaning out from the veranda, her hands on the rail.

'Chicago,' came Blanche's voice. 'I saw the postmark.'

'Where did she put it? Run and get it, Blanche.'

There was the sound of footsteps moving away behind her and Myra turned from the fence, from the early twilight and Dora scattering petals on Joy's prostrate skirts.

'No, Blanche!' She lifted her voice to stop her, though it had no effect. 'It is my letter.'

Ellen clapped her hands, lifted her palms towards Myra, dropped them and said scornfully, '"My letter"! Whatever do you mean? William would intend you to share it with your sisters. We are anxious for news of him. You should not allow them to do that. They're ruining the garden,' she finished, gesturing at the twins. Myra ignored her.

'He would write to you if that were the case.' She felt heated and brave.

'Would he indeed? Have you written to him?' She didn't wait for an answer. 'We know you have not. You can scarcely write.' Her sister-in-law's wounded eyes told her she had been cruel, but plain speaking was necessary to achieve her end. William was the family's responsibility, not that of faraway Americans on whom he would inevitably be imposing himself. He was in as much need of care and protection as Henry. She had come to this conclusion soon after he left and had prayed and thought about it since: it was clear that whatever influence made Henry excitable and careless affected William also, but obscurely. Henry, she had decided, may well have been the same even if he hadn't met with his babyhood accident. Where Henry's responses were entirely predictable, William's were not. Where William, for his beauty and passion, drew people close, Henry's fat and dribble repelled them. Neither of them had any thought for the future or concern for those who loved them. His sister's love was as necessary to Henry's survival as air, though he seemed oblivious to it. William, it was obvious, depended on ill-considered and inappropriate intimacies with strangers and constantly sought them. The sooner he returned to Myra, where she, Ellen, could act as counsel, the better. She would write to him herself, taking his address from this new letter.

'How would his letter find me?' she said stiffly. 'He doesn't even know that I am Mrs Clement Baxter.'

Fanny giggled and Myra saw how her eyes shone and how precariously she balanced her teacup on her knee.

'Excuse me?' Ellen snapped. 'What could possibly amuse you, Fanny?'

'It sounds so funny!' Fanny gurgled. 'Mrs Clement Baxter! No one ever thought you'd get married, Ellen!'

Ellen glared at her and thought again how fortunate it was that William had not married this vacuous creature. Myra was stupid too, of course, but at least she was quiet and for that reason alone was a better choice. One must be thankful for small mercies.

The Reverend Sanderson, who stood on the path nervously buttoning his jacket though the heat of the day stood heavy and close around them still, was suddenly aware that the eldest sister had fixed him with her ferocious eye and was drawing breath to make a pronouncement.

'We are not ashamed of our brother, Vicar.'

His blond eyebrows shot up to meet his salt-laden thatch of hair: the Reverend was a sea-bathing enthusiast and reminded Ellen in that moment of a freshly cooked piece of corned silverside, brined and steaming.

'I did not imagine you were,' he began. 'It's just that I think . . . well, I do feel that Mrs McQuiggan ought to . . . yes.

Read the letter first, alone and in peace. It was addressed to her, was it not?'

'How do we know?' Ellen demanded. 'The envelope may read differently to the letter's head.'

'Oh! Oh. Yes. That thought had not occurred to me.' He looked around, took a step towards Myra. 'Well. Thank you for your hospitality,' he said. 'I will be going. Please bid –'

'Are you going, Rev?' Blanche had appeared at the door, William's letter in her hand. Her eyes were bright and Clement, whose dozing pipe had been interrupted by his wife's clapping hands moments before, thought that she may have had a nip of something, or taken a powder. Her foot stumbled at the lip of the door.

'I am, yes. I will perhaps see you at All Saints –' He bobbed his head and hurried out the gate and up the hill. Blanche pushed the envelope into Ellen's hand and followed him out into the street.

'Come with me, Myra.' Ellen held out her empty hand and enclosed her sister-in-law's fingers. 'We will go downstairs. Fanny, watch the children.'

They stood together at the window, the paper angled towards the light.

Dear Myra

'It will be easier if I read it aloud for you and you have nothing to hide,' said Ellen.

> *Find enclosed a letter to the bank. Give it to Mr Edmond who is the manager, and he will give you enough money for you and our daughters to make your way to Zion City to join me. Dr Dowie asked me in passing the other day how my wife and children were fending for themselves without me and in doing so brought me to a remorseful state of mind. My sisters have been very kind in caring for you for as long as they have and no doubt will be desirous of an end to your dependency. You may send notice of your expected date of*

departure to the above address so that I might estimate your time of arrival. I enclose a separate piece of paper with instructions of which trains to take once you leave the steamer at San Francisco. The new City of God is on the shores of Lake Michigan, a very long way from the western coast, but I do not wish you to take a second steamer to New York and so to Chicago.

Ellen paused and noted the still eyes of her listener. Though Myra bent her head to the page she gave no indication of actually reading it. Her face had paled around her mouth and nostrils and she seemed to be leaning a little into the window frame.

'So he has left the Mormons, then?' Ellen asked. 'Or is this another Mormon settlement, this Zion?'

'I don't know,' said Myra. She looked out the window. Riha's pink nightgown was stretched over the privet by the wash-house. In the glowing dusk it looked like a fallen piece of pink cloud, or sugar, as if it would dissolve in a moment, fade away to nothing.

'Dr Dowie,' Ellen said thoughtfully. 'You know, I have heard something of him . . .' She deepened the already considerable furrow in her brow, her fingers lifted lightly from the paper's edge. Myra took the letter from her and sat at the kitchen table. The light was not as good here and was made immediately worse by Ellen coming and leaning into it at her shoulder, but at least she could go slowly. With a finger under each word she began again, from the address:

3210 Ezekial Avenue,
Zion City,
Illinois.

She wondered at a street that could contain so many houses, if that's what so many numbers meant written close together. And what was the long E word, and how did you say it, and what was the last word that began with 'I'?

Ellen watched the finger with its nail bitten so low that the bed of the nail, tender and translucent, showed at its edge. It traced what she had already read, rolling from word to word on its lumpen edge, so slowly it set her teeth on edge. She held quiet, though, suddenly sorry for the bent dark head, the way the thumb of Myra's right hand caressed the top corner where William had written the address. It was unconscious surely, not a gesture of affection or longing. She darted past the stumbling indicator, read on from where she had earlier broken off:

I am staying with friends while I build our home, although I have other commitments in the building of our city, which slows its progress. At present I am engaged upon finishing Shiloh House, a grand residence for the good doctor, and in the spring will begin on a splendid hotel for the Feast of Tabernacles. You will see these marvellous things for yourself when you join me. You will find me a different man. God walks among the Zionites and his name is Elijah the Restorer. There is no fear here. I am at peace, and so will you be.

I remain your ever loving husband,
William F. McQuiggan.

Ellen still held the envelope in her hand and she opened it now, saw the letter to the Colonial Bank. While her sister-in-law plodded on she read it quickly – it was a request for an advance on his allowance – and replaced it. There was something else in the envelope – a piece of newsprint, something torn from a page. She pulled it free and read it, though she knew she should hand it to Myra first, but she couldn't help herself.

'Listen, Myra! Listen to what your husband has found in America! These must be the rules of the town!'

Myra looked up at her quizzically, her finger paused near the bottom of her husband's page.

No Breweries or Saloons, Gambling Halls, Houses of Ill-Fame, Hog-Raising, Selling, Handling, Drug or Tobacco Shops. No Hospitals or Doctors' Offices, Theatres or Dance Halls, Secret Lodges or Apostate Churches, Bad Books, Pictures or Papers or Any of the Curses or Abominations which Defile the Spirits, Souls and Bodies of Men.

Myra shook her head slowly, as if she could not imagine such a place, and Ellen, as she refolded the soft paper and replaced it in the envelope, felt a small envy for her brother. Perhaps he had found a kind of paradise on earth and maybe he could bring a little of it with him when he returned home to Auckland. Her sister-in-law was folding the letter and rising from her place at the table to tuck it behind an ornament on the mantelpiece, a rather nasty blue boy.

The twins were coming, and Blanche and Fanny with them, down the stairs and bursting in with expectant faces, even the little girls.

'Did our father send a letter?' asked Dora, and Myra knew Blanche and Fanny had talked about William in front of the children, and that Dora had questioned them and been answered.

'Where is it? What does he say?' asked Blanche, while beside her Fanny looked around the low-roofed room and would have wrinkled her nose at the part-earth floor and some ants scurrying in some fallen sugar on the bench, if Ellen had not astonished them all by announcing: 'Myra is to go to America to bring him back to New Zealand.'

'Really?' Blanche gazed at Myra. 'When will you leave?'

'As soon as possible,' said Ellen. 'There is no call for any delay.'

'No,' whispered Myra, wishing she could take a breath and shout at Ellen. She found it in herself, somewhere, a nerve that let her meet Ellen's narrowing eyes, but Ellen was talking on as if Myra had made no response at all.

'Of course it's not ideal. I would have preferred for William to make his way back alone but it is obvious he will not be capable of that while he is still in this man's clutches. There was something about him in the *Herald*, I remember – he came here, I think, this Dr Dowie. He's an Australian, I think. I must ask –' and she pushed past Myra and went to the door as the twins recognised their mother's consternation and went to her, leaning hard into her legs.

'Clem!' Ellen called from the foot of the stairs. 'Come down at once!'

She waited expectantly until she heard the sound of someone shifting above, then hurried back into the kitchen, dispatched the twins to play with Henry and encouraged Myra to build up the fire and put the kettle on. There was much to organise. She would write to William herself and tell him – it was high time he knew – of the truth of his father's will. She would explain to him in simple, forthright language that it would be better for everyone if he returned home. That would help Myra persuade him. The twins would be left here, of course. They could not possibly make such a long journey. They would live with Clement and herself –

It was not Clement obeying his wife's order in uncharacteristically short time, but Riha who came stumbling down the stairs, her eyes bleary and face creased from brief, heavy sleep. At the sight of her, Fanny let out a little gasp and looked at Blanche with astonishment. Hurrying to Riha, Myra took her hands and drew her down into a kitchen chair, aware of Fanny's haste to depart at her back. She would leave now and hurry home to her sisters to regale them with the news: Myra is to go to America and there is an old Maori lady, most peculiar in appearance, who is a house guest in Summer Street.

Myra was glad she was leaving. She wished they all would. Ellen was gazing at her now, thoughtfully, with a faraway steely look that all the McQuiggans fell into at times. It was the one characteristic they all shared: a sudden focus that was not focused in any real sense at all, at least not on anyone present, or the present itself, or any likely vision of the future. She would not go to America. She could not.

Suddenly, she found she had sunk into the chair beside Riha and was weeping. Yes – she put her hands to her face and found her cheeks were wet. Tears had come before she had known she would weep, and at the sensation of moisture beneath her fingers her stomach and breast heaved in a sob. Riha's arm hooked around her heavy and quiet, and Myra feared with her rational mind, which went on functioning away from the dictates of her body, that Fanny would hear from the steps, which she ascended now with Blanche.

'Stop that immediately,' said Ellen. She went irritably to the range and, taking a cloth against the heat, opened the firebox door. The fire had gone out, which of course it would have done: Myra had set it with half a mind.

'You are hopeless, Myra. It is time you stood on your own two feet.'

'I do,' whispered Myra to her back. 'I do.'

'I beg your pardon? Let us speak plainly now.' She slammed the firedoor shut and came back to the table, sitting down and taking Myra's hands from where they sat clenched on the table.

'You are in possession of what rightfully should have been our brother's. You will go to him and bring him home, where he can administer his inheritance in a more equitable fashion than my father intended.' Ellen did her best to ignore her sister-in-law's companion, who still had not uttered a word since her entry. Her head down, Riha listened intently, like an outlandish judge or jungle animal, thought Ellen. It was unnerving, as if she would spring across the table at any moment.

Clement was suddenly at the door, startling them. He had taken his shoes off on the veranda and was in his stockinged feet.

'That is enough, Ellen –' he began.

307

'I will be plain!'

Myra tried to pull her hands away but Ellen tightened her grip at her wrists.

'Clement and I will not have children. I wish to start a school for girls.'

Myra understood then. It was not that she wanted William returned for his own sake – how could she? She never spoke of him fondly, if she spoke of him at all. Once, getting off the tram in Queen Street, she and Ellen had passed a young man drunkenly leaning against a lamp-post. He was well dressed, handsome in the way William was with thick dark hair and full mouth, his pallid complexion belying his nurturing class. A look of recognition had passed from Ellen to Myra, with the unconscious thought behind it, and they had hurried on, wordless.

'I will give you money if that is what you want,' Myra burst out. So Ellen had seen it too, her shameful parsimony. She should have thought of it before – should have offered the day the will was read.

'And Blanche too,' Ellen said. 'Why should she live in penury because she is unmarried? She is unused to it, unlike you. And she will make a dreadful clerk – she is untidy and easily bored.'

'Have a moment of pity! Must we all be dreadful and hopeless?' Clement shook his wife's shoulder, roughly, thought Myra, and felt her stomach contract in fear. Ellen, glancing quickly up and away from her husband, carried on regardless.

'I have a strong conscience, though, Myra, and I would not take that money, should you place it on the table right now, without my brother's permission. It must be a just exchange. His financial assistance for my tempering of his obsessions and manias. I have always been the only one who could speak sense –'

'Why don't you write to him yourself and ask him?' interrupted Riha, speaking slowly and deliberately, at a pitch low enough to set the last of Ellen's voice twittering and harping in the room.

'A letter would not do. Myra must go herself, though what business it is of yours I cannot imagine.'

'Go? Go where?' Riha asked Myra softly. She pressed her lips against Myra's brow. It felt cool, clammy; she sensed the young woman's exhaustion.

'To America,' whispered Myra. 'To Zion.'

'Without the children,' Ellen interjected. 'It would be too risky. Besides, if the children are here, then William will be further compelled to return.'

'Why would he indeed?' asked Riha. 'The man does not love his children. He did not care for the first one.'

'Men rarely enjoy small babies,' snapped Ellen. 'Please do not interfere.'

'I will come with you,' whispered Riha, and Myra remembered how they'd whispered that night in Riha's hut, made quiet by the vast surrounding hills, Riha's whisper as echoing as the emptiness outside, louder than the shrieking bush.

'You will not!' Ellen slapped her palms down. Clement was hauling her out of her chair and Myra saw how she gripped at the table's edge for a moment.

'This is not the time, so soon after the letter –' began Clement, but Riha had stood to face him, eye to eye.

'Myra and I will make the voyage to America, with the twins. We take the babies with us or we do not go at all. We will bring him home to you, and you can have his money.'

'Myra can speak for herself.' Ellen glared at Riha and then at her husband while she rearranged her collar, which had been rumpled on her ascent. 'She knows what is right.'

'We do not require your brother's money,' hissed Clement. 'I am weary of this, Ellen. You gave me your word you would not bring it up again, and least of all to Myra herself.'

Turning her head sharply, Ellen jutted her chin at him. She lifted her skirts. 'We will go now, Mr Baxter.'

She moved towards the door, and Myra forced herself to stand, to see her out. Her bones felt weighted, soft, like heavy clay, her eyes gritty and sore. No matter what decision she made, she realised, nothing would ever be the same again. Ellen despised her for her greed, and Blanche resented her: they could not pretend otherwise.

Riha had not taken her eyes from Clement's face. Her breath rose and fell, her nostrils flared.

Oh, if only the confrontation were over, if only he had never written. Myra swallowed, pressed her hands into her stomach. She wanted to sob and howl as she had immediately after little Alithea's death, in the interlude between finding the child and laying her out. She had forgotten, until that moment, how she had run from the house, blood roaring in her ears, her heart louder than the thump of her feet on the wooden boards, out to the white pines where she tipped her head back and howled at the dawn, howled at God to forgive her and restore the child to her. He did not, He would not, perhaps He could not – and she had stopped almost as soon as she had begun, and she wondered if she had called out at all, if it were true the child was dead. Perhaps she had made a mistake. She'd run again, faster than she had on the way out, back to the house and reached for the little body, held the tiny frame against her, loving her, willing her to come back to life, weeping when she felt the wizened face still warm against her neck.

'Will you go, Myra?' demanded Ellen. Myra could not see her – she stood in the passage at the bottom of the stairs. Clement watched for her response and Myra nodded, which sent him fast after his wife. They passed up and outside and the voices of Henry and the twins gusted in on the draught of the opening door.

'America,' breathed Riha. She sat again, gazed into Myra's face. 'I would like to see it. I will take care of you there.'

Myra felt herself recoil from her, even from her dear friend, and felt as alone as she ever had, but it was not the plain, uninhabited solitude that she had experienced after her father's death in Yarrabin. She was crowded around by the demands and needs and opinions of Ellen and William and Riha, none of whom had faith in her. She was at worst a parasite, at best a naïve child. Perhaps William really had changed as he said he had and he would love her as she had believed he would when they were first married. All that had ever been missing from William was happiness, she thought, though she had it herself – she had it even while she nursed the old man, and she had had it here in Summer Street. If William had contentment now, they could live together like other husbands and wives: he will be a true, gentle husband to me and I will improve myself, be his proper wife, she told herself. We could pick up from how we were on the farm, before everything went wrong.

PART THREE

NORTH AMERICA, 1904–1912

CHAPTER 18

On the day of Dr Dowie's return to Zion City, Riha did not want to be left alone in the house. She wanted to accompany Myra and William and the children to Shiloh Boulevard, to see the fifty-foot-high archway with the words 'Welcome Home' at its apex, and the names of all the cities he had visited up the sides. She wanted to carry little Audrey on her hip, to save Myra the effort, which might be bad for her, given her condition, and she wanted to see with her own eyes Dora and Joy in their white muslin dresses standing guard at either side of the arch. The fair-haired twins had been chosen from all the children at Zion to be the ones who stood before the giant gates to welcome Elijah. It wasn't that Riha particularly wanted to see the doctor himself. He had failed to captivate her as he did the thousands who had flocked to his new city, laid out in a grid beside Lake Michigan.

A long time ago, before she got sick, Riha had seen an African on one of the wide Zion boulevards, his face shining with health and contentment. Dr Dowie welcomed all to Zion, black and white and all shades in between, to work in the factories and on the building sites, to contribute to his utopia. He taught that all God's people were equals and spoke out against the lynch mobs of the south. He was a good man in that respect, thought Riha, but he talked too much and gave himself airs. After the first rally she attended, two years ago now, which had lasted for four hours, she never went again. Neither did she obey, as all others in Zion did, the shrill whistles that blew over the city three times a day for prayer.

Leaning out from her bed, she took her walking stick from where it leaned against her dresser and hooked the door open. The three older children sat at their breakfast at the narrow table. Joy saw her first, heard the whine of her bedsprings as she fell back against the pillows.

'Nanna is awake!' she announced to her mother, slipping down from her place and coming to stand at the door. In the dark room there was the smell of liniment that Nanna Riha rubbed on her aching legs, and the smell was nice, though it worried Mother because it might not be allowed in Zion. Liniment was, after all, a kind of medicine and medicines belonged to quacks, whatever they were, and the Devil.

'Open the window, Dora,' said Nanna.

'It's Joy,' said Joy, but opened the window anyway. She had to climb up onto the end of Nanna's bed, which took up nearly the whole room. It wasn't a proper room, it was supposed to be for storing trunks and boxes and broken things that Father might fix, but when Nanna first got sick, last winter, Mother had moved her downstairs to be closer to the kitchen and the warmth from the stove. Father had wanted her to go to the big new Elijah Hospice, built for all the people who came from all over the world to be healed by Dr Dowie, but Nanna had cried and said she didn't want to go and Mother had stood up to Father and said Riha had to stay. She would never have come to America if Riha hadn't come with her, she told him, and she and Father owed their new happiness to her. Dora and Joy, playing with some pieces of dough on the hearth, rolling and pinching them to shades of grey and black, thought it was an odd thing for Mother to say. She did not seem at all happy, not since the new baby came. Father had smiled though when she said it and had taken her in his arms the way he liked to, with his hands on her seat.

When Mother had tried gently to push him away, he'd tightened his grip and told her to go upstairs. They were always going upstairs, since the furniture factory closed in February and Father stayed home most of the time. After half an hour or so they would come downstairs again and Father would be jolly and Mother's cheeks would be flushed. Sometimes she would be cross and other times distracted and dreamy, as if whatever they did up there had two different effects on her. Nanna Riha would just shake her head and pretend she hadn't noticed either their going or returning.

'Eh, Tama, get my dress off the hook,' said Nanna now, when the curtains had been parted to reveal in the morning light the shabby room, the dusty black dress on the back of the door.

'Are you going to get up?' Joy asked, and Riha nodded, sitting up, though her back ached and her arms throbbed from bracing herself upright. She closed her eyes to gather the impetus for pushing back the covers and swinging her legs around. Her eyelids felt sticky and heavy, as if they would stay closed for ever.

'What are you doing?' Alarmed, Myra stood at the door, the baby Edna over her shoulder and Audrey holding on to her skirts. Riha could just make out Dora, the pale glimmer of her face above her porridge bowl, and she could hear the circular scrape of her spoon, round and round and round and round.

'Stop that!' came William's voice, and the scraping stopped. So he was there too, thought Riha, though he was out of her view. There was the rustle of paper: he was either at his Bible reading or absorbing this week's Bible lesson from the *Leaves of Healing* newspaper.

In the kitchen William folded away his reading and looked irritably at his boots, one nuggeted and the other not, the smell of their sweated leather strong in the dim, hot room. Audrey tottered towards them, towards the loaded brush and open tin that her mother had laid aside on the hearth when she went in to Riha. She remained there still, her voice pleading and anxious, as she urged the old lady back to bed. William listened, his head on one side. His wife's wheedling voice, Riha's brief, querulous replies, back and forth. The Maori lady was old now, he realised: he'd never thought of her as old before.

Riha knew she was old. She knew she'd got as old as she was going to get last winter when the snow lay thick in the treeless town, on the gabled roofs of the frame houses and on the bare, wide plain, and she was colder than she had ever been or ever believed possible. The last time she'd looked in a mirror, a while ago now, her hair was grey and her face thin and muddy, the skin grown coarse and lined.

'Myra!' William lifted one stockinged foot to rest on the table. Dora scowled at it and shifted her bowl of cold oats sideways. The murmuring in the other room continued. Riha was saying something in her own language, the springs creaked, the quilt was pulled up from the foot of the bed.

'The kid's in the nugget!' William called, impatient now. His wife came in and gave Dora the baby to hold while she cleaned up the older child. She said nothing to William, just raised her eyes to the clock on the mantel. She did not want to miss Dr Dowie's return and sermon. Her heart, since he left for his world tour, had felt dry and shrivelled and small and she missed him as she had never missed William when they were parted, or her father after his death. The General Overseer's love for his people was inexhaustible – it sprang from God Himself – and his good, his healing, filled the thousands who had come to build Zion to overflowing. She would beg him to come to their house and he would cure Riha. Overseer Hart had visited, weeks ago now, but he was not as beloved by God as the doctor, and his prayers and laying on of hands had had no effect.

There was Overseer Hart himself now, coming from his house on the corner with his wife and flock of children and carrying, oddly, given the drought, a black rain umbrella. Myra would have liked to hurry to join them on the walk to the Boulevard but William hung back, putting Audrey down and holding her hand while she stomped slowly beside him. Traces of black nugget still darkened Audrey's cheeks and hands.

'Hurry, Father!' called Dora, who skipped along, holding Joy's hand on one side and her mother's free hand on the other, the hand that wasn't clasping Edna. 'We can't be late!'

From the train station down by the lake came the strains of the brass band, the music blowing louder and softer in the wind, the wind as gusty and hot as it had been for weeks. At this distance the band sounded almost like insects, like the Australian cicadas of her childhood. The heat too reminded her of that country: the lack of rain, the vast state of hundreds of square miles. No wonder Riha had weakened – this country was a place of extremes: of hot and cold; of good and evil; of impulses so pure they could heal what was bad in William; of ignorance so wicked that people in other towns and states railed against Dr Dowie's truth. Freeing her hand from Dora's clasp, Myra rearranged Edna in her arms and laid the child against her shoulder. This child was different to the first four: there was little of the McQuiggans in her. Whereas Dora and Joy grew daily more like their father, with their narrow, deep-set eyes and broad brows, and Audrey already displaying his unguarded temper, this child had her mother remembering fairytales about changelings. Her sparse hair was tinted red and her widely spaced eyes were calm and almost unnervingly tearless. A phrase kept running through Myra's mind as she tended little Edna – balm to my soul, she thought, balm to my soul – and it seemed right and true that such a child should have been born to her in this wondrous place. In a few months her fifth child would be born and she had asked the Lord to send her a son.

A plume of smoke rose from above the roofs, blowing eastward across the lake. The doctor's train had arrived then, and they must hurry.

'Could you carry Audrey, please, William?' she asked, and felt a flush of pride at the way she addressed him now. Gone was the childish voice she had cultivated on the farm. She had forgotten how to use that voice during her time at Summer Street and more than once, when they were first reunited, William had said, 'You're different now to how you were. Even your voice has changed.' He wasn't sure if he liked it or not, its firmer, more resisting tone. He caught up to her, waved his arm at the expanse of Sharon Park.

'Look how brown it all is,' he said. 'I will speak to the elders about taking up a farm. We need men like myself, experienced at working the land.'

Myra pressed her lips together and said nothing. Dora and Joy were ahead of them now and she quickened her step to draw level with them.

'If it had not been for the drink,' William continued quietly, earnestly, 'I would have been an excellent farmer. I have the gift for it.' He waited for his wife's response but she gave him none. At least she did not disagree, he thought.

Myra was admiring the back view of Mrs Hart's dress, the fine drape of the skirt, the narrow black band at her waist, and longing for a new dress of her own: she was still a young woman, she thought, only twenty-six, and she'd had nothing new since she left New Zealand. There was the old man's money still – she could spend some of that on herself, but she did not want to rouse William's suspicions: he still knew nothing of it. It weighed heavily on her, that money. She should sign it all over to Dr Dowie, she knew, just as all the other people in Zion had given theirs, and he would take care of them, body and soul, as he did all of his people, but something in her resisted. It was not what the judge would have wanted; it was the shade of his voice that rang in her ears whenever she debated it.

'The lace factory has not closed,' she said gently, 'and there is still a need for carpenters. Families are still coming to Zion and needing houses built –'

'I am a better farmer.' William scooped Audrey around from his front to have her ride on his shoulders. 'I must work where I can best serve Zion and Dr Dowie. Give me a flock of sheep and I'll be happy.'

Myra looked quickly into his face to see if perhaps he were joking, but he was gazing up at the hard, adamantine sky. His happiness in Zion – for he loved Dr Dowie with every fibre of his being – had softened his mouth and eyes. Sometimes on Sundays at Shiloh Tabernacle, or while they were exchanging scrip for food at Zion Stores, Myra was aware of other women looking at her husband but not, she thought, as if they wanted him for themselves. Their admiring faces were the same ones they wore when they asked a store worker to roll out a bolt of fine silk, or open the glass china display cabinet. There was a thousand thousand times more adultery in the Bible than there was in the whole of Zion.

'It won't rain for weeks,' he said. 'It would certainly be a different kettle of fish farming here. But the Lord wants me to give it a go.' He was staring at her now, willing her to ask what signs the Lord had given, but Myra was hastening the children through the crowds on the Boulevard towards the corner of Elijah Avenue where the giant archway stood. One of the women overseers had spotted her and was hurrying over, taking Dora and Joy by the hand and positioning them carefully before the gates. They were each given a bunch of flowers, which were wilting in the heat, and their hats were tipped back on their heads to better show their faces. William watched them proudly: they were beautiful children, and they were his. Once, soon after William had come to Zion, Dr Dowie had talked in a sermon about what pleasure it gave him to see a family of nineteen, the twelve older children helping with the seven younger ones. It gave William pleasure now, as he saw his wife come back to stand near him, the baby still sleeping in her arms, to think of how many more children waited for him and the praise he would earn from the doctor.

The faithful, several thousand of them, stood four or five deep on either side of the wide boulevard, all in their Sunday best. Many carried umbrellas and William felt excluded suddenly from some secret understanding: he wished he'd brought an umbrella himself, the better to demonstrate his faith and love. He pushed his way through the crowd and although those he elbowed muttered the customary 'Peace be with thee' and he replied, as he should, 'Peace be with thee multiplied', he sensed their annoyance. Leaning out into the road, he saw the fine carriage turn the distant corner. In it were three heads, those of the great man himself, his wife Jane and son Gladstone. As William made his way back to Myra and his youngest daughters, excitement and anticipation filled his veins and his heart thumped. He had the peculiar sensation of his brain fizzing in his skull as if it floated in soda. The carriage wheels rolled in the dust closer and closer, and many of the faithful whom the carriage had already passed turned out into the road to follow it. Before the gates, the carriage stopped and Overseer Speicher unlocked them. Taking Dora and Joy by the hand, he led them towards the carriage, where he handed the key to the doctor, the key to the city of Zion, then lifted the twins one after another to hand their bouquets to Mrs Dowie and Gladstone. The Prophet rose, arms outstretched, his grand silver beard ruffling and shifting in the hot wind, as the gates swung open and the carriage rolled through to the other side.

Clouds. Some of the throng were pointing and exclaiming – there were clouds! Grey, heavy with rain, rolling in from the north: a miracle. William held his wife and daughters close as they pressed with the crowd through the gates and thanked the Lord for his height, which allowed him to see over the heads of most of the people, between the umbrellas, to see how Alexander Dowie beamed at his people, how the love of God Himself shone from his dancing eyes. When at last he spoke in his strong rich voice with its sweet Scottish lilt, the words twisted and tugged at William's heart, and under his embracing arm he felt his wife's shoulders tense and lift with delight. The Prophet was home.

'No words which human thought or tongue could frame would express the feeling of my heart at this moment. God has answered prayer and sent this glorious sunshine. But I have heard requests of many people here, and have prayed that His reviving and refreshing rain may follow.'

'Amen,' called the crowd.

'I tell you my journey was a success. Success demands progress, and soon the ringing of hammers will fill all the world as cities of Zion are built in every continent: wealth and abundance will be known all over the globe, as it is here. Zion was rejected only by a noisy minority. The vast majority, even in Australia, I believe, were in sympathy with me. You will have had reports of how I barely escaped with my life from a mob of Royalists in Australia, a mob blind to the excesses of King Edward, adulterer and wastrel. Pity the British Empire, my people, and rejoice that you are not part of it. I stand here before you, glad to be in America, in Zion, in this City of our Lord. Listen to the Father now, hear how He speaks to us —'

Thunder boomed in the high domed sky above the crowd, growing louder the longer it rolled, on and on, while children clung to their mothers and the wooden Administration Building that stood near the arch reverberated like a vast wooden drum.

'The artillery of Heaven is answering Amen!' the doctor shouted above the thunder and the cheering crowd. As the first drops began to fall, thousands of umbrellas unfurled and opened, one after the other. Out of deference to his height, the woman beside William gave him hers to hold over herself and his wife and babies. The storm came thick and fast: all the rain the Lord had withheld during Dr Dowie's absence poured at once on the earth. The half-day holiday was over and the people of Zion began to melt away, back to their places of work and their homes.

With his face tipped to the beneficent sky, John Alexander Dowie, General Overseer of the Christian Catholic Church, Elijah III, Prophet of the Restoration of All Things, was driven to Shiloh House, his three-storeyed brick residence in the city. As his carriage moved beneath him, he whispered his thanks to God: He had not deserted him once, not in his healing mission, nor the times on his journey when he feared for his life, nor when he needed to give his people a miracle, some showy proof of the Lord's regard for him.

His staff waited on the broad wooden veranda, the women's faces wet with grateful tears, as wet as he was himself from the miraculous rain, and the men who took his hand in greeting were choked and trembling. The doctor suddenly felt tired and every one of his fifty-seven years. He made his way up the two flights of polished, golden-hued stairs to his quarters, where he bathed and rested before preparing for his momentous announcement in the Tabernacle the following morning.

For months he had been surrounded by people – people of all nationalities, the sick and the sad, and at close proximity to his wife and troublesome son. It had been relentless. Now, he had his manservant lock the door so that while he lay in his marble bath he would be uninterrupted and could focus on the beginning of all this, on the Creator Himself. As he reclined in the warm soothing water, he felt His presence strong around him.

There had not been an opportunity to gain the doctor's attention, not with so many of his people gathered together in one place. Then the rain came and he departed before she could push her way through and ask him to come to Riha. He would remember Riha, she was sure. He had spoken to her soon after their arrival. Her face had captivated him: there had been no Maoris in Zion before.

The men around them kissed their wives and took their leave, and Myra felt a glimmer of envy, a thought that she immediately quashed: it was a self-imposed part of her own role in the new understanding with William that she not have these thoughts – envy of other wives or, to her shame, speculation about their intimate lives. It would only make her own lot more difficult. For all of their journey home, the rain fell around them in soft swinging whips, and William, she could see, was as excited as the children were by the drenching, though he did not run and skip as they did. He strode ahead of her, humming, his hands clasped behind his back. Myra fell further behind with Edna against her shoulder and Audrey's little hand in hers.

Once, she thought, before Zion was built, not so long ago, this wide flat plain on the shore of Lake Michigan was covered with groves of hickory and oak and maple. Progress had felled them and now young trees, only four or five years old, struggled up in the brown gardens and verges. Some of them had dropped their leaves in the drought and the rain pattered and coursed on their bare twigs and sapling trunks. Myra had listened to Dr Dowie's sermons for two years now and he was, among so many other things, she thought, a poet. It was perhaps from listening to him that she began to think a little like a poet herself. The young struggling trees – why, they were like her and the rain falling around them was Dr Dowie's love. It fell around her – it was there for her roots to take up, it was soaked into the soil she walked upon – but somehow she felt he had failed her, or she him. She could not apply his simple principles to her life: she could not give up her inheritance, her only means of escape.

In the kitchen William waited impatiently, watching Myra as she undressed the little ones and put them in dry clothes. The youngest daughter, Edna, he had not warmed to her. There was a little of Henry there, he thought, though he did not share that observation with his wife.

'Put it in its cradle,' he told her.

'But I have to feed her now, William.' She had turned her back on him and was gathering up the twins' sticky porridge bowls. Audrey had taken up her customary position behind her mother, one hand in her mouth and the other clinging to the stuff of her dress. In the porch room, Dora and Joy were chattering, one over the other, to Riha. William caught the words 'Dr Dowie' and 'flowers' and 'rain' and Riha's soft replies, which were in Maori and grated on his nerves. Neither did he like them calling her Nanna: she was a Maori, a heathen who had not accepted the Prophet's word. It must have been on the long journey on the steamer across the ocean and the trains across the continent that they had begun to love her and learn her language. He had told her often enough that she wasn't to teach them it and he would have gone in to her now and said it again, but for a more urgent, pressing need.

He bent to Audrey and pulled her hand free, took Myra by the arm and led her out of the kitchen, slamming the door against the child's startled yell with a backward kick of his heel. Myra gave him no resistance but neither did she look at him, keeping her gaze on her feet as they slipped one after another from under her hem and up the stairs to the bedroom.

He was quick and as gentle as he could be. Always, when he knew she was acquiescent, the energy and passion he would otherwise have needed to subdue her tore and bit at him, reducing his pleasure. When he had finished, he kissed her once, on her cheek, as her face turned away from him into the bedclothes. He wished she would smile at him, or reach up and touch his face, but she didn't. Her eyes remained closed until he lifted himself and she stood up, smoothing down her rain-dampened skirts. Turning himself around, he lay back on his pillows and watched while she let her rumpled hair down and began to pin it up again.

'Are you not happy with our arrangement?' he asked her. 'Most husbands insist their wives share their beds with them every night.'

'It's better that I sleep with the children. Then you are not disturbed if the children wake. It's sensible,' she murmured placatingly.

'You are beginning to show,' he said, after a pause.

'Yes.'

'Soon you will begin to refuse me. Then our arrangement will not be "sensible".'

Myra said nothing to this, though he fancied she lifted her shoulders in a careless shrug.

'There are other ways you could satisfy me. I could teach you.'

She looked away from herself in the mirror, focused on the reflected square of grey sky in the upper sash. He had talked of this before – how she could use her hand, or mouth. Bile burnt her throat at the thought of it, at the memory of his hand at the back of her head.

'It's my right,' William went on. 'You must obey me.'

'It would be a sin. I won't do it.'

'You are a fine one to talk about sin.'

She hurried with her hair, slid in the last pin and moved towards the door. As she went, she was aware of her husband leaning from the bed and picking something up – it was one of his carpet slippers. He flung it at her and it struck her painlessly on the hip.

'Why do you say that, William? I obey you in every way. It is you who misuses me.'

'You are my wife!' he shouted, 'God help me!'

'You promised you would not do this. Strike me, or raise your voice.'

'It didn't hurt you.' He gestured at the slipper on the floor. Myra bent and picked it up, tossed it to join its mate beside the bed. William laughed then, a low, provoking chuckle.

'Thought for a moment you were going to let me have it. Show a bit of fire.'

Turning her back on him, she opened the door.

'That's all it is, you know, Myra. I'd be putty in your hands if you looked as if you enjoyed it.'

'I do, sometimes. But you . . .' She trailed off, her face burning again.

'What? I what? I don't hurt you. What do you think about when we're . . . What goes on in that dull little head of yours?'

Myra opened her mouth to tell him, closed it again.

'Go on.'

'You won't like it.'

'Won't I?'

'I think about the bit that says −'

'The bit? What bit?'

'In the marriage service. The part that says that marriage is not to satisfy men's carnal appetites like brute beasts that have no understanding.'

'Is that all?' He was reaching towards the floor again, both hands this time.

She nodded. 'Just that. Over and over. Brute beasts with no understanding. I heard it many times, you see, not just at our wedding, but when my father married people in his church −'

The slippers missed her entirely, finding a mark resoundingly on the back of the door. On the other side, Myra wiped the nervous sweat from her palms and found to her surprise that she was smiling − just a little smile, almost triumphant.

Oh, but she was tired. She would go downstairs and see if she could get Riha to eat something.

Dora and Joy waited at the kitchen door, each holding one of Audrey's hands. Audrey was still crying, but softly, and the twins' faces were stricken.

'Something's wrong with Nanna Riha,' they said. 'She's breathing funny.'

All the time she ran, the ten minutes it took her, with her skirt lifted to her knees, along Ezekial Avenue and into 27th with the rain falling steadily, more gently than it had earlier in the afternoon, Myra was blind to the startled stares of passers-by. She saw only Riha's grey, thin face against her pillows and heard the terrible, frightening rattle in her chest. When she turned to run up Elisha Avenue, the grey face shifted and changed to the smiling Riha on board the steamer, her wide, excited eyes, her calm, deliberated responses to Myra's panics at train stations across America. With pain sharper than the rasp of wet air in her heaving lungs, she saw how far they had drifted apart since their arrival in Zion. Once the arduous journey was over and they had settled in William's house, with its curiously narrow weatherboards and kitchen as dark as the one in Summer Street, and Riha had comforted her through storms of tears and bathed a black eye and strapped a sprained wrist, the older woman had implored her to leave.

'You have your own money. We could go while he is at work – take the train to Chicago and find out how to get back to New Zealand.' Myra's remembered voice rang falsely in her ears as she tried to explain why she must stay, how she loved Dr Dowie, how she could see the beginnings of change in William, how the change was happening already, couldn't Riha see? And then in the last part of her frightened, now stumbling run she calmed herself, sweetened her conscience with the memory of how she had told Riha she would give her the money for her own return, that Riha could go back alone. But Riha wouldn't. She stayed too – not for love of the doctor but for Myra and the children. She watched Myra, saw how she made a deal of sorts with her husband, and prayed every night that William would die, that the Lord would see fit to take him. Myra knew that her friend watched her and was disappointed in her new life, and a sudden impatience welled in her as she flung herself up the steps of Shiloh House and pounded on the front door: Riha should have gone when she offered her the money; if she'd gone then, before the last long, bitter winter, when howling storms were flung up from the lake across Zion, and William's little house froze and chilled its inhabitants – if she'd gone then she wouldn't be dying now.

A young man in a black suit came to the door. Gladstone, the son. His dark hair was oiled and his lips were very red against the pallor of his face. He put out a hand to prevent her from advancing any further into the wide, sepulchral lobby.

'You will drip all over the floor,' he said, and Myra looked at him with amazement, gasping, unable to reply, still trying to catch her breath.

'What is it?' he asked. 'Do I know you?'

'I'm Mrs McQuig –' she managed, finally, but a man was coming from the dining room behind Gladstone, brushing biscuit crumbs from his jacket, a man she recognised. It was Overseer Hart, their neighbour.

'Riha is dying!' Myra burst out. 'Dr Dowie must –'

'Peace be with you,' interrupted the overseer. He had, Myra noticed, a new gold tooth. Dentists were permitted to practise in Zion, though doctors were not. Her mind raced – perhaps she should have taken Riha to a doctor in Waukegan; perhaps she still could if Dr Dowie would not come; perhaps there was still time.

'Peace be with you multiplied,' she responded dully. There was a footfall on the stair above and she glanced up – it must be the doctor, please God let it be the Prophet himself. The footsteps went away into a room on the second floor and a door shut after them.

'Please let me see Dr Dowie,' pleaded Myra. Somehow, and she seemed unable to prevent it, she was sinking to her knees, her wet skirt bunching up around her, while Gladstone watched. Was that a smirk on his face, she wondered, and tried not to care if it was, while the other man, her neighbour, was hurrying towards her, embarrassed, taking her by the shoulders and trying to lift her.

'What is the matter? Are you ill?' The wet fabric clung to the woman's body and he saw she was with child. Her bones under his hand felt thin and hot.

'Riha, my friend, she . . . I think she is dying. Please call the Prophet.'

'He is upstairs being fitted.' It was a woman's voice, coming out from a doorway on Myra's right. A green velveteen chaise longue and pink glass lamp were visible behind her, as elegant as the woman herself in her lilac voile blouse and black satin skirt, a small volume in her hand. Myra had never seen the doctor's wife so closely before. She was not only his wife, but also his cousin, and she could see the family likeness. Both were broad of face, with strong noses and chins, but there the similarity ended. Where the Prophet was bald and stout, Mrs Dowie was slight, and her glossy brown hair was piled ornately in a bun at the crown of her head. What would it be like to be the wife of the great man, Myra wondered, to be loved by him above all others?

Jane Dowie had been disturbed in her Bible reading, which she did not mind so much. Reading was difficult as she was long sighted and her husband did not allow her a pair of spectacles. Here was a diversion, though, in the shape of this little woman who, if she remembered correctly, was the New Zealander's wife, the New Zealander who had been cured by John of an affliction that had no visible manifestation. The evil had been firmly rooted in his brain and over several long winter nights in Chicago at the end of 1902 John had cast it out.

'Fitted for what?' asked Gladstone. He closed his eyes.

'His robes for tomorrow,' said Mrs Dowie, and Myra had the feeling she would have gone on but the overseer had begun to stride towards the staircase.

'I'll get him,' he said.

Gladstone continued to stand in the centre of the lobby on the fine Persian rug, his eyes closed and one finger pressed to his temple. His mother watched him for a moment, quietly shut her Bible and then snatched it to her breast in exasperation.

'Gladstone!'

Her son swivelled on the rug.

'Have you not business to attend to?'

'No doubt, no doubt,' he murmured and swivelled again, this time so he faced away from Myra. He hurried off through another door that gave out beside the foot of the staircase. Mrs Dowie gave Myra a watery smile. She passed out into the room she had come from and returned a moment later with a light chair, which she placed just inside the door. Carefully, Myra lowered herself onto it: the lobby floor of the hastily built Shiloh House was uneven and the chair wobbled on its spindly legs.

'Thank you,' she mumbled. How wet her dress was. It clung to her swollen belly. Mrs Dowie was studying her intently.

'I don't believe you have attended any of our Dorcas meetings to help with our charity,' she observed gently and immediately regretted it. The woman flinched, as if from a harsh criticism. 'But I imagine you are busy at home. How is your husband these days?'

'He . . . he is without work,' ventured Myra. During the Dowies' absence she had more than once been at the receiving end of the Dorcas women, rather than the giving.

'There is work for all in Zion,' Mrs Dowie said sternly. After a moment, when there was no rejoinder from Mrs McQuiggan, she made her way to the cloak stand at the far wall. She lifted down her waterproof and was in the act of buttoning it as her husband came down the stairs. She would accompany him to the McQuiggans' house and have a word with the indolent husband. The heavy clouds outside obscured the sun and the dark sky, the sliver of it that she could see through the open door beneath the overhang of the veranda seemed not to belong to Illinois at all. It was oddly sub-tropical, as if her husband's miracle had drawn the storm from the South Pacific, from the homeland of the dying woman.

CHAPTER 19

In the dim kitchen the three older children were huddled on the floor near the cradle. Despite Dora's vigorous rocking, Edna was in full cry. Wordlessly, Joy took the Doctor by the hand and led him through to Riha's room. Mrs Dowie followed and soon after Myra, with Edna over her shoulder and a lamp in the other hand. It was not until the lamp was lit and placed on the narrow bedside table to glow around the room, and the twins came to stand at the bed with Dr Dowie, that they saw the end had come: Riha's mouth and eyes were open and her jaw twisted in evidence of some final searing pain. The doctor took up one of her long hands, which clenched on the blanket in an attitude of resistance, and patted it. Myra began to cry, quietly at first, and then with terrible renting sobs that drew Mrs Dowie towards her to put an arm around her shoulders. She tried to guide her out of the cramped room but Myra shook her head violently, thinking only that Riha had died alone. Dr Dowie felt for a pulse in the wrist he still held, and Dora and Joy, under-standing that he searched for a sign of life and found none, began to weep too. By the hopeless, falling tone of their grief, Mrs Dowie knew that the children were exhausted, and by the soot and grime on their faces also ill cared for. Perhaps, she thought, this poor dead woman had been a guide and source of strength to the family. She did not recognise the little girls as being the same ones who had offered the bouquets of drooping flowers that morning, nor could she possibly know that their frothy white dresses, drying now on the backs of chairs in the kitchen, had been sewn by the woman in the bed, painstakingly pin-tucked and embroidered through the last weeks of her long illness.

'Please wake Nanna up,' one of the twins cried out, and clung fiercely to the Prophet's leg. He bent and prised the child away, turning its blind, wet face towards its mother.

'I should like you all to leave the room,' he said, and nodded to his wife. She took Mrs McQuiggan's arm firmly, and the hand of the bewildered toddler who squatted in her vest and napkin at the door.

'Come, dear,' and she led the mother out into the dishevelled kitchen and pushed her into a chair at the table. After her long cry, the baby was drowsy and Myra thought dully that she ought to feed her, though her breasts felt slack and, besides, she could not open her blouse now, not with Mrs Dowie moving about, taking a cloth and wiping the crumbs from where the twins had helped themselves to the last of the bread. She watched her sit the children at the table and search the safe for some food for them. It was empty.

Where was William? she wondered suddenly. Upstairs still no doubt, oblivious to the cries of his children, Audrey now wailing in distress at the stranger in the kitchen and the bowed head of her weeping mother.

Myra stood abruptly and returned to Riha's door while behind her Mrs Dowie found a tin containing some Scotch oatcakes and gave them to the children.

'Is there any milk?' she heard her ask, but Myra's attention was taken entirely by the General Overseer, his hands on Riha's chest, his eyes closed and his mouth, the opening in his curly silver beard muttering, praying, as he moved up and down Riha's body.

'And he that was dead came forth –' He lifted his voice a little when he saw her standing there and it seemed in the soft glow that another light hovered around his head, his pate shiny and reflective, his rich sweet voice going on: 'Jesus said unto her, "I am the resurrection and the life, he that believeth in me, though he were dead yet shall he live –"'

It was from John or Luke, Myra wasn't sure: he was quoting from the story of Lazarus. The dear, great man lifted his face towards Heaven and began to pray, his hands moving all the time on Riha's stilled, wasted limbs.

'Lord, command me as you did the twelve apostles. I have gone among the lost sheep, I have healed the sick and cast out devils – why then do you not give me the power to raise the dead as you did them?'

Myra kept her gaze from the poor face on the pillow, though she could see without looking directly that the Doctor had closed her mouth and eyes.

'The kingdom of Heaven is at hand! Freely ye have received, freely give . . .' He paused for a moment and bent his head to Riha's quiet mouth. When he straightened, Myra saw there was a rage and fire in him.

'And he that was dead came forth!' He was shouting now. 'And he that was dead came forth –' He repeated the phrase again and again, impossibly louder each time, his great orator's voice reverberating in the small room, his fist striking the foot of the bed. Myra dropped to her knees to pray too, for why shouldn't the Lord let Dr Dowie raise Riha to walk among them: he had saved so many from illness and death, why could he not go at it from the other side?

'I will raise thee up and you will walk again.' The Doctor's face was contorted and wet with tears, and Myra's heart swelled with love for him. He loved her, he loved Riha, so boundless was this man's love for all his followers. Mrs Dowie had come to stand beside her, and the look on her face as Myra gazed tearfully up at her was one not of adulation but alarm.

Behind the women, the kitchen door flung open and slammed again and heavy footsteps came into the room.

'Myra?' It was William, in his nightshirt. His voice broke the flow of the older man's passion. Dr Dowie lifted his hands, clasped his fingers together and gazed uncomprehendingly at William, who had laid a firm hand on Myra's shoulder.

'Doctor – what –'

'Riha has died,' whispered Myra, 'but Dr Dowie will raise her.'

'Hush!' Mrs Dowie's face had the white, deathly appearance of bleached bone. She held out a hand towards her husband.

'My dear, you are overwrought. You should be sleeping now after our long journey today. You have done what you can for these people. Let us go home now.' She spoke slowly, deliberately.

Suddenly it seemed to Myra that the room was darker and the Prophet smaller and she hated William and Mrs Dowie for interrupting him, for if they hadn't, she knew he would have completed his work. William's hair stuck up on one side from his pillow, and Mrs Dowie was reaching for her cloak, her face set with disapproval. Disconsolate, Myra stood to let the Prophet pass. He stopped and tilted her chin towards him.

'Lay her out now, my child,' he said, 'and tomorrow attend the Tabernacle for service.' Myra nodded and the Prophet went on, 'Pray for her poor disbelieving soul at your Family Altar tonight, for if she had had faith, Satan would not have worked his wickedness upon her. Peace be with thee.'

She followed the Prophet and his wife down the hall to their waiting carriage and saw the lights gleaming in porches up and down Ezekial Avenue and the shadowy figures of neighbours through the rain, all intent on their leader as he left the McQuiggans' house. Though they could not see, as Myra had, how blue his lips were and how haunted his eyes, they saw from the angle of his gait that he was strangely stooped and defeated. The carriage rolled away, rain falling to its roof and bouncing away like silver forks dropped tines first from a great height, and for a moment Myra heard the rain as if it were she who sat in the carriage beside him, not Mrs Dowie. She closed her eyes and allowed herself to feel the immense comfort that such a moment would afford her: his strong, miracle-working hands holding hers, the dark, wet, closing night outside the narrow windows.

William stood barefoot in the narrow hall, his arms raised as Myra came towards him, and she thought he would embrace her but it was a gesture of wonder and he dropped them against his sides as she came level with him.

'Our house?' he said to her, awestruck as she passed. 'Why did he . . .? How did he know Riha was . . .?'

She turned her face away and hurried in to the baby, snatched her up and took a dry napkin from the rack above the range. She wanted to be able to think, to sit with Riha and mourn for her, and for the Prophet's failure, if it could be termed a failure – for he could have succeeded, indeed it seemed as if he almost had, she could feel the miracle pressing up against her even now, like a living, breathing creature – but she quietened herself, stilled her mind, concentrated her thoughts on the needs of the children. There would be time later.

Audrey had climbed into the easy chair in the corner and fallen asleep, and Dora and Joy were quarrelling over the doll Blanche had given them for their third birthday, which seemed part of another lifetime. William came in and sat at the table and she wondered if he expected supper as she lifted Edna, half-asleep, to her shoulder. She wished she were strong enough to lift Audrey too and so save herself a return journey up the steep stairs. William was gazing at her with tear-brimming eyes, and she realised with a start that it was adoration that shone from them, that he was pleased with her.

'Did you fetch the Doctor?' he asked her. 'I fell asleep you see, after we . . . I didn't hear you go and the children were quiet –'

'William,' she interrupted, bravely, firmly, 'could you carry Audrey upstairs for me? Dora and Joy, quickly now, bedtime.' She took a candle from the sill, lit it with a taper while William picked up the sleeping child and she saw with a little burst of tenderness how gently he cradled her as he negotiated his way to the kitchen door, even setting his lips to the nape of her neck while he paused to let her past him with the candle.

Perhaps he is learning to love us, she thought, as she climbed the stairs, feeling the weight of his tread behind her, his breath at her back – Riha's death will be easier to bear. She knew he would not grieve beside her because he had made no secret of his dislike for Riha: his dismayed face at first sight of her at Zion Station stood forever in her mind. Perhaps, she thought now, because the Doctor came after Riha's death, perhaps we will be happy together.

In the bedroom Dora, Joy and Audrey were tucked up, still weeping, in the big bed and Edna in a drawer, which she had almost outgrown. Silently, the mother and father went about drawing up sheets and smoothing quilts and as they came out into the landing again, closing the door after them, Myra felt William's arms close around her waist. He kissed her tenderly and she whispered then, while she felt his mood still soft and accommodating, 'We must not forget it was Riha who brought him here.'

He tensed against her while he meditated on that.

'It was,' he mumbled eventually, before he took her hand and led her to his room where he undressed her entirely, seeing how her pale shoulders glimmered in the candlelight, the candle set on the lowboy. She kept her eyes steady on his face, gauging his mood, wondering how long it would hold. His lips were moving, muttering something, as he brought her to the bed to sit astride him.

'What did you say?' she asked him.

'What you think about when we are together – I don't want you to think that. You must think this' – he pulled her close and whispered in her ear – 'With my body I thee worship.' His hand was warm against her back, his other stroked her breast, and she felt a tightening across the little swell in her belly, a sensation as strong as an early birth pain. It was fiery and jagged; it wrenched her heart and enlivened her tired limbs. It was what she had wanted on the farm, though she had not had the words for it, still did not. It was a pressure and a burning, an intense feeling of being . . . yes, of being blessed. God must have planned all this when he created us, she thought, that men and women could do more than just fit together.

'With my body I thee worship,' he said again, arching underneath her, rising again. She moved with him, her grief for Riha sharpening all her senses, thinking now that he was all she had, he and the children. She gave herself to him without shame, and though her mind slipped away down to Riha and returned again, slipped away and returned, she drew some comfort and sweet solace from the act, bringing her hands to lie flat against his chest in the way she knew he liked and brushing his hair away from his hot forehead when at length he pulled away, and lay almost instantly asleep beside her.

Early in the grey dawn, she rose and went to Riha, taking the baby with her and setting her at her breast while she sat beside the bed. It was always the same in the company of death – the loss of little Alithea, even the old judge, and before that, when death occurred as it had with dulling frequency at the Home – she could not believe it. She half expected Riha's eyes to open, her full lips to part on her fine white teeth and her beloved deep voice to rumble: 'You see, I am here. Dr Dowie brought me home to you,' or, what was more likely, more true to Riha: 'I am not really dead, I was just playing a trick – now you can see the Doctor believes he is an apostle and can raise the dead! He really is a crazy man.'

She shot out her free hand and touched it lightly on Riha's brow. It was cold, colder than she could have believed it to be, colder by far than the warm midsummer dawn, and she withdrew it as rapidly as she had extended it, bringing it instead to cup Edna's warm fuzzed head. Beneath her palm, the fontanelle pulsed, a fainter rhythm beneath the one set up by the feeding mouth, and dispelled the chill even as it crept up her arm. She settled back, let her eyes rest on Riha's face, and her mind drifted from thought to querying thought, alighting on each one until the next one occurred, though there was no resolution to any of them. What would Riha have wanted, what kind of funeral? Her people, her people in New Zealand – what would they want? None of them had come to see her off at the wharf, and neither had Riha corresponded with them. Perhaps they would be indifferent to her passing . . . She could try to write to the Waylands, if she could find someone to help her with her spelling, and the Reverend could make the trip to the pa, though he would be frail now, truly elderly; it seemed years since she had seen him though in truth only five. How strange it was to see Riha's mouth still, the mouth that in life had been quick to laugh and jest, to bestow kisses on herself and the children, to shoot deadly barbs at William, barbs he most often richly deserved.

Oh, my dear Riha – how I loved you, she thought, and realised she'd said it aloud, and that she'd never before declared her feelings, not for anyone and she wished she'd said it when Riha were alive to hear it, though surely she'd known. Since the births of Audrey and Edna there had been so much to do, so much hard work, and so little time for talking and she thought now how strange that was when they'd worked together in the house side by side for hours in each day, and often in complete silence. Was it that there had been nothing to talk about? William had somehow stood between them.

Sated, the baby pulled away and Myra sat her up gently, rubbing her little back and thinking how she should start the range now and wake the children to ready them for Tabernacle. Even in her mind she could not approach the thought of laying out her dear friend, who in life was always so modest. Even on board ship, in their tiny third-class cabin, she would always dress and undress inside her capacious gowns, her arms pulled free of the sleeves to struggle in and out of undergarments, a contortionist exercise accompanied by much snorting and grunting. Perhaps she could just sponge her poor grey face, Myra thought, and lift her hands to lie on her chest with the fingers, broad and brown, interlaced one after the other the way she'd set them before the Prophet dislodged them in his strenuous prayer. She could take a comb and tidy her bed-tousled hair, the thick steely curls hardly grown since they were cut short at the beginning of her illness. Even as she longed to do these things for Riha, her body remembering the warmth and safe harbour of the other woman's circling arms, she recoiled from the idea of touching her. When little Alithea died, so close to the beginning of her life, how she had clung to that little shawl-wrapped parcel, willing her own warmth to set the tiny heart beating again. And the judge – he died at the end of his time, in what his wife and Dr Pollock had both called a merciful release. But Riha – dear Riha – she should not have died at all, not being at either the beginning or the end and Myra, tipping her body forward over the child in her lap until her brow rested on the bed's edge, wished she could rage against Satan as passionately as the Doctor had called on God, that she could shake her fist and cry out instead of falling ever deeper into this dry-eyed and hopeless despair.

There was a tap at the door and with the baby's head nodding against her shoulder Myra went to answer it, not thinking as she would have any other day how odd it was for a visitor to call at six in the morning.

On the stoop stood two neighbours, women older than herself. One of them was Mrs Hart and the other was a New Zealander called Mrs Trench. This latter was from Wellington and had applied herself, these past months since her own arrival in Zion, to making a friend of young Mrs McQuiggan. So far her overtures had been rebuffed – once she had sat for half an hour in the grim and ill-equipped kitchen without so much as an offer of a cup of tea – and she had come to the conclusion, one she had shared vociferously around town, that Mrs McQuiggan's attachment to the Maori woman precluded her from any natural friendship with women of her own kind. She had brought with her a basket, which was covered with a cloth. The smell of freshly baked bread rose from it in the damp morning air. Mrs Trench smiled, her tight grey curls gleaming in the beginning, watery light like a cauliflower past its best, her pale eyes squinting to the point of disappearance.

'Breakfast for the children,' she said, gesturing towards the basket. The Maori woman was dead, so now she and Mrs McQuiggan could embark on their long-overdue association.

'We have come to help you lay Riha out,' said Mrs Hart. 'Will she be buried after Tabernacle this afternoon?'

Myra nodded, relief flooding her veins, and wordlessly led the women to Riha's room. She brought them a basin of warm water and a length of muslin torn to strips as they required them, but kept her face turned away from the bed.

The Tabernacle was filled almost to its capacity of seven thousand. The McQuiggans found a row of empty chairs high at the back and for once Myra did not have to reprimand Dora for kicking the chair legs or twisting her sister's plaits or whispering, or any of the other pastimes the boisterous twin usually found to amuse herself in the long, airless moments before the service began. The child was subdued, as pale faced and ashen eyed as her father, though for different reasons. Riha's death had struck the child forcibly when she met the neighbours at the end of their work. She had run up against them at the threshold of Nanna's room as they emerged, closing the door firmly after them. Mrs Trench had gently tipped the child's face towards her and bestowed a kiss on her forehead. At this unexpected tenderness and since her own mother had spared her none, Dora had wailed and kicked. Barely concealing her disapproval, Mrs Hart had then taken her leave but Mrs Trench had stayed on, helping the young mother with the children and the silent, strange husband, who came downstairs only moments before they left for service.

William, seated between his wife and the twins and with Audrey on his knee, worried silently about the cost of the coffin and how in the absence of any tools of his own he would have to see the joiner at Zion Stores and buy one from him. He had hocked his roll – his hammer and spanner and plane, his chisel and set of three screwdrivers and leather pinny – in Waukegan, the visit to the pawn shop being the last thing he remembered before a gap of some twelve hours. He jolted his mind away from that – no one knew and he would keep it that way, just as the episodes on the long journey from Salt Lake to Chicago were kept hidden, even from himself. It was a damnable truth, his mind lurched on, that his allowance dwindled and became less and less effective with a wife and four mouths to feed. The old rage he had experienced when he first saw his wife and the Maori woman disembark from the train returned in a savage spurt, though if he had wondered at Myra's brave alacrity in accepting his invitation to join him, which he had not, he would have realised that the timorous little wife, the woman he remembered, would not have been able to make the long hard journey alone. She needed the assistance of someone stronger than herself. At least she had not brought Ellen – who had written to tell him his wife was on her way – or Blanche, he thought now, watching Myra's profile as she bent to rearrange the cotton shawl of the child on her knee.

On the back wall behind the choir stalls there were crutches nailed at right angles to one another to form two crucifixes, and above them a row of twelve crutches placed side by side in a gentle arch to form the front half of a crown. A semicircle of surgical boots suggested the crown's rear arc. There were trusses, casts, pistols, flasks and tobacco pouches, medicine bottles, braces and brass knuckles, eye-glasses and callipers, all captured from the devil by Dr Dowie and arranged aesthetically on the walls by his followers. Still more crutches formed two Stars of David on either side of the crown and below that the inscription that had drawn William to the Christian Catholic Church and kept him there – Christ Is All And In All – was written proud and clear. In this church the scriptures were pure and true: there was no invention such as the *Book of Mormon*, no perversity such as that which dogged the inhabitants of Salt Lake City. A man took one wife, cleaved her to him and lay with her skin to skin without guilt or remorse or undergarments. If only he could point out to his wife now the evidence of his own healing on the church walls – but his own healing had no tangible form, it had been invisible. He had not cast off any of the objects that decorated this place of worship.

Gleaming in white robes, their heads topped with black mortar boards, two hundred choristers filed in from the side doors and made their way up the steps to the loft. The thousands in the congregation, most of them inhabitants of Zion and some worshipful commuters from Chicago or Kenosha, fell quiet. The great man would make his entry at any moment, and most knew, as Myra did because Mrs Trench had told her, that this morning he would make an announcement so consequential, so earth-shattering, that the whole world would want to come to Zion.

A startling figure in robe and hat, the latter heavily embroidered in gold and purple and scarlet, ascended the stairs at the left of the podium in front of the choir. The vast congregation stood and at first did not recognise the Prophet, though he led his wife and senior officials to the platform as he always did, and when he turned to face his flock, arms spread, there was a gasp of recognition and astonishment. Gone was the dusty black suit. Instead, scarlet traced his gown; the tip of a red, gold-rimmed cross hid beneath the extremities of his beard. The hem of the gown fell low over white slippers; a red-tasselled overskirt hugged his round belly. The hat was rounded too, puffed above a gold band low on his forehead and embroidered with a purple 'V'. The Prophet lifted his white-clad arms and made his usual greeting, 'Peace be with thee', and the hearty reply, 'Peace be with thee multiplied', was infected with more than the usual enthusiasm. William's hand grasped for Myra's and she closed her fingers around it. The man on the platform gave a sign for his people to be seated and they obliged in one neat movement, with scarcely a chair scrape or cough.

'I declare in the name of the Lord Jesus Christ, in the power of the Holy Spirit, in accordance with the Will of God our Heavenly Father, that I am, in these times of Restoration of All Things, the First Apostle of the Lord Jesus Christ, in the Christian Catholic Apostolic Church in Zion.' There was no evidence of last night's defeat: the Doctor's voice was strong and pure.

William turned to look at his wife and, feeling his eyes on her, she turned to meet his gaze and they saw reflected in each other's face such delight and wonder and Myra felt she could lift above the crowd and hover in the wooden rafters. Such happiness took hold of her that the misery and despair that had wrapped her around that morning dissipated, and never would return again. The young century that she was part of, that she herself was still young in, would bring joy for all through the holy, beautifully attired man on the podium.

'The work of the past has made it possible for me to stand in this position and make this Declaration today. God has led me and graciously used me as a teacher throughout the world for many years. He has blessed me as His Prophet, Elijah the Restorer. Now He has given me that which I declared to you eight and one half years ago, when I formed this church, was the Goal of the Ecclesiastical Organisation: the Restoration of the Apostolic Office. Divine Order is Heaven's First Law. These are the Times of the Restoration. The key-note of this discourse is that the church must get back to its Primitive Order if it would have its Primitive Power. I put it to you now – do you accept me as John Alexander, First Apostle?'

There was a moment of hush, where it seemed as if God Himself had lowered his mouth to the door of the Tabernacle and drawn away the breath of the Doctor's flock, holding it a moment before exhaling it as a sweet, glorious air which the crowd inhaled in a single lifting of their chests before they stood cheering, the men flinging their hats high into the gabled wooden roof. Myra was standing with them, leaning into William, tears streaming down her face. Now that the Doctor was truly an Apostle he would come to raise Riha, and surely this time he would succeed. There would be no more death: Zion was Paradise on Earth. The exaltation around them was so loud it set Edna to wailing and Audrey to clinging to her father's trouser leg. William's arms were raised above his head. Smiling tearfully down at her twins, Myra saw that Dora's brow was puckered, because she did not understand, but Joy's face, with its cool blue eyes steady on the Apostle, was hidden from her.

The Apostle was reading from the Bible now, standing at a new lectern, the desk of which was the spread wings of a brass eagle. His voice boomed above the delighted cries of his people, which were lessening now as many of them sat again to hear him. As ornate as the Prophet's gown, the lectern was a sign of the changing power of the church, a solid acknowledgement of its antiquity.

'And Jesus told his apostles, go, preach, saying the Kingdom of Heaven is at hand. Heal the sick, cleanse the lepers, raise the dead, cast out devils: freely ye have received, freely give.'

Myra felt a tug on her skirt and saw that Joy had pushed her way between her father's knees and the chair backs of the row in front to stand before her. Her face, Myra saw, was bewildered. More than that, it spoke of betrayal and outrage, the same expression it wore when her father too strenuously punished either herself or her twin. She lifted a small hand and crooked a finger to draw her mother's face close to hers. Wondering, Myra bent her ear and the child cupped her hand to it. 'Can you hear her?'

Her mother frowned slightly. 'What? Sit down, Joy.'

But the child shook her head. 'Nanna's calling me.'

Myra made a grab for the child's arm to hold her back, a reprimand forming already on her lips, but Joy was pulling away, moving swiftly down the row to the aisle and flitting down towards the door that stood open to admit latecomers and the sweet cloying smell of the damp, baking earth and brown grass beyond. Unnoticed by the shiny-eyed parishioners, she ran across the porch and down the path, tracing the well-worn path between Shiloh Tabernacle and Ezekial Avenue, running as fast as her small legs could carry her through the sticky mud of the last of last night's puddles, away from her father and the beating he would surely give her, though she ran towards it because she was running home. When she reached the house she hurried to the back door, her chest heaving and lungs burning, the hot air making her eyes dry as sand. The back door stood ajar and a light – was it a holy light? she wondered – streamed through the eastern window of Nanna Riha's room into the kitchen. Her pinched feet, in shoes too small for a season at least, pounded on the boards. She pulled up short at the door: the bed was empty, the mattress rolled back, the blankets folded neatly at the foot.

Evidently Nanna Riha had gone away. Even her clothes were gone. Riha had not liked Dr Dowie – she had told the little girl often enough – and Joy, as she climbed under the bed to hide from her father, who was coming this moment through the front door and calling her name in a thunderous angry voice, knew what had happened. Nanna had not risen because she had not died. She had merely packed her bags and gone home to New Zealand.

CHAPTER 20

The tavern in Waukegan was low roofed and thick with smoke. The woman called Laura was serving alongside Doc – William didn't know her attachment to him, didn't care to know. She was either his daughter or his wife, an ugly little thing with bucked teeth, protuberant, fearful eyes and sharply sloping shoulders. He supposed her shoulders were her best feature. She worked, while Doc leaned on the bar trading insults with his regulars.

William now, Doc recognised him, not the least because he'd once made use of the back room with the girl and tried to pay for it with Zion scrip. Doc had had him thrown out onto the street. Since then the Zionite had arrived with real money – crisp new notes withdrawn from the bank across the street. Obviously he was some kind of remittance man and one who hadn't signed everything he had over to Dowie at Zion City, not as the old fraud expected his followers to. There had been some sorry tales told around this very bar, by men who after years of abstinence had come to drown their sorrows. When William had staggered in tonight, stamping off the snow and shrugging off his coat, Doc had curled him a brown-toothed snarl and poured his tot even before William had asked for it. The drinker hadn't looked at him as he'd handed him the money; he'd kept his head down while he shuffled into a dark booth in the corner.

The publican tossed the money into the till and smirked. Dowieites were all the same: guilty, haunted-looking men and, from what he heard, rats off a sinking ship.

William knocked back his third scotch and waited for the soft burring fire to spread from his chest and stomach, to his arms and legs, to warm his brain and quieten his panicking heart. If you could see that fire, he thought, it would be blue or green, like the flames around a copper nail in a building-site fire. But thinking about it, waiting for the sensation, was like pouring cold water on his head. Three drams would not do it, he'd known that before he came in – he knew it every time he made the trip south down the lakeside. It took longer to get properly drunk now. Was it because he was out of the habit for so many years, he wondered, or because he was nearly forty years old? There was grey at his temples, a few of his teeth had fallen – but still, he felt like a young man. Sometimes, pushing home through all weathers and at all hours of the night, either on foot or catching a ride on a passing carriage or automobile, he felt waves of exhilaration and vitality, all his appetites aroused: for God, for adventure, for women.

Beyond the small grubby window, flurries of snow fell and the bank across the road was closing its doors. Above its low façade the lake glinted, steely, shifting and glinting like poison in a pewter cup. Someone had once told him – maybe it was when he was a boy – that the whole of New Zealand could fit inside Lake Michigan. He hardly believed it was a lake. Sometimes in a storm there were waves as big as those on an ocean coast. It was only when he bathed at Hosea Beach on Zion's lakefront and the fresh water foamed in his nostrils, without the sting of salt, that he remembered the mass of land on the other side – that there was land that stretched all the way to New York City and the Atlantic Ocean.

He held his hand up to Laura, one finger raised, for another. She saw him with a quick sideways slip of her owl eyes and hurried over to him, ignoring the other men who stood at the bar. Of course she'd be watching him, thought William: women always did. He watched her now, her oily head inclining as she picked up his glass. The hair reminded him of Myra. In all the women since Myra, there had been something to remind him of her, though he didn't enjoy their small resemblances. There was Jeanie in Colorado with Myra's sharp chin, Goldie in Missouri with her high round breasts, sad broken-down little Annie, scarcely more than a child, who'd snivelled the whole time he'd had her in a Kansas City back alley, and many others who'd disturbed him with a look or gesture – even Sister Eliza with her tiny feet, not that he'd had her, or wanted to.

His thoughts drifted now to Brother Everett and Paora and their fine rich lives in Salt Lake. He wondered if it would all crash around their ears like Zion was around his: the Apostle was dying. For a year or more rumours had circulated that he had lost his mind. The city's finances, with Dr Dowie as theocrat and purse-keeper, were in disarray even with the new overseer in control, a man whom William intensely disliked. He was a man of rigid opinions with none of the passions and gifts of the old man. Voliva was not, in William's opinion, divine. The Apostle was in close collaboration with the Lord – for years he had proved it by his healing – but now the Lord had forsaken him and so had most of his people. It was said now around Zion, even in *Leaves of Healing*, that the people put their faith behind the new leader, but William had yet to meet a man of passion who did, a man who like himself bargained daily with Satan for the possession of his soul, a man who knew the cosmic pull of evil, who like himself had almost looked upon the face of God. The men of Zion, the men who remained, for there was now a steady exodus, were mostly domestic, weasely creatures whose souls were steeled as much by a cup of hot tea as they were from a blistering sermon from their old, now dying leader.

William wished the girl would hurry with his drink. He could feel tears prickling at his eyes: he couldn't bear to think of the Prophet dying. He had loved him from the moment he had laid eyes on him in Chicago in 1902, loved him for his toughness, his workmanlike approach to the power of his healing and to God. Dr Dowie was a man of the world. Voliva had come in on his coat-tails and turned against him, a soft-handed, book-learned man, ordained at nineteen when he was scarcely more than a boy. What would he know about anything, about any of the tests William daily faced?

The door blew open, letting in a bitter draught of chill damp. A group of young men stood at the threshold peering into the grey, shifting air. Immediately William pulled further back into his booth. They were deacons, on the lowest rung of ascendancy in the church. William himself had been a deacon. For God's sake, he thought, he was still a deacon, nobody had told him otherwise, and if these men challenged him he would answer them. He turned his face towards the wall, one hand shielding his cheek, but it was too late. The one with the sharpest eyes had followed Laura's dogged and stooping path towards him with the whisky. She was knocked aside, William's nearest arm was seized, he was pulled roughly to his feet and propelled between the larger of the men across the greasy floor, through the door held open by the third man and out into the night. They would beat him before they returned him home, William knew, and his body craved it suddenly, the absolution it would bring. They had caught him before, these same three men, whipped into the fervent detective work by Overseer Voliva. They had not been gentle.

The first blow took him by surprise, a violent kick in the seat of his pants that must have been administered by the younger man who had opened the door. As he fell forward and landed in the filthy slush at the tavern step, a second kick caught him in the side of his head and a splintering pain wrenched his jaw and ear. He felt his cheek split. Then he was being held up by the two men who had hauled him out, his arms twisted painfully behind him, while the smaller one punched him twice, once in the chest and once in the stomach. None of the men uttered a word. He heard the impact of their fists on his bones and flesh, the puffs of air rising from their throats with the exertion of each blow. The only other sound was the wind, whistling in over the roof of the bank and swirling the powdery snow in the street. Nearby, her breath frosting, a horse stood quietly between the shafts of a closed carriage, waiting to convey William back to Zion. At length, when the three deacons had each had a turn at his punishment, he was thrown into the carriage, their parting shot a triumvirate kick, one to each of his thighs and one to his groin. As he curled agonised on the floor, a strange peace filled him: the sense of beginning anew, a conviction that God now watched him more keenly than He ever had before and might save him when next he stood at the brink. It was not the watchfulness he'd sensed during his father's beatings – that of a living, breathing being concealed behind a near wall – and not the impassive horse, but someone who trembled with him at each stroke. This presence was glorious, just and punitive: God did not save him from his beatings because he deserved them.

'What was that, Brother?' The deacon who was closing the doors heard him mumble.

'I said, thank you.' William tried to sit up but his back and arms, his stomach, his aching face, his entire body complained. He contented himself with turning his bloodied eyes towards the black, featureless shape of his benefactor and saw that the man had paused, his hands at the catches of each of the doors.

'You poor sod,' he said, and slammed William in.

After Mr Trench was sent to Zion's new enterprise, the new Paradise Plantation in Mexico, Mrs Trench made a habit of joining the McQuiggans at their Family Altar. On the night of

William's second arrest, she made her way across her dark snowy yard to the McQuiggans' – though it was difficult to tell where her yard ended and theirs began: there were no fences in Zion. She looked forward to the pleasure she would have listening to the children's lisping prayers, the sweet purity of which was even more enjoyable when the unpredictable and gloomy husband wasn't there. As she had told Myra many times – and each time with a hushed, confiding air as if she were imparting something new and fresh – she and Mr Trench had been blessed only once, with a daughter who was grown up and married and had stayed behind in New Zealand.

The little McQuiggans – and there were six of them now: Dora, Joy, Audrey, Edna, Riha and little Theo, who was the precious boy and not quite a year old – would gather around her and make her feel quite the grandmother. She was generous with her advice, as a good grandmother should be, offering her wisdom on everything from the foolishness of giving the last daughter the Maori woman's name, to how Myra could better launder the linen and in what respects the children's diet was lacking.

It was six o'clock when Mrs Trench pushed the door open. The children were there and the table was cleared and the little mother was lighting a candle, as if she had expected her neighbour at that very moment. Mrs Trench was comforted by the idea that on evenings when the weather was truly inclement, or when she herself was too tired to make the short walk and failed to join the family, she was greatly missed.

Myra opened the Bible. Behind her Mrs Trench held Theo on her lap and tut-tutted while she inserted his chilled, plump foot into a discarded baby shoe. Myra wished she would go away. Most often the neighbour brought gifts of food, which were appreciated more than her company. A new, brutal honesty cloaked Myra round these days: she was too tired to soften her perceptions of people, least of all William, with the little fictions encouraged by the Apostle –

who, as it had turned out, was not truly an Apostle. He could cure the sick, but hadn't he failed Riha? He did not have the full powers promised by the Saviour.

There were some people, she thought now, who belonged entirely to God Himself and a lesser number in league with the Devil, but the greater number belonged to neither, being neither good enough nor evil enough. They floated in the grey choppy waters that lay between the good country and the bad, drifting blindly between them. Dr Dowie could well be one of God's own, and Mrs Trench, possibly, but William certainly was not. She turned carefully away from the table so that her visitor would not see how she favoured the rib that still pained her. It was surely strange and a little sad that in a town of healers she could go to no one for the rib to be strapped or prayed for, for no one should know about William or the family would lose their place. Her injuries were secrets she guarded as carefully as she had once guarded the old man's bequest.

'Will we say the Zion Psalm, Mumma?' asked Joy at her hip.

'Mother,' corrected Mrs Trench.

'Can I say it all by my own?' asked Audrey. 'I know it all.'

'We'll say it together,' announced Mrs Trench, bouncing Theo on her knee and clapping his sticky hands together, but Dora turned on Audrey and shouted.

'You don't know the psalm! You're a liar! You're only five! I'm eight and I'm going to say it.'

'Sit down, Dora.' Myra gestured towards the chair next to the one she had taken at the table, glad of the chance to sit. If William were here for Family Altar he would insist on them all standing.

'But Mumma —' Dora's voice escalated to a whine and Myra, seeing the rage and wounded pride in her face, wrong headed though it was, patted her lap. After all, more than once, the child had seen her father . . . she had seen . . . Myra could not bear to think of it.

Needing no second invitation, Dora catapulted herself to her mother's narrow embrace, fastening her arms around her neck, oblivious to her sharp intake of breath. From the armchair by the fire Mrs Trench shot her neighbour a reprimanding glance – she was too soft with the children, though the father was too hard, so perhaps the parents achieved a balance.

'He that dwelleth in the secret place of the most High shall abide under the shadow of the Almighty –' began a small voice that Myra thought at first was Dora, but Dora's face was pressed in quietly at her neck. It was Joy, her eyes screwed tightly shut, whether in piety or memory's endeavour Myra couldn't be sure. The candlelight flickered on her pale face and smooth, fair hair and Myra thought how sad the child seemed, though the quiet words moving on through the psalm spoke of strength and glad faith.

'He shall cover thee with His feathers, and under His wings shalt thou trust –'

Dora flung herself upright on her mother's lap.

'You've missed out the snare of the fowler!'

Joy's eyes sprang open and not pausing went on: '. . . His truth shall be thy shield and buckler –'

'Joy!' Dora's fury mounted.

'Hush, love, it doesn't matter so much –' Myra ran a soothing hand up and down Dora's ridged back and Mrs Trench joined the reciter now: 'Thou shalt not be afraid for the terror by night, nor for the arrow that flieth by day –'

'Shshsh!' said Dora suddenly, and the psalm singers would have gone on but for the earnest, nervous tone in Dora's voice, which had lost all trace of aggression. In the sudden silence, she slipped down from her mother's knee, went to the door and rested her head against it. There were men's voices outside, the heavy feet on the porch, the sound of something being dragged. The voices were low and close and arguing mildly, though the words were muffled. Dora stepped out into the dark hall, peering towards the narrow panes of glass in the front door.

'They've gone,' she announced as the two shadowy heads with the soft street-light behind them turned, their boots thumping on the wooden stoop before hushing into the snow of the yard.

'Well, who on earth –' began Mrs Trench. 'They didn't even knock! Were you expecting a late delivery, Mrs McQuiggan?'

Myra shook her head. 'I'll go alone. Could you keep the little ones with you for a moment? Come with me, Dora and Joy.'

'But it may not be safe –' Mrs Trench was standing up, holding Theo.

'I think it will be,' said Myra, and saw that the older woman understood what she had left unsaid: that Myra knew who it was and would not say. The realisation slipped into the woman's narrow fleshy eyes.

'Has your husband been hurt, then?' Mrs Trench asked, but all she got in response was the back view of the wife's shrugging shoulders as she hurriedly lit the lamp from the candle stub, with much shaking of the hand judging by the trembling flare of light on the patched kitchen wall. With the twins following, Myra left the room, hurried down the hall and opened the front door.

The detectives had beaten him severely, more severely than the first time. Blood stained the fine dusting of snow that had been blown up onto the boards. Perhaps, thought Myra, as she held the lamp over William, who was curled on his side like a sleeping child, perhaps the next time, the third time, they would kill him. Ridiculous! she admonished herself in the next second. The Blue Laws had killed nobody yet. The men who transgressed were certainly left as bruised as the laws promised they would be, but nobody had actually died. How miraculous it was, what the human body withstood, she thought, while the heat of the house escaped through the door behind her, out into the bitter night. In life the body is more resilient than the soul, though the Bible tells us otherwise.

She bent to her husband and shook his shoulder, unable to meet her daughters' eyes as she passed the level of their gaze. 'William. William?'

He gave no response.

'William, you are too heavy for us to move you. You must help us get you inside.'

His uppermost eyelid flickered but did not open.

'If I leave you out here you will die. Is that what you want?' she hissed, aware at her back of the approaching footsteps of Mrs Trench. 'Go back to the kitchen!' Shame and grief had her almost shouting as she spun to face her. 'Please,' she added, to the surprised arch of Mrs Trench's pale silver eyebrows.

'I just came to see what the fearful draught was. You've clean sucked the heat out of the house. Come on. I'll give you a hand.' She pushed her way past the young wife and took hold of William's shoulders, twisting him straight and onto his back, while Myra went wordlessly to his feet and, gritting her teeth against the pain in her rib, took up the weight of his legs in her hands.

'What were you thinking of, letting the children see?' demanded Mrs Trench the moment the door was closed behind them.

'Leave him here,' ordered Myra.

'In the hall? He'll catch his death.'

Very likely, thought Myra, but she did not say it. She put an arm around Dora and Joy and guided them back to the kitchen, where Riha was balancing on a kitchen stool at the safe and reaching for the honey. Mrs Trench threw her hands up in alarm and rushed towards her but Myra, thinking fondly of how this Riha sometimes reminded her of the first Riha, the way she had just the right idea at the right time, ideas of comfort and solace, went towards the child with a smile and a step ahead of Mrs Trench. The honey was lifted down and all the children given a large spoonful each and no one, not even Dora and Joy, their eyes wide and meditative above their sticky spoons, uttered a word about the man, their father, who lay dead drunk and bruised in the hall. Mrs Trench left soon after and Joy, who was set to watch from the parlour window, reported that she had not gone to her own house but to Overseer Hart's, which was just as Myra had expected.

Myra didn't hurry. There was no need for any kind of haste. She built up the fire with the last of the coal the Dorcases had brought, and gave the children a cup of warm water with a dash of milk. Then, with Dora and Joy helping her with the little ones, she put them all to bed and went downstairs to her husband.

He was snoring loudly. The offending letter – the letter that had changed everything – protruded from his inside pocket, his jacket having fallen open, buttonless from the fracas. His shirt too was unfastened and torn, and his belly, under its thick coat of hair, rose and fell with each of his deep, shuddering breaths. Myra sat on the bottom step and watched him, the candle guttering beside her. Despite the privations of recent months, William had grown stout. His neck, with its new folds of fat falling away on either side and his wider, now swollen face, made him look older. He was getting older, of course, thought Myra, as was she: her thirtieth birthday would come in the spring.

Her fingers itched to retrieve the letter and spirit it away down to the kitchen to read in peace. When it arrived, William had read it to her, terse and abrupt. She could not believe Blanche would write such a letter – she was sure William had picked bits out, or even made it up: the bitterness, the accusations, the inevitable revelation that had curled William's hands to fists.

There – the envelope was in her hand, with never a crackle, and lightly, so lightly, she was slipping past him, with her feet leading her not to the kitchen as she had imagined, but in her urgency to read the letter to the parlour, a small uncurtained front room, unfurnished but for a single chair. She spread the letter out and saw what she had not noticed when

William had bellowed his chosen lines at her: there were two pages, not one, and the upper sheet was bordered in black. Who had died? William's rage would have been bad enough with the news contained in the second letter. She saw now that it was grief roused by the first that had made it uncontrollable.

Dear William, it began. Myra crouched over it on the floor, the candle positioned for the best light, her hand pressing against her complaining rib.

> *Our dear brother Henry passed away a week ago on Tuesday. He died peacefully in his sleep. Since you last saw him he had grown very large and Dr Pollock is of the opinion that his poor heart was weakened by his obesity. We miss him greatly as for all his faults he was a cheery soul and a firm favourite with all the children round about. He was buried on Saturday and Ellen and I were both surprised and delighted by the number of mourners. He had friends we never knew he had. We pray he is with our Lord in Heaven.*
>
> *I remain, your ever loving sister,*
> *Blanche*

Henry's face came to Myra more clearly than she had remembered him for years: smiling, delighted with the twins' antics; then bewildered at his father's funeral; now weeping among her boxes and trunks in the hall at Summer Street on the morning of the departure, when he finally understood that she and Riha were going away. Poor, dear Henry. He was as different from William as a brother could possibly be, and Myra wondered now if he would have been as unlike if he had not hurt his head, if Ellen had not dropped him . . .

There was still no sound from the hall, but he could wake at any moment. She hurried on to the second page.

> *Dear William,*
> *It is now, though I can scarcely believe it, five years since Myra and the twins left to join you in Zion. Ellen and I –*

Myra saw the letters' genesis, the sisters composing them together, their heads bent over the fine copies. Was it the Summer Street kitchen they worked in, or at Ellen's tidy table in Grey Lynn?

When Ellen and I bade farewell to Myra and the children, we were hopeful that Myra would very soon return, and in your company. For years now there have been reports in our newspapers of Dr Dowie's delusions and his misuse of his people's private fortunes and estates.

I trust Myra has been an honest wife and revealed to you what was revealed to us upon our father's passing: that is, that it was she and not yourself who was named as the chief benefactor of his will.

This last sentence, familiar to Myra because it was one William had read aloud, rang in her ears not in his voice but in Ellen's, as it must have been dictated to her sister and transposed to paper in Blanche's flowery copperplate. It struck her how odd it was that five years had passed before they had felt it necessary to go against their father's wishes and tell William the truth of her bequest. Something else must have happened, apart from Henry's death, to urge them on.

Myra sighed heavily and the candle spluttered, almost expired, wavered and resumed its dim light. Beyond the open door, William groaned and turned on the hard floor. She held her breath and listened, waited. He mumbled something, his voice muffled. Perhaps it was her name. Again, clearer, the two syllables: 'My-ra,' croaking, pleading.

We are deeply worried that you have perhaps given your fortune away to Dr Dowie, whom we hope, dear brother, you now recognise as the charlatan he is.

Pausing, she saw again the tables in the Tabernacle, piled high with the last valuable belongings of the people of Zion:

ladies' jewellery, gentlemen's tie-pins, a violin, unredeemed coupon books, even a fine English skeleton clock, its glass dome rising above the jumble. And there were hundreds of cheques, some for thousands of dollars. Overseer Voliva himself had given a fob watch and urged the congregation on to greater and greater beneficence. The gift-giving continued for over a week. That Myra, the Myra of two years before, had looked on, having not yet given up hope of William's reformation of character, but keeping her promise to her father-in-law. Racked with guilt, she had kept her fortune secret and placed on the table only a pair of earrings, two drops of heavy green glass, a long-ago gift from Alithea and probably worthless.

Our father was a fine man and we hold his memory in the highest esteem, but Ellen and I are of the strongest opinion that the changes to his Will were made when he was not of sound mind. He may even have been led in this course of action by Myra herself.

A great surge of indignation ran through Myra's body as a physical jolt. How dare Ellen say that, how could she even think it? The old man had altered it soon after the twins were born, at a time when she had had only one conversation with him, before she had nursed him through his last weeks . . .

Times have changed and Father perhaps was not aware that his daughters, two of them at least, would choose to lead more independent lives than did the women of his generation. For this reason we believe his Will to be inequitable in the extreme. Dear brother, Henry's death is not the only shadow we labour under here. Clement is unwell and unable to work, indeed, for the most part he is bedridden. Ellen and I are thrown entirely on our own resources. You will be aware that I was married two years ago. For many reasons, most of which are unpleasant and not worth recounting, my marriage was not a success and my husband now lives apart from me. Ellen and I plan to unite our two households, as there are only three of us to live together. We understand, from information imparted by our late father's lawyer, that the funds inherited by Myra amount to some twenty thousand pounds, a not inconsiderable fortune. This includes a sum of money we did not know existed until recently, a further bequest from our ancestor Farquhar of Aberdeen. We entreat you, our dearest brother, to take this long-overdue matter into your own hands, and forward to us what is only our just and fair share of Father's estate.

You are with us always and in our prayers,
We remain your devoted sisters,
Blanche Sanderson and Ellen Baxter

There was no noise from the hall now, not even his rasping breath or snore, and Myra wondered briefly, as she stood, whether she had been so engrossed in the letter that she had not heard him call out again, but she repressed that thought, and with it a vision of his insanely glittering blue eyes and raging fists. She took the letter and candle stub to the cold grate. The paper flared up immediately and died down, and in the sudden light and equally sudden darkness she was aware that not only had her candle given out its final pulse of life but that William stood, weaving, at the parlour door.

'What are you doing?' he asked, and though she could not see his swollen mouth she heard how it cost him to speak. The dark shape of his body put out one hand to steady itself against the door frame.

'I am on my way to bed,' she said simply and took a step towards him. He shivered pathetically, hunching himself into his damp coat.

'Go down to the kitchen,' she told him, keeping her voice level and soothing. 'It is warm there and you can take off your wet things.'

When Myra had gone upstairs, William threw off his damp clothes onto the floor, went into the log room, which had been Riha's room and was now returned to its proper use, and gathered up a blanket. The blanket smelt musty and had some holes, but he wrapped it around himself, shut the porch door and stuffed some pages from the *Leaves of Healing* into the gap beneath it. He unlaced his boots, opened the firedoor in the range, fell into the easy chair that earlier had been occupied by Mrs Trench and curled his toes over the fender. An enamel jar stood open on the table at his back and a sweet smell rose from it. His stomach rumbled painfully, both with hunger and from the blows he had sustained. He took up the jar, heard a spoon clank inside it and saw a small brown beetle making its gravitative way down the spoon's shaft. He plucked it off and flung it into the glowing coals. The small, sharp action hurt him and he groaned, fell back, letting the jar drop from his hand.

Five years. Five years in Zion, a town he had helped to build with his own hands, and he only now discovers that his wife had betrayed him for seven. But he would not go home – not back to that dead little country at the edge of the world. Nothing waited for him there, yet everything waited. He saw his sisters' reproachful faces, heard the invective of men who had known his father, hunched his shoulders against the watchful windows of the little wooden houses that would border his own little wooden house, where he would live miserably, crowded around by his children, collecting his pitiful allowance while Myra governed the family's finances. That is how it would be for his physical self, the shell that would go about the taverns and streets. His soul, his inner self, would shrivel and die, unattended and ill-nourished. A wife should care for a man, body and soul. In both respects Myra failed him. How bravely he had stood tonight and taken his punishment – if he had cowered they would have beaten him more. That was how it was with Myra. Pusillanimity, as his father would tell him when he was a boy, deserved a longer and harder beating. Her bowed head and tears were tacit agreement that she had done wrong and deserved his chiding hand.

Upstairs a baby cried and was immediately hushed, too quickly for Myra to have made her way along the corridor to the children's room. She must have gone to her bed there, the bed she shared with Edna. She would rather share her bed with a dribbling, snot-nosed child than sleep with her own husband, thought William. He should have known from the moment he met her that she was an unnatural woman. She had none of the normal instincts and desires.

An ember fell from the fire to the hearth and glowed there. He would bend and pick it up but his body felt stiff and unpliant. Only his mind, racing on now to tomorrow's contrition, was swift and responsive. He would take Myra with him. Her confession would overwhelm his by its sinful duplicity. The Apostle would be more interested in Myra's gift, which in reality, of course, was William's gift, and they would not be expelled from the city, not with twenty thousand pounds. They may even, perhaps, be accepted into the Prophet's inner circle.

A pungent steam rose from the damp wool of his socks. In his last conscious moment he slid his feet away from the fire before sleep overwhelmed him.

CHAPTER 21

At six-thirty the following morning, they stood on the steps of Shiloh House. Myra had put up no resistance. While he had stood at the bedroom door, she had dressed quickly and quietly, instructing the twins in an undertone not to fret or cry, as Dora was threatening to do. She would be back soon, she told them. She'd put on her coat, which was threadbare and worn, and pinned on her hat, a dun-coloured concertina that had once belonged to Riha.

After he knocked, he watched her carefully, keeping his grip on her arm even though he was no longer afraid she'd scarper. She had that scheming look again, which had not been apparent in the last week since he'd read his sisters' letter. She could have used some of the old man's money to buy a new coat and hat and he wondered dully, shifting his weight from one bruised limb to the other and back again, why she had not. The answer came to him as footsteps sounded in the hollow, unlit lobby beyond the door: because then he would have realised, he would have worked it out. She had gone almost too far in her endeavours to make nothing of herself, to keep herself as unattractive as a woman could humanly be. He wondered now how he had not even suspected the truth. It seemed suddenly as if it had been staring him in the face for years.

The door opened to the starched apron and black face of one of Shiloh's housemaids. She regarded them with suspicion, one eyebrow arched.

'Peace be with thee,' William greeted stentoriously to announce his continued allegiance to the old leader. The maid ignored him.

'The Doctor is still in bed.' She had a southern accent, William noticed.

'We will wait, then,' he said smoothly, taking a step towards her. The maid paused a moment, looking back over her shoulder, before she admitted them. After the door closed, William relaxed his grip on Myra's arm and guided her over to a wooden bench set in the alcove at the foot of the stairs. A tall coat-stand stood beside it. Together they divested themselves of their coats, her tired old sealskin and his stylish Chesterfield, bought in Salt Lake for his first winter in America. William pushed his wife into the bench and positioned himself at the lower banister.

Myra shivered. The maid had not lit the oil heaters and perhaps would not. Like everybody else in Zion, the old Doctor now lived on the edge of penury. His family had deserted him: the cavernous house was empty but for a handful of servants.

The maid stood before them, still staring at William. Myra supposed he did cut a strange figure without his concealing coat. He had put on his spare clothes, worsted trousers and cutaway jacket, but he had not washed. Dried blood hardened his hair, dirt trailed down one battered cheek and one hand cushioned the elbow of the opposing arm. Myra wished the maid would go away and busy herself. There was plenty to be getting on with – a scurf of dirt flung out over the vast pale carpet square that covered the lobby floor.

'He may not be able to see you,' the maid addressed William, who continued staring up the dark stairwell as though she were not there, his ears cocked to the first sounds of awakening. 'He was not in his right mind yesterday, the day before the same. He's as weak as a baby.'

'We want to give him some money,' said Myra. 'He may do with it what he will.'

William had ascended the first two or three steps. He turned now and leaned over the balustrade.

'Such generosity!' he exclaimed with deadening sarcasm. 'Considering the money was not yours in the first instance.' The faces of the women tipped up towards him, one shiny black, the other so pale it was almost grey. The maid narrowed her eyes at him.

'Ah, so it was you the deacons caught last night,' she said. 'They gave you a mighty fine tanning.' Suddenly, as if she anticipated his next move, the maid put out her broad hand to cover William's long fingers, which rested on the polished rail. But he was quicker than she was and pulled away, his teeth gritted against the pain in his resisting legs, and bounded up the stairs two at a time as if he were ten years younger. Behind him the maid loudly called out a name, no doubt that of another servant. She called again but William had reached the first landing and then the second without meeting anyone.

He had not been inside the Dowies' house since he had worked on its construction. Dr Dowie's private apartments filled the top floor of the house. Which way lay the great man's room? Two floors below, heavy and echoing, a set of footsteps raced across the lobby floor and mounted the stairs. He must hurry. A step down to his left led to an open door and he peered in. It was the bathroom, with its marble sitz-bath and shower. Of course – it was coming back to him now – when he'd worked on the house he had seen the plans. The bedroom was here, on his right – but the bed was empty, unmade. The Doctor must be at work already, in his library or study. Where was that? He stood on the landing, his head swivelling. Footsteps thundered up the stairs.

'Who is there?' came a querulous elderly voice, hardly recognisable as the Apostle's except for its Scottish lilt, and

William saw at last the soft glow of an oil-lamp in a room ahead of him. He flung the door open and there sat the Doctor at his desk in his night attire, a silk robe thrown clumsily over his shoulders.

'It's McQuiggan, Elijah. William McQuiggan.'

Both the desk and the room it sat in were in great disarray: papers, many of them covered with his lucid rounded script, and books and multitudes of copies of *Leaves of Healing*. The floor and every available surface were covered. The old man looked up at him without alarm, and William saw how long his hair fell now, white and thin below his shoulders. A dreamy soft smile spread across his face, and William went towards him as if he would embrace him.

'I'm sorry, Doctor –' A man dressed similarly to his leader burst into the room and took hold of the back of William's collar. He shoved him against the wall, face first, and William cried out at the impact, bruise on bruise.

Myra, holding her skirts at her knees and hurrying up the stairs behind the maid, heard the crack of her husband's head against the wood. And there, at the breach of the only lit room off the landing, was her husband, slumped, apparently unconscious. A man in a white flannel nightshirt was behind him, dragging him by the shoulders. The man was attempting to prop him in the corner between a desk and wall. Another man – it was the Doctor, greatly changed – sat at the desk.

John Alexander Dowie saw the young woman come in and a long-lost drifting shaft of clarity struck him like light through an uncurtained window. He remembered suddenly who she was and also the face of the Maori woman, which seemed to hover near her, the face that in death had gained the colour of an old tree, a weathered silvery bark. Then, just as suddenly, he would rather not have remembered that day of utter madness when he had tried to raise the woman from the dead. The nearly dead – those who gave no vital signs and appeared to have passed away – he had raised those but

Riha – yes, that was her name – he had been too late. He had thought when he first met her that he would make her one of his own – he wanted the opportunity of having her closer – but there had been so many daily calamities to deal with and temptations to resist, not to mention the burden of his work, that he had missed her, he was too late. There she had been, Riha, dead, and though her death caused him no true grief, the sense of loss that had clapped him around as he entered the house of the bereaved, as fierce at his head and shoulders as a cast-iron cape, had resolved him to experiment. The stench of the devil had risen from the walls of the hall as he made his way towards the glow of the kitchen, a stench even stronger than the evil he had smelt during the Royalist riots in Sydney or in the cesspits of New York. His time had come. In the face of true evil he would raise Riha from the dead.

He had been utterly insane, he saw it now.

His will exerted itself and dismissed the memory of this unfortunate woman, replacing her tired and slightly bitter countenance with his late daughter's broad Scottish cheeks. He concentrated on the dark shape of his desk, since he could not see Esther's harmonium from where he sat. Three-tiered and narrow, all polished wood and knobs, the desk was brother to its sister the harmonium, which stood at the far end of the room before the bay window, to catch the western light on the open pages of music. He had had the same configuration of furniture in his room at the Zion Hotel on the corner of Twelfth and Michigan in Chicago, and Esther had played the harmonium for him there, soothing, slow and pious music while he worked at his newspaper or wrote speeches, sermons, poetry and hymns. In the early days his thousands of pages a week had come to him in that room drawn in on golden threads from On High and from Esther, whose music, as she and the instrument learned to wheeze and squeak less, grew more congruous to prolonged concentration.

How great a healer is our Lord, mused John Alexander, there is no sign of the burning in her skin or hair, the fire from the spirit lamp Esther had used to heat her curling tongs. Poor, foolish Esther . . . But the woman spoke and her voice brought back the memory of that ill-starred family, the inhabitants of the grim house in Ezekial Avenue.

'What have you – William!' Myra McQuiggan came right into the room to stand behind him. The man who slumped near the doorway, at such an angle that the Doctor had to lean slightly from his chair to see his face, was the dipsomaniac Ephraim of Gilead, forever joined to his idols and to be left well alone. Who was he himself, he thought, other than Hosea's Prophet who fell in the night? He was useless to him.

The young woman had put her hand on his shoulder, gloveless and cold.

'Do not touch the Doctor,' the maid called out from where she stood in the doorway. Against the wall William groaned, Ephraim as blotched and bumpy as a cake not turned, a lost cause.

'It's all right, Martha,' the Doctor said. He looked around suddenly, irritably. 'Is there still a daybed? Or did they take –' He seemed to be talking to himself, but Myra saw the maid and the man exchange a glance. Together they bent to her husband and, with much straining and negotiation of the scholar's books and papers, they brought him to the divan under the window, his head knocking once or twice against wood or solid horsehair. Myra went to him. His eyes were shut tight.

The Prophet was struggling to stand.

'Don't get up,' said Myra, pressing on his shoulder.

'Could you leave us, please?' asked the Doctor. 'Both of you? It will be quite safe.'

Obediently, the pair left the room, though Myra, as she listened to their departure across the landing, did not hear them descend the stairs.

The old man did not like having his back to William and was fidgeting again, agitatedly, his hands flying out to the sides of his chair, and Myra saw that he had not been trying to stand at all. It was a bath-chair he sat in and he wanted it turned around. As carefully as she could, she pulled the heavy chair out from the desk and worked it in short diagonal trajectories on its rigid, difficult wheels until he faced the divan and William lying along it. Pain leapt and flared at her side, and she bent away from its bite, feeling her breath catch in her throat. She watched the back of the Prophet's head, hoping he would not hear her panting and turn to see her angled, aching body. It was too shameful, her injuries on top of her parsimony and deceit.

The Doctor's alarmed hands softened and released the sides of his chair. She waited for a sign that she could speak. Did he nod then?

'My husband believes I have betrayed Zion City by not giving up an inheritance,' she began tentatively, moving around to face the Prophet and taking up a position between him and her husband, so that he could better hear her. The old man did not lift his gaze to her face.

'The funds were bequeathed to me by my father-in-law and I –'

'How long ago?'

'Six, nearly seven years.'

'A long time, then.'

'Yes! Yes, I know.' Myra fell on her knees before him, her eyes filling with tears. 'As soon as the bank in Waukegan is open I will go there with one of the overseers and withdraw the money.'

'There is no need for that,' the old man said gently, meeting her eyes quickly and then looking away. He rested his gaze once more on William.

'Oh, but I want to – I want to make you a gift of it,' insisted Myra.

'Is that what your husband wants?' came the Prophet's voice eventually. The conversation was like the ones she had had with Elisha in his last weeks, full of pauses and gaps.

'It is what I want.' The old man gave no response and she wondered if he had heard. Myra went on. 'To give you most of it. I will keep a little back for myself and my children.'

'And what will you use that "little" for?' asked the Doctor adding, 'Wheel me a little closer please.'

Myra rose to her feet and propelled him forward closer to the bed, pondering her reply. Was he so removed from his people now that he no longer comprehended the realities of their lives?

'Why, to live off.' She spoke softly.

'Then you must keep more than a little. Do you have family in New Zealand?'

'His family.'

'Will you be welcome there?' As he spoke, the Doctor lifted his hands from his lap and laid them, one on William's chest and the other on his forehead.

Myra shook her head. 'No. Perhaps. I don't know.'

'Where are your family?'

'I am an Australian, like you. None of my family survive. I was an only child.' But the Prophet was oblivious to her, bending forward, his hands on William. Suddenly he recoiled as if he had been burnt, his hands flying up and startling her.

'You must leave this man, my dear. Go somewhere he will not find you. I do not want any of your money, not if it will take away your freedom. With the grace of God given through me I absolve you from your sin, your neglect of your duties to Zion. Unshackle yourself from your guilt. It is too late now.'

'But we are married. I cannot be free of him.' Myra wanted to sit down. Her head felt light suddenly, her legs weak at the joints.

'I know this man, I remember him well. If I were younger, if things were different, I would try to help you. But he is lost and I am tired. My work is finished.'

She sat heavily on the harmonium stool with the stops and keys at her back and felt herself grow lighter still: she was leaning back, the keyboard catching her and digging at her waist, her head continuing its passage until her hair brushed against a loose sheet of music on the stand. She righted herself and heard the paper rustle to the floor.

'He is breathing normally and his forehead is warm. He will sleep for twenty minutes and then I will rouse him. Quite probably he will want to sleep again. My man has given him concussion.'

'He is not lost, then. He stays with us.'

'Oh no, he is not entirely lost, not in that sense.'

'How can . . .' Myra began but lost her courage. The Doctor had turned his eyes on hers. The strange dreaming expression that had rested in them when she had come into the room was gone. Now they were bright, alive, full of love, the way she had seen them before. He nodded at her gently, wishing her to continue.

'How can he be lost to God? I sometimes think that myself, but then I worry that the thought is a sin. If we think that, then we must . . . we must be −'

'Doubting the power of God?' asked the Prophet. 'Is that what you are saying? No, my child, we are not doing that. God's work is magnificent and we see it in all except the truly evil. We are reeling away from the work of Satan.'

'You think my husband is evil?' she whispered. But the Prophet didn't reply. He had turned his face away to look at William again.

Waves of stinkpot fumes, of drink and tobacco, had risen off the young man who had staggered up to him across the small floor between his podium and the mass of his people in the first meeting house beside the Chicago Colombian Exposition. 'International Divine Healing Association' was written in circular style high on the building façade and behind that front was the Zion Tabernacle, the first, the one the Chicago press had dubbed 'The Little Wooden Hut'. That was where he had first laid eyes on William, one night in 1902, pushing through those who waited in orderly lines to be healed – the halt, the diseased, the blind. The young man had danced from one foot to the other, drunk as a fool, pointing to his head and grinning, his narrow bright eyes like splinters of blue ice.

Dr Dowie, remembering himself as younger and more vital, looked now at the prone head on the divan and recalled the sensation of William's head that day as he had reached up with his strong arms and taken hold of it, a hand over each overheated ear, and drawn him down until the man knelt and he had stood above him, his hands firm. He had prayed long and hard for the man's soul. He did not release him with a jerk and sudden thrust backwards as charlatan healers did, but laid him down gently a full hour after he had begun calling on the Great Healer. As the power of the Saviour passed through him and worked through his hands, Jesus had given the Doctor to understand that drink was only a small part of this man's problems, that his disorder was the work of the Devil at his most labyrinthal and deceiving.

Two nights later William had come again when he was holding a private healing session at the Zion Hotel. All night he had worked on him then: when the man ranted and shouted a story about being lifted heavenwards above the South Pacific jungle, Dr Dowie had shouted him down. When he wept, the Doctor comforted him through prayer; when he talked about Salt Lake City and whined like a disappointed child, the Doctor scolded him. At the end of the session, he bid him go to Zion. 'We need carpenters there,' he'd told him, and that was the last he'd heard or seen of the man until the Maori woman's death.

The pause had been so long this time that Myra wondered if the Apostle had gone to sleep. His hands curled softly in his lap.

'Doctor?' she said, softly.

'Come here, Mrs McQuiggan.' He had begun to speak in the same moment she had. He held out his hand as she came across to him.

'We will pray for your husband and then you will go home to your children. Pack only what you can carry, then take them and your fortune –'

'It is not a fort –' began Myra, but the old man was going on, his voice hoarser and quieter with each word.

'. . . to the train station. Zion is finished. Look at Voliva and his wolverine friends. They are tearing our city to shreds. Just go, my dear, while your husband sleeps. Go while you can.'

'But William –'

'The home is the most sacred thing outside the church and God. If I had examined your husband as a candidate for marriage when . . . When did you marry?'

'Ten years ago.'

'Then I would have pronounced him unfit for it, as I have many other slaves of the bottle. I pronounce him unfit now.'

Myra held tightly to the Prophet's hand, warm and dry as a corn husk, warm and small for a man's hand, much smaller than William's.

'Are you putting us apart, then?' she whispered. 'Are you divorcing us?'

He pulled away from her grasp. 'You go too far, Mrs McQuiggan.'

It was a spurt of anger, almost, and she saw him suddenly, a flash of his old self, pacing the platform, shaking his fist at stinkpots, backsliders, adulterers, doctors, drunks and devils, the lynch mobs of the South and the factory lords of Chicago. But this anger came and went as fast as she had perceived it: it could not approach the depth of rage that had governed him then. This displeasure was almost pettish, his mouth turned down, moist at the corners in his beard.

It seemed impossible that he was the man who had reduced her to helpless giggles while other people laughed around her. After the sermon they had risen to their feet and sung – how they had sung! It was her first Sunday in Zion. She and Riha and the children, only the twins then, accompanied William to church – he was fair jumping out of his skin to show off his family. He had bought new clothes for everyone, except Riha, and had obviously had some guidance from the store clerks: the dresses fitted everyone.

' "Lot was a very bad lot," ' she murmured, and then louder as the memory took hold: ' "Shame! Shame, you dirty old beast of a Lot!" '

'What was that?' The old man inclined his head.

Her first glimpse of Zion, the quiet walk to the Tabernacle through the unfinished town on the wide flat plain. There were birds and the voices of children, a family of quails crossed their path, and they came to the high wooden building that William had helped to build. It was just a large wooden barn in the middle of a treeless and muddy paddock, she'd thought. But the love of the people inside, for one another and for the man on the platform, and the passion of that man who raved and cajoled, hooted and whispered, laughed and wept and called God down among them, aroused her heart to such a clamour that she scarcely noticed the following day when the air filled once again with the ringing of hammers on the building sites, the clangour of trains in the lumber yard and the rumble of wagons to the lace factory, the sweet factory and the furniture factory, all the thriving enterprises of Zion.

'Lot?' asked the Prophet. 'Why does he occupy your thoughts now, my dear?'

'You were the most wonderful preacher I ever heard.' The young woman had come to kneel before him. She gazed up into his face now; he could feel her gaze warming his cheeks but he would not meet it. He shook his head gently and closed his eyes. They sat in silence then for a long time and Myra wondered again if he had gone to sleep; his head inclined gently towards the high back of the chair. When his voice came it was a tiny, silvery whisper:

'Great Merciful Parent and Healer of all Pain, observe thy servant William and his wife Myra. Have mercy on him, though You weary of his diabolical nature as do we, his earthly compatriots. Guide Thy daughter Myra away from him, for her physical safety. Guide her, Lord, to my sister Theodora in Vancouver, who will help her find a living. Keep Thy mighty eye upon her at all hours of the day and night and until her passing. As for William, let him be of use in Zion, yea, even to Voliva, whom You have sent to test me. Make him strong in body and spirit and keep him with us so that we may school him in practicality and kindness. Keep him from the Enchanter Fear and the Angel Abaddon, who between them drag him to the bottomless pit.'

He turned to his guest now and laid his hands upon her head. 'I will give you the Benediction, child, and then you will go. Now may the Grace of our Lord Jesus Christ, the love of God our Heavenly Father, and the fellowship and communion of the Holy Spirit, the Comforter, abide with you, bless you and keep you and all the Israel of God everywhere, for ever. Amen.'

All the time the prayer went on above her, Myra's mind went over and over the prayer before, swinging back and forth like a pendulum over the word Vancouver, a pendulum of glass, the word distorted in its illusory bowl, Vancouver and sister, my sister Theodora in Vancouver. A living. Her own living and the money still her own. Vancouver.

The Apostle shifted his hands from her head to the underside of her jaw and exerted a gentle pressure for her to stand. Myra did so, her legs stiff and sore from the long kneeling, her rib as cold and brittle as the branch of a broken tree. Her time with the Prophet was over. Vancouver – she was not even sure where it was: in Canada, yes, but where now? She began to move away but the Doctor's sudden movement arrested her. Laying a hand against her rib, on the place she had feared would come apart as she'd shifted his chair, he held it there, the warmth of his palm just beneath her breast. She looked down at his bent, old head, and marvelled at how he knew. She had given him no sign or clue.

William stirred, his head moved slightly to one side, his full upper lip peeled apart from the other leaving a sticky white rind.

'Go now,' said the Apostle. 'I will pray for you.'

Downstairs she gathered up her coat and ran home through the dawn streets, picturing the children's excitement – a train journey! – and planning what little they could take: only what they could carry. It was the right thing to do: she had the Apostle's blessing.

Two things were remarkable, and all her life afterwards whenever she thought of that early-morning race she wondered at how she had accepted them, as if they weren't remarkable at all. They were simply existent, like the bare trees she ran between in Sharon Park and the frozen ground beneath her feet. One was that her rib gave her no pain or discomfort, there was only warmth, as if the Prophet's hand rested there still. The other was that she could have sworn, though she did not look around, that Riha ran just behind her, in the pink gown she had worn at Pukekaroro, a soft, blurring glow of colour just beyond the corner of Myra's eye, and she was laughing softly and saying,

at last,

at last,

at last,

in the rhythm of a train crossing a long, wide plain.

CHAPTER 22

The summer the twins were eleven, they both agreed then and for years after, was the best time of their lives. They were old enough to know, as the other four children were not, that it was because their mother was happy. She had never been so carefree, not in their memory.

Time was divided into parcels, the kind of eras that most people don't recognise in their lives until well into adulthood. It was a game Dora and Joy played early some mornings if Mrs de Feranti let them into the kitchen of the boarding house. The older ones battered and black, the newer ones still shiny, the men's dinner pails would be lined up on the scrubbed table, ready for the journey to work at the lumber yards and sawmills. Inside them were rough-cut sandwiches with a tin flask of water tucked in beside and, if Mrs de Feranti was feeling generous, or if the season was right, an apple or an orange.

'This is New Zealand,' Dora would announce, shifting a pail to balance precariously on the table corner, though she didn't remember Summer Street, not clearly: she was only three years old when they left. There were images, disconnected and fleeting: the steep stairs to the kitchen she fell down once, Auntie Blanche's and Aunt Ellen's faces, dear Uncle Henry whom Mother said was dead now. The grocer's horse. The day they found Nanna Riha at Three Lamps.

'This is the steamship,' contributed Joy, pushing a teaspoon away from the pail towards another.

'And here we are at San Francisco.' Dora patted that pail, the pail of the teaspoon's arrival. Joy stood the teaspoon up.

'Don't cry Myra, little bird,' she said in a deep voice, just like Nanna Riha. She made the teaspoon wriggle, as if it were looking down at a group of smaller beings gathered around it. In the game either Dora or Joy always had to say that line, in case they felt again the fear that had engulfed them every time they had looked into their mother's face. Nanna Riha had made everything all right. She'd taken the money to the little booths at each stop, bought the rail tickets for the next day's journey and taken directions to the railway hotels for a crowded night's rest, rest disturbed by the restless sleep of the others and jumbled dreams spawned by the sights of the day.

'Here is Zion.' Dora moved along to a third dinner pail. Mrs de Feranti would sometimes not be looking at this stage of the game. She would either be bringing in a ewer of water from the scullery, or have her scarlet face in the full blast of the hot plate over the range, the frying bacon and spluttering eggs, or have her back to them counting out the cutlery for the lodgers' breakfasts, those who took it. If she were safely otherwise occupied, Joy would take a knife – the pointier the better – and stand it on its handle and declare, 'Here is Father waiting at the station for us.'

Dr Dowie was always the pepper shaker from the kitchen cruet set, not because of its contents but its shape. Mrs Trench was always a bit of food, since that's what the children remembered her for. The saddest part of the game was here when the spoon, which had been the steamer and was now Nanna Riha, must lie down and die, but would shortly be resurrected to live again as their mother.

Far, far away from the pail that was Zion, at the furthermost end of Mrs de Feranti's table, stood the pail that was Vancouver. The spoon would hurry towards it, zigzag fashion, in the same harried way their mother had, from Zion to Canada. It rode atop a saucer, if there were one, or a cloth or scrap of paper, which represented the *Chicago Burlington* and *Quincy* from Chicago to Minneapolis, and then the *Northern Pacific* to Seattle.

'*Chicago Burlington* and *Quincy!*' chanted Dora and Joy, each time shouting Quincy loud enough to earn a startled gaze from the landlady. The pepper shaker, which lately had been Dr Dowie, would be resurrected as their friend Mr Quincy, who was likewise round and short with a top to his head as shiny as his representative. He was not, he had informed them on their first acquaintance, at all associated with the railways, though he was, the twins knew in their bones, responsible for their mother's continuing happiness.

Neither spoon nor pepper-pot nor knife represented Theodora, who would have been a kind lady they were sure, if they had been able to find her. How could she not be, with the first part of her name belonging to their only brother and the last to Dora herself? Mother had said that though Vancouver was bigger by far than Zion, it was not such a large place that they would not locate the Prophet's sister. Their first view of the city, from the deck of the steamer from Seattle as they came into port, showed a town pushed between the snowy mountains and a sea of the same icy blue as Father's eyes, a town that had looked in late winter like a cluster of broken china scooped on the edge of a dustpan. But Theodora was nowhere to be found, and Mother had said, again and again, so many times that Dora and Joy had begun to sigh with the tedium of it, that she'd wished she'd asked the Doctor for his sister's surname. Was she still a Dowie, or had she married? Or was she estranged from her brother and so went by another name? Myra was never to know.

They took first some rooms in Grandview which was not at all grand and Mother, who was certainly not happy then – the children endured slaps and scoldings for the slightest misdemeanour – had them move from there after only a few weeks. Mrs de Feranti's house in Hastings Street East was between the Wilbur Apartments – the abode of Mr Quincy – and the Empire Hotel, and backed onto the Chinese Market Alley. Its location did not endear it to their mother, but the two rooms the family shared were larger than the ones in Grandview and not only was Mrs de Feranti a fierce housekeeper and preserver of moral standards, she also took a liking to the blond, pale children.

One summer Sunday, when they had been in Vancouver for three years, Mr Quincy took Myra and the children to English Bay: in the summer it was their favourite excursion. Mr Quincy was in real estate and would point out, as the streetcar made its way through the town, what had sold recently and for how much. When the buildings of commerce and trade gave way to the wealthy homes of West End, Mr Quincy would grow ever more animated, identifying various vast-roofed residences and enthusing about them.

'What would you give to live there, Myra, my duck, eh?' And Dora and Joy, listening, because the fine houses aroused their curiosity, would wonder why the grown-ups that loved their mother gave her birds' names. Nanna Riha had called her 'little bird' though she was not like a bird at all: she had been more like a twiggy branch then, all sharp ends and corners. Now she was a princess or a queen. Under Mr Quincy's attentive eye, she had grown plumper and smoother. Resting in the streetcar after the flurry of getting the children ready and repeated assurances to Mrs de Feranti that she would be back to help prepare the evening meal, Myra would sit close to Mr Quincy – but not too close – and listen to all his facts and figures with rapt attention. It seemed every second man in Vancouver was a realtor, and for this reason she did not think any the less of her friend for failing to strike it rich. His small apartment was modestly furnished, and on this warm and windy day he was in a suit: broadcloth trousers, waistcoat and jacket. It was quieter than most of his clothes, many of which would have been more at home on stage in a vaudeville than a day at the beach, and Myra, though she had still in her possession the bathing dress bought so long ago in Auckland with Blanche, always left that garment in the boarding house in order to keep Mr Quincy company on the sand. Besides, Mr Quincy may well have misread her intentions if she had appeared before him dripping wet with the dress clinging to the swelling curves of her body. He was her dear friend and seemed to accept, though the subject remained unbroached, that friendship was all Myra offered. To Myra and Mrs de Feranti, who more than once had offered her opinion on the subject, it was a great surprise that he persisted at all. A woman in her thirties with six children would not be an attractive proposition to many men. Times had changed since the early days in Vancouver when the men outnumbered the women one hundred to one.

A small pang of guilt pained Myra as Mr Quincy helped little Theo and Riha along the beach towards the Bathhouse. She had told him, because she feared she would lose him altogether if she did not, that her husband was dead. Watching him now, as he paused to set Riha's sun bonnet on her head, she pondered her mendacity, faced it squarely, and wondered for a moment if it were true. Three whole years almost, of peace of mind and body, and the black shape of danger had receded. She was careful with her money; she mostly kept to herself, save for the children and her landlady and her friend. Besides, unless Dr Dowie had told William which city she had set off for, he would have no idea where to find her.

The girls, under the wing of Dora and Joy, raced into the Bathhouse to change.

'One of the ground-floor rooms!' Myra called after them. 'Don't go upstairs –' She watched them vanish heedless into the fine brick building, three storeyed, with the uppermost level a shady veranda.

'That's where I'd like to live,' she told Mr Quincy with a smile, pointing.

'In the Bathhouse?' he asked, surprised.

'Why not?' said Myra. 'You'd like that too, wouldn't you, Theo? To live at the beach?'

'No,' said the little boy.

Myra sat down on the sand and changed Theo into his bathing costume. Later he would clamour to be taken out along the pier. He liked to be above the sea, to lie on his stomach and watch the waves ripple beneath him, between the wooden boards. She watched him now, seated between Mr Quincy's bare feet, that gentleman's shoes and stockings discarded, all scuffed leather toes and torn weave. The child had found the tail feather of a Canada goose and mounted up a pile of sand and stuck the feather in, like a flag. Of all the children, the boy resembled his father the most. His unruly hair spiralled in its double crowns and promised already, the darker stripes of hair among the blond, to darken in adulthood. He had large hands and feet, and a little barrel chest. Perhaps he would be like his father in other ways too and act thoughtlessly and selfishly. She would bring him up to be otherwise, she resolved; she would keep him away from the bottle and ships and men of God. They would never leave Vancouver.

Mr Quincy was smiling at her, reaching out to pat her hand. She returned his smile but pulled away her hand. He did not often touch her and she was grateful for it. Putting her head down and blushing for her coolness – he was a kind man, after all – she busied herself with unlacing her own boots and tucking her white cotton skirt around her bare feet, hiding them from Mr Quincy's continuing gaze, which she knew without looking had shifted to her hems.

'There's Joe! We're going in, Mother!' Dora and Joy dropped their bundled clothes – and those of Edna and Audrey and Riha as well, Myra hoped – and ran for the sea, the smaller girls trailing after them. Waist deep in the water,

Joe Fortes held a small body by its arms while its legs kicked and frothed. He watched the small swimmer intently, not turning his head away from the flung spray.

'That Joe deserves a medal,' said Mr Quincy, as he always did at the sight of the lifeguard. 'Even though he's a coloured man.'

What would Mr Quincy have made of my friend Riha? Myra wondered, watching Trinidadian Joe, his head as hairless as Mr Quincy's, his arms black and strong. The twins had reached him now and were wrapping their arms around his shining, wool-costumed waist. They were almost too old for such displays of affection, thought Myra. Audrey and Edna splashed out after them, calling out to Joe. He smiled and nodded and Myra saw his lips form their names. He had a gift for that, to be sure. All the children who swam at the bay were known by him, whether they were the children of lawyers and judges, or merchants and loggers, or thieves and prostitutes. From the shallows Riha bellowed for Dora to carry her out. Joe cast a protective eye over her, and Myra waved to show him Riha was all right, that she was watching her.

Mr Quincy had found her hand again and taken it up in his. She knew by the way he pumped it gently, up and down, that he was about to recite. Most often he did so with his own hand before a poem, like a conductor beginning an overture.

> *In the sloped shadow of my hat,*
> *I lean at rest, and drain the heat,*
> *Nay more, I think some blessed power*
> *Hath brought me wandering idly here:*
> *In the full furnace of this hour*
> *My thoughts grow keen and clear.*

'One of your own, Mr Quincy?' she asked him softly when she was sure he had finished.

'If only!' he snorted. 'I could never cast words into gold, as does Mr Archibald Lampman, who wrote the verse. He is an Ottawa bard, like myself, but his poetry is better.'

'No, no,' Myra demurred. She could not bear to see Mr Quincy's face as pained and defeated as it was at that moment.

'Do not disagree with me, my dear. I know it in my bones, as I know certain other things. About you, for instance, and your children.'

'Oh,' said Myra doubtfully. Mr Quincy's hand was damp and sticky but retained its firm clasp.

'And your future,' he went on.

'Our future? Oh, but you needn't –'

'But I am concerned with it. Your husband, God rest his soul, appears – though you have never confided in me the details – to have left you reasonably well provided for, but his funds will not last for ever.'

Myra stole a sideways glance at Mr Quincy. A little drop of perspiration had gathered at the end of his round red nose and though his chosen poem had included a hat, he himself wore none. She cast her mind back: he certainly had had one when they boarded the first streetcar in Hastings Street. A straw one, with a navy band.

'I think you have mislaid your hat, Mr Quincy,' she said.

Theo twisted around and squinted at the bare, reddening head above him. 'It blowed off,' he announced, solemnly.

'Where?' asked Myra. 'Did you see it?' Mr Quincy cleared his throat.

'A hat is a trifle,' he said, with a twinge of irritation. 'I am trying to talk to you, Myra, of far more important matters.'

'Yes, Roland,' she said, and knew she would have pleased him by calling him by his Christian name, though she never thought of him as that. Mr Quincy he was and ever would be, the little fat man she and the children had passed any number of times on the street before the day he had steeled his nerve and invited them all to tea. She had thought he meant to a tea shop, but it was into a ground-floor apartment next to their lodging house that he led them. Myra had sat at his table, the children ranged around her, while he boiled the kettle and poured out. So strange it had been, to be waited on by a gentleman and a stranger. Later Mrs de Feranti had asked if she had been frightened, going alone to an apartment with a man she didn't know from Adam. Myra had almost laughed. How could anyone be frightened of Mr Quincy? Why, he was the same height as she was, he had small soft white hands, and kindness, such kindness, shone from his eyes.

'One sweet moment, in the not too distant future —' The hand was beating again, holding hers. It was another poem, though she could tell by his nervous tone, his slightly strangled pauses, that it was one of his own.

> *I will declare my heart to Myra,*
> *A modest ring I will slip on her finger,*
> *And forever beside me my love will linger.*

During the poem little Theo rose to his feet and placed a sandy palm on either of Mr Quincy's knees, and stared into his face. Mr Quincy looked pretty funny with his eyes closed, Theo thought, and he was all wet, though he hadn't been in the sea. When their friend had finished talking, his eyes sprang open again in time to perceive the child's sand-encrusted hand reach out for his brow, wipe it tenderly and return to his knee. Mr Quincy's eyes filled with tears, though with emotion or from the sand trickling into them Myra couldn't tell. She took up a towel and handed it to him, speechless, her mind racing. Why hadn't she told him the truth about William? What a position she had got herself into. At the corner of her own now moist eye she perceived the towel move on Mr Quincy's head, up and down, a white blur, but she kept her gaze fixed on the swimming children. Joe had Dora standing on his shoulders. She lifted her arms above her head, Joe's hands steadying on her calves, and she dived gracefully into the water. Myra longed suddenly to join them, wished she'd brought her costume. More painfully, she wished Mr Quincy would let go of her hand.

'I don't expect an answer now, Myra. Take your time to consider it.' He let go. He stood up.

'Come on, Theo, let's go to the pier.'

There was no invitation for Myra to join them. Mr Quincy did not even look down at her as he bent to lift Theo. She watched them go, hugging her knees, though the angle of her body made her corset pinch. When they reached the hard sand, Mr Quincy put the child down and they made their slow way, hand in hand, towards the northern end of the beach and the pier.

Even if William were truly dead she would not marry again. She knew that. Not even Mr Quincy, who had never been angry or ill-tempered or even discouraging. He was, she supposed, at least ten years her senior and seemed never to have been married. At least there was no evidence in his apartment of any other woman, save for a photograph of a small white-haired lady who was most probably his mother. What would it be like to be with Mr Quincy in that way, as man and wife, after knowing only William? She felt memory making it real, suddenly, heat in the pit of her stomach, and William's hard, demanding body lying along her own, his grasping hands, her body resisting him until, against her own will and resolve, she would feel herself melt, give way, want him, more of him, even while he was having her. It bewildered her to feel this way after all this time, but it was as if he had laid claim for ever to that part of her. Now he was as lost to her as that part of her was almost lost to herself. It was only the skin of the milk she could offer to Mr Quincy, not the true nourishing love that lay beneath, and surely he would not accept an inconsummate marriage? She could not imagine he would, for were not all men the same in the night? She would never be able to find the words to explain, though she would have to try. They would have to be tender words, as tender as those he had offered her in his little poem.

She rested her forehead on her knees, and the miles she had come to join William, and the miles since then away from him numbered themselves in the pulse of her heart, thudding against the walls of her chest, inside her sticky blouse. If she were a child, Riha's age perhaps, she would fling herself on the sand and kick and scream.

A little hand patted her shoulder. It was Edna, her wide, normally smiling face furrowed and worried.

'What's wrong, Mumma?' she asked. 'Are you sick?'

'No, my darling.' Myra stretched out her legs and pulled Edna onto her lap. The child's costume was damp, cool, welcome. She closed her hot arms around the small sandy body, kissed the nape of her salty neck.

'Where has Mr Quincy gone? You're hot.'

'He'll be back soon.'

Edna leaned back against her mother, lifted her cool face to press it against the base of her throat. Mumma was thinking about something, she could tell, though the soft underside of her jaw and gently flaring nostrils gave no clue as to what, nor did the floating veil on her big white hat, or her fingers that interlocked now over Edna's round belly. The child closed her eyes to the sun glancing off the water.

Far, far away at the breach of the pier there were two figures, a hatless little man and a tiny boy, moving along towards the floats. The floats lay bumping against the long pier and were crowded with bathers, diving off, swimming and returning to dive again. There were canoes and dinghies coming and going between the floats and the far end of the pier and all the activity, though Myra could hear the delighted yells and shrieks, seemed utterly removed from her, as if the view were one caught on a postcard displayed under glass. She felt as numb as if she were the inanimate pier herself, with the children and Mr Quincy the swimmers and the divers, frantic, clinging, letting go, returning.

'Mumma?' It was Riha now, who was hungry. Myra found her an apple in the canvas bag.

'When Theo and Mr Quincy come back we will have our picnic,' she told them. Nothing would be any different, perhaps; Mr Quincy was not an insistent man – perhaps he would deduce her answer from her silence and would not ask again.

The moment she saw the man and boy regain the sands, she spread the rug and dispatched Edna to fetch Audrey and the twins. Glumly, the adults picked at the food, the pork pie and cupcakes that Mr Quincy had packed that morning. The children ate and squabbled and ran again for the water. He did not speak to her again and neither did he beat time in the air or recite another poem or hold her hand. She sensed that the day was over early and that some trust or comfort that had existed between them was now broken. No matter, she told herself, for she had no real need of him. He had introduced her to things she had not previously experienced, like poetry and recitals and vaudeville at the Orpheum Theatre and most importantly of all friendship, the first real friendship she had known since Riha, which until today had not been demanding or prescriptive. But she had not accepted gifts from him, or kissed him, or given him any indication that their association would blossom into courtship or marriage. He was mistaken, she decided. The fault lay with him. She would be able to get along without him.

Mid-afternoon she sent the children to the Bathhouse to change and they began the journey home.

Chapter 23

Mrs de Feranti was in a state. Myra could see that from the moment they alighted from the streetcar outside Wilbur Apartments. There was the landlady on the fire-escape of the second floor of the boarding house, buffing the windows though they sparkled still from the polishing of only a few days ago. She waved her rag at them and leaned out over the railing.

'Oh, thank God, Mrs McQuiggan – thank God you come – oh hurry, hurry! I have left the door open downstairs – hurry, come up to me – I go inside –' And even while she spoke, the broad form of Mrs de Feranti disappeared back through the open window.

In their haste to obey her urgent entreaties, none of the McQuiggans noticed the quiet departure of Mr Quincy, laden with the rug and remains of his careful picnic. Nor did they hear the final soft click of the door to the apartments or behold his last despairing glance along the pavement at the disappearing heels of Myra.

On the second-floor landing, Mrs de Feranti was gesticulating wildly towards the gentlemen lodgers' bathroom, the door of which, the first off the long corridor on that floor, stood closed.

'He been in there for hours. Since you left.'

'Who, Mrs de Feranti? Who is in there?' asked Myra, puzzled.

'He come in. I know who, you know who. I tell him, you not here. He say he wait. He go in there –' She pointed again, agitatedly.

'Who? Who are you talking about, Mrs de Feranti?'

'All my hot water! All of it! You go and see –'

'But I can't go in there. It's the gents –'

'There are no others but him. Go you. You go and see –' and Mrs de Feranti, larger by half than Myra, was pushing her towards the door, turning the handle and flinging it open.

At first clouds of steam obscured all but the shape of the white bath and the black alternate tiles. Then Myra perceived a pair of boots propped on the bath's end with a pair of still-trousered legs attached to them. The man was in his clothes, though the water lapped at the rim. At the far end, between the taps, through the steam clearing in the draught from the open door, rose a neck and a dark, bearded face. The children pushed in around her, and Myra was aware of Mrs de Feranti at her back, clattering away down the stairs.

'Father!' Joy yelled, and the man rose up then, his boots submerged, and stood, his arms out wide, water spilling from the bath to the floor and an impossibly red, shining mouth opening in the beard. Myra saw that it was indeed William, his hair streaked with grey and reaching to his shoulders, his clothes ragged and soaked. The older children were squealing, the sound ricocheting off the hard damp walls, and running towards their father, who now vaulted out of the bath to the drenched floor. With no concern for his sodden state, he gathered the twins and Riha to him.

Theo and Edna hung back with their mother, silently clinging to her skirt.

'Why are you in the bath in your clothes?' asked Theo, when the strange man's eyes alighted on him over the heads of his sisters. The twins were laughing, wringing water from their father's sleeves.

'Come away,' Myra whispered to them. She felt as though she had become part of the wall she leaned against, lumpen, stationary. Her tongue lay in her mouth like a piece of dead meat, her bones pulsed with the impulse to flee. He had found her. She could not go to poor Mr Quincy or even to Mrs de Feranti. Here was William, walking towards her, the older girls hysterical with laughter at the squelching of his boots. He took her chin, hard, between thumb and forefinger and forced her face up towards hers.

'I found you,' he said, and she heard the barely suppressed anger in his voice. The twins heard it too, and over William's shoulder she saw their eyes widen, heard their laughter shut off.

Audrey, who had hung back at a midpoint between Theo and the older ones, now took her chance and lunged for her father's legs to embrace him. But William's mind, Myra could see by the fury in his eyes, had moved rapidly away from whatever delight he had experienced in his first sight of the children. Firmly, he pushed Audrey away with his knee and the child slipped, caught her head on the edge of the bath. It was a slow, sliding impact and she was not badly hurt, though she howled loudly.

'Which is your room?' His voice was level, implacable, and Myra saw she had no choice but to show him to it. She scooped up the sobbing child and led them down the hall.

Dora and Joy watched them go, their arms around each other. The door closed after their mother and father and the younger children. After a moment it opened again and their mother re-emerged, carrying their father's bundled, dripping clothes. She thrust them at Dora.

'Take these outside into Market Alley,' she whispered, 'and careful – they're crawling with lice.'

'But why has he –' began Joy, but her mother brought her finger to her lips and shook her head. At the open door loomed the shape of their father, a towel around his waist. The smaller children were herded before him, their heads swinging from him to Myra and back to their father again, like a flock of bewildered geese.

'Dora and Joy,' he said, 'take the others downstairs and leave your mother and me in peace.'

Their mother's face was a mask, her small features drawn away, blank, unreadable.

They went downstairs with Dora in the lead, Audrey snuffling and whining, and the others following. Dora carried the clothes, a brown, soaking bundle, with the smell of wet wool rising off it, the smell of their father's sweat and the indefinable traces of whatever roads he had taken and beds he had slept in during his mysterious absence. As she stomped loudly onto each tread of the stairs, she examined it closely for movement, hoping to see one of these lice that had so recently lain against their father's skin. He had turned into a gypsy, she decided, or a native, with his long hair and wild eyes. He had been out in the weather, he was brown skinned and his hands, when he had laid them heavily on her head in the bathroom, were hard and callused.

They passed through the hall and out the front door, which still hung ajar. Market Lane was at the back of the house and more quickly gained by the back door, but Dora knew that Mrs de Feranti would loudly bewail the trail of water from the clothes, spread by the feet of her siblings following after her. Anyway, the way Dora felt right now, a chill and a burning all at the same time, the return of her father thrumming inside her and the sea salt and heat of the day's sun on her skin, she knew it would be best not to encounter the landlady. Why, she was so excited she might yell right back at her, and run away, and drop the infested clothes right on her precious floor.

Quickening her pace, she led the others down the steps into the dusk. They turned right and hurried around the corner into Columba Avenue, past the Empire Hotel. It being a Sunday evening and continuing fine, the earlier wind dropped and still, there were people milling around. Men and women looked in shop windows and came in and out of the hotel. There were other children too, some of them ragged and bony, running or sitting on the porches. Columba Avenue was crowded with automobiles and horses and carts. There was the faint sound of gunshot from the shooting gallery next to the restaurant on the other side of the street and more strongly, as they turned into Market Alley, the smell of the Chinese's suppers cooking: cabbage and pork and fish.

Dora could recognise the back of the boarding house by the shafts of a cart, long unused, which lay on its tail-board against the house. As soon as you turned into the alley you could see it, and a moment later, on the other side of the Empire, you could see the top of the wooden rickety stairs that led up to the back door.

The Hastings Rooming House was the only building on the alley with a wall, which Mrs de Feranti had had built in order that the Chinese, who were their neighbours on this side, would not indulge their natures and steal from her. All Celestials, she had told the children, were sly thieves who would not ignore an opportunity and she planned not to give them one. The wall was about five feet high, cement, with a low wooden gate. On the other side, between the wall and the house, was a narrow dusty strip of ground, strewn with cinders and rubbish and knobbly unburnt bits of coal that either crushed to a powder beneath your feet or dug into them. Dora dropped the clothes and fetched a strong stick from the kindling under the stairs.

Joy sat the children in a row on the bottom step and stood before them, regarding them. Probably Theo would begin to cry now that Audrey had left off. He was still in his bathers and she supposed Mother hadn't changed him because he was still dry, he hadn't gone in at the beach. He was such a sook. Now he was pulling at the itchy wool around his waist. The others were glancing about, amazed at being turned out of doors at this time of day. Unlike other mothers in the neighbourhood, who let their children run around until after dark, their mother had not let them out alone in the evening before. Audrey, who suddenly felt very tired, as if she were dreaming while she was still awake, pulled her dress down over her knees and curled into the corner of the step, her eyes drooping.

'How long will we have to stay out here, do you think?' asked Joy.

Dora didn't answer, engrossed in her search for lice. Stepping away from the children, her sister crossed her arms over her pinafore and gazed up to the second floor, to the lit room that contained their mother and father. Her hair ribbon had come untied so she drew it around and sucked on the end. It tasted of salt and a hint of pie from Mr Quincy's picnic. The lunch pail game she played with Dora would change soon, she thought: there would be another journey. Father would take them all away somewhere else.

Her parents had not drawn the curtain. Joy could see their shapes quite clearly, her father close to the window, his naked arms and back, his hair shining from his bath. Her mother stood a distance away, on the other side of the bed. She was not looking at Father, but a little to one side of him at a bear, a small bear that stood beside Father on its hind legs with its head slumped, the hind legs concealed below the window. Father had his hands on its shoulders.

Thick brown fur, black tipped, ruffled around the huge collar and fell in a swathe to the heavy hem. William turned it so that she could see the lining. It was sliver, shining, fluid as water. The coat would drown her and smother her all at once.

'Here,' he offered, 'try it on.'

She shook her head quickly, without thinking.

'Bloody try it on.' His voice hardened.

'It's the middle of summer,' she said quietly. 'I don't need a fur coat.'

William threw it onto the bed, into a square of late-afternoon light. Its pelt took on the golden sheen of the sunset. It was beautiful – she wanted suddenly to stroke it and would have done so, but William was spinning and thumping his hand into the window frame.

His eye caught the upturned face of one of the children. It was Joy, or was it Dora? He couldn't tell: they had grown more alike in his absence. One of them gazed up at him, while the other was bent over beside her, stirring his clothes around with a stick. He pulled the curtains closed, pounded the same fist on his forehead; without even looking at her he knew Myra was shrinking back against the wall.

'Don't be frightened of me,' he muttered through clenched teeth. 'Don't do that to me, not after all this time.'

Myra took a tiny step towards the door that connected the two rooms. Beyond that door, in the other room, lay the door to the hall – she could run and fetch the children inside, they could sit safe with Mrs de Feranti in the kitchen while she worked out what to do.

'Myra?' He was looking at her now – had he seen her try to move away?

She took a deep breath and without knowing it mirrored her daughter outside, on the other side of the closed curtain, leaning against a wall with her arms across her chest.

'How could I not be frightened of you?' she whispered. 'The terrible things you've done.'

But William had started talking before she had finished, urgent, hushed. 'He didn't tell me where you'd gone, the Prophet. He kept your secret. After he died, Mrs Dowie found your letter among his things and passed it on to me.' He moved around the foot of the bed towards her.

The letter about the Doctor's sister, the letter he'd never replied to. She'd sat nine-year-old Joy at the table in the Grandview Rooming House and dictated it to her, Joy writing it out in great childish loops. Perhaps the Doctor had been unable to read it.

'I didn't come straight to you. I went north to the Yukon to look for gold.'

'Did you find any?'

'No.'

She looked directly at him then, saw how hard and whip-like his body had become. He was stringy, brown, his eyes shadowed with exhaustion.

'I've only been in Vancouver for a week,' he said.

There was a long, deep scar on his upper left arm, healed but still pink and lumpy. He saw her gaze travel to it.

'Cove took to me with a knife –' he began, but Myra, with the same impulse that had had her shake her head to the fur, held up a hand for him to stop.

'Please go away, William.' There, she'd said it. She stepped rapidly through the door into the children's room but he was right behind her, ahead of her, slamming the door into the hall even as she opened it, forcing the handle out of her grip. He leaned against it and held her hands, his thumb pressing and caressing her wrists.

'I've prayed for you and the children every night since I saw you last. The Doctor told me that even if I ever found out where you were I wasn't to go to you. But he had no right to ask that of me, did he, Myra?' His hands travelled, took hold at her elbows. 'You're my wife.'

On the floor peeping out from under Theo's narrow bed was a toy Mr Quincy had given him. It was a jack-in-the-box, made of tin, brightly painted. The laughing jack's face was half in shadow, half in light, and she remembered Theo when the toy was sprung for him the first time as Mr Quincy held it out, and the uproarious laughter of Mrs de Feranti and the girls at Theo's wonder-filled face, his sweet gurgle and endless demands for the jack to go back in, back in, back in – and the hook swung and caught up and released and the jack bounced again and again. She saw Mr Quincy in his outrageous mustard suit with large black checks, kneeling before Theo in the rooming house hall on the worn Turkish rug and smiling and laughing with the child, growing ever more cacophonous in his hilarity until one of the lodgers put his head out from his room.

Was that life gone from her then? She had grown so used to it, her careful governing of the money that she supplemented by her hard work, side by side with Mrs de Feranti, who traded it for a reduction of the family's board. Myra would walk the children to school down the road, return and cook and clean, scrub and polish, and very often she and Mrs de Feranti talked of God. He was the same one for both of them, she decided, only Mrs de Feranti had him on a cross in the kitchen, a small black ebony crucifix with a pearly white Christ all yellowed on the toes by her touching. She was glad their gods concurred. It seemed more and more that there were many gods: ones who blessed and ones who punished. The one she shared with Mrs de Feranti bestowed them with blessings and miracles: the range drawing on a day when they thought it would not because it was too cold and windless outside; the bread rising when they thought it would not because the yeast was old; the children's small successes at school; the departure of an obstreperous lodger – apart from Myra and her daughters they were all men; and even the generous friendship of Mr Quincy. Was there a religion anywhere in the world, she wondered now, her gaze resting on the fuzzed white roll of William's towel, where there were many gods?

She lifted her eyes to meet her husband's and searched them for evidence of his God – his wild, punishing, terrible singular God that put him through such agonies. The Yukon. A good twenty years after the gold was exhausted. She felt leaden at the prospect of hearing about it.

'You are a fool, William.' Suddenly she didn't care if he tried to kill her. She would scream, batter at the door, and if she was lucky someone would hear her. Mr Ogden in Room 25, he might be there, or Mrs de Feranti would hear from downstairs. 'Let go of me.'

William's eyes – how they spiralled and whirled, or seemed to. The longer she held them the more still they became. She felt him see her, an almost audible click at the back of his gaze as he saw how she had changed. Then she saw him shy away from the truth of it like a startled horse.

A slow smile, disbelieving, only half amused, spread across his face and he did indeed let go of her elbows. He turned and sauntered towards the bed, allowing as he did so the towel to fall from his hips. His pearly rump shone like two new potatoes below the brown of his back. His legs were sinewed and still youthful, and when he reached the bed he did not turn to confront her but flung back the sheets, climbed in and covered himself. He lay back against the pillows.

For a moment he said nothing. Myra opened the door and looked out into the hall. There was no one about.

'Well, go on,' said William in profile from the bed. He had his arms crossed behind his head, was attempting to appear nonchalant. 'I won't stop you.'

She didn't move.

'No doubt you've got slavvying to do with the mick downstairs. She told me about your arrangement.'

'It's sensible. I want the money to last as long as possible.'

'A Catholic boarding house! You've got no class!' This last was spat out with such vehemence that Myra found she had been drawn by it to the foot of the bed to face him, though she knew she should be running – oh, God, she knew it, running helter-skelter down the stairs to the children. At least the door was open and would enable her to hear them when they came inside.

William's gaze swept over her on its way to the ceiling.

'You could do much better than this,' he said, and then in an undertone, 'we could.' He picked up the fur coat from the bed and laid it gently beside him, stroking it, the soft rich pelt under his hand.

'I will not take you back, William.'

It was as if she hadn't spoken. She gave the bed a sudden jerk and shake, but he continued his stroking, unperturbed. 'You see, you don't know about money. How to handle it. It's always been handed to you on a plate, first from your father sponging off his parishioners, then by me and now my old man. It's not as if you ever had any real money –'

'William –' Why was her face burning so? Was it rage or shame?

'. . . and it seems to me to be a little stupid for you to have a part of it, and for me to have the little that comes to me by way of my allowance. It would be far more sensible for the money to be pooled. When the Doctor told you to run away, he was not at all pragmatic. He was old and half insane.'

'Did you stay in Zion?' she asked suddenly. 'Were you there when he died?'

'Left in 'eight,' he answered, 'a year after . . .' He trailed off, as if his mind were on other things, and went back to stroking the fur. There was a curious sense of something repeated and Myra searched for it. It was the night before he sailed for America, the night she arrived in Auckland heavy with the twins. He had been in his bed, his hands white, indolent, soft. But the hands now working the fur were hard and dark, a thin line of dirt under the chipped nails: there was a slip and sheen as his palm rode up, the darker side peeling away from his fingertips as his palm rode down. He was watching her steadily.

'Come here.' He patted the fur now.

'No,' she said. Oh, but she wanted to suddenly, even though God had sent her a warning, a prescience of this, on the beach – of how her body would betray her. He had sent it to her so . . . to . . . her mind grappled, she could not concentrate . . . so that she could resist it now.

William threw back the covers and laid the coat out flat, the lining uppermost, and lay back again, stark naked. She averted her eyes, but she had seen it, the part of him she had thought she would never miss – though she had ended up missing only that.

'We would ruin the coat,' she blurted. How foolish! Why had she said that? Now he would know she was thinking about – at least, that she perceived –

'Would we? Doing what? Shut the door.'

Myra took a deep breath and hurried across the room. She would keep going, she would, through the open door, she would not derail herself from her purpose, she would not allow him –

But she closed the door. Was she mad? Either that, or her gods were warring, or the devil was whispering in her ear. There was only one devil. She looked to him again, on the bed, the startling presence of him, exposed, looked to him as if he would give her strength to do the very thing she knew she should not. He had his hand on himself, but not to cover himself from her: it was curved around and moved as languidly as it had on the fur.

Hands, her own, were undoing the button at the back of her skirt, reaching beneath her petticoat to undo the string on her drawers. She bent, unlaced her boots and kicked them off and then she was walking, her blouse coming open beneath her trembling fingers, her arms arched behind her head at the high neck, until she could pull the thing over and off and she was, in chemise and corset, climbing onto the bed, one leg on either side of him, her knees slipping on the silk, and he was touching her there, on the place that longed for him, at least as much as did the part inside her, the part he'd claimed that long-ago time in the bush, by the still, when she'd conceived the twins.

A hard voice asked then, even as she moved to take him in, how she could possibly know that was the time she'd got the twins and not the night of the fire when he had forced her? Rising up in her then, black, inchoate, just the messy, deadening shape of them, were all the times since then that he had hurt her and left her, as if he couldn't care less if she'd lived or died. Her eyes cleared suddenly – had she had them almost closed? she wondered – and there he was beneath her, his hands loose at her hips, his face vulnerable. She took hold of the stubbly flesh at his jaw and pulled it hard, viciously, as full of rage and spite as she had been of want of him, but the want was still there: it was all confused. In response to the pain she had inflicted on him he was turning her over, but with infinite grace and gentleness, and entering her again, his hands on either side of her face, his brow against hers for a moment, then his hot mouth was on her neck and she laid her hands against his working flanks, and there was such urgency and despair in him it was as if he would mix his very blood with hers.

It was Mrs de Feranti who fetched the children in eventually, just before dark, opening the back door with a bucket in one hand. Dora now had a collection of lice, fifteen or twenty at least, scraped from the stick into a discarded oil bottle she had found in the rubbish heap. They congregated mostly in the seams, she had discovered. On the brown wool they were almost indistinguishable from the stitches – in pursuit of one elusive captive she had ripped a sleeve clean off.

She looked up just in time, at the click of the opening door, to see Mrs de Feranti's astonished face, which reminded her suddenly of a clown she had seen only a week ago at the Vancouver Exhibition. It made her giggle, and Mrs de Feranti fixed her with a frosty eye. Heavily she descended the stairs, scooping up Theo on the way. His legs were getting longer, Joy noticed: his ankles hung midway down her apron.

'What you doing?' Mrs de Feranti wrested the bottle away from Dora and looked with disgust into its greasy, murky depths. 'Pidocchi del corpo!' she shrieked and flung the bottle over the top of the cement wall where it did not collide with a Chinese, though it could well have. Passing at that very moment was Ying Yee, the second son of Ying Po the laundryman. The bottle exploded at his startled feet, on impact with the cement floor of the alley.

'What is that?' The landlady pointed now to the mound of cloth, the torn sleeve tossed to one side like the peeled skin of a giant saveloy.

'Our father's clothes,' answered Joy, when she saw Dora would not, her mouth set into a silent straight line.

'It is disgusting!' Mrs de Feranti emphasised with fervour, the word being one of her favourites in the English language. Disgusting! Disgusting! The word chimed daily in the children's ears. She grabbed up the stick, which Dora had discarded some time ago in preference for her bare hand, and used it to drag the offending pile towards the gate, where she kicked it into the alley. The stick was then employed to administer several sharp cracks across the backs of Dora's legs and only tossed away at the top of the back steps when Dora had reached the safety of the hall.

Their mother came downstairs soon after Mrs de Feranti dished up the soup. It was hot and peppery and the younger children did not like it. Theo was hungry but not for minestrone and had begun to cry at the sight of it. His volume doubled at the sight of his mother, his itchy bathers and coke-bruised feet compounding his misery.

'Where is Father?' Joy asked.

Myra picked up Theo, hauling him out of his chair into her arms. Immediately she felt a tug on her skirts and looked down into Riha's furious, jealous eyes. She hooked her in with her spare arm and the child wiped her grimy face on her mother's flanks.

'Good evening at last.' Mrs de Feranti got up from the table. Carefully she looked Myra up and down, her eyes coming to rest on her flushed face, and though Myra had brushed and re-pinned her flyaway hair and buttoned her blouse as neatly as it had been before, it seemed the landlady knew what had passed between her lodger and the man upstairs.

Could she smell it on her? Myra wondered, and though she felt she should be ashamed she wasn't. She had told Mrs de Feranti nothing about William, though at times she had longed to, just as she had with Mrs Wayland in Hakaru. She had never told her an outright lie, such as she had to Mr Quincy. In answer to the landlady's questions, Myra would always feel herself recede, that old fainting away that she only ever had at the thought of William. Her face would close over and she was deaf to the question. In any case she would not know where to begin. She made a point of never asking Mrs de Feranti about Mr de Feranti, in the vain hope that this would prevent, by example, further interrogation about the children's father.

'He is staying?'

Myra nodded.

'For how long?'

She shrugged.

'Not long?' Into this question the landlady injected a querulous, tremulous note, and it seemed to Dora that she was almost singing and she hummed the note under her breath. The large, glittering brown eyes of Mrs de Feranti fixed themselves on her once more. 'Hush up.'

'I don't know.' At the stove Myra ladled out a bowl of soup.

'He is your husband?'

'Yes.' Myra moved towards the door with the bowl.

'And what will you do? You will take him back?'

'I don't know.'

'Phuff!' Mrs de Feranti threw her hands up in exasperation but paused mid-gesture to take the soup bowl out of Myra's hands.

'Siddadown,' she said and handed the bowl to Joy, whom she considered infinitely more sensible than her twin. 'You take this to him up there.'

The twins stood as one and Joy took the soup through the door into the passage, her sister beside her, their hearts pounding. Not only must she carry the soup without spilling a drop, Joy thought, but it was Father she was carrying it to. Father! What was he doing upstairs? she wondered. Maybe he was looking at a map wondering where they would go next, or maybe . . . and her spirits sank a little . . . maybe he was reading his Bible and would want them to pray together like he did all the time in Zion. Maybe Bible reading would be better – or praying – than map reading. She didn't want to move away from the Hastings Rooming House, or her friends at school, or even Mrs de Feranti whom she liked a lot better than Dora did. Imagine never seeing Mr Quincy or Joe at English Bay again. Beside her Dora moved up the stairs, silent as a shadow.

As soon as Myra sat down, the remaining children flew to her, Riha and Audrey to one side and Edna behind her, with her arm around her mother's neck. Theo pushed into the soft stomachs on either side of his claimed lap and shoved them away. Audrey howled, loudly.

'Shoosh!' said Myra, more sharply than she had intended, but the child blinked with surprise and quietened.

'He come to get you. Where you go? Don' say again you don' know.' Mrs de Feranti had her back to her, ladling out another bowl of soup. Myra sighed and dipped her nose into Theo's hair.

'So he is a good man in the bedroom, eh?' Mrs de Feranti winked, and Myra felt a blush rise from her toes to her head, so violent that the rush of it made her momentarily nauseous.

'Three years is a long time,' continued Mrs de Feranti. A bowl, floating with white beans and tomatoes and cabbage, was deposited before Myra. A fine yellow veil of pungent cheese lay over the surface. How hungry she was, thought Myra. The crust bent under her urgent spoon.

Mrs de Feranti put out her arms for Theo. He remembered her earlier dangerous, groaning lean towards infinity as she had earlier carried him up the steps, and instinct compelled him to put a foot to the floor as he stepped out from his mother's lap. The moment he was close enough, Mrs de Feranti kissed him with her hard-lipped mouth and her weighty arms crossed about him as he watched his mother eat in a way he had never seen her eat before. She spooned up vegetables and beans and smelly cheese, heavy liquor spilling at each laden ascent. Riha, who had refused the soup, now opened her mouth to every second spoonful. When she had finished, Myra neatly wiped her mouth and said, very quietly, 'Mr Quincy would call it an epoch.'

Theo didn't know what she meant. Neither did the owner of the lap he snuggled in.

'Eh?' said Mrs de Feranti.

'A very long time.'

There was silence then, the girls leaning into their mother, their soft breath ruffling her hair. Audrey reached up and stroked Myra's cheek. The soup bubbled and hissed and outside there was still a little traffic: the last tram rumbled by, there were distant shouts and a little closer a man whistled the new tune of 'Bill Bailey'.

Carefully, Joy settled the bowl, still steaming and entire, on the little table their mother had bought for when she wanted to keep the children away from the lodgers. It stood in the children's room, just inside the connecting door, and was cluttered with belongings: Riha's hat and sandy towels and a jumble of wet bathing dresses and – she yanked it out from under the latter – her very own copy of *Anne of Green Gables*, a gift from Mr Quincy. One buff corner was sodden and swollen and tucked inside was Theo's treasure from the beach, the tail feather of a Canada goose. She opened the book and ran her finger down the feather, separating the tight-knit, greasy black ribs.

In the bedroom Dora tiptoed closer and gazed at her father. Under the covers he was on his side, as if he had fallen asleep curled around something that was no longer there. Closer still she padded, stepping from the tatty round sisal rug to the rag-rug beside the bed, without letting her boots connect with the floorboards. Against the curve of Father's back lay a lick of thick shadow, convoluted and gleaming. In the lamplight, low and spluttering, its surface sparked on myriad fine fibrous points. Quickly, she grabbed it up and dragged it away, stepping loudly in her haste on the echoing floor. Father gave a little groan, whether at the sound or the lightened sensation at his back she did not know.

The coat was beautiful: heavy, soft, thick, a faint smell of animal – not horse or dog, but something other, exotic, a wild creature perhaps, a bear. She shouldered her way into it, the vast collar falling over her head so she thought it must be a hood, though it made it difficult to see. Lifting the weighty swathe away from her feet she went to show Joy, whom she could see at the open door laying her book aside and shooting a nervous sideways glance at the man in the bed.

Shambling towards her out of the dim room was the bear Joy had seen earlier through the window. It was small and crumpled; its arms hung against its side; it had no ears. What kind of life had it led with Father, she wondered, to leave it in such a tragic state? She let out a sudden sharp wail of horror and Dora flung the bear's earless head away from her own, her eyes white with alarm.

'Who's that?' said their father.

William had been dreaming of finding Myra. It was a dream he'd had recurring for two years: the way she will look when he finds her, her warm welcome, his forgiveness of her, the house in the dream small and pink and near the sea, the children reduced in number though there is another son among them. Every tin and jar and box he opens in the house is stuffed with paper notes, and as he counts it into its denominations he does not recognise its country of origin. Through a window he catches a glimpse of Henry surrounded by a mob of cats.

It was strange to wake from that dream and see the reality: the shabby room, the kerosene lamp with its cracked shade, the cluster of battered children's shoes on a lower shelf, his baggage disgorged on the floor, the acrid aroma of his own piss in the chamber pot under the bed. But there was the smell of Myra all around him – in the sheets, on his lips and pillow. The twins, one of them in Myra's coat, watched him breathlessly from the door.

'Take that off, Missie.'

The child obliged immediately, letting it slide to the floor and giving it a tiny irritable kick as if it were to blame for its momentary hang on her back. He would take a closer look at this one, work out which one she was.

'Bring it here.' William leaned out and turned up the wick of the lamp in order to study them better.

The child bent to pick up the coat at one end, her sister wordlessly going to the other, and they carried it together, laying it across the foot of the bed. They watched the stretch of his back, saw the knobbled scar on his arm. He was infinitely mysterious.

'We're not going to tell you which one we are,' said Dora with a challenging air.

'Haven't you got a nightshirt?' asked Joy, concerned.

'Who can tell you apart?' asked their father. 'Can your teacher?'

The twins looked doubtful. 'No,' said one; 'Yes,' said the other.

'Mrs de Feranti can,' said the first.

'And Mother, of course,' added the second.

'I haven't seen you for a long time.' William patted the bed in an invitation for them to sit down. Neither twin moved.

'Why haven't you,' asked the one who'd asked about his nightshirt, 'seen us?'

'Because the Lord told me to stay away from you for a while. I knew Mother would look after you.'

'Did the Lord tell you himself? Did he send an angel?' asked the other twin.

'The Father speaks to all of us. Does your mother take you to church?'

This time they had the same answer: they shook their heads.

'Sometimes we go with Mrs de Feranti to Mass,' said the more talkative one, who he guessed was Dora. When they were three years old and first arrived in Zion, he had been able to differentiate easily between them. The uneven nourishment of their confinement still showed. The smaller, paler one was Joy; the shining, big-boned child was Dora.

'And do you like Mass?'

'Not much,' replied Dora.

He shuddered at the thought of them, his own daughters, surrounded by the perversions of papism, the traditions and clanking trappings of the ancient church. It was what was wrong with Dr Dowie's church: its frantic endeavours to accommodate and mimic all that, going even so far as to include the word 'Catholic' in its title. It seemed to William, as he had moved alone through the world, that what must come into being is a thoroughly modern church, one that by its reason and science would draw all men to it. It would devastate and reshape all of mankind, much as he had seen machinery do to whole hillsides and landscapes. The new God would be a kind of machine: solid, dependable, beyond desire for punitive response. On the long road to Vancouver from the Yukon, he'd thought he would begin a church like this himself if he could not find one already in existence. Hadn't he offered himself again and again to the Lord's service, so many times he'd lost count? But the Lord continued not to show Himself, not in a real, tangible sense as He had at Pukekaroro. Steadily his conviction grew that the Lord was terrible, mighty and inanimate, a celestial tool that mankind must take up and use like a hammer. In the new modern world God did not push Himself forward or force his will.

Dora looked worriedly at Joy: could she see how Father was glowering, his eyes focused, distracted? She wondered if he would notice if they left. Taking her sister's arm she gave it a little tug.

'Come and sit here,' said Father suddenly. He smiled and Joy thought how even when he smiled he still looked sad – there were deep lines in his cheeks, which she didn't remember from Zion.

'Do you know what I'm going to do?' he went on as they perched side by side on the bed. 'I'm going to buy us a house and a motor-car, and since you like that coat so much I'm going to buy you a coat too, one each, everybody, right down to a tiny small one for Theo. What do you think?'

Without looking, Joy knew that Dora was smiling and smiling, beaming at their father who she saw now had the same eyes as they did, narrow and bright, eyes that almost disappeared when you grinned. But at the back of her own eyes she felt tears, prickly and hot as embers.

'What about Mrs de Feranti and Mr Quincy?' she asked.

'We'll say goodbye to both of them, whoever Mr Quincy may be,' said William, categorically. He sniffed the air. 'What can I smell? Onions?'

'Oh!' Rubbing at her foolish eyes, Joy hurried away from the bed to fetch her father's forgotten soup.

CHAPTER 24

There were coats, one for everyone, and many dinners in the dining rooms of many of Vancouver's hotels – the eight of them around a table with Mother spoon-feeding Theo, who in Riha's opinion was quite old enough to feed himself. She would never have dared say so, or offer any opinion at all on anything, for Father had proved himself, ever since he came back, to be a stickler for manners and resentful of opinions offered by children. He'd given the stick to Dora and Audrey in his first week home: Audrey for grizzling and Dora for her infestation of lice, which she'd got from playing with his clothes.

There were coats and dinners in hotels and then, a few months after Father's return, there was the house in Kitislano with shingled siding and a veranda with brick posts for climbing. There were toe-holes in the mortar that Riha was sure none of the other children knew about.

There were coats and dinners in dining rooms and two motor-cars, one that had broken down soon after Father had bought it. He'd prayed over it for hours and ended by leaving it on the side of the road, never going back to retrieve it. Outside the house, on blocks in the street, was the newest motor-car, another Ford identical to the first one, which didn't go any more either and Mother said there was no money left to fix it. Just now, as Riha gazed out from the upstairs window of Mother and Father's bedroom, the Ford's canopied roof below was as snow-laden as the trees and all the surrounding roofs of Kitislano. The teacher had said at school it was the coldest winter she could remember and she was old, older even than Mother. She liked the children to be as quiet as mice, and Riha wished she could somehow be here now and watch her play statues, which is what she was doing brilliantly in front of the window. One day, when she was grown up, she would keep so still she would fade away altogether, and in so doing would discover the secret of invisibility. She would become the colour of air, and then those glaring, terrifying eyes of her father's would never alight on her again because he wouldn't be able to see her.

A while ago, a long time ago, it seemed like hours, when she first froze herself into a statue at the window, a holy statue with its hands clasped before it in an attitude of supplication, she had seen her father and Joy come down the front path and out onto the street. Father was wearing his hat and greatcoat. Joy had her fur coat on, which was too small for her now, and her new green muffler that Mother had knitted for her. Under her arm she carried a black book, which was Father's Bible. One coat pocket bulged with the *Book of Mormon*, the other with a hardcover notebook that contained Father's handwritten notes and cuttings from Dr Dowie's newspaper. They had made their way down the street, Father towing Joy along beside him, and vanished around the corner towards the train station.

Riha turned back into the room and surveyed the two beds. The one closest to the window was Father's and the other one Mother's. Between their beds was a small white bow-legged table, which only ever had on it two things: the Bible, which had gone out with Father and Joy, and a small carved wooden box, which remained. Riha liked opening the box, though what it contained unsettled her because she didn't know what the strange object was, or what it could possibly be used for. She opened it now and peered in. There was the faint smell of sandalwood, which came from the wood, and a smell of something else, which was not always pleasant. The second smell came from a skin that lay curled in the box: a grey tube, closed over at one end. Sometimes the skin thing was damp, she supposed because Mother had washed it as Mother washed most things. Most often these last few months it was dry and crackly, undisturbed, in exactly the same position as it had been last time she opened the box lid. There was something sad about it, like a cast-off snake skin or locust shell. She wondered what Father used it for. It was definitely Father's because the box lay closer to his bed than it did to Mother's, and once she had found some collar studs inside it, which he must have dropped inside by mistake. She memorised the position of the skin so that she could put it back exactly as it was, then picked it up and put it over her finger. It flopped over against her wrist.

'Hello,' she said in a sad, squeaky sort of voice, the sort of voice it would have if it could talk. 'Merry Christmas.' She took it over to the window and let it look outside at the gloomy afternoon, but that seemed to make it even sadder and floppier, so she put it back in the box, snapped the lid shut and went downstairs to the kitchen, where Mother was mixing dough for dumplings. The air was warm with the smell of stew.

'Oh look, the sky has fallen in!' said Mother when she saw her long face and there was a derisory snort from the table where Dora sat equally glum-faced with a cabbage, which she had been set to slicing for the pot. The other children's voices, rising in delight or squabble, came through from the parlour where Mother had lit a fire.

'Where's Father gone?' asked Riha.

Myra turned on the tap and held her dough-flecked arms and wrists under the icy flow.

'The girls at school,' Riha continued, 'their fathers go out to meetings all the time, just like ours. Lodge meetings, they go to.' Dora put the cabbage on the chopping board and took up the knife. Myra watched warily and hoped the cabbage would be good all the way through. By her calculations the stew would yield two little cubes of meat each and a few rounds of carrots. The dumplings would have to fill everyone up. At least there was plenty of gravy.

'Is Father at a lodge meeting, then?' persisted Riha. 'You know, there's the Masons and the Orange. He could be in the Knights of Pythias. What do they do, Mother?'

'I have no idea,' said Myra. 'It's only men. Women never go.'

'Is that where he is, then?' asked Riha. She came around to stand beside her mother, watching the dumplings drop from the spoon to the stew, the landing of the oval sticky islands in the bubbling sea concealed by the rim of the pot.

'No,' said Myra, 'he's gone to preach on the streets.' There was a tiny, infinitesimal connecting glance between Dora and Mother then, the meaning of which eluded Riha though it made her jealous by its intimacy.

'Why?' she demanded.

'Why what? Why – because in the town there will be a lot of people. It's Christmas Eve.'

The cabbage showed itself to have a brown core. Myra took the knife from her daughter and carved it out, or most of it.

'Joy and I were born the night before Father went to America,' Dora told Riha, though Riha knew that already. 'Father held Joy in his arms. He likes her better than he likes me. That's why he's taken her to hold the hat.'

'I don't care,' said Riha. Brown, brown, brown, everything was brown. Her mother's dress, the tiny flowers speckling her pinny, the table, the wainscoting, the knife handle, the silly rotten cabbage, the smelly stew, even the electric light, gloomy and dim. She opened the firedoor of the range to look at something bright.

'Close that,' said her mother immediately. 'The wetback is heating for the bath water. We'll have baths for Christmas.'

'It's only half past two,' yawned Dora, and then she grimaced, bringing a hand to her open jaw. That was another thing that was brown. One of Dora's teeth.

'Joy went with Father last time.' Riha brought her Viyella cuff to her nose and wiped the ruffle across it.

'Have you been upstairs?' asked her mother. 'You'll sicken again. It's too cold upstairs. You stay down here now, in the warm.'

'I could have gone with Father instead.' Riha clamped her arms around her mother's upper legs and pushed her face into her skirt. Close up the tiny brown apron flowers danced and blurred. One of her mother's hands stroked the back of her head.

'He always takes Joy,' said Dora, 'though I'd be better. What's he reading?'

'Luke. He said he'd read from Luke because it tells the Christmas story best.'

'Why don't you ever read the Bible, Mumma?' asked Riha.

'I do, you just don't see me doing it. Everybody reads the Bible sometimes,' Mother replied, snippy.

'Why does Father read it all the time?'

Mother's hand altered its stroking to a quick pat, half pushing her away, and Riha knew she wasn't going to answer her.

'Why does he?'

Mother continued to ignore her.

'Because he's a crazy man,' said Dora.

Mother ignored even that. It was strange, the things Mother let them say about Father. She never agreed with them, or added to their remarks. Right now she was starting up, with a sharp intake of breath and a distracted look. It was something Mother often did, when she remembered a chore or task she'd forgotten, or if she saw one of the children doing something she considered dangerous. Dora giggled, pleased with her pronouncement on her father. She caught her mother's eye and gasped too, much louder than Mother had. It made Mother jump.

'Cheeky miss,' said Mother, though she was smiling.

Myra put on her hat before the glass. The idea had come to her, not five minutes ago, when she realised the stew was ready, or on the way at least, and that it wasn't yet three o'clock and that there would be time, if she were quick, to take a train to Mrs de Feranti's. Her old landlady remained her closest friend in Vancouver, and Myra visited her when she could, sometimes as often as once a week. From its hiding place at the back of her closet, she took the lustreware cream jug and sugar bowl, which were wrapped still in their brown shop paper. As soon as her eye had lit on them in the shop on Waters Street, she had seen them glowing prettily on the rooming-house sideboard. Mrs de Feranti's dining room was sparsely furnished. There was the sideboard and a heavy shellacked table and eight chairs. The lustreware would sit sweetly at the back of the sideboard against the wall, beside Mrs de Feranti's crucifix of shells, at the base of which fought St Michael. Like the smudged little figures on the china – for it was not real lustreware, but what the man had called the fairground kind: St Michael lacked definition of feature. Gold and blue, like the little jug, he was a construction of time-blurred pelleted wax, his tiny golden sword grown misshapen, the point drooped.

At the sight of her mother in the doorway of the small parlour, in her fur coat and gloves and hat and carrying a string bag, Dora scowled. Her mother lifted a finger to her lips and gestured to her to come closer. The other children had not noticed her, gathered happily as they were around the warm fire, and she would keep it that way. A quiet exit and a quiet return, and nobody would be any the wiser, she hoped. On the vast chesterfield, a foolish purchase of

William's that almost filled the room, Audrey was reading aloud from Joy's old Christmas annual from last year and Theo was snuggled into her, his scrap of six-year-old blanket in its customary position under his arm. It only came out of hiding when William wasn't home. Edna and Riha were invisible though she could hear their chattering voices, each instructing the other in the making of a house between the sofa and wall. So vast was the stuffed curl of its rolled back that it held the chesterfield away from the wainscot and provided a roof for their narrow nest.

Dora approached her warily. Before she'd gone upstairs with a secretive expression on her face, Mother had set her up with some mending in the armchair closest to the fire, and that had been tedious enough. Now it seemed she was going out.

'I'll be back by five,' Myra said. 'Look after the others and keep an eye on the stew. The dumplings will be done in twenty minutes, then just shift it back to the warm and make sure it doesn't catch.' She dropped a kiss on her daughter's head, directly parallel now to her pursed lips. It landed on Dora's crown, at the end of the parting in her dark blonde hair. The child smelled musty, shut up, and Myra remembered too late the planned baths – but a window had opened out into the world, the chance of a small escape, and the bubbling wetback was not enough to keep her at home.

Only one change and the train took her to the station on Carrall Street at the bottom of Hastings Street East. From there it was only a short walk, and as she hurried along with her head down, the better to avoid frozen clods of horse manure and slushy piles of snow, she thought only of the time and of how little of it remained and how she must force herself up and away from Mrs de Feranti after only half an hour in order to be home in time for William.

'Myra?'

At first she thought it was William, that somehow he'd seen her from an upstairs window, or the other side of the street, and hurried across to join her, but then her eyes filled with the mustard and black checks of a suit, and the size of the man inside it, who was so very much smaller than William and his voice not nearly so deep, in fact a kind of sharp, light voice, which he used now to repeat her name and she looked up and smiled.

'Mr Quincy!'

He reached out abruptly and took her closest hand. The string bag with the parcel inside bumped and swayed.

'How are you?' The cold air had made Mr Quincy's cheeks as red as the sun had that summer of 1910 and his eyes, which she had forgotten were that exact murky shade of brown, streamed lightly as if he were about to cry.

'Where are the children?' He would keep her on the street, Myra saw, wasting precious time, so she hurried on, gesturing for him to accompany her.

'At home with Dora.'

There were two pool rooms on Mrs de Feranti's block and outside each stood crowds of young men, smoking and talking, their breath frosting. They parted in an amused sort of way for Mr Quincy, whom some of them knew and doffed their hats to. Myra avoided their eyes, which she knew without looking were not as curious as they would once have been. Or were they ever, she wondered in spite of herself – did young men ever look at her so? Certainly they did not now, nobody did, not even William. Mr Quincy's attentions were that of a neglected child.

'Is Dora able to look after them all safely?' he was asking now, with a hint of disapproval.

'Of course. The twins are thirteen.'

'I wish you had brought along little Theo. How tall is he now? Here?' He held out a hand at waist height and Myra felt a tremor of irritation.

'It is not as if I have not invited you to call on us –'

'How could I?' They had reached the rooming house and Myra had taken the lower step. 'How could I possibly come to visit you when you have been reunited with a ghost? A dead man, Myra.' He was patting his pockets and Myra feared he was searching for a recent poem. He had written many for her since she had gone to live in Kitislano and was apt to read her excerpts on the rare occasion they met at Mrs de Feranti's.

'Oh, Mr Quincy!' Myra shook her parcel with exasperation and heard the china rattle and tinkle inside, 'haven't we already been over this?'

'It's just that —' It was a red handkerchief he pulled from his pocket. 'It's the loneliness, the loneliness is so terrible. Enough to lay a man as low as he can go.'

'I'm not going to apologise again. It's foolish. If I explain to William what a good friend you were to me and the children he'll most likely be so grateful as to welcome you with open arms. I've not done so only because you don't want me to.' Mr Quincy, diminutive on the pavement, dabbed at his nose. Suddenly, while she watched him, he drew himself up and met her gaze. His eyes, the brown surrounded by moist pink, glinted with outrage.

'It amazes and astonishes me how a lady can never see the true nature of her husband. My own dear mother was the same, God rest her soul. Mr McQuiggan, though I have only observed him from afar on the day he carried out your furniture, is not the kind of man to allow his wife the friendship of a stranger.'

'Mr McQuiggan allows me a great deal of freedom.' Myra felt the heat of anger rise in her, blood flushed her cheeks. 'Here I am, out on Christmas Eve!'

Mr Quincy pursed his lips, as though he disapproved of that as well.

'Come with me,' Myra said on impulse. 'Come inside and see Mrs de Feranti.'

Tears fell lush and round from the landlady's eyes, at first on perceiving Myra at the door, then on perceiving the absence of little Theo — though she did agree with Myra that it was too cold to bring the little soldier out – and then fresh and rounder still at the cream jug and sugar bowl, which she immediately freed of their wrappings and held against her breast. She hurried her guests down the hall to the kitchen at the back, where three young men scarcely more than boys sat around the table smoking and playing cards.

'My nephews. They just come last week from Italy.' She spoke to them rapidly in their own tongue, and Myra discerned only her own name and that of Mr Quincy. The young men shuffled their cards together, grinned shyly at Myra.

Mrs de Feranti picked up the coffee pot that stood on the table between them and squeezed out a final cup, which she placed before Myra. The three nephews scraped their chairs back, extinguished their cigarettes and followed one another out into the hall. She heard them make their way into the front parlour, and though she understood none of their language she could tell by their huffing and blowing that the rest of the house was icy. By contrast, the kitchen was hot, the coal range roaring and the air thick with the last exhalations of their strong tobacco. She shook her coat away from her shoulders, letting it fall around her chair.

'Now, you tell me everything,' said Mrs de Feranti. 'How your husband is treating you. He drive you here in his motor-car?'

Myra shook her head and smiled. 'No, he's out preaching.'

'Preaching what?' Impatiently Mrs de Feranti patted the chair beside her and Mr Quincy did as he was bid, sitting down with an air of melancholy. He pulled off his gloves and heaped up a little pile of tobacco ash on the table before him.

'You have his religion yet?' Mrs de Feranti carved off a slice of the high yellow cake that stood on the table. 'You eat. Italian Christmas cake. Is hard when a husband believes one thing and a wife another.'

'William has no . . .' began Myra. It was impossible to explain, but both Mrs de Feranti and Mr Quincy were gazing at her expectantly. She went on. 'He has no real religion. Not an organised one. He takes a little from here and a little from there. From Dr Dowie and the church in Salt Lake City and even . . . even from your faith, Mrs de Feranti. He believes in the saints.'

Mrs de Feranti looked blank. 'Here there what? He thinks he is a saint or what? A holy man?' Narrowing her eyes, she flicked her gaze to Myra's lap and stomach. 'So holy he not a proper husband to you. By now – two years! – there should be another baby.'

Mercifully, Mr Quincy gave no sign of having heard the remark, though of course he must have. As always, Mrs de Feranti made no allowances for his presence. It was as if she regarded him as another woman, somehow not a real man. Myra sipped quickly at her coffee, which was thick and dark and not at all like the coffee she drank at home.

'Maybe next year,' crooned Mrs de Feranti. 'Maybe you have a baby in 1913.'

'William doesn't want any more children. He says the world as we know it will end in 1914,' Myra said mildly. Mr Quincy allowed himself a response to that.

'Rubbish! He's been reading the *Watchtower*, eh? Pastor Russell's drivel.'

'William says the hundred and forty-four thousand, of which he hopes to be one, will meet the Lord in the air in a fiery chariot,' Myra continued, 'and then the children will play with wild beasts and all marriages will be perfect.'

'Pure Pastor Russell!' exclaimed Mr Quincy while Mrs de Feranti laughed out loud.

'I think he is a little mad, your husband.'

Mr Quincy concurred with her by nodding. 'Pastor Russell would have done better to write down his fancies as stories for children. Any sane man gives them no credence at all.'

'He is not the only one who believes these things. Thousands of people do, all the International Bible Students.'

'But why?' Mrs de Feranti leaned closer to Myra, her broad hands cupped under her chin. 'Why would anybody believe these things? Who would want the world to end?'

'So that . . .' Myra thought hard, drumming her fingers against the base of her coffee cup. The truth for William, or the pursuit of it, she had understood since he came back to her, was his only refuge from the bottle. That and their congress, their coming together. But after his carpentering job on the *World* Newspaper Tower had finished at the end of the summer and he had spent the autumn studying afresh St Paul to the Corinthians, he had taken his vow of celibacy.

'It is good for a man not to touch a woman,' William had read aloud to her in their bedroom late one night when four months of abstinence had already passed. 'He that is unmarried careth for the things that belong to the Lord . . . he that is married careth for the things that are of the world, how he may please his wife . . .' He was inspired in his reading by her licentious behaviour, climbing as she had from her bed into his that night with the lamp still on, and taking the French letter from the box on her way. He explained to her the Mormon principle of marriage, which he had adopted as part of his own. Even though he had put her apart from him, he said, they would be together for all eternity.

'He thinks that by his reading and searching he will create a perfect faith, one that combines the best of everything, and he will be the best prepared,' she said lamely, though Mrs de Feranti could see by her blush and racing eyes she was thinking about something else altogether. She was right, then.

'So he puts in nothing of himself? He is merely collating other men's theologies?' asked Mr Quincy.

'It is not quite so,' said Myra. 'He has one belief I have never heard before.'

'And what is that?'

'Heights,' she said. 'William likes to climb up high to be closer to God.'

Mr Quincy and Mrs de Feranti stared at her, amazed. Then they looked at each other and burst out laughing. The laughter seemed to go on for hours, though Myra supposed it was only a few moments. Mr Quincy's eyes streamed more than ever and Mrs de Feranti fairly shook.

'It's not such a foolish idea,' Myra said quietly, though neither of her friends was listening.

She felt now as if she were under attack. Perhaps she shouldn't come again: it often ended this way, with Mrs de Feranti's disapproval of William leaving her feeling comforted in one sense, but guilty and disloyal in another. Her friend was wiping her eyes, patting her heavily on the shoulder.

'You tell him from me to write a book. Everyone will read it to have the joke.'

'No he's not . . . He's not the type to write a book. He struggles even with his reading, though he reads aloud with great expression –'

Mr Quincy was watching her now rather sadly, she noticed: his earlier melancholy seemed to return. Or was it pity?

'Not like Mr Quincy,' she finished to cheer him up. 'Mr Quincy is a true poet.'

'I was,' Mr Quincy corrected, 'but no longer. I lost my muse.'

'Find another muse,' said Mrs de Feranti, hard. Mr Quincy had wept on her shoulder too many times after Myra had gone to live in Kitislano.

'More coffee!' the landlady announced. But Myra leaned across the table and took her hands and drew them to her, kissing them on their work-hardened knuckles.

'Not for me. I have to get back to the children. Merry Christmas, Mrs de Feranti.'

Mrs de Feranti was standing too, hurrying around to wrap Myra in her broad, soft embrace, instructing Mr Quincy to see her safely onto the train and entreating her to come again soon, before the New Year.

'Next time bring the children!' she called after her down the street.

CHAPTER 25

William ended up on Homer Street before the *World* Tower. He hadn't meant to preach there; he'd meant to stop on Hastings Street outside Woodwards, where the people were. There were such crowds there that the streetcar was forced to stop several times and he could easily have disembarked, grabbing Joy's hand and slipping out among it all, the people and horses and vehicles and motor-cars. Already, at two in the afternoon when they'd passed through, electric lights had glittered and burned on the other side of the shop windows. But the throngs had unnerved him – he wouldn't have been able to find a place. And Joy, moving around with the hat, would have been lost to his view.

It was better around the corner on Homer Street where there was next to nobody and a man could breathe properly and keep an eye on his daughter. He read for a while from the second chapter of Matthew, the Christmas story, but failed to catch the attention of the few passers-by. Five young Chinamen jostled by in a group, laughing and talking, ignoring him completely, and soon after an elderly woman passed, struggling home with a sack of coal half as big as she was. As he began reading, he'd had the newspaper building at his back but he ended with it before him, its tower peak lost in the lowering clouds of the afternoon. Memory blew a cold bracing wind in his face and he was there again, as he had been in the summer, way up, looking out over the city with False Creek to one side and Burrard Inlet to the other, feet firm on the scaffolding, his hammer raised as he nailed in the boxing for the concrete. How good it had been to be a working man again, to be part of the army of construction workers who set off in streetcars every morning from points all over Vancouver to converge on sites where great buildings took shape. He hadn't wanted to go out to work – he had resisted it – but there had been a problem with the New Zealand lawyer, who had decided in his dotage to act upon some half-insane instruction of the old man's and withhold the money. And Myra, when he'd questioned her, told him Elisha's instructions. She was to discharge his debts, she said, but the old man wanted her to keep the money to herself. His own father! Expecting him to scrape by on the allowance.

Now, with funds slim again, the allowance all but dried up, William waited on the lawyer once more, this time for evidence of Mr Ryde's communication with the Colonial Bank of Auckland. All he wanted were two facts, simple facts, and he couldn't fathom the reason for the delay. Firstly, he wished to ascertain how much of the estate remained exactly, in pounds, shillings and pence. Secondly he required the lawyer to inform him of the exact percentage of the estate that owed its origins to his Scottish ancestor, Gunpowder Farquhar. He cursed himself for having left the only copy of Gunpowder's letter in the keeping of the bank manager – the letter he had stolen from his father's ledger that day at the end of the last century. Gunpowder's bequest was mostly, it seemed, in the form of interest earned from investments. But investments in what? William wondered. Stocks and shares, lands and industries? The old crank had not been able to build a university as he had wanted to, and his vast fortune must have been invested by the Scottish lawyers.

William wanted the controlling seat. He felt the possibilities of the wealth, the muscle of the money rise and buck

427

beneath him, a surge of power from the very earth. He would build a church in New Zealand – not immediately, but in a year or two. For now he was content to wait, work hard on building sites if he could, and meanwhile, with the help of God, construct his theology. Then, with his investments cashed, the capital all in the Colonial Bank, he would steam home to where his life's true work awaited him. He pictured the church, stone, high on a South Island mountain, the faithful happily working the alpine farm, the vast underground reserves of food and medical supplies laid in for Armageddon.

Tonight he would write to the lawyer again, he decided; he would have a letter ready for when the post office opened again after Christmas.

'Come with me, Joy,' he said suddenly. The girl was leaning against the brick wall of the newspaper building, pulling threads from her gloves. He led her up to the main doors and they passed into the high, wood-panelled lobby. The draught from the closing door set the lofty globular lamps swinging, the filament in their opalescent depths flickering. Joy had never been in such a grand room before, not that she remembered. There was a tall polished desk that was unattended, and behind that a large painting of a red-faced, important-looking British Columbian. Her father walked purposefully, in large strides, as if he owned the place. Perhaps he did, she thought. He had owned other surprising things, like the motor-cars. And he had worked on a tower last summer, somewhere in the city, before he'd taken up preaching again, taking herself and an extra hat with him.

'Where are we going, Father?' Joy asked quietly. 'We should be going home.'

'Soon,' he replied, taking her hand, too tightly as usual, and mounting the wide marble stairs.

'Can I help you, sir?' The speaker was a young clerk, bundled in greatcoat and scarf on his way out. 'The offices are closing for Christmas –'

William nodded at him in greeting but passed on.

'Do you have an appointment, sir?' persisted the young man. William nodded again and the clerk, imminent escape into Christmas Eve uppermost in his mind, and seeing that the lobby was empty of witnesses, allowed the stranger leading the pale slender girl to continue his ascent.

At the top storey, William crossed the polished floor to the door he remembered led out onto the roof. It was unlocked, though he struggled to push it open against the snow that had banked up on its outer side. Joy stepped out after him, the snow covering her boots and stockings to just below her knees. The cold hit her in the chest like a fist, even through her coat and knitted muffler. She could feel the bones in her chest, thin and aching. Her father was grinning, beckoning with one large square hand, paddling it against the low grey sky, the air heavy with the smell of lifting coal smoke from the surrounding chimneys.

'Look,' he said softly, leading her across the flat roof, not giving her time to look behind her, where she had the sense of another, higher structure rising up.

All before her was white and grey and brown, even the sky and the evergreens of the forested hills of the north shore, which was so far away as to attain a distant shade of ash. Hard and close, at the edge of the city, the mountains rose up, the grey fuzzy light not softening but intensifying the black of the flanks below heavy white caps of snow. Father put up his collar. It was so much colder up here than down on the street, and Joy thought to ask him why that was, because didn't heat rise as Father said most things did, sooner or later, but her lips were so achingly cold they could not move. Instead she looked quietly down on Hastings Street: the men's hats moving about, the bobbing derbies and trilbies, the women's hats rare among them. It had always struck her on her wanders with Father how women were less on the street than men, but it was stranger still tonight, Joy thought, that so few of these people – and there were so many of them – carried Christmas parcels or gifts. Perhaps it was true what

Father had shouted at Mother, that they were not the only family having no Christmas, that he would work if he could but work was scarce.

Father flapped one of his large gloved hands to the east.

'Mountains,' he said, and then, his hand to the west, 'the ocean.' He turned her head around in the usual careless manner he had whenever he touched her, unmindful of the pressure of his fingertips on her skull or the natural inclinations of her neck. He tilted her back so that she looked up at the tower, her body against him, while he steadied her shoulders.

'I've been to the very top,' he said. 'From there you can see all over. This is the tallest building in the British Empire!'

The roof they stood on was black pitch, as Joy could see in the places the snow had not covered, and the low wall that surrounded them concrete, but the tower that rose before them was shining steel. It didn't look as if it belonged to the building at all, but as if it had been an afterthought, a rigid steel tent pitched on top of its parapet roof. It rose to a point, its sides slippery and tractionless. Not even the snow clung to its sharp edges. Her father, Joy knew, was thinking about climbing it. She knew this without even looking at him. She often knew what he was thinking during their excursions: she could anticipate his request for his Bible, or for the *Watchtower*, or an old faded copy of *Leaves of Healing*, or, more rarely, the *Book of Mormon*. She knew when his senses had swung around to perceive a listener who had deep pockets, a man or woman Joy could successfully approach with the battered felt hat.

'Around here.' He pushed her upright, over-correcting the angle of her body so that she almost fell forward. 'Around on the other side there's a ladder.'

And he was moving away, climbing over a low parapet to a narrow ledge that ran along the eastern side of the building. Reluctantly Joy followed in his wake, but only as far as the drop to the ledge, which she could see now was only the corniced eaves of the building, a two-foot-wide concrete projection. At Father's left was a plinth, a small level expanse, on which stood the concrete base of the tower. He walked along the ledge, arms outspread, one foot placed exactly in front of the other, as if he were utterly unconcerned about losing his balance. Joy watched him pensively, wriggling her numb toes inside her boots and trying not to draw the cold air too far into her lungs in case it made her cough and drew his attention back to her, but he had taken a quick glance over his shoulder and seen she wasn't behind him.

'Joy!'

It was impossible, she thought, but he had done it: executed a turn almost in mid-air, his arms waving madly, like birds' wings, and was making his way back. He turned again, and she understood he wanted her to climb onto his back.

'No, Father, I –' she whispered, frozen with cold and fear.

'Do as you're told!' He was snarling now, and she knew if she didn't obey him he would strike her. She climbed onto the parapet and launched herself onto his back, keeping her face away from the dizzying, terrifying fall at her right, staring only up at the tower. Now her father's steps were not so assured: each foot was settled into its place with a tiny side-to-side motion that she could feel in the movement of the muscles of his back, under his thick coat.

Slowly, his breath coming shallow and concentrated, his arms outstretched as before and with the child clinging painfully to his throat, he reached the bottom rung of the black cast-iron ladder that lay against the shining eastern side of the structure, its narrow treads between the rails widely spaced.

It was like a steeple, thought Joy, and she wondered if there were a cross at the top, though why this newspaper building would have a cross when the *World* was the sort of newspaper Father now frowned on she did not know, nor could she fathom why the ladder was there in the first place.

Perhaps above them in the clouds there was a flagpole and perhaps men sometimes climbed it to unfurl the flag or free it when it tangled . . . Her father lurched below her, his leather-gloved hands reaching for the bottom rung, taking hold, his right foot lifting from the ledge and scrabbling onto the plinth. A small flurry of wet snow blew into her face – it was windier on this side of the tower – and she closed her eyes, brought her legs around under her coat to grip more firmly her father's hips. There was a lump in her throat, as if a piece of bread were caught there, but she hadn't eaten for hours. Father was muttering to himself and she thought at first he was praying.

'And they said, "Go to, let us build a city and a tower, whose top may reach into Heaven" ' – Genesis, thought William. Yes, that was it. The ladder was grasped, the first three rungs taken. The child was heavier than he'd thought she would be. He had never lifted her before, he realised, at least not since she was a tiny baby, a newborn. Now her bony thighs were vices at his side, his Bible in her coat pocket wedged hard into his kidneys. He hauled himself up another few feet.

' ". . . and let us make a name, lest we be scattered abroad upon the face of the whole Earth –" '

Their ascent was stalled, Joy realised, opening her eyes again, but keeping her face close to the dark cloth of his coat. Both of Father's feet were on the same rung, his hands gripping the icy bar above his head.

'The Bible, Joy,' he said, turning his face towards her, his hot breath ruffling the hair below her hat, 'Pass me the Bible.'

The lump in her throat threatened to choke her.

'But I can't – I'd have to –' How her arms ached. She was going to cry, though she didn't want to. He would insist, he would shout, he would tell her to do as she were told. But he was silent, his feet shuffling side by side as far to the right of the ladder as they could go. Then he leaned to the left and she knew without instruction that he expected her to grasp the left-hand rail and swing herself away from him. Her hand flailed: there was no sensation in the fingers inside her knitted gloves. Her left leg kicked out and caught the rung on the heel of her boot, her palm struck the rail and she willed her fingers to close around it.

'There's no need to be frightened,' her father said, shoving his hand hard into her pocket and retrieving the Bible. She couldn't turn her head to look at him, could only press her forehead to the cold iron, her eyes open to a lump of molten metal on the underside of the rail, the means by which the ladder was welded to the steel. Colder now than she had ever believed possible, she felt the origins of the tower, the Earth its elements had been mined from, the fire that had shaped it. A small, entirely rational voice told her that she was not at all clinging to a near-vertical plane high in the sky on Christmas Eve beside her father who she could hear was now ruffling through the fine pages of his Bible, but that she was instead walking among the high fire of an iron foundry, such as she had seen pictures of in books, the planes of her face licked by heat.

' "I will stand me upon my watch and set me upon the tower, and will watch to see what He will say unto me, and what I shall answer when I am reproved —" ' Father had found his place. At least with her mouth so frozen her lips were stuck to her teeth, she would not be tempted to ask him questions. He did not like to be interrupted. Idle questions were not tolerated, even when he had no audience. A sudden flashing hand, heavy at the side of the head and hard enough to knock her sideways, was the usual response to the most tentative curiosity. Father could preach into empty space, with no answer, for hours.

' "For the vision is yet for an appointed time, but at the end it shall speak and not lie, though it tarry, wait for it because it will surely come, it will not tarry —" ' Despite the cold, Father was in full voice. His breath fluffed around his mouth, he held his Bible high.

433

'"Yea, also because he transgresseth by wine, he is a proud man —"' William's stomach bucked and swooped with the words. How he loved this passage, this well-thumbed page. He'd come across it in the Yukon one bitter drunken night when he could scarcely focus on the tiny lines. The Bible he'd had then, now retired, was almost worn through at Habakkuk's corners.

'". . . who enlargeth his desire as hell and is as death, and cannot be satisfied"!' He offered the last word to the heavens as a challenge, his face tipped back. Habakkuk was the tiny, fifth-to-last book of the Old Testament, only two pages long, after which came Zephaniah, Haggai, Zechariah and Malachi. The prophet was not mentioned or even referred to anywhere else in the entire Bible and it seemed to William that his angry and righteous voice was tucked away like a secret, a talisman reserved exclusively for himself.

'Oh, Lord, my God,' he shouted now, '"The Lord is in His holy temple: let all the Earth keep silence before Him." I could love you, Lord, for Habakkuk alone. Joy! Joy!'

The sudden insertion of her name into his monologue lifted her head, though she suspected he intended its other meaning, one that was quite distinct from herself, but he was looking at her, his gap-toothed smile huge, ecstatic.

'Habakkuk knows what it is to live on this Earth. He doesn't just rail against his enemies, he sees into their hearts, he knows his own heart to be black. Listen, Joy: "Drink thou also and let thy foreskin be uncovered: the cup of the Lord's right hand shall be turned upon thee, and shameful spewing shall be on thy glory —" The child stared at him, uncomprehending. He supposed there was no chance she could understand Habakkuk, who addressed himself to men of the world. The charming salutation at the end – 'To the chief singer on my stringed instruments' – spoke of generous masculine spirit, a respectful comradeship. Brotherhood. William laughed at her, shoved the Bible into his pocket and climbed, quickly, to a point several rungs above Joy's head. He turned himself then, hooking his elbows under the rails so that he lay on his back against the ladder, his face open to the frosty sky.

'I love you, God! Everything you show me.' He was bellowing, his throat reddening and swelling. 'Make me a decent man, a shining jewel like your servant Habakkuk! Satisfy me, Jesus!'

Below them there was a waving black thing – it was an arm, Joy realised. There was a man's face looking around the corner of the tower from the plinth. He was standing on its far corner, on the adjacent face of the tower. The man was three or four lengths of Father below her, about twenty feet down.

'Hey! What the devil do you think you're doing?'

Father glanced down then and Joy saw an expression very like fear cross his face. He held up one finger to the man, as if he were asking him to wait a moment, and turned himself again, this time with difficulty, his feet slipping and banging on the rungs. Seeking to obey the stranger, Joy let one foot reach out behind her to search for the rung immediately below, but quickly brought it back to sit beside the other. There was nothing but a looming sense of space, purpled and shining, like the inside of a vast china bowl.

Now Father was facing the tower, and his boot – she could see the nails still shiny from the last re-soling as it came down – was on track for her right hand and Father was moving fast. She was still crying and frozen, and though her mind instructed her hand to move, it wouldn't soften its grip on the bar. She knew the tractionless woollen gloves would slide, that she wouldn't be able to shift her hand in time. The heel caught her fingertips. She pulled away – not sideways, as she intended, but backwards, her elbow jabbing out, the thrust of the movement strong enough to dissociate the rail from her left hand. Her feet, grown numb entirely, had no warning of their imminent passage. Unresisting, her body arched away from the tower, childhood's proportion still evident enough in her body to flip her head first.

Her small body struck the plinth of the tower's base.

There was someone gathering her up.

She had not at all rolled heavily to the narrow ledge above the curling concrete cornices. There was someone gathering her into an ample, aproned breast.

She had not at all fallen again, this time out into the heavens above Homer Street.

Was it Nanna Riha? The face was broad, like Nanna Riha's, but it was white, its features as blurred and indistinct as Mrs de Feranti's St Michael. Grey wispy hair flung out on either side of a small white cap.

How the air rushed past her ears still, though she was closely gathered in. She saw the face more clearly now, above the far end of endless proffered spoons in a room – it was a kitchen with a vast, frowning, black iron range and a gloomy photograph of a wizened baby in a cradle. She was warm and her sister sat in the pram opposite her, her identical chubby knees under the pink blanket. The light, gas-lit and golden at first, grew steadily dimmer, then the dark was coming in as fast as the rushing sound had stopped, abruptly, owing no logic or reason to time or speed at all, at least not to the kind of time taken by ordinary arrivals and departures in the ordinary, living world.

PART FOUR

THE VINE IN
AUCKLAND, 1915

CHAPTER 26

Out of the front door of the Vine and down St Martin's Lane from Symonds Street came Dora, carrying the baby on one hip, her other hand held firmly by Riha. The summer rain had made the lane slippery, but Mother wanted the children out of the house. They followed along barefoot in a draggly line, Edna and Audrey and Theo, through the cemetery gate and in among the trees and tombstones.

'Will the man in the black coat be here?' asked Riha, peering into the shadows under the Grafton bridge. If she saw him she would look away immediately, before he had time to beckon to her.

'How would I know?' snapped Dora, shifting the baby to the other side. Myrtle wasn't really a baby any more: she had turned one in September and she was heavy.

'Shall we play the game?' Theo came to stand in front of her, his hands on his hips, squinting into the sun.

'You little kids can. I'm going to sit down.' She flung away Riha's hand and switched the baby to the other side.

'Only you have to go to your grave,' said Theo, 'to make it fair.'

'Anything for peace,' said Dora. She could be eighty years old.

Light on her young feet with Myrtle gurgling tight against her, she made for the plot further up the gradient of the gully. Someone had visited her grave recently: red geraniums glowed in a jar. They were short stalked, picked by a child.

Dora flopped down on the grass, hauled her skirt up over her knees and pushed her black stockings down to her ankles to let her legs see the sun. She plonked the baby between her feet for safe keeping, loosened the top button at her neck and reclined on her elbows. Immediately Myrtle climbed upright, hauling with her plump hands on her sister's legs, and trained her eyes on the children who were moving together down the hill, through the trees, until they met a cluster of graves. Dora's grave used to be down there as well, until she decided she was too old for the game and mostly abandoned it, even though she had been the one who'd made it up two years ago when they first came back to New Zealand. Now, on the rare occasion she accompanied the children to the gully, she chose this grave, which was out on its own, peaceful under a shaggy cypress that had grown up since the grave was dug. Edward Trenwith, 1875, aged 18. He was buried with his mother and father and Dora pitied him more for that than she did for being dead.

The baby plopped down on her bottom again and sunlight dappled her white bonnet. Auntie Blanche and Auntie Ellen said she was the one most like the twins: fair haired, big boned, with William's eyes and full mouth. At least she didn't grizzle all the time like Edna and Audrey did when they were smaller. She uprooted a heavy-headed stem of paspallum, tickled Myrtle's chin with it and wondered why Mother had let her out like this, in the middle of the day. Ever since they had left Vancouver, she had helped Mother with the children – first on board the ship, then while they stayed with Auntie Blanche and now in the boarding house on Symonds Street – and Mother was always so tired and strained that even though Dora had long-ago made up her mind to despise her, she felt guilty every time she left her side. But just then, only ten minutes ago, when they'd finished clearing Sunday dinner in the hot, stuffy, fly-buzzing dining room and the lodgers had all left the table to go back to their rooms or out into the afternoon, Mother had said she could go, if she wanted, and she had seemed to mean it, even though it was the maid's afternoon off. Dora was grateful she hadn't been sent to find William. It being a Sunday the shops were closed, so he was probably up in his room on the third floor, the one across the landing from the maid's. It had a high dormer window that looked east, over the gully. When he was home he spent most of his time up there, poring over plans for the church he said he was going to build, and making notes in the margins of his Bible and endless yellowing newspapers he'd brought back from America.

At first on that last Christmas Eve in Vancouver, when they'd brought him in, Mother had fallen to him and she and Father had wept together. She couldn't recollect actually seeing them embrace, though she remembered her father coming right into the parlour with the snow thick on his shoulders and in the brim of his hat, and he seemed shorter, as if the dark and cold outside had somehow shrunk him. She was sure they must have stood for a moment in each other's arms because wasn't it her mother's cry, that strange strangled little scream she gave as she recoiled from him, spinning away and groping for the fat arm of the chesterfield – wasn't that the moment Dora knew Joy was dead? Her mother had known already, known by the horror in his face that she was, but the cry – Dora knew now that that was when Mother had realised he was responsible for Joy's fall. Dora hadn't understood that for months, not until the voyage home in the spring, the night he climbed the ship's derricks.

Now that she was sixteen, she knew a lot of things. She could see what had happened that Christmas, how she'd gone away from everything and everyone. The moment of departure had come when she'd first met her mother's eyes while Mother sat crumpled on the settee, and seen it there – that Joy was gone for ever. Back and away Dora had gone – the soul of her it must have been, she thought, because didn't she still stand upright with her back to the fireplace? But she felt herself reel away from her mother, knowing at the same time that the abandonment was mutual: Mother was vanishing in her own way, in another direction. It was something Mother did when things were too much for her; it was instinctive, like her gasping. She departed and Dora did it then too. Perhaps it was something she had learned from Mother, or something inherited. She hadn't inherited anything else from her mother: she was fair and tall and too full of feeling. For three months Dora had taken Riha into her bed in place of her twin, and slept with her body spooned around her. It was nothing like sleeping with Joy: when Joy had lain against her Dora had felt her hard, beginning breasts pressed against her back, as they nestled flank to flank for warmth. With Riha it was more comfortable around the other way, with the smaller body cupped in the curl of hers. Neither could Riha play the dream game.

'Tell me what to dream about,' Joy used to say. And Dora would think of something. Nanna Riha, or school, or Mr Quincy, or going to English Bay or Stanley Park or Heaven. And Joy would dream it, a huge long story, which she'd tell her sister when they woke up.

Some mornings, before they left Vancouver, before the voyage home, the back of Riha's nightgown would be wet at midpoint, between her shoulders, and Riha would turn and put her arms around her sister to comfort her, even though it was Joy she had loved best. Everybody had loved Joy best. It wasn't until after that night on the *Makura* that the dream-crying stopped.

Theo had darted away from the others to a grave a short distance away, closer to Dora, and was returning, his hand glowing with orange marigolds. It was a good haul, Dora considered: they looked fresh, as though they had been placed only yesterday, or earlier this morning perhaps, the mourner coming in before the church bells rang. Theo left the small jar behind, scattering the marigolds over the slab, his feet wedged into the iron rails of the fence that surrounded his little grave. It had been a rule, when the game first started, that your grave had to match your age, or as near as possible. And that once you'd chosen it, you couldn't un-choose. Theo's belonged to Dear Little Norman Aged 5 Years, and below the dedication it read: Your favourite Lilly, Mama. It always had arum lilies, a sheath of them left lying against his headstone. Theo had been only seven when he picked it and now he was nine. He'd got older while Norman had stayed the same. He wanted to choose another one but Audrey, who was the new boss of the game, said he couldn't. Besides, if Dora wasn't there to hide behind – and she hardly ever was nowadays – your grave was the only place you were safe from the tall bent man in the black coat who lived under the arches of Grafton Bridge.

A cart rumbled over the bridge now, and Dora watched the horse and driver flicker between the concrete palings before she lowered her gaze and peered into the shadows under the bridge. The man wasn't there today.

Riha's grave had a stone urn with tiny stone roses. It belonged to Jessie Clarke Ewen, 1890, nine years of age. From Dear Little Norman, Riha, who had turned eleven, took the arum lilies and wove them in and out between the iron palings of the grave fence.

'Come and see!' she called to Dora, but Dora shook her head and watched Theo, who was standing back now, contemplating his handiwork, before he ran for an oak, scooping up pebbles to his pocket as he went. Rapidly he scaled the trunk, his bare toes gripping the dull bark, until he reached the first bough. Out and up he swung himself until he sat astride it and the first pebble met its target: a marigold in the centre of the slab jumped with the impact. Suffer the little children, said Norman's tombstone.

Click, click. Pause. Click, click. The stones that missed the flowers struck stone and ricocheted away. High on the other side of the gully a vast corrugated roof glowed bright beneath the hot sky. Dora wondered if her father was looking out at it too, seeing how the red bled into the blue above, how a single white gull wheeled against the tall white walls of the house. From William's window you could see Rangitoto on the other side of the channel, and the green mound of Mt Victoria. You could see, closer, the end of Stanley Street and the tram lines, the low hill that was the further reaches of the domain, and beyond that the reclaimed land at the edge of the harbour. You couldn't see west to the graveyard though, thought Dora: he won't be watching us. The boarding house stood on a small promontory into the gully and this part of the cemetery lay behind it, hidden by trees.

Perhaps Mother had gone up to him. Dora wouldn't put it past her. She had no pride. It pained the daughter, angered her even now while she lay in the peaceful cemetery with the baby staggering about. It made her ears hot with rage: Mother had accepted Father's great evil. She still loved him; Dora had seen her put her hands on his shoulders, stroke his upper arm when there was no need to. She let him get close to her, close enough to get another baby, even though it was his fault Joy had died. Mother had called the baby Myrtle Joy, and though it was traditional to name a living child after a dead one, it seemed a brutal trick to Dora. Every time her mother ran the two names together, it struck her like a knife to her throat, or a hand, tight, momentarily cutting off her air.

'Hello, Myrtle Joy,' her mother would say as she passed the pram with Myrtle chortling and dribbling in it, shiny and fat between sleeps or meals, and a little smile, new and peaceful, would rest on Mother's lips for an instant. Did she think she'd replaced her older daughter? It was a stupid and cruel tradition in Dora's opinion. Anyway, she was sick to death of babies and hoped with all her heart that there wouldn't be another one.

She tore her mind away from the boarding house and its occupants and tried instead to think of her own future, of how she could stand up to Mother and take a job away from the house. If silly Gertie could get a job as their maid, then so could Dora. Not that she would be a maid: there were plenty of other more interesting jobs because of the war. She could get a man's job, outside maybe, or she could get a position in a shop on Karangahape Road. She was good with numbers, she was good with money . . . but the vision of herself serving people, smiling, helpful, faded almost as soon as she had conceived it.

Instead, she was on the ship again, standing on the third-class promenade among a small but growing crowd, looking up in the moonlight to her father clinging to the derricks. She had put her hands to her ears but they failed to block out his tearing, sobbing voice, or the consternation of two of the ship's crew who were climbing after him and shouting for him to come down.

'Forgive me, Father!' she heard him cry. 'Absolve me!' And then it was scripture he shouted at the stars, at the heaving dark ocean around them – scripture he knew from memory. It was either Habakkuk or St Paul – they were all he ever read, those two short books. Dora didn't recognise it; besides, she wasn't trying to. She was running as fast as her legs could carry her to Mother in the stern, the full length of the ship away. All four hundred and fifty feet she ran, though of course she ran further, she thought, when you took into account the corners and steps, the circuitous route she took partly of necessity, and partly because she couldn't think properly. The McQuiggans' cabins were in the stern on B Deck and Father was howling at the moon on C Deck's third-class promenade. She could not have cut through the first-class Dining Saloon: it was impenetrable, especially to a thirteen-year-old girl in a faded summer frock, with her too-small fur coat thrown over the top for decency rather than warmth, who would clatter along in heavy brown shoes and disturb the toffs at their dinner. Up the third-class companionway she tore to B deck where she pounded along first-class promenade, many of the cabin doors on her left open to the evening. There were one or two heads, she saw them out of the corner of her eye, turning at the sound of her feet. There was the smell of perfume, Bay Rum and cigarettes wafting across the deck.

On she sped, effortlessly, the four hundred and fifty feet falling away beneath her. Eight thousand and seventy-five tons the ship weighed, with a breadth of fifty-seven feet, a thumping twin-screw engine and a consumption of one hundred and fifty tons of coal every twenty-four hours: these facts she had gleaned from a chart of the ship's arrangements in the Union Office in Vancouver when they had gone to buy their tickets. Numbers stuck in her head: she had liked arithmetic at school but Pastor Russell taught that too much learning was a bad thing, and even though Father wasn't a real International Bible Student he had made up his mind to believe it too. Anyway, after Joy died she had wanted to stay home. It was easier there to keep up the pretence that she was still entirely alive herself, instead of her true state of existence, which was that bits of her fell away every day, as if she were rotting away as casually as an autumn leaf under a big pile of leaves, a leaf no one would miss.

At the end of the promenade, she turned to starboard where a flight of metal steps led down to the small cabin-class promenade, which she crossed in bounds, then up another short flight and around the corner, throwing herself against the doors into the corridor.

On the other side of the door to number eighty-one sat Mother, who had paused a moment with the younger children once she'd got them into bed. Now they had fallen asleep and so had she, her head back and mouth agape, her scuffed shoes undone and kicked aside. It seemed to Dora that it took her an age to get ready. First she wouldn't listen and kept shushing her agitated whispering, then she had to put on her shoes and carefully lock the children in behind her, Theo and Riha top-and-tailing, the other two in their own single berths.

By the time they arrived in the bow of the ship, Father was gone and the crowd had vanished. Mother's breath rasped loudly in her chest from her rush along corridors and companionways, through parts of the ship she had never ventured to before. As she searched the derricks for her husband, she tipped her face back further and squinted against the shadows cast by the lattice work.

She doesn't realise what's happened, Dora thought. She can't see that he has fallen into the sea and been left behind in the foaming wake, that Father is drowned. Would she weep at the news, she wondered, and went to take her mother's hand when a loud crack and flap in the air above their heads startled her and drew her focus upwards again. A sweeping, triangular shape like a coat thrown from a roof was falling towards them. A flashing, intelligent eye caught in the spreading light of the Music Saloon and Dora felt herself lift towards it, that eye, her whole self lifting towards the outspread dark wings, the gored panels of the swelling coat. It was Joy, the weight of Father's doctrines in her pockets hurling her to the street below. And Father himself was somewhere above her, looking down, not as Dora had always imagined, at the place of her sister's arrival. It was so obvious, she thought now: of course, he had been there with her when she had lost hold. Joy had always had to climb in company, to be encouraged at the hard parts.

She must have cried out because her mother was hushing her, hooking an arm around her shoulders.

'It's all right – look, it's only an albatross.'

The huge bird, disturbed earlier from its night perch by William's ranting, had been unable to find another. It flung now out into the wheeling sky, disoriented, to hang in the dark and wait for the dawn.

Dora gazed up at the neck of the derrick, saw it illuminated in the lights of the wheel-house and thought how pretty it looked, the weave of the steel with the endless stars behind. It was as if she had been asleep under a stifling heavy blanket that had now been lifted away from her face. She could breathe, her life shone with a sudden simplicity. She remembered the time she and Joy and Father had climbed the tree in Stanley Park, and how Joy had remained on the lowest bough of the tree, the one Father had lifted them to from the ground, before he had swung himself up. That time Dora had climbed as high as Father and they had sat up in the tree for hours, even after Mother had taken the other children home. Father sang sea shanties and hymns and Dora had laughed and laughed with the thrill of it all, of being with Father, high above all the world. Joy had waited quietly for her father to lift her down again.

Dora knew now what he had done and she would hate him for ever.

A woman was talking to Mother, leaning out of the window of the first-class Dining Saloon.

'They took him to the doctor,' she said, pointing towards the stern with a clanking, braceleted wrist. 'On this deck, near second class.'

'But we came that way. We would have passed them –' Mother said, gripping Dora's hand harder now.

'Oh no. You see, they brought him through here, right through the saloon. We all saw him.'

She was smirking. Dora looked past her into the Dining Saloon. It was crowded, she saw now. The women were dressed for the evening in low-necked gowns; the men all wore the stiff collars Father had given up wearing. Another curious face appeared at the window beside their informant and stared at them. A man.

'Oh,' said Mother. 'We'll go back the way we came.' She picked up her skirts to go but the woman hadn't finished.

'He was raving,' she called. 'A complete lunatic.'

At their backs they heard her companion snigger and snap the window shut.

High in his room in the Vine, above Grafton Gully, William was not looking out at the early afternoon at all. He lay on his narrow bed, his book open on his chest, his eyes closed. He was not asleep, though he appeared so. Instead, his mind was running over that night on the *Makura*, the same scene that his daughter's mind returned to. Whenever his mind was left idle, away from its calculations and stores or plans, it played the same pictures over and over, like a demonic, smoking, magic lantern. The sailors had tied him to the wooden stool and one of them stood behind him, restraining his arms. Pot-bellied, his dinner wine on his breath and reaching William's sensitive nostrils, the doctor had prevailed upon one of the sailors to roll up a sleeve. William's mouth was dry with fear and panic, from talking without pause since he'd first ascended the derricks. He remembered now, on his bed in the Vine, how he'd persisted with the Word, but none of the men had listened.

When the doctor had taken up a black case lined with scarlet plush and taken from it a needle and glass syringe, William had felt a pressing need to explain himself, to enter the temporal cause-and-effect world of the surgeon.

'I am a man of leisure, Doctor, but I have not abused this privilege. Instead I have worked as hard as it is humanly possible to do. I have made it my business to struggle against my natural antipathy for the written word. I have worshipped in all the great temples of the world; I have read the texts.'

'Are you still preaching at me, my man? Or may we talk?' The doctor had followed William and the crew members from the Dining Saloon, his napkin still at his neck. It was discarded now and lay in starched, gravy-stained peaks on his desk.

The needle drew fluid from a vial. William saw it glitter transparently in the glass shaft of the syringe and his dry tongue peeled away from the roof of his mouth with an audible click.

'I do not believe in doctors, sir. Not one iota. This I take from the teachings of John Alexander Dowie, who I was with in Zion. Christ is the Healer.'

'You were a Dowie-ite?' The doctor's curiosity was aroused.

'Until the end.'

'There was a scandal, I remember. In the papers. Polygamy and treachery.' His tone was as dry as William's mouth.

'Polygamy is our instinct, sir. It is given by God to us and heeded by many faiths.'

'Not so many.' The doctor held the needle to the light, a bulb reflected many times in the glossy white wall of his shipboard clinic. He depressed the plunger an inch or so. Thick and shining, the cruel needle discharged a little of its load.

'But St Paul offers us refuge from it, should you so choose. "It is good for a man not to touch a woman."'

'Where is your wife, Mr McQuiggan?'

William did not recall having given the doctor his name. Perhaps the doctor had heard him preach last Sunday on the cabin-class promenade, though the crowd he drew was small enough for him to remember every face. Besides, why would the ship's doctor, who hobnobbed with first class, have cause to be in the stern at all? The preaching that day had ended when some wit had hauled up a bucket of water on a long rope and emptied it over him. William had hit the fellow – he couldn't help himself – and the man had picked himself up from the deck and run off. There had been no brawl, no gathering crowd, no reason for the doctor –

'Your wife? Where is she?'

'Myra? She will be asleep.'

'Are you sleeping yourself of late? How do you pass your nights?' asked the doctor.

'I am full of plans for my great design. I am dispensing with contradiction in the scriptures. Dissent among the prophets only leads to misery and bewilderment in ordinary mankind. My course through the gospel will be simple and true.'

On the other side of the locked door a hand beat rapidly. The handle rattled, a woman called softly, and the doctor bent with the needle, nodding at the sailor at William's back to take a firmer hold. The other went to the door and freed the snib and Myra came into the room with one of the twins. Dora of course, it could not have been Joy, he would never make that mistake because he was not insane. He only envied Joy her escape, the bliss that was hers in Heaven. She would surely be one the Lord would keep close to Him; she would be part of His inner circle. When his own time came he would find her in the City of God and she would draw him close to the Holy Flesh and Blood.

He struggled against the sailor, bit the hand at his shoulder. There was a mess of voices: the child crying out, her hands against her mouth; Myra's voice forming around his name; the bitten sailor cursing; the doctor exhorting the crewmen to hold him steady while he struggled against them, thrashing his bound torso against his restraints, setting the chair rocking. Cold steel pierced his flesh, a thick current ran up his veins, and in the painful buzz that all of a sudden besieged his ears he heard only one word, a long word beginning with B, like a Frenchwoman's name, almost a beautiful word. Barbiturate. Then the vibration at his ears invaded his eyes, first as a violent, swiftly deepening red, then in a thrumming, billowing black. It was what hell might be away from its fires: an absence of pain, an absence of consciousness, a dark existence that was not life, nor death, nor the afterlife.

There were footsteps now, dogged and steady, on the stairs beyond his open door. They were at the landing, now in his room itself. Myra, he thought, with a tray. He could hear his books being shifted, papers rustling across his leather-topped desk; he could smell meat and roasted vegetables. There was the squeak of the casement and a cool breeze edged in the window, over his ruffled pages and across the room. He wouldn't open his eyes, not until she touched him.

'It's very hot in here,' said his wife.

There. Her hand on his knee. He looked and saw how one sliver of hair had slipped from her bun, the black streaked with grey. He saw how, with her face falling forward, the skin around her eyes was crinkled, her forehead lined. She met his hard, evaluating eye and straightened.

'Your dinner,' she said, putting a hand into the small of her back and rubbing the flesh below the fabric of her skirt. William sat up. Why would she remind him of her physical self, of her body's failings? "The wife hath not the power of her own body."'

She touched him lightly under the chin and lifted his face. 'Are you all right, William?'

He could not bear it, her sympathy, her tenderness. She had a surfeit of it because she encouraged it so much in other people. In Vancouver there had been Mrs de Feranti and a miserable sodomite called Quincy who had smothered her in it. They had even come uninvited to Joy's funeral. Then here, on the family's arrival off the boat, his sisters had poured it on her, and they were bewilderingly angry with him. Even the lawyer was all empathy with Myra and wanted to speak to her alone. William wouldn't allow it. It was too late anyway: he'd already cashed in the brewery investments. Old Farquhar's money was tainted beyond use and he'd purified it by sending it to representatives of the Family of Faiths: to Pastor Russell, to the Catholic Christian Apostolic Church in Zion, to Brother Ridge in Salt Lake. Enough had remained to procure the Vine, to have the earth dug away on its southern side and a cellar built, and invest in stores. God would provide the rest, he knew, for the land and the church.

She was stroking his forehead now with a coarse-skinned thumb.

'Why don't you come downstairs for a little? We could sit on the veranda together, in the cool.'

He shook his head. 'I have work to do.'

'On a Sunday?' He loathed the tone of her voice: humouring, gentle. His nurse.

He got up, went across to the window and looked out.

'The children have gone to the gully,' she was saying now.

'What for? What do you want me to do? You've got the maid and Dora to help you.' His words built in speed and pitch. Myra waited a moment, pacing him out. His breathing steadied.

'Have your meal –' she began, neutrally, but William was speaking over the top of her.

'Where is Gertie, by the way?'

'It's her afternoon off.'

'Did she go to church this morning?'

'She doesn't, William. You know that.'

'Make sure she is at Family Altar tonight, then,' said William, his voice suddenly distant, as if he were thinking about something else. She wished he would turn around so she could gauge his mood. Whatever had she been thinking of, she wondered, why had she come up to his room? It was only that she had thought some fresh air would be good for him. Often on a Sunday night he slept badly. She would hear him in his room, which was directly above hers, crashing around until all hours, praying and singing, taking the stairs before dawn down to the kitchen for bread or cake. She wanted him to sleep tonight, so that she could.

'Are you sure she hasn't gone down to the cellar?'

'How could she? She doesn't have a key. Nobody does, except you.'

'Sometimes I am convinced there is an intruder, a thief. It is a long way in the night.'

'It's perfectly safe.'

He was quiet for a moment again. A hum of cicadas lifted from the trees lower in the gully. Downstairs the Vine's open front door blew closed in the bright westerly. A scraggy, long white cloud flew over the roof to rent the blue afternoon.

'Ah,' said William suddenly, lifting a hand as if he had just solved a problem. 'That is what we will do, then. We will go down and complete the inventory.'

He swung round, took her arm and hauled her downstairs, their rapid footsteps echoing in the empty wooden house. Out of the kitchen door he led her, across the crest of the steep garden, around the southern side of the house to where a fern, heavy and green from the humid summer, leaned over a short flight of cement steps leading down to a low door, which William unlocked with a heavy key.

A cloth-bound notebook, candle and matches sat on a nogging-piece in the unlined brick wall. William struck a flame and kicked the door shut after them.

'You haven't been down here for a while, eh, Myra?'

Myra stood rubbing her arm at the bite of his grip. His candle made a half circle, its single light flaring on the bright labels of hundreds of tin cans, their shining stacked rims leaping and receding. There was corned beef, sardines, tomatoes, peaches, pears and peas. There was corn, cocoa, carrots, apricots and asparagus. Some of the labels she did not recognise at all. When she had first uncovered his store, soon after Myrtle's birth, there had not been nearly so many, nor had the variety been so great. Fat brown sacks of flour and rice bulged in a huddle just as they had then, though some had since been nibbled by mice and spilled their contents on the carpet of newspapers on the dry mud floor. The mound of potatoes in one corner had grown to reach the ceiling and some of them sprouted white tendrils, little falling veils of roots. Never to ripen in the dark, a hand of green bananas dangled above William's head. The cellar smelt of damp and rot. Here and there William had spread sheets of newspaper, where the rain got in.

If I were not so tired I would be angry, thought Myra. How often had she kept Theo from the bread because of the lodgers' breakfasts, or luncheons, or suppers? She thought of how careful she had been with her portions: the endless repetitive grind of her economy in the kitchen. Her husband stood among the piles of food, grinning at her.

'Come Armageddon we will be safe and well, my dear. I will build my church with the angels. What do you say?' William asked, waving the arm with the candle expansively. The flame flickered and jumped, shedding wax. Carefully, he set it down in a saucer that he had attached to a strut below a crucifix. The cross was simple and plain: two unpolished pieces of wood with a central, hurried nail holding them fast. William opened the cloth-bound notebook and took a pencil from his breast pocket.

'Now, where shall we start?' he asked, businesslike.

Myra sighed. 'I don't know how far you've got. Some of the food is spoiling, you know.'

'Then I will replace it. You tell me what is ruined and I'll make a list.'

Immediately Myra regretted her remark. William tore a page from his notebook and looked at her expectantly.

'May I open the door a little?' she asked him. 'It's stuffy in here.'

The only egress for light and air was a tiny barred vent, which now that she looked for it was half hidden by the stacked tins. William nodded, distracted by his list. He inscribed the date: 11 March 1915.

You must keep him calm, the ship's doctor had told her. Try to keep him from any undue excitement. He was not, in the doctor's opinion, harmful to any other but himself: it was a nervous disease, brought on by grief perhaps. Had there been a bereavement?

'My sister,' Dora had said. 'He killed her.'

In her shame, Myra had found herself shaking her head at him, and the doctor had looked from the father to the daughter as if he thought them tarred with the same brush, before he hurried away to resume his interrupted dinner.

The open door let in a wedge of gusty afternoon sunlight. Myra looked longingly up the steps to where a fern shimmied in the breeze.

William had followed her, holding the book out so that she could see. 'I haven't updated the inventory since before Christmas.'

Neatly and closely written, his figures progressed in orderly columns down the page. In the left-hand margin he had listed the items themselves: a gross of potatoes and the name of the merchant he had got it from; tins of biscuits and cabin bread and fruit and vegetables, their brand names and places of purchase. The names of the grocers repeated themselves in unvarying order: William went all over the city to different establishments, rotating his custom, never giving it to the same merchant twice in a row.

'3.9.14. Two pounds of Bermuda arrowroot. Mr Fischer, Parnell,' read Myra. '10.9.14. Two pecks cider vinegar. Mrs O'Brien, Ponsonby.' At the bottom of the opposing page he had written: 'I estimate that in tinned produce alone we have two dozen bushels.'

More astonishing were the sums of money at the base of the far right column. On each page William had tallied up his expenditure since stores began. The figures were like the street numbers in Zion: Myra could not comprehend them. She stared at the final sum on the last page. What was it? she wondered. The sterling symbol, then a one, a nought and twenty-five, then seventeen shillings and sixpence.

'It's hundred and hundreds of pounds,' she said to him. She wanted suddenly to dash the book from his hands. William's eyes, previously shining with pride, now narrowed at her displeasure.

'It is our future,' he said.

'It's three years away, if it happens. It didn't come to pass in 1914.'

He turned his face away as if she had slapped him.

'At least let me take some of it upstairs now,' she hurried on. 'The things that will perish. Some flour and potatoes and rice.'

In answer he turned his back on her. Ducking his head for the low beam he made his way behind the cans, under the sharply sloping roof to a pile of empty wooden crates stacked against the wall. He pulled one free with a dull, scraping thud and brought it back to her.

'For the potatoes,' he said. 'Pick some out.'

She stared at him. 'Are you sure?'

He nodded and she lifted her hands to take the crate from him but he held fast to it. He was smiling so warmly now she could not keep up with him, with his rapid changes of mood: see now, she thought, though his mouth is smiling his eyes are filling with tears. He bent, laid the box on the floor and took hold of her face. It was his first tender gesture for months and she remembered how the same caress had preceded his lovemaking on board the *Makura*, two nights after the doctor had sedated him. He had come to her narrow berth defeated, wordless, as he had been for the two days since the drug wore off. Dora was sent from her bed in their cabin to sleep with the children next door. William had taken Myra's face in his hands, stared at her for a moment before taking his hurried, despairing pleasure. Myrtle had come from that, and from Myra's faint, reluctant arousal, a raft of confusion that led only to the knowledge that she had comforted him beyond measure. Afterwards he had lain beside her into the night, awake, breathing softly, and now and then increasing the pressure of his gentle, encircling arms.

He bent to her now, pressed his wet cheek against her dry one. She could feel his stubble against her skin.

457

Dora's voice rang suddenly in her ear – 'Mad as a maggot' – and for a moment Myra thought she had come down the steps into the cellar, but she had not, she had just imagined it. Instead of replying, she lifted her arms to his waist and held him close. She could sense his mind racing, as if he ran about in an arid landscape, turning over stones and rocks, wanting his world mapped, clear and smooth.

'It's all right, William,' she told him. 'You mustn't worry so much.'

'I am alone.' He was sobbing now. 'There is no one who has any faith in me.'

Myra closed her eyes, listened to his gulping breath and searched for something to say. Dora's voice, so loudly scathing before, had vanished. The old man came into her mind – Elisha – what would he do if he were still alive? Most likely he would have acted on the ship's doctor's advice and taken William to a physician who specialised in mania and nervous disorders. Unhinged minds were not his province, the ship's doctor had said: take him to someone who knows before he comes to the notice of the police. Myra hadn't told him it would be impossible, that her husband would never willingly see a doctor.

'It's not that . . .' she began hesitantly. William waited for her to go on, quieter now. 'You should not concern yourself with whether or not people believe in you. It's God you should lead them to.'

'You will come with me to Pukekaroro? When I'm ready to build the church?'

It's hopeless, thought Myra. Dry-lipped she kissed him on his cheek and stepped away to pick up the box. Together they filled it with potatoes and William carried it for her, upstairs to the kitchen, leaving the cellar door ajar.

The children were running squealing up the slope towards her, and Dora, squinting against the sun, could see the man in the black coat flitting between the arches under the bridge.

458

She had made a daisy-chain for Myrtle and fitted it around her neck. The baby had broken it and was chewing on one of the soft green and white links. She crowed delightedly now, green dribble on her chin, as her brother and sisters flung themselves on the grass behind Dora.

'He's there! He's there!' shrieked Audrey.

'He beckoned at Riha,' said Theo.

'He did not. It was you.' Riha gave him a shove and Theo rolled over onto his back, kicking his legs in the air.

'He beckoned at Riha. Riha! Riha!' he chanted. 'Riha's going to die!'

Squalling like a cat, Riha flung herself on top of him. 'It was you!' she shouted. 'I saw him first and he wants you!'

The man came out from under the bridge and made his way towards a sunny patch not five yards away. He sat down, his back against an oak, and pulled his greasy hat over his eyes, seemingly oblivious to Theo and Riha's racket.

'Hush up,' said Dora. 'It's only the game. I made it up. I never saw him beckon anyone. How can a poor old crazy man kill you just by crooking his finger?' She watched the tramp carefully to see if he heard her. The hat covered his face still.

'How do you know he's crazy?' asked Theo.

'Why else would he live under a bridge?' responded Dora. 'He must be mad as a maggot.' She had a fancy suddenly that she could get up, purposefully, and walk over to where the man rested, his shabby coat wrapped around his skinny legs, and knock his hat off. The face she would reveal would be different to the one he'd had before, when he'd tugged down his brim. It would be her father, drowsy and flushed, the way he looked on these hot summer Sundays when Mother sent her up to his room with meals or cups of tea to rouse him from sleep over his papers.

It would be a brilliant solution to all of their problems, Dora thought, if their father came to live in the cemetery with the man in the black coat. It would solve the problem of how

Mother never had any money from the allowance, though he had plenty judging from his new black suit, which was necessary he said, if people were to believe in him. What people? Dora had wondered to her mother. None ever came to the Vine, save the lodgers and the grocers who delivered goods to the house, those mysterious parcels he spirited away down to the cellar. When she'd asked Mother about that, the money he spent, she'd said something about turning a blind eye, and how we should look after him as best we could.

The afternoon had drawn on, the shadows of the trees and stones stretched and narrowed. The man in the black coat remained immobile against his oak.

'Let's go home,' said Dora, though she wished she could go somewhere else. Perhaps she would be a tourist, like her father, and travel the world. There would be no religion though, not for her. No trying out churches as if they were different kinds of meat from the same beast. And no marrying, either. If only she were a boy. Then she would enlist, put her age up a year and go to France to fight the war.

The children made their way back to the gate on the upper corner of the steep lane. Theo had produced an orange from his baggy short trousers and was sharing it around. He wouldn't be a selfish man like their father, thought Dora. He'd turn out different because of Mother. He'd learnt the path of least resistance from her.

As they came across the back porch of the boarding house, they heard Father's voice in the kitchen.

'That's all you can have.'

He wasn't shouting, Dora thought. He was whining, like Audrey.

'I've locked up now.'

Quick on their muddy feet, the younger children ran to him at the table: he was still mysterious to them, passing into their days so rarely, and then out again. Some of the lodgers talked to them more. They clustered around him and stared. Father looked as though he'd been crying.

Dora, with Edna and Riha flanking her, hung back and watched him. A great surge of violence ran through her: she would shake him if she could – shake him until his teeth fell out. He was either like this – little boy lost, with his hair rumpled, mouth turned down and collar untidy – or striding the floor blue with fury.

From an assortment of stained and tattered brown paper bags Mother and the maid, who was supposed to have Sunday afternoons off, were filling crocks and jars: arrow-root, soda and salt. There were two pounds of sultanas that had been found to be full of ants. Mother looked up and saw Dora.

'Take these into the scullery and wash them in a sieve,' she said.

'Please,' Dora hissed at her under her breath, picking the broken bag up and taking it through. She emptied them into the colander and ran the tap.

'What's that for?' Theo asked, putting out his hand to touch the heavy brass key in William's hand.

He'd had no answer. Father hadn't even looked at him. The only person he ever looked at was Dora. Theo was glad he never looked at him that way – glinty eyes narrowed to slits below their fleshy lids, as if Dora were something disgusting on the sole of his boot.

Dora brushed off any tiny black bodies that still stuck and divided the sultanas evenly among the children. They were allowed to eat them then, giggling in a row on the back steps, hooking their muddy toes around the warm wood. Their father had proved uninteresting, daydreaming, sad, deaf to their prattle.

She would go upstairs, Dora decided, lie on her bed and read her library book. It was by a man called Joseph Conrad and it was called *The Mirror of the Sea*. It wasn't a novel. What was the point of reading something someone had made up? There was a danger you could be fooled into believing it, into thinking it was true, like her father did. Not only did he spend hours crouched over the words of born liars, men who were the outcasts of their time, but he made up lies of his own. It seemed to Dora that the more you took away from the real world, the more it had to struggle to exist.

'The anchor ready for its work is already overboard, and is not thrown over, but simply allowed to fall . . .' She remembered that bit: it had stuck in her head because it made her think of Joy, though the book was about sailing and ships. She struggled with the long sentences and sometimes felt riled that the only girls were the ships themselves, but she persisted. It was hard and true and beautiful. She pictured the book now, small and blue on the cluttered bedside table she shared with Edna, as she made her way along the back passage beyond the open kitchen door.

'Where are you going?'

Her father. He was scraping his chair back, standing, coming towards her. She stopped but didn't enter the room.

'Upstairs.'

'What for? To lie around while your mother works?' William still held the key. He saw her eyes travel to it and dropped it immediately in his pocket.

'That's what you're good at, isn't it?' She didn't remove her gaze from his pocket and spoke so quietly he couldn't hear her. He only saw her lips move.

'You get in here!' he exploded.

Perhaps he'd learned to lip-read. The maid exchanged a nervous glance with Myra, and Dora glared at her. She was a tall woman, taller than Dora who already towered over Mother. If Dora could stand up to William then Gertie could too – refuse some of his embarrassing gifts, such as the blouse the servant wore now, pale green, too small by half. The lawn pulled across her chest, the mother of pearl buttons strained. It would better fit Mother than her. She was a great lumbering mouse, with her timid watery blue eyes and ugly carrot hair.

'Dora!' her father bellowed. Blood had rushed into his previously pallid face and made it blotchy. If they were alone he would strike her, knock her to the floor. She half-expected him to do it now and cowered away from him as he grabbed a handful of her skirt at the hip and thrust her towards the laden table. She went to stand beside her mother, who pointed wordlessly at the filled jars, which were ready to be conveyed back to their shelves in the pantry.

William watched his daughter go back and forth for a moment or two until he was satisfied she was obedient to him, then he turned on his heel and went to his room upstairs.

CHAPTER 27

On the evening of the day that Myra sent Dora to the gully with the children, Blanche and Ellen came to visit. They lived together in the little house in Summer Street on the money left to them by Grandmother, who had died years ago in Scotland, and of whom the children had no recollection. They often came in on a Sunday evening when the maid wasn't there and sat with Myra in the kitchen, drinking more tea than was good for them. Sometimes Dora joined them when she wasn't busy looking after the children, or cleaning up after one of the lodgers, but she couldn't stand the way the three women talked in hushed tones about William, as if he were someone important. Sometimes Mother wept and Auntie Ellen would pat her hand; sometimes the aunties would apologise for sending the letter to Zion, but nobody elaborated on the letter or its contents – what the aunties had actually written. It was a letter to William and it had had far-reaching consequences. What they were exactly, Dora couldn't fathom.

'How's the maid? Are you happy with her?' asked Auntie Ellen, cutting the sponge cake she'd brought. She had also brought Dora a book, which looked suspiciously like something made up. For a few months after the family came back to Auckland, Auntie Ellen had given Dora lessons, in

defiance of her brother. It had so upset William that Myra
had begged her to stop. Now she brought her niece books:
the Victorian novelists, and sometimes the latest Farnol or
Guy Thorne. *Little Women* this latest was called, which Dora
thought was pretty wet. She sat at the table leafing through it.
She would read one page, she decided, and if it had people
arguing, or thinking about one another in a certain cosy, sick-
ening way, then it would be added to the unread pile under
her bed.

'Gertie, do you mean?' Myra asked.

'Well, of course I mean Gertie,' snorted Ellen. 'Who else?
There isn't another maid.'

'Dora –' Mother had placed a cup of tea in front of her.
Dora picked it up, blew on it, watched Blanche looking at
Ellen as if she were worried about what the older aunt would
say next.

'She's a good plain maid,' said Ellen in a soothing voice.

'Whatever do you mean?' Myra almost laughed. 'A good
plain cook – but a good plain maid?'

'She means nothing by it,' Blanche said quickly, opening
a paper bag of rock cakes. Dora took one and nibbled on it.
Auntie Blanche was a rotten cook. She would have bought
these cakes and judging by their dry crumbs, that was several
days ago.

'Father has taken a shine to her,' said Dora through her
rock cake.

'A shine? Whenever are you children going to stop speaking as if you're Yankees?' asked Ellen, bending to Myrtle who
was pulling at her skirts. She lifted her to her knee.

'He buys her little presents,' Dora continued. 'Never buys
us anything at all.'

Mother stared at her, and Dora thought perhaps she
hadn't noticed Gertie's blouse or the new black Bible she
brought to the tedium of Family Altar.

'Oh dear,' said Blanche, and Ellen nodded at her as if she
were giving her permission to go on. 'She'll have to finish,

then.' Blanche was patting Myra's hand. 'We'll have to find someone else.'

'No, no.' Myra drew her hand away. 'It's perfectly all right.'

'But –' began Ellen.

'He does give her little gifts, but it's perfectly innocent,' Myra assured her sisters-in-law.

'I don't think . . .' Ellen turned to Dora. 'Take your book upstairs, dear.'

Dora wriggled more firmly into her chair. Her mother glanced at her and away again.

'You know – St Paul and all that,' said Myra. 'It's almost as if . . .' She was looking at her daughter again as if she were carefully choosing words that would obscure the truth. 'As if he has become a kind of monk.'

'More a grocer than a monk,' Dora suggested, helpfully, sipping her tea.

'A grocer?' repeated Blanche, bewildered.

Ellen, flustered, waved her hands. 'That's quite enough! Why don't you switch on the light? We are almost in the dark,' she continued, almost in one breath.

It was very quiet, Dora thought, and wondered where the children were. They had vanished after Family Altar. Mother was standing in her place and reaching for the string hanging from the ceiling. The light flickered on, the whole apparatus squeaking and clunking, the enamelled conical shade heavier on one side than the other with its weight of plugs and wires. Its electrical connections snaked and wove away across the ceiling. One black wire was pinned down the matchlined walls to feed a bulb that Dora had rigged over the kitchen sink; another hung in a loop to just outside the kitchen door where the suction-sweeper stood idle in the hall, the excess of its tether wound around the handle. Gertie had left it there since yesterday. The pool of light swung away from it, relegating it to the shadows once more. On Ellen's knee the baby gurgled and clapped as the light passed over the table to the hearth, where the closed cinder-sifter cast the shadow of a squat, fat child, and back again to wobble above them.

'Where are the children?' Ellen asked suddenly. Dora sighed. Now she would be sent away to search for them. She wished the conversation would return to the subject of Father's shopping. She'd tried to get them started on it by mentioning the word 'grocer' but Auntie Ellen had side-tracked them. How much did the aunties really know, she wondered, of what actually went on at the Vine? Sundays were quiet days for Father and that was the only day they visited. Sometimes, if Mother had the time, she took some of the children to visit them in Ponsonby on a Wednesday after-noon, but William never went. The aunts couldn't possibly know how different he was on different days of the week, depending on the strict routine he had mapped out for himself. Monday to Wednesday he stayed in his room read-ing and making notes; Thursday and Friday he concentrated on the building of his church, or rather the raising of funds for it. This latter was undertaken in the form of letter-writing: Theo was always being dispatched to the post office with another letter for Pastor Russell in Philadelphia, or to Overseer Voliva in Zion City, or someone called Brother Ridge in Salt Lake City, Utah. As far as Dora knew, none of them had ever replied.

On Saturdays he emerged from his room and was active enough to make up for the rest of his week hunched over his desk. On this day, the day he devoted to his stores, it was dangerous to be around him. Even if she didn't do anything wrong, he was in the mood for remembering past misde-meanours and punishing her for them all over again. Recently he'd recalled the lice she'd caught from his clothes and spread to the other children, a crime five years old. Dora pictured now the 'Saturday William': his rapid-fire speech, his almost comical small-stepped and frenzied gait as he raced up and down from the cellar. It was as if a part of him were making a failed attempt to resist his own haste. Mother said they had to pretend they knew nothing about the cellar, Edna and Dora and everybody except Myrtle, who wouldn't understand anyway. Probably no one had told the aunts. They hadn't even known about him climbing the *Makura*'s derricks until she had told them herself.

'Dora!' Mother was flapping her hand in her face. 'Go and find the children. Are you deaf?'

With a tragic air, Dora pushed herself up from the table and went out onto the darkening porch. Beyond the cemetery trees, Grafton Bridge arched white over the gully, the deep sky above it purple-black and patched with streaming, effulgent blue in the cloud gaps. Here at the back of the house, the steep garden was quiet, and as she came around the corner to the south-facing wall she could hear nothing from the narrow veranda at the front. Surely they wouldn't have gone to the graveyard. Even she herself, fearless as she was, wouldn't be so brave as to go down St Martin's Lane at this time of night. It was late – it must be after eight o'clock, she realised.

'The–o!' she called softly, then louder. 'Ri–ha!'

There was no answer. The ground was still lumpy here from where the earth was moved to dig out the cellar. Grass had grown over it, but you had to watch your step if you were off the path. She picked her way carefully over to where the steep narrow steps led down to the cellar door.

Ah – there now – there was a light flickering, candlelight perhaps, tiny dancing squares in the air vent set in the cellar wall. At the foot of the steps the underground door stood open and there was the sound of whispering, hoarse and urgent, as if the whisperer only just managed to stop himself from breaking into full voice. Dora went down the steps until she drew level with the grid and held her eye close.

Most of the cellar was hidden to her by the close proximity of a stack of tins and jars, but she doubted that it obscured anything more startling than what was easily visible. Sullen and perplexed, close together on a wooden box with a great mound of potatoes at their back, sat Riha and Theo. On either side of the maid stood Edna and Audrey, holding hastily gathered bunches of flowers, marigolds and arum lilies and some short-stalked geraniums, which seemed oddly familiar, but Dora wasted no time thinking about that, being more taken with Gertie. Her veil – it was a net curtain from one of the lodger's rooms – hung unevenly from her head to one side of her body. Another curtain, which Dora recognised as coming from the upstairs parlour, hung from the beam overhead. A huge hole had been slashed in it, big enough for a grown-up to pass through. All around the room, on noggings and on a low bench, burned as many candles as Dora had ever seen gathered together in one place. Her father must have lit half his candle store.

William stood before the little group with his back to Dora, but she could see that he was touching Gertie, dipping his fingers each time into the cup of water he held in his other hand.

'I wash you that you may be clean from the blood and sins of your generation,' he was whispering, his fingers on her brow, 'that your brain may work clearly,' then at her ears, 'that they may hear the word of the Lord,' then at her mouth, lips and breast, 'that you may be fruitful in propagating of a goodly seed.' He finished with a light brush at the front of her skirts and then stepped towards the hanging curtain. As he moved away, he revealed Gertie's apron, which Dora saw now was roughly in the shape of a fig leaf, clumsily cut from the green baize Mother hung in the kitchen door on draughty winter days. It was attached to Gertie's dress by means of safety pins and William's wet fingers had left a dark smudge on its thick nap. Gertie's eyes bulged, even more than they did ordinarily. Her cheeks were flushed, flaring red in the frame of her orange hair and she pressed her lips together, softened them, tensed them again, over and over, while her tongue worked inside her mouth, bulging against the walls of her cheeks. It was fear, thought Dora at first – fear and something else, something she struggled to define.

The protuberant eyes were full of reverence. Gertie believed in her father: he had found a follower. Awe settled over the maid's face like a death mask.

He was taking Gertie's arm now, leading her towards the hole in the curtain. Dora turned and ran up the stairs without a sound. It was a trick she had learned since they had come to the Vine: she could pass around the echoing house, spy on the lodgers without them suspecting, she could watch her father from his landing, she could leap out at her playing sisters and scare them half to death. All you had to do was pretend your body's weight rested just above your knees, that your shins and calves and rapid feet flew along unburdened, that the air did not hinder your upper half but bore it along. There was no sound, not even at her progress along the gravel path.

'You'd better come and see,' she said to her mother and aunts in the kitchen. Myra was rinsing the cups at the wooden sink, her back to the room. The aunties were putting on their coats.

'Did you find the children?' asked Blanche.

'Father is baptising Gertie in the cellar,' announced Dora, and Mother gasped with such ferocity that she startled Ellen, who held up a hand and demanded of her niece, 'I beg your pardon?'

'I think that's what he's doing. Or maybe he's marrying her,' she called after her mother, who had already left the room, wiping her hands on a cloth, her feet echoing on the hollow boards of the porch.

William must have heard them coming, thought Myra. He had vanished from the low room, or perhaps he was hiding in it, leaving poor silly Gertie draped in a raggy curtain she had given the younger girls to play with. At first sight of his mother, Theo sprang up from his box and hooked an arm around her. Behind him Riha pointed at the red curtain, one that William must have taken down from the parlour window while she sat in the kitchen with his sisters. It was almost torn in half.

'Oh, my goodness,' said Blanche.

Dora, her face white and jaw set, took Riha's direction and pulled the curtain open. On the other side stood William, in his best suit, his hands clasped like an actor.

'You're just in time,' he said quietly. 'We are about to take our Pledge.'

'Don't be ridiculous, William,' snapped Ellen. 'You –' She jabbed a finger at Gertie, who blushed and hung her head. 'Get upstairs and collect your things. Dora – take the children up to the kitchen.'

'No!' shouted Audrey, from the other side of motionless Gertie. She came forward to glare at her aunt. 'This is a wedding. Theo even went down to the gully and got flowers, the ones I put on Dora's grave.' She held up her red geraniums. 'Father is taking Gertie to be his Spiritual Wife.'

For a moment Ellen was speechless, and the children, shifting their gaze from her to their mother, saw that she was shaking her head and sighing and . . . surely not. She was. She was smiling. More than smiling: a shrill, hysterical giggle broke from her lips.

'Myra!' said Ellen sharply. She put her hand on her sister-in-law's shoulder. Myra shook her off.

'That's it, then,' Myra said to nobody in particular. 'He's blind to me.'

'What do you mean?' Ellen whispered at her. 'Pull yourself together.'

The maid was staring at her mistress, tears gathering in her eyes.

'Don't cry now, Gertie,' Myra told her. 'It will be all right. You won't lose him.' She pushed the children ahead of her, one arm around Edna, who yawned hugely in the silence.

William stepped out of his curtain altogether and would have gone after them, Myra and Gertie and Dora and all the children, trailing out the low door and up the crumbling steps, but Ellen took hold firmly of the cloth at the side of his jacket, laid her other hand flat against his chest.

'The food, Ellen,' Blanche was saying. 'Look at it all.'

'It won't be enough.' William was suddenly agitated. 'Don't think you can share it. There won't be enough for all of us.'

'We don't want it, dear,' said Blanche, soothingly. 'Don't worry about that now.'

'Is there a cellar key?' asked Ellen. He dug in his pocket and handed it to her. His sister's eyes blazed at him, narrow, grey and furious, feminine versions of the old man's. He would not think of disobeying her.

'Sit down,' she said to him then, pushing him down onto the box that had lately been pew to Theo and Riha. 'We won't be long.' They left then, quickly, locking the door after them.

He didn't notice they had made him a prisoner. Knees apart and his big hands linked to hang between them, he sat on his box with his head bowed not in prayer, but in meditation on what he had achieved so far: his church plans, his stores, his biddable Spiritual wife. Myra he would put apart from him just as surely as Brother Everett had Sister Eliza. He remembered that long-ago day at the Central Hotel and Eliza's arch tones before his audience with the American. She had not truly believed in her husband, and neither did Myra in himself. Although she loved him, her love was tinged with pity, and for that he must relinquish her. He did not require a nurse but a help-meet, a woman who put all her trust in him, who regarded him with respect, who would assist him to realise his dreams.

Footsteps, those of his sisters, crossed the porch above his head. The kitchen door slammed shut.

In a moment, thought William, I will go upstairs and explain it all to them. I will have to be very patient, especially

472

with Blanche and Ellen, who are ignorant of the Everlasting Covenant as I have incorporated it into my own faith.

An object on the floor, shining and fluid, caught his eye. He bent to it, picked it up: Gertie's veil. It must have fallen from her head as she left the cellar. He stood, the veil limp in his hand, and began to play the scene back in his head, up until the interruption. Had he completed the ritual, he wondered? He was about to pull Gertie through the hole in the curtain, he was whispering the incantation 'Health in the navel, marrow in the bones, strength in the loins and in the sinews' when the women came in. Yes – they had stopped him too soon. He would go and get Gertie now, fetch her back and complete it.

The door was stuck fast. The knob rattled and jammed in his hand.

'Gertie!' He tipped his face up and bellowed. 'Gertie!'

'Pay him no heed,' Ellen snapped. At least the older children would not hear him. They had been sent to their beds upstairs, where his voice would not carry.

'I'm going to let him out.' Blanche stood up. 'We shouldn't have locked him in, Ellen. He's harmless.'

'Is he? How do we know?' Ellen turned on Myra now. 'You should have told us how ill he was. How long has he been like this?'

White faced, Myra sat at the table with Myrtle on her lap. She shook her head slightly.

'Months? Years?' Ellen went on. 'What possible good do you think you've done by keeping it a secret? He needs to see a doctor.' She glared at Myra, who remained unresponsive. 'We will bring a doctor to him then. Tomorrow morning.'

'It won't do any good,' said Myra at last. She felt numb, her stomach churned acid and molten, as if the charade in the cellar had somehow melted her insides. There was a pause while Ellen strode to the passage and looked out. There was no sign of the maid.

'We must decide what to do before Gertie comes back.'

'There's nothing we can do,' said Myra, wearily. The baby had fallen asleep, hot and heavy in her arms.

'It's all so ghastly!' Blanche was weeping now, groping in her coat pockets for a handkerchief. 'Imagine if Father were still alive – oh, it would kill him. It would kill him!'

'My God, you're a silly goose, Blanche!' Ellen had begun to make her way back to the table when her brother's voice reached them again.

'Gertie! Come down!'

She shook her head. 'He'll have to stay there overnight. At least he won't starve,' she added dryly.

'Poor Will . . .' Blanche began to sob in earnest, sinking into a chair opposite Myra.

What would it be to have such strength of feeling, to be covered in tears? Myra wondered, watching her. She had not cried since Joy's death. She felt calmer suddenly; a sense of finality took her. It was as if William had at last done the thing that had been inevitable, as if she should have expected it, or something like it, for years.

'William will be all right,' she said quietly. 'Perhaps we should just let him go.'

'Go? Where?' Ellen demanded.

'Wherever he wants. With Gertie.'

'But the children –'

'The children will stay with me.'

There was a dull kicking and thumping from the cellar, and William's voice again, enraged.

'The neighbours will hear him,' Blanche whispered.

'Right!' Ellen marched out the door and across the porch.

'It's all right,' Blanche told Myra. 'She's going to let him out.'

To the vent in the wall, the same spot Dora had watched at, Ellen bent her eye. The candles were burning low but she could see her brother clearly, bisected by the grid, gazing at the cellar roof as if he were waiting for an answer. The net curtain that had formed Gertie's veil was looped around his neck. She watched him take a deep breath and fill his capacious lungs to bellow again.

'William!' she said sharply, cutting him off. His head swivelled. 'Up here.'

'Unlock the door, Ellen.'

'You are to be quiet now, Will. No more yelling out.'

Two bounds onto a crate below the window, between the wall and the pyramid of tin cans, and his face was inches away from hers.

'Unlock the door,' he repeated. His eyes blazed with righteous indignation. 'I put you all away from me.'

'You're not well, William. We'll arrange for a doctor to come in the morning.'

'You are a devil!' he screamed at her. She felt his spittle spray her face through the grill. 'All you bitches are scions of Satan!'

He saw her rear back at his curse, her white face blur into the gloom of the night. A moment later her busy feet crunched away on the gravel path.

Boiling with rage, he shifted backwards off the crate, his fury fuelling too great a step, his shoulder connecting with a tin labelled British Best Corned Beef. It slid away from its niche in the construction, the pyramid wavered and though he stretched his frantic hands towards it it fell, cans and jars crashing and rolling around him. A candle, one he had carefully positioned on the pyramid's shoulder, fell onto the nogging that held his open inventory. Over the fallen tins he stumbled, reaching for it, but he was too late. All his careful calculations were lost and flaring, the pages curling to black while Gertie's veil, flung upward by his flailing arm, caught the flame and ignited, hissing, wrapping its orange length around his sleeve. As he banged his burning arm against the stone of the wall, helplessly wheeling, his hands desperate to peel the veil away, his sleeve scorching, both sleeves now, now his shift-front, he saw the fire had taken hold of the cellar. Other candles had been knocked by the falling tins to the newspaper spread on the floor, and the sacks of potatoes and rice were on fire, the stack of empty wooden crates flowered yellow and red, long fingers of flames reaching inexorably for the gallon tins of kerosene.

'It's as well he built the door so solid,' said Ellen. 'Listen to that. He's truly demented.'

Dora stood with her arm around her mother, their heads inclined towards the noise from the cellar: muffled unearthly screams and bangs and thumps.

'Blanche and I will stay the night –' began Ellen, when a colossal explosion shook the floor under them.

'My God – what –' Blanche sprang out of her chair.

'Smoke – look!' Dora pointed through the open door to the porch, where a thin grey tendril lifted between the planks. A sudden orange flame licked along the tread of the top step.

'He's set the cellar on fire! Dora, run for help; Myra, the children!' Ellen shouted orders, and Dora, a terrible pain spreading in her chest, ran down the hall, through the front door, across Symonds Street, breathless, her skirt hitched and fair hair tumbling loose, her long legs carrying her towards the fire station on Pitt Street.

On the corner of Karangahape Road and Queen Street she pulled up short. It was not for traffic, to let pass a horse and cart or motor-car, for at this hour on a Sunday night there were none. It was because, quite suddenly, she saw with that logical, cool part of her mind – the part that had counted the distances of the *Makura*'s decks the night she ran for her mother, the part that longed for facts and figures and stories that were true – she saw that to call the fire brigade would not be rational, it did not make sense. As suddenly as it had appeared, the pain in her chest vanished. If she were a character in one of Auntie Ellen's novels, well then, of course she would run for the firemen and they would come and spray water about, and the father – who would not at all be locked in a cellar full of food and crushed flowers and torn curtains, the detritus of a tawdry, crazy marriage – the father would be saved. There would be embracing and gratitude and a whole new beginning. But there had been too many beginnings, thought Dora, and not enough endings.

Her mind clicked over rapidly, as if she were ringing up a sum on a till. Mother and her aunts would save the children and the lodgers and poor silly Gertie. There might even be time to save some clothes and pots and pans.

She went on, but walking, and as she walked her mind ran on speedily. She must be sure that she wanted this, her father's certain death. It must not ever translate into guilt or remorse, a bad conscience to plague her for the rest of her life.

'It's what he wants,' said a small voice in her head, the voice of a girl not quite on the cusp of womanhood, and a small woollen gloved hand, warm on the inside but with a dusting of snow on this humid summer night, a hand identical to her own in every way, except three years younger, slipped into hers. The logical, clear part of her mind went on, click, click, click, in time with her steps, telling her that this waking dream of Joy was only her own mind offering comfort and solace. 'It is what he wants,' she agreed with the small voice and shoved the hand that pretended Joy held it deep into the pocket of her apron.

'He has wanted it for years and years,' the small voice went on, 'since before we were born.'

'Dora!' A young man overtook her on Pitt Street. It was one of the lodgers. 'It's all right – I'll go,' and he passed, sprinting down the hill to the fire station while Dora stopped and gazed up at the sky. There was no moon, and great swathes were obscured by cloud, but now and then stars showed through, brilliant, eternal, full of promise.

'If you're there, God, I hope you're ready for him,' she said, then she turned, making her way back to the Vine, which was visible even from the corner of the Jewish cemetery, flames leaping high as the chimneys.

Chapter 28

He is ascending, and as he ascends he remembers the first time, seventeen years ago, when he was a young man with a wife who loved him and would call him back. Below him he sees the cypress of the cemetery, the oaks of Grafton Gully and the burning roof of the Vine; he sees Dora strolling nonchalantly to join the little group on the street – Gertie, Ellen, Blanche with Myrtle in her arms, Riha, Edna, Theo, Audrey and in the middle of them all, her face lit by the flames, the woman with whom he shared his life's journey. The children cling to her, watch the avid fire.

Myra hardly looks around at the grunting and clanking snorting of the fire engine as it pulls up before the house and begins to unwind its hoses. Instead she raises her face to the sky and he could swear she's looking right at him. From this height her face is just an upturned smudge; he could not possibly read its expression.

On and on he speeds. He does not remember the distance being so great before and it occurs to him that Heaven is perhaps moveable, that it does not stay in the one place.

'Oh, Lord, my God, would you deny me judgement?' he cries, and his head, cooled by pure celestial breezes, leads the rest of his body into an expanse that is dark and chill and inexpressibly empty.

EPILOGUE

1920

In the garden, not the boarding-house garden but a small backyard in Ponsonby, Myrtle lies under the lemon tree peering up through the glossy leaves at the racing clouds. Nearby Myra kneels to apply her garden fork to the clods of earth in the silverbeet patch.

'If Father looked down on us now, he would only be able to see my legs,' Myrtle announces. She lifts her head to check, to see if that is exactly right. 'Only the end of my legs,' she corrects. 'Father is in Heaven, isn't he, Mother?'

'I expect so,' replies Myra, puffing a little as the yellow clay crumbles and breaks.

'When did he die?' Myrtle rises up on an elbow to watch her mother, though she can see only her back. Clotted with mud, the heels of Mother's boots push against her bottom, marking her skirt. The pale material of her blouse shifts and pulls at her shoulders.

'At the boarding house. When we lived in the boarding house in Symonds Street.'

'I said when not where.'

'Ah-ah!' says Mother, warningly. Myrtle supposes because she had taken a tone.

'I was a baby at the Vine,' she says carelessly, as if she hadn't heard. Crab-wise on her knees, Myra shifts along the ground. Myrtle thinks she saw her nod.

'Now I'm six.'

'You are indeed.'

'Did you love our father like Dora loves Freddy?'

Mother's head stays down, she digs around the roots of the silverbeet. Why does she grow so much of it? Myrtle wonders. Nobody likes it, not Riha nor Theo nor Edna nor herself, the children who hadn't grown up enough to leave home. Dora was so grown up she'd got married.

'Mumma? Did you?' Myra stands and brushes herself down. There are two brown ovals where her knees had pressed, streaked with green on the front of her skirt.

'Mother?' But Mother has that look on her face, her lips press together and her eyes are distant, glazed over.

'Will we see Father there?' On her hands and knees Myrtle crawls out from under the tree.

'Where?'

'In Heaven. When we die.' She stands up.

'It depends. Myrtle – look at your pinafore!'

'Only if we can find his house? Your skirt is dirty too, Mumma.'

'Yes, but it's the one I use for . . . oh never mind.' Myra bends to the vegetable patch, taking a small knife from her apron pocket to cut away some of the dark seersucker leaves.

'Do you believe in God, Mother?'

But there is only the sound of the silverbeet tearing away and a soft flopping sound as Myra lays the leaves one on top of the other on the grass. 'Mumma? Do you?'

'Shall I boil up some rhubarb for pudding?' With the child following, Myra moves away towards the rhubarb patch, which is with the parsley against the fence.

'When I go to Heaven I'm going to live with Father. Will I go to Heaven, Mother?'

'If that's what you believe.'

'What do you mean?'

'Not everybody in the world believes the same thing.'

482

'What do they, then? What do they believe in?' Myra straightens, her hand at her back: it aches all the time, more so in the garden and the garden is a necessity to help feed them all. Perhaps Theo could do more of the heavy digging. He is thirteen now. Where is he, Myra wonders? He has a great knack for making himself scarce . . . Myrtle gazes at her expectantly.

'There are some religions which have many gods,' Myra begins slowly. 'They have a god for everything. They believe there is no Heaven, that we come back and live again.'

But Myrtle isn't listening, she's drawing breath for her next volley of questions. She reminds Myra of William sometimes, this one, the way her mind fastens on to an idea or story and won't let go.

'What will it be like in Heaven? Will we all be the same up there? Will you be the same Mother?'

Mother smiles a little, and Myrtle feels a softening in her chest, a release of tension. Mother will come with her now, there's no danger she'll send her away. There will be a lovely curly drift of talk and bright, interesting pictures popping into her mind, she will forget about how she has to eat silverbeet for tea.

'In Heaven my back won't ache.'

'And?'

'I will be able to read properly.'

'I can teach you to read. I can write my name.'

'I'm too old now, my dear.'

'How old are you, Mumma?'

'It's not polite to ask that.' She is forty-two. How extraordinary, she thinks. Forty-two. William was forty-five when he died.

'Will there be books in Heaven?'

'I hope so.'

'What books?'

'Well . . . maybe in Heaven everybody writes their own book. Maybe everybody writes down their lives, as they really happened, the good they did and the bad.'

'Whose book will you read Mother? What will be in Father's one?' But Mother doesn't seem to want to answer this question. Myrtle rubs her tummy before the hard lump comes back and runs after her to where she stands beside the little pile of cut silverbeet, the tines of her fork pointing down. The rhubarb pokes out of her apron pocket, green and red.

'Pick those up for me, will you?'

Myrtle gathers up the leaves and shakes off a snail. 'Mother?'

'Mother what?'

'What will be in Father's book?'

'Oh . . . well . . . lots of different times. When he was young he had a farm.'

'And after that?'

Myrtle follows her up the back steps into the kitchen, where Myra runs the tap over the rhubarb. Perhaps she shouldn't have started this game, she thinks, as the water plashes and gurgles. On the curved end of a rhubarb stem there is a persistent fleck of dirt, which she scrapes with her thumbnail. Behind her Myrtle rummages in the dresser drawer.

A rustle of paper.

'Look! I've got a pencil,' comes the child's voice. 'I can write f a r m.'

'Myrtle – I must get on with –'

'Farm. What would be the next chapter?'

'Well I suppose . . . when he went to America. The steamer. The first city, the trains . . .' Mother sighs heavily, and Myrtle knows the game is nearly over. Once Mother sighs like that it's hard work keeping her at it, but Myrtle isn't about to give up just yet. She crouches over her piece of paper on the floor, positioning it so that the pencil doesn't push through a gap in the floorboards. The tap is still running, and outside it's starting to get dark.

The child waits expectantly still, but her mother has fallen quiet. She sees herself sitting over her husband's book, poring over it, seeing it all in the order it happened, his boyhood, the poor farm, his voyages, his drinking and his other women, the cities he lived in, the different beliefs he had and the one he made up. Her own love for him would be there, and how in the end he lost it, and the children's forgotten childhoods, and Riha and Joy, and Gertie's belief in him, and whether he was mad or entirely sane. She would see it all as he had seen it, laid out in chapters, and perhaps she would come to understand him. Will she forgive him then, she wonders? In Heaven, are understanding and forgiveness one and the same?

The child's arms are around her, her little white face upturned in the dim light.

'Mother? Why are you crying?'

Myra would like to say that she's not, to say it's the water splashed up from the sink, but Myrtle is standing on her tiptoes, one gentle hand patting her mother's hip.

'Mother,' she says gently. 'Here, bend down and I'll give you a kiss.'

ACKNOWLEDGMENTS

I am indebted for information supplied by Zena Journet. Thanks are also due to my aunt, Lorraine Johnson, for the loan of papers and photographs; to Melissa Rogers for her conversations with me about Mormonism; to Jene and Pudge Neave of Zion, Illinois, for their hospitality; to the Zion Historical Society; to train buff Joe Piersen for his help with turn-of-the-century American routes; to Douglas Lloyd-Jenkins for architectural advice; to my brother Bruce for Elisha's will; and to my agent, Lois Wallace.

I am also in debt to the librarians at the Maritime Museum in Auckland who gave me their assistance on steamships of the period. Grateful thanks also to my editors, Harriet Allan and Rachel Scott, for their careful and inspired contributions.

The author gratefully acknowledges receipt of a leading writers' grant from Creative New Zealand.

Many thanks and all my love to Tim, Stan, Maeve, and Willa.

Belief could not have been written without
the following resource books:

Zion City, Illinois: Twentieth Century Utopia by Philip L. Cook (Syracuse University Press, New York, 1996); *John Alexander Dowie* by Gordon Lindsay (Christ for the Nations, Texas, 1986); *Utah: A People's History* by Dean L. May (University of Utah Press, Utah, 1987); *Mormon Polygamy: A History* by Richard S. Van Wagoner (Signature Press, Salt Lake City, 1986); Teachings of Presidents of the Church: *Brigham Young, Book of Mormon, Doctrine and Covenants, The Pearl of Great Price* (all the Church of Jesus Christ of Latter-day Saints, Utah); *Making Vancouver 1863–1913* by Robert A. J. McDonald (UBC Press, British Columbia, 1996); *Vancouver: A History in Photographs* by Aynsley Vogel and Dana Wyse (Altitude Publishing, Vancouver, 1993), *Auckland by the Sea: 100 Years of Work and Play* by David Johnson (David Bateman, Auckland, 1988); *Auckland Through a Victorian Lens* by William Main (Millwood Press, Wellington, 1977); *Te Mete* (Smith) by Glenise Rolfe (self-published, Tauranga, 1991), *Pleasures of the Flesh: Sex and Drugs in Colonial New Zealand* by Stevan Eldred-Grigg (Reed, Wellington, 1984).